ISLANDS IN THE STREAM

"A complete, well-rounded novel, a contender with his very best . . . It is 100-proof Old Ernest!"
—The New York Times Book Review

"There are brilliant descriptions in the famous Hemingway style . . . When he describes the close bonds of love and hate between a group of men who are engaged in a tight and dangerous adventure with death as the ultimate stake, he remains unbeatable in his craft."
—Maxwell Geismar, Chicago Sun-Times Showcase

"Remarkably alive with voice and muscle . . . Hemingway never displayed a brawnier wit . . . There are memories of Paris as pungent and vivid as anything in A Moveable Feast. And the fishing episode . . . is only slightly less dazzling than Santiago's struggle in The Old Man and the Sea."
—Charles Lee, Philadelphia Bulletin

"Incredibly moving and powerful."
—Robert Kirsch, Los Angeles Times Calendar

"This book contains some of the best of Hemingway's descriptions of nature: the waves breaking white and green on the reef off the coast of Cuba; the beauty of the morning on the deep water; the hermit crabs and land crabs and ghost crabs; a big barracuda stalking mullet; a heron flying with his white wings over the green water; the ibis and flamingoes and spoonbills, the last of these beautiful with the sharp rose of their color; the mosquitoes in clouds from the marshes; the water that curled and blew under the lash of the wind; the sculpture that the wind and sand had made of a piece of driftwood, gray and sanded and embedded in white, floury sand."

—Edmund Wilson, **The New Yorker**

"Many of the episodes contain the most exciting and effective writing Hemingway has ever done."

—John W. Aldridge, **Saturday Review**

"Marvelously alive, moving quickly and showing glimmers of joy and humor that you might never have noticed in his work before."

—Bruce Cook, **National Observer**

PARAMOUNT PICTURES PRESENTS

GEORGE C. SCOTT

A BART/PALEVSKY PRODUCTION

A FRANKLIN J. SCHAFFNER FILM

ISLANDS IN THE STREAM

Also Starring
DAVID HEMMINGS
GILBERT ROLAND
and
CLAIRE BLOOM

Screenplay by
DENNE BART PETITCLERC

Produced by
PETER BART and MAX PALEVSKY

Directed by
FRANKLIN J. SCHAFFNER

Music
JERRY GOLDSMITH

ISLANDS
IN THE
STREAM
ERNEST HEMINGWAY

BANTAM BOOKS
TORONTO · NEW YORK · LONDON

*This low-priced Bantam Book
has been completely reset in a type face
designed for easy reading, and was printed
from new plates. It contains the complete
text of the original hard-cover edition.*
NOT ONE WORD HAS BEEN OMITTED.

$$\text{RLI:} \quad \frac{\text{VLM 4 (VLR 3–6)}}{\text{IL 8+}}$$

ISLANDS IN THE STREAM

*A Bantam Book / published by arrangement with
Charles Scribner's Sons*

PRINTING HISTORY

*Scribner's edition published October 1970
2nd printing .... October 1970*

Book-of-the-Month Club edition published October 1970

Bantam edition / February 1972

2nd printing .... March 1972	6th printing .. February 1977
3rd printing ..... April 1975	7th printing .... March 1977
4th printing ... January 1976	8th printing .... May 1977
5th printing .. September 1976	9th printing ...... June 1977
	10th printing .... January 1978

Excerpts appeared in ESQUIRE *September 1970*

*Cover Art courtesy Paramount Pictures Corporation.
Copyright © 1976 by Zeeuwse Maatschappij N.V.
All rights reserved.*

*Map by Samuel H. Bryant
Copyright © 1970 by Charles Scribner's Sons*

ISBN 0-553-11868-4

Published simultaneously in the United States and Canada

PRINTED IN THE UNITED STATES OF AMERICA

NOTE

Charles Scribner, Jr. and I worked together preparing this book for publication from Ernest's original manuscript. Beyond the routine chores of correcting spelling and punctuation, we made some cuts in the manuscript, I feeling that Ernest would surely have made them himself. The book is all Ernest's. We have added nothing to it.

MARY HEMINGWAY

CONTENTS

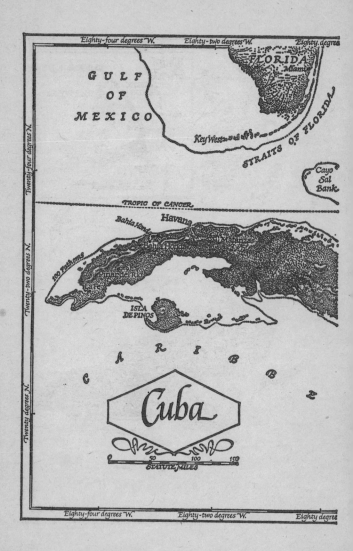

Seventy-eight degrees W.   Seventy-six degrees W.

5 W.

Great Isaac I.
Little Isaac I.

Bimini
Islands

Bimini
Islands

North Rock

NORTH
BIMINI   EAST BIMINI

Bailey Town

Alice Town

Middle Cay

Rabbit Keys

SOUTH
BIMINI

0 1 2 3 4 Miles

ANDROS ISLANDS

GREAT BAHAMA BANK

Santaren Channel

OLD
Cayo Francés
BAHAMA
Cayo Guillermo   Guinchos Cay
CHANNEL
Cayo Coco   Cayo Paredón
                  Cayo Megano   Cayo Lobos
                  Cayo Cruz
                  Confites
                  CAYO ROMANO

100 Fathoms

Cayo
Sabinal

Cayo St Domingo

Camagüey

100 Fathoms

Guantánamo

Guantánamo Bay

N

S   E   A

Twenty-four degrees N.

Twenty-three degrees N.

Twenty degrees N.

5 W.

Seventy-eight degrees W.   Seventy-six degrees W.

Stan' Bryant

Part I

BIMINI

BIMINI

I

THE house was built on the highest part of the narrow tongue of land between the harbor and the open sea. It had lasted through three hurricanes and it was built solid as a ship. It was shaded by tall coconut palms that were bent by the trade wind and on the ocean side you could walk out of the door and down the bluff across the white sand and into the Gulf Stream. The water of the Stream was usually a dark blue when you looked out at it when there was no wind. But when you walked out into it there was just the green light of the water over that floury white sand and you could see the shadow of any big fish a long time before he could ever come in close to the beach.

It was a safe and fine place to bathe in the day but it was no place to swim at night. At night the sharks came in close to the beach, hunting in the edge of the Stream and from the upper porch of the house on quiet nights you could hear the splashing of the fish they hunted and if you went down to the beach you could see the phosphorescent wakes they made in the water. At night the sharks had no fear and everything else feared them. But in the day they stayed out away from the clear white sand and if they did come in you could see their shadows a long way away.

A man named Thomas Hudson, who was a good

3

painter, lived there in that house and worked there and on the island the greater part of the year. After one has lived in those latitudes long enough the changes of the seasons become as important there as anywhere else and Thomas Hudson, who loved the island, did not want to miss any spring, nor summer, nor any fall or winter.

Sometimes the summers were too hot when the wind dropped in August or when the trade winds sometimes failed in June and July. Hurricanes, too, might come in September and October and even in early November and there could be freak tropical storms any time from June on. But the true hurricane months have fine weather when there are no storms.

Thomas Hudson had studied tropical storms for many years and he could tell from the sky when there was a tropical disturbance long before his barometer showed its presence. He knew how to plot storms and the precautions that should be taken against them. He knew too what it was to live through a hurricane with the other people of the island and the bond that the hurricane made between all people who had been through it. He also knew that hurricanes could be so bad that nothing could live through them. He always thought, though, that if there was ever one that bad he would like to be there for it and go with the house if she went.

The house felt almost as much like a ship as a house. Placed there to ride out storms, it was built into the island as though it were a part of it; but you saw the sea from all the windows and there was good cross ventilation so that you slept cool on the hottest nights. The house was painted white to be cool in the summer and it could be seen from a long way out in the Gulf Stream. It was the highest thing on the island except for the long planting of tall casuarina trees that were the first thing you saw as you raised the island out of the sea. Soon after you saw the dark blur of casuarina trees above the line of the sea, you would see the white bulk of the house. Then, as you came closer, you raised the whole length of the island with the coconut palms, the clapboarded houses, the white line of the beach, and the green of the South Island stretching beyond it. Thomas Hudson never saw the house, there on that island, but that the sight of her made him happy. He always thought of the house as *her* exactly as he would have thought of a ship. In the winter, when the northers blew and it was really cold, the house was warm and comfortable because it had the only fireplace on the island. It was a big open fireplace and Thomas Hudson burned driftwood in it.

He had a big pile of driftwood stacked against the south wall of the house. It was whitened by the sun and sand-scoured by the wind and he would become fond of different pieces so that he would hate to burn them. But there was always more driftwood along the beach after the big storms and he found it was fun to burn even the pieces he was fond of. He knew the sea would sculpt more, and on a cold night he would sit in the big chair in front of the fire, reading by the lamp that stood on the heavy plank table and look up while he was reading to hear the northwester blowing outside and the crashing of the surf and watch the great, bleached pieces of driftwood burning.

Sometimes he would put the lamp out and lie on the rug on the floor and watch the edges of color that the sea salt and the sand in the wood made in the flame as they burned. On the floor his eyes were even with the line of the burning wood and he could see the line of the flame when it left the wood and it made him both sad and happy. All wood that burned affected him in this way. But burning driftwood did something to him that he could not define. He thought that it was probably wrong to burn it when he was so fond of it; but he felt no guilt about it.

As he lay on the floor he felt under the wind although, really, the wind whipped at the lower corners of the house and at the lowest grass on the island and into the roots of the sea grass and the cockleburs and into the sand itself. On the floor he could feel the pounding of the surf the way he remembered feeling the firing of heavy guns when he had lain on the earth close by some battery a long time ago when he had been a boy.

The fireplace was a great thing in winter and through all the other months he looked at it with affection and thought how it would be when winter came again. Winter was the best of all seasons on the island and he looked forward to it through all the rest of the year.

II

WINTER was over and spring was nearly gone when Thomas Hudson's boys came to the island that year. It had been arranged for the three of them to meet in New York to come down together on the train and then fly over from the Mainland. There had been the usual difficulties with the mother of two of the boys. She had planned a European trip saying nothing, of course, to the boys' father when she planned it, and she wanted the boys for the summer. He could have them for the Christmas holidays; after Christmas of course. Christmas itself would be spent with her.

Thomas Hudson was familiar with the pattern by now and finally there was the usual compromise. The two younger boys would come to the island to visit their father for five weeks and then leave to sail from New York, student class, on a French Line boat to join their mother in Paris where she would have bought a few necessary clothes. They would be in the charge of their older brother, young Tom, on the trip. Young Tom would then join *his* mother, who was making a picture in the south of France.

Young Tom's mother had not asked for him and would have liked him to be at the island with his father. But she would love to see him and it was a fair compromise with the unmalleable decision of the other boys' mother. She was a delightful and charming woman who had never altered a plan that she had made in her life. Her plans were always made in secret, like those of a good general, and they were as rigidly enforced. A compromise might be effected. But never a basic change in a plan whether that plan was conceived in a sleepless night or on an angry morning or on a gin-aided evening.

A plan was a plan and a decision was truly a decision and knowing all this and having been well educated in the usages of divorce, Thomas Hudson was happy that a compromise had been made and that the children were coming for five weeks. If five weeks is what we get, he thought, that is what we draw. Five weeks is a good long time to be with people that you love and would wish to be with always. But why did I ever leave Tom's mother in the first place? You'd better not think about that, he told himself. That is one thing you had better not think about. And these are fine children that you got from the other one. Very strange and very complicated and you know how many of their good qualities come from her. She is a fine woman and you never should have left her either. Then he said to himself, Yes. I had to.

But he did not worry much about any of it. He had long ago ceased to worry and he had exorcised guilt with work insofar as he could, and all he cared about now was that the boys were coming over and that they should have a good summer. Then he would go back to work.

He had been able to replace almost everything except the children with work and the steady normal working life he had built on the island. He believed he had made something there that would last and that would hold him. Now when he was lonesome for Paris he would remember Paris instead of going there. He did the same thing with all of Europe and much of Asia and of Africa.

He remembered what Renoir had said when they told him that Gauguin had gone to Tahiti to paint. "Why does he have to spend so much money to go so far away to paint when one paints so well here at the Batignolles?" It was better in French, "quand on peint si bien aux Batignolles," and Thomas Hudson thought of the island as his *quartier* and he was settled in it and knew his neighbors and worked as hard as he had ever worked in Paris when young Tom had been a baby.

Sometimes he would leave the island to fish off Cuba or to go to the mountains in the fall. But he had rented the ranch that he owned in Montana because the best time out there was the summer and the fall and now the boys always had to go to school in the fall.

He had to go to New York occasionally to see his dealer. But more often now his dealer came down to see him and took canvases north with him. He was well established as a painter and he was respected both in Europe and in his own country. He had a regular income from oil leases on land his grandfather had owned. It had been grazing land and when it was sold the mineral rights had been retained. About half of this income went into alimony and the balance provided him with security so that he could paint exactly as he wanted to with no commercial pressure. It also enabled him to live where he wished and to travel when he cared to.

He had been successful in almost every way except in his married life, although he had never cared, truly, about success. What he cared about was painting and his children and he was still in love with the first woman he had been in love with. He had loved many women since and sometimes someone would come to stay on the island. He needed to see women and they were welcome for a while. He liked having them there, sometimes for quite a long time. But in the end he was always glad when they were gone, even when he was very fond of them. He had trained himself not to quarrel with women anymore and he had learned how not to get married. These two things had been nearly as difficult to learn as how to settle down and paint in a steady and well-ordered way. But he had learned them and he hoped that he had learned them permanently. He had known how to paint for a long time and he believed he learned more every year. But learning how to settle down and how to paint with discipline had been hard for him because there had been a time in his life when he had not been disciplined. He had never been truly irresponsible; but he had been undisciplined, selfish, and ruthless. He knew this now, not only because many women had told it to him; but because he had finally discovered it for himself. Then he had resolved that he would be selfish only for his painting, ruthless only for his work, and that he would discipline himself and accept the discipline.

He was going to enjoy life within the limits of the discipline that he imposed and work hard. And today he was very happy because his children were coming in the morning.

"Mr. Tom, don't you want nothing?" Joseph the house-boy asked him. "You knocked off for the day, ain't you?"

Joseph was tall with a very long, very black face and big hands and big feet. He wore a white jacket and trousers and was barefooted.

"Thank you, Joseph. I don't think I want anything."

"Little gin and tonic?"

"No. I think I'll go down and have one at Mr. Bobby's."

"Drink one here. It's cheaper. Mr. Bobby was in an evil mood when I went by. Too many mixed drinks he says. Somebody off a yacht asked him for something called a White Lady and he served her a bottle of that American mineral water with a lady in white kinda mosquito netting dress sitting by a spring."

"I better be getting down there."

"Let me mix you one first. You got some mails on the pilot boat. You can read your mails and drink the drink and then go down to Mr. Bobby's."

"All right."

"Good thing," said Joseph. "Because I already mixed it. Mails don't look to amount to anything, Mr. Tom."

"Where are they?"

"Down in the kitchen. I'll bring them up. Couple with women's writing on them. One from New York. One from Palm Beach. Pretty writing. One from that gentleman sells your pictures in New York. Couple more unknown to me."

"You want to answer them for me?"

"Yes sir. If that's what you want. I'm educated way beyond my means."

"Better bring them up."

"Yes sir, Mr. Tom. There's a paper too."

"Save it for breakfast, please, Joseph."

Thomas Hudson sat and read his mail and sipped at the cool drink. He read one letter over again and then put them all in a drawer of his desk.

"Joseph," he called. "Have you everything ready for the boys?"

"Yes sir, Mr. Tom. And two extra cases of Coca-Cola. Young Tom, he must be bigger than me, ain't he?"

"Not yet."

"Think he can lick me now?"

"I don't think so."

"I fought that boy so many times in private life," Joseph said. "Sure is funny to call him mister. Mr. Tom, Mr. David, and Mr. Andrew. Three of the finest goddam boys I know. And the meanest is Andy."

"He started out mean," Thomas Hudson said.

"And boy, did he continue," Joseph said admiringly.

"You set them a good example this summer."

"Mr. Tom, you don't want me to set those boys no good example this summer. Maybe three four years back when I was innocent. Me, I'm going to pattern myself on Tom. He's been to an expensive school and he's got good expensive manners. I can't look like him exactly. But I can act like him. Free and easy but polite. Then I'm going to be smart like Dave. That's the hardest part. Then I'm going to learn the secret of how Andy gets that mean."

"Don't you get mean around here."

"No, Mr. Tom, you mistook what I meant. That meanness isn't for in the house. I want that for my private life."

"It will be nice to have them, won't it?"

"Mr. Tom, there won't be nothing like it since they had the big fire. I rank it right along with the Second Coming. Is it nice? you ask me. Yes sir, it's nice."

"We'll have to figure out plenty of things for them to do to have fun."

"No, Mr. Tom," Joseph said. "We ought to figure out

how to save them from their own fearsome projects. Eddy can help us. He knows them better than me. I'm their friend and that makes it difficult."

"How's Eddy?"

"He's been drinking a little in anticipation of the Queen's birthday. He's in tip-top shape."

"I better get down to Mr. Bobby's while he's still in that evil mood."

"He asked for you, Mr. Tom. Mr. Bobby's a gentleman if there ever was a gentleman and sometimes that trash comes in on yachts gets him worn down. He was wore down almighty thin when I left."

"What were you doing there?"

"I went for Coca-Cola and I stayed to keep my hand in shooting a stick of pool."

"How's the table?"

"Worse."

"I'll go down," said Thomas Hudson. "I want to take a shower and change."

"I've got them laying out for you on the bed," Joseph told him. "You want another gin and tonic?"

"No thanks."

"Mr. Roger's in on the boat."

"Good. I'll get hold of him."

"Will he be staying here?"

"Maybe."

"I'll make up a bed for him anyway."

"Good."

III

THOMAS HUDSON took a shower, scrubbing his head with soap and then rinsing under the prickling drive of the sharp, jetted shower. He was a big man and he looked bigger stripped than he did in his clothes. He was very tanned and his hair was faded and streaked from the sun. He carried no extra weight and on the scales he saw that he weighed 192 pounds.

I should have gone swimming before I took the shower, he thought. But I had a long swim this morning before I started work and I'm tired now. There will be plenty of swimming when the boys come. And Roger's here too. That's good.

He put on a clean pair of shorts and an old Basque shirt and moccasins and went out the door and down the slope and through the gate in the picket fence onto the white glare of the sun-bleached coral of the King's Highway.

Ahead a very erect-walking old Negro in a black alpaca coat and pressed dark trousers came out of one of the unpainted board shacks along the road that was shaded by two tall coconut palms and turned into the highway ahead of him. Thomas Hudson saw his fine black face as he turned.

From behind the shack a child's voice came in an old English tune singing mockingly,

> "Uncle Edward came from Nassau
> Some candy for to sell
> I buy some and P.H. buy some
> And the candy give us hell—"

Uncle Edward turned his fine face, looking as sad as it was angry, in the bright afternoon light.

"I know you," he said. "I can't see you but I know who you are. I'll report you to Constable."

The child's voice went on, rising clear and gay,

> "Oh Edward
> Oh Edward
> Buff, rough, tough Uncle Edward
> Your candy rotten."

"Constable going to hear about this," Uncle Edward said. "Constable know what steps to take."

"Any rotten candy today, Uncle Edward?" the child's voice called. He was careful to keep out of sight.

"Man is persecuted," Uncle Edward said aloud as he

walked on. "Man has his robe of dignity plucked at
and destroyed. Oh, Good Lord, forgive them for they
know not what they do."

Ahead down the King's Highway there was more
singing coming from the rooms up above the Ponce de
León. A Negro boy slipped by hurrying along the coral
road.

"Been a fight, Mr. Tom," he said. "Or something.
Gentleman off'n a yacht been throwing things out of a
window."

"What things, Louis?"

"Any kind of things, Mr. Tom. Gentleman throw
anything he can get his hands on. Lady try to stop him he
say he going to throw the lady, too."

"Where's the gentleman from?"

"Big man from up north. Claims he can buy and sell
the whole island. Guess he could get it pretty cheap if he
keeps throwing it around the way he's doing."

"Constable taken any action, Louis?"

"No sir, Mr. Tom. Nobody has called in Constable yet.
But way everybody figures, Constable's time is coming."

"You with them, Louis? I wanted to get some bait for
tomorrow."

"Yes sir, I'll get your bait, Mr. Tom. Don't worry
about bait. I been with them right along. They hired me
to take them bonefishing this morning and I been with
them ever since. Only they ain't been bonefishing. No *sir*.
Unless throwing plates and cups and mugs and chairs
and every time Mr. Bobby brings him the bill he tears
up the bill and tells Mr. Bobby he's a robbing thieving
bastard and a crook is bonefishing."

"Sounds like a difficult gentleman, Louis."

"Mr. Tom, he's the damnedest gentleman you ever
saw before or since. He had me singing for them. You
know I can't sing good like Josey but I sing as good as I
can and sometimes I sing *better* than I can. I'm singing
good as I can. You know how it is. You heard me sing.
All he wants to hear is that mama don't want no peas
no rice no coconut oil song. Over and over. It's an old

song and I get tired so I said to him, 'Sir I know *new*
songs. Good songs. Fine songs. And I know old songs
such as the loss of John Jacob Astor on the *Titanic* when
sunk by an iceberg and I would be glad to sing them
rather than that no peas no rice song if you so wish.' I
said it polite and pleasant as you want. As you know I
would say it. So this gentleman say, 'Listen you ignorant
black little bastard I own more stores and factories and
newspapers than John Jacob Astor had pots to, you
know the word, in, and I'll take you and shove your
head in those pots if you try to tell me what I want to
hear.' So then his lady said, 'Darling, do you really have
to be so rude to the boy? I thought he sang very well
and I would like to hear some of the new songs.' And
the gentleman said, 'Listen you. *You* won't hear them and
he won't sing them.' Mr. Tom, he's a strange gentleman.
But his lady just said, 'Oh darling, you are difficult.' Mr.
Tom, he's difficulter than a diesel engine is to a newborn
tree monkey out of its mother's womb. Excuse me if I
talk too much. This has aroused me. He's got her feeling
very bad."

"What are you going to do about them now, Louis?"

"I been to get conch pearls," he said.

They had stopped in the shade of a palm while he had
been talking and he brought out a quite clean cloth from
his pocket and unfolded it to show a half dozen of the
shiny, nacreous pink, unpearllike pearls that are sometimes found in conches by the natives when they clean
them and that no woman Thomas Hudson had ever
known except Queen Mary of England has ever cared
for as a gift. Of course Thomas Hudson could not think
that he knew Queen Mary except through the papers
and in pictures and a profile of her in *The New Yorker*
but the fact that she liked conch pearls made him feel
that he knew her better than he knew many other people
he had known for a long time. Queen Mary liked conch
pearls and the island was celebrating her birthday tonight,
he thought, but he was afraid conch pearls would not
make the gentleman's lady feel very much better. Then,

too, it was always possible that Queen Mary said she liked them to please her subjects in the Bahamas.

They had walked down to the Ponce de León and Louis was saying, "His lady was crying, Mr. Tom. She was crying very bitterly. So I suggested I might go up to Roy's and get some conch pearls for her to inspect."

"They ought to make her very happy," Thomas Hudson said. "If she likes conch pearls."

"I hope they will. I'm taking them up now."

Thomas Hudson went into the bar where it was cool and almost dark after the glare of the coral road and had a gin and tonic water with a piece of lime peel in the glass and a few drops of Angostura in the drink. Mr. Bobby was behind the bar looking terrible. Four Negro boys were playing billiards, occasionally lifting the table when necessary to bring off a difficult carom. The singing had stopped upstairs and it was very quiet in the room except for the click of the balls. Two of the crew of the yacht that was tied up in the slip were at the bar and as Thomas Hudson's eyes adjusted to the light it was dim and cool and pleasant. Louis came downstairs.

"Gentleman's asleep," he said. "I left the pearls with his lady. She's looking at them and crying."

He saw the two sailors from the yacht look at each other but they didn't say anything. He stood there, holding the long, pleasantly bitter drink, tasting the first swallow of it, and it reminded him of Tanga, Mombasa, and Lamu and all that coast and he had a sudden nostalgia for Africa. Here he was, settled on the island, when he could as well be in Africa. Hell, he thought, I can always go there. You have to make it inside of yourself wherever you are. You are doing all right at that here.

"Tom, do you really like the taste of that stuff?" Bobby asked him.

"Sure. Or I wouldn't drink it."

"I opened a bottle by mistake once and it tasted like quinine."

"It's got quinine in it."

"People surely are crazy," Bobby said. "Man can

drink anything he wants. He has money to pay for it. He's supposed to be taking his pleasure and he spoils good gin by putting it into some kind of a Hindu drink with quinine in it."

"It tastes good to me. I like the quinine taste with the lime peel. I think it sort of opens up the pores of the stomach or something. I get more of a kick out of it than any other gin drink. It makes me feel good."

"I know. Drinking always makes you feel good. Drinking makes me feel terrible. Where's Roger?"

Roger was a friend of Thomas Hudson's, who had a fishing shack down the island.

"He ought to be over soon. We're going to eat with Johnny Goodner."

"What men like you and Roger Davis and Johnny Goodner that been around stay around this island for I don't know."

"It's a good island. You stay here, don't you?"

"I stay to make a living."

"You could make a living in Nassau."

"Nassau, hell. There's more fun here. This is a good island for having fun. Plenty money been made here, too."

"I like to live here."

"Sure," said Bobby. "I do, too. You know that. If I can make a living. You sell those pictures you paint all the time?"

"They sell pretty good now."

"People paying money for pictures of Uncle Edward. Pictures of Negroes in the water. Negroes on land. Negroes in boats. Turtle boats. Sponge boats. Squalls making up. Waterspouts. Schooners that got wrecked. Schooners building. Everything they could see free. They really buy them?"

"Sure they buy them. Once a year you have a show in New York and they sell them."

"Auction them off?"

"No. The dealer who shows them puts a price on them. People buy them. Museums buy one once in a while."

"Can't you sell them yourself?"

"Sure."

"I'd like to buy a waterspout," Bobby said. "Damn big waterspout. Black as hell. Maybe better two waterspouts going roaring over the flats making a noise so you can't hear. Sucking all the water across and scare you to death. Me in the dinghy sponging and nothing I can do. Waterspout blow the water glass right out of my hand. Almost suck the dinghy up out of the water. God's own hell of a waterspout. How much would one like that cost? I could hang it right here. Or hang it up at home if it wouldn't scare the old woman to death."

"It would depend on how big it was."

"Make it as big as you want," Bobby said grandly. "You can't make a picture like that too damn big. Put in three waterspouts. I seen three waterspouts closer than that across by Andros Island one time. They went right up to the sky and one sucked up a sponger's boat and when it dropped the motor went right through the hull."

"It's just what the canvas would cost," Thomas Hudson said. "I'd only charge for the canvas."

"By God, get a big canvas then," Bobby said. "We'll paint waterspouts that will scare people right out of this bar and right off the damned island."

He was moved by the grandeur of the project but its possibilities were just opening up to him.

"Tom, boy, do you think you could paint a full hurricane? Paint her right in the eye of the storm when she's already blew from one side and calmed and just starting from the other? Put in everything from the Negroes lashed in the coconut palms to the ships blowing over the crest of the island? Put in the big hotel going. Put in two-by-fours sailing through the air like lances and dead pelicans blowing by like they were part of the gusts of rain. Have the glass down to twenty-seven and the wind velocities blown away. Have the sea breaking on the ten-fathom bar and the moon come out in the eye of the storm. Have a tidal wave come up and submerge every living thing. Have women blown out to sea with their clothes stripped from them by the wind. Have dead Negroes floating everywhere and flying through the air—"

"It's an awfully big canvas," Thomas Hudson said.

"To hell with the canvas!" Bobby said. "I'll get a mainsail off a schooner. We'll paint the greatest goddam pictures in the world and live throughout history. You've just been painting these little simple pictures."

"I'll start on the waterspouts," Thomas Hudson said.

"Right," said Bobby, hating to come back from the big project. "That's sound. But by God we can make some great pictures with the knowledge you and I've got and with the training you've put in already."

"I'll start on the waterspouts tomorrow."

"Good," said Bobby. "That's a beginning. But by God I'd like us to paint that hurricane, too. Anybody ever paint the sinking of the *Titanic?*"

"Not on a really big scale."

"We could paint that. There's a subject that always appealed to my imagination. You could get in the coldness of the iceberg as it moved off after they struck it. Paint the whole thing in a dense fog. Get in every detail. Get that man that got in the boat with the women because he thought he could help because he was a yachtsman. Paint him getting into the boat stepping on a few women just as big as life. He reminds me of that fellow we got upstairs now. Why don't you go upstairs and make a drawing of that one while he's asleep and use him in the painting?"

"I think we better just start with the waterspouts."

"Tom, I want you to be a *big* painter," Bobby said. "Leave all that chicken stuff behind. You've just been wasting yourself. Why there's three paintings we've outlined together in less than half an hour and I haven't even started to draw on my imagination. And what have you been doing up until now? Painting a Negro turning a loggerhead turtle on the beach. Not even a green turtle. A common loggerhead. Or painting two Negroes in a dinghy bullying a mess of crawfish. You've wasted your life, man." He stopped and had a quick one from underneath the bar.

"That don't count," he said. "You never saw me take that one. Look, Tom, those are three great paintings. Big paintings. Worldwide paintings. Fit to hang in the Crystal Palace alongside the masterpieces of all time. Except the first, of course, is a small subject. But we haven't started yet. No reason why we can't paint one to end them all. What do you think of this?"

He took a very quick one.

"Of what?"

He leaned over the bar so the others could not hear.

"Don't shear off from it," Bobby said. "Don't be shocked by its magnitude. You got to have vision, Tom. We can paint the End of the World," he paused. "Full size."

"Hell," Thomas Hudson said.

"No. Before hell. Hell is just opening. The Rollers are rolling in their church up on the ridge and all speaking in unknown tongues. There's a devil forking them up with his pitchfork and loading them into a cart. They're yelling and moaning and calling on Jehovah. Negroes are prostrated everywhere and morays and crawfish and spider crabs are moving around and over their bodies. There's a big sort of hatch open and devils are carrying Negroes and church people and rollers and everyone into it and they go out of sight. Water's rising all around the island and hammerheads and mackerel sharks and tiger sharks and shovelnose sharks are swimming round and round and feeding on those who try to swim away to keep from being forked down the big open hatch that has steam rising out of it. Rummies are taking their last swigs and beating on the devils with bottles. But the devils keep forking them down, or else they are engulfed by the rising sea where now there are whale sharks, great white sharks, and killer whales and other outsized fish circling outside of where the big sharks are tearing at those people in the water. The top of the island is covered with dogs and cats and the devils are forking them in, too, and the dogs are cowering and howling and the cats run off and claw the devils and their hair stands on end and finally they go into the sea swimming as good as you want to see. Sometimes a shark will hit one and you'll see the cat go under. But mostly they swim right off through it.

"Bad heat begins to come out of the hatch and the devils are having to drag the people toward the hatch because they've broken their pitching forks trying to fork in some of the church people. You and me are standing in the center of the picture observing all this with calm. You make a few notes and I refresh myself from a bottle and occasionally offer you refreshment. Once in a while a devil all sweating from his work will brush by us hauling on a big churchman that's trying to dig into the sand with his fingers to keep from being put into the hatch and screaming to Jehovah and the devil will say, 'Beg pardon, Mr. Tom. Beg pardon, Mr. Bobby. Very busy today.'

"I'll offer the devil a drink as he passes, sweating and grimed, going back for another churchman and he'll say, 'No thank you, Mr. Bobby. I never touch the stuff when I'm working.'

"That could make a hell of a painting, Tom, if we can get all the movement and the grandeur into it."

"I believe we've got about all we can handle outlined for today."

"By God, I think you're right," Bobby said. "Outlining a painting like that makes me thirsty, too."

"There was a man named Bosch could paint pretty well along those lines."

"The magneto man?"

"No. Hieronymus Bosch. Very old-timer. Very good. Pieter Brueghel worked on that too."

"He an old-timer too?"

"Very old-timer. Very good. You'd like him."

"Oh hell," said Bobby. "No old-timer will touch us. Besides the world's never ended yet, so how the hell does he know any more about it than we do?"

"He'd be pretty hard to beat."

"I don't believe a word of it," Bobby said. "We've got a picture that would put him out of business."

"What about another one of those?"

"Yes, damn it. I forget this is a bar room. God bless the Queen, Tom. We're forgetting what day it is, too. Here, have one on me and we'll drink her health."

He poured himself a small glass of rum and handed Thomas Hudson the bottle of Booth's yellow gin, some limes on a plate, a knife, and a bottle of Schweppes's Indian Tonic Water.

"Fix your own damn drink. The hell with those fancy drinks."

After Thomas Hudson had made the drink and shaken a few drops of bitters in it from the bottle that had a gull's quill in the cork, he raised his glass and then looked down the bar.

"What are you two drinking? Name it if it's simple."

"Dog's Head," one of the sailors said.

"Dog's Head it is," Bobby said and reached into the ice tub and handed them the two cold bottles of ale. "The glasses are out. Rummies been throwing the glasses away all day. Everybody got their drinks? Gentlemen, The Queen. I don't think she'd care much for this island and I'm not sure she'd do extremely well here. But gentlemen, The Queen. God bless her."

They all drank her health.

"Must be a great woman," said Bobby. "Bit on the stiff side for me. Always fancied Queen Alexandra myself. Lovely type. But we will try to give the Queen's Birthday full honors. This is a small island but a patriotic one. Man from here went to the last war and had his arm shot off. Can't be more patriotic than that."

"Whose birthday did he say it was?" one of the sailors asked.

"Queen Mary of England," Bobby said. "Mother of the present King Emperor."

"That's the one the *Queen Mary's* named after, isn't it?" the other sailor asked.

"Tom," said Bobby. "You and I will drink the next toast alone."

IV

IT was dark now and there was a breeze blowing so that there were no mosquitoes nor sand flies and the boats had all come in, hoisting their outriggers as they came up the channel, and now were lying tied up in the slips of the three docks that projected out from the beach into the harbor. The tide was running out fast and the lights of the boats shone on the water that showed green in the light and moved so fast it sucked at the piling of the docks and swirled at the stern of the big cruiser they were on. Alongside in the water where the light was reflected off the planking of the cruiser toward the unpainted piling of the dock where old motorcar and truck tires were tied as fenders, making dark rings against the darkness under the rock, garfish, attracted by the light, held themselves against the current. Thin and long, shining as green as the water, only their tails moving, they were not feeding, nor playing; only holding themselves there in the fascination of the light.

Johnny Goodner's cruiser, *Narwhal,* where they were waiting for Roger Davis, was headed into the ebbing tide and astern of her in the same slip, made fast so that the two cabin cruisers lay stern to stern, was the boat of the party that had been at Bobby's place all day. Johnny Goodner sat in a chair in the stern with his feet on another chair and a Tom Collins in his right hand and a long, green Mexican chile pepper in his left.

"It's wonderful," he said. "I bite just a little piece and it sets my mouth on fire and I cool it with this."

He took the first bite, swallowed, blew out, "thew!" through rolled tongue, and took a long swallow of the tall drink. His full lower lip licked his thin Irish upper lip and he smiled with his gray eyes. His mouth was sliced upwards at the corners so it always looked as though he were about to smile, or had just smiled, but his mouth told very little about him unless you noticed the thinness of the upper lip. His eyes were what you needed to watch. He was the size and build of a middleweight gone a little heavy; but he looked in good shape lying there relaxed and that is how a man looks bad who is really out of shape. His face was brown but peeling across the nose and the forehead that went back with his receding hairline. He had a scar on his chin that could have been taken for a dimple if it had been just a little closer to the center and his nose had been just perceptibly flattened across the bridge. It wasn't a flat nose. It just looked as though it had been done by a modern sculptor who worked directly in the stone and had taken off just the shadow of a chip too many.

"Tom, you worthless character, what have you been doing?"

"Working pretty steadily."

"You would," he said and took another bite of the chile. It was a very wrinkled and droopy chile about six inches long.

"Only the first one hurts," he said. "It's like love."

"The hell it is. Chiles can hurt both ways."

"And love?"

"The hell with love," Thomas Hudson said.

"What a sentiment. What a way to talk. What are you getting to be? A victim of sheepherder's madness on this island?"

"No sheep here, Johnny."

"Stone-crab herder's madness then," Johnny said. "We don't want to have you have to be netted or anything. Try one of these chiles."

"I have," Thomas Hudson said.

"Oh I know your past," he said. "Don't pull your illustrious past on me. You probably invented them. I know. Probably the man who introduced them into Patagonia on Yak-back. But I represent modern times. Listen Tommy. I have these chiles stuffed with salmon. Stuffed with bacalao. Stuffed with Chilean bonito. Stuffed with Mexican turtledoves' breasts. Stuffed with turkey meat and mole. They'll stuff them with anything and I buy them. Makes me feel like a damned potentate. But all that's a perversion. Just this long, drooping, uninspiring, unstuffed, unpromising old chile with the brown chupango sauce is the best. You bastard," he blew out through his pursed tongue again, "I got too much of you that time."

He took a really long pull at the Tom Collins.

"They give me a reason for drinking," he explained. "Have to cool my damned mouth. What are you having?"

"I might take one more gin and tonic."

"Boy," Johnny called. "One more gin and tonic for Bwana M'Kubwa."

Fred, one of the island boys Johnny's captain had hired, brought in the drink.

"Here it is, Mr. Tom."

"Thank you, Fred," Thomas Hudson said. "The Queen, God bless her," and they drank.

"Where's the old whoremaster?"

"Up at his house. He'll be down."

He ate some more of the chile without commenting on it, finished his drink, and said, "How are you really, old Tom?"

"OK," Thomas Hudson said. "I've learned how to live by myself pretty well and I work hard."

"Do you like it here? I mean for all the time."

"Yes. I got sick of moving around with it. I'd rather have it here. I get along well enough here, Johnny. Pretty damn well."

"It's a good place," said Johnny. "It's a good place for a guy like you that's got some sort of inner resources. Hell of a place for a guy like me that keeps chasing it or running away from it. Is it true that Roger's gone Red on us?"

"So they're saying that already."

"That's what I heard on the coast."

"What happened to him out there?"

"I don't know all of it. But it was something pretty bad."

"Really bad?"

"They've got different ideas of what's bad out there. It wasn't St. Quentin quail if that's what you mean. Anyway out there with that climate and the fresh vegetables and everything it's like the size of their football players. Hell, girls fifteen look twenty-four. At twenty-four they're Dame May Whitty. If you're not a marrying man you better look at their teeth pretty close. And of course you can't tell a damn thing from their teeth. And they've all got mothers and fathers or one or the other and they're all hungry. Climate gives them appetite, too, of course. Trouble is, people get enthusiastic sometimes and don't ask for their driving licenses or their social security cards. I think they ought to measure it by size and weight and general capabilities and not just by age. Wreaks too many injustices just going by age. All around. Precocity isn't penalized in any other sport. Other way around. Apprentice allowance claimed would be the fairest. Same as racing. They had me pretty well boxed on that rap. But that wasn't what they got old Roger on."

"What did they get me on?" Roger Davis asked.

He had dropped down from the dock onto the deck in his rope-soled shoes without making any noise and he stood there looking awfully big in a sweatshirt three sizes too large for him and a pair of tight old dungarees.

"Hi," said Johnny. "Didn't hear you ring. I was telling Tom I didn't know what they got you on but that it wasn't jailbait."

"Good," said Roger. "Let's drop the subject."

"Don't be so powerful," Johnny said.

"I'm not being powerful," Roger said. "I asked politely. Do you drink on this boat?" He looked at the cabin cruiser that lay with her stern toward them. "Who's that?"

"The people at the Ponce. Didn't you hear?"

"Oh," said Roger. "Well, let's have a drink anyway even though they have set us a bad example."

"Boy," Johnny called. Fred came out of the cabin. "Yes sir," he said.

"Enquire what the pleasure of these Sahibs is."

"Gentlemen?" Fred asked.

"I'll take whatever Mr. Tom is drinking," Roger said. "He's my guide and counselor."

"Many boys at camp this year?" Johnny asked.

"Just two so far," Roger said. "My counselor and I."

"My counselor and me," Johnny said. "How the hell do you write books?"

"I can always hire someone to put in the grammar."

"Or get someone free," Johnny said. "I've been talking with your counselor."

"Counselor says he's quite happy and contented here. He's hit the beach for good."

"You ought to see the place," Tom told him. "He lets me come in for a drink once in a while."

"Womens?"

"No womens."

"What do you boys do?"

"I've been doing it all day."

"But you were here before. What did you do then?"

"Swim, eat, drink. Tom works, read, talk, read, fish, fish, swim, drink, sleep—"

"No womens?"

"Still no womens."

"Sounds unhealthy to me. Sort of unwholesome atmosphere. You boys smoke much opium?"

"Tom?" Roger asked.

"Only the best," Thomas Hudson said.

"Got a nice stand of marijuana planted?"

"Any planted, Tom?" Roger asked.

"Was a bad year," Thomas Hudson said. "Rain gave the crop hell."

"Whole thing sounds unwholesome," Johnny drank. "Only saving aspect is you still take a drink. You boys gone in for religion? Has Tom Seen The Light?"

"Tom?" Roger asked.

"Relations with the Deity about the same," Thomas Hudson said.

"Cordial?"

"We are tolerant," Thomas Hudson said. "Practice any

faith you wish. Got a ball field up the island where you can practice."

"I'll give the Deity a fast one high and inside if he crowds the plate," Roger said.

"Roger," said Johnny reproachfully. "It's after dark. Didn't you see twilight fall and dusk set in and darkness come? And you a writer. Never a good idea to speak slightingly of the Deity after dark. He's liable to be right behind you with his bat poised."

"I'll bet he'd crowd the plate, too," Roger said. "I've seen him crowding it lately."

"Yes sir," Johnny said. "And he'd step into your fast one and knock your brains out. I've seen him hit."

"Yes, I guess you have," Roger agreed. "So has Tom and so have I. But I'd still try and get my fast ball by him."

"Let's cut out the theological discussion," Johnny said. "And get something to eat."

"That decrepit old man you keep to tool this thing around the ocean still know how to cook?" Thomas Hudson asked.

"Chowder," Johnny said. "And a yellow rice tonight with plover. Golden plover."

"You sound like a damned interior decorator," Tom said. "There's no gold on them this time of year, anyway. Where'd you shoot the plover?"

"On South Island when we went in to anchor and swim. I whistled the flock back twice and kept knocking them down. There's two apiece."

It was a fine night and after they had eaten dinner they sat out in the stern with coffee and cigars, and a couple of other people, both worthless sporting characters, came over from one of the other boats with a guitar and a banjo and the Negroes gathered on the dock and there was some sporadic singing. In the dark, up on the dock, the boys would lead off with a song and then Fred Wilson, who had the guitar, would sing and Frank Hart would fake along on the banjo. Thomas Hudson could not sing, so he sat back in the dark and listened.

There was quite a lot of celebration going on at Bobby's

place and you could see the lights from the open door over the water. The tide was still ebbing strong, and out where the light shone fish were jumping. They were gray snappers mostly, Tom thought, feeding on the bait fish that fell out with the tide. A few Negro boys were fishing with hand lines and you could hear them talking and cursing softly when they lost a fish, and hear the snappers flopping on the dock when they landed one. There were big snappers out there and the boys were baiting them up with chunks of marlin meat from a fish one of the boats had brought in early that afternoon and that had already been hung up, photographed, weighed, and butchered.

There was quite a crowd on the dock now with the singing and Rupert Pinder, a very big Negro who was said to have once carried a piano on his back, unaided, from the Government dock all the way up the King's Highway to the old club that the hurricane blew away, and who fancied himself as a fighting man, called down from the dock, "Captain John, boys say they getting thirsty."

"Buy something inexpensive and healthful, Rupert."

"Yes sir, Captain John. Rum."

"That's what I had in mind," John said. "Why not try for a demijohn? Better value, I think."

"Many thanks, Captain John," Rupert said. Rupert moved off through the crowd which thinned rapidly and fell in behind him. Thomas Hudson could see them all heading toward Roy's place.

Just then, from one of the boats tied up at Brown's dock, a rocket rose with a whoosh high into the sky and burst with a pop to light up the channel. Another went whooshing up at an angle and burst, this time, just over the near end of their dock.

"Damn," said Fred Wilson. "We should have sent over to Miami for some."

The night was lighted now with rockets whishing and popping and, in the light, Rupert and his followers were coming back out onto the dock, Rupert carrying a big wicker demijohn on his shoulder.

Someone fired a rocket from one of the boats and it burst just over the dock, lighting up the crowd, the dark faces, necks, and hands, and Rupert's flat face, wide shoulders, and thick neck with the wicker-covered jug resting tenderly and proudly alongside his head.

"Cups," he said to his followers, speaking over his shoulder. "Enameled cups."

"Got tin cups, Rupert," one boy said.

"Enameled cups," Rupert said. "Get them. Buy them from Roy. Here's money."

"Get the Verey pistol of ours, Frank," Fred Wilson said. "We might as well shoot up those flares and get some fresh ones."

While Rupert waited grandly for the cups someone brought a saucepan and Rupert poured into it and it was passed around.

"For the little people," Rupert said. "Drink up, unimportant people."

Singing was proceeding steadily and with little organization. Along with the rockets some of the boats were firing off rifles and pistols and from Brown's dock a Tommy gun was skipping tracers out over the channel. It fired a burst of threes and fours, then loosed off a full clip, rattling the red tracers out in a lovely looping arc over the harbor.

The cups came at the same time as Frank Hart dropped down into the stern carrying a case with a Verey pistol and an assortment of flares and one of Rupert's assistants started pouring and handing cups around.

"God bless the Queen," Frank Hart said and loaded and fired a flare past the end of the dock directly at the open door of Mr. Bobby's place. The flare hit the concrete wall beside the door, burst, and burned brightly on the coral road, lighting everything with a white light.

"Take it easy," Thomas Hudson said. "Those things can burn people."

"The hell with take it easy," Frank said. "Let me see if I can bag the Commissioner's house."

"You'll burn it," Roger told him.

"If I burn it I'll pay for it," Frank said.

The flare arced up toward the big white-porched house but it was short and burned brightly just this side of the Commissioner's front porch.

"Good old Commissioner," Frank reloaded. "That will show the bastard whether we're patriotic or not."

"Take it easy, Frank," Tom urged him. "We don't have to play rough."

"Tonight's my night," Frank said. "The Queen's night and mine. Get out of my way, Tom, while I nail Brown's dock."

"He's got gas on it," Roger said.

"Not for long," Frank told him.

It was impossible to tell whether he was trying to miss each shot to devil Roger and Thomas Hudson or whether he was really being bad. Neither Roger nor Thomas Hudson were sure either but they knew no one should be able to shoot a signal pistol with that much accuracy. And there was gas on the dock.

Frank stood up, took careful aim with his left arm down at his side like a duelist, and fired. The flare hit the dock at the far end from where the gas drums were piled and ricocheted off into the channel.

"Hey," someone yelled from the boats that were tied up at Brown's. "What the hell?"

"Almost a perfect shot," Frank said. "Now I'm going to try for the Commissioner again."

"You better damn well cut it out," Thomas Hudson told him.

"Rupert," Frank called up, ignoring Thomas Hudson. "Let me have some of that, will you?"

"Yes sir, Captain Frank," Rupert said. "You got a cup?"

"Get me a cup," Frank said to Fred, who was standing watching.

"Yes *sir*, Mr. Frank."

Fred jumped and came back with the cup. His face was shining with excitement and pleasure.

"You figure to burn down the Commissioner, Mr. Frank?"

"Only if he catches fire," Frank said.

He handed the cup up to Rupert who three quarters filled it and reached it down.

"The Queen, God bless her," Frank drained the cup.

It was a terrific slug of rum to take like that.

"God bless her. God bless her, Captain Frank," Rupert said solemnly, and the others echoed, "God bless her. God bless her indeed."

"Now for the Commissioner," Frank said. He fired the signal pistol straight up in the air, a little into the wind. He had loaded with a parachute flare and the wind drifted the bright white light down over the cruiser astern.

"Sure missed Commissioner that time," Rupert said. "What's wrong, Captain Frank?"

"I wanted to illuminate this beautiful scene," Frank said. "No hurry about the Commissioner."

"Commissioner'd burn good, Captain Frank," Rupert advised. "I don't want to influence you in it but it hasn't rained on island for two months and Commissioner's dry as tinder."

"Where's Constable?" Frank asked.

"Constable's keeping out of the way of things," Rupert said. "Don't you worry about Constable. Nobody on this dock would see shot if shot was fired."

"Everybody on this dock lay flat down on their faces and see nothing," a voice came from back in the crowd. "Nothing has been heard. Nothing will be seen."

"I give the command," Rupert urged. "Every face is averted." Then, encouragingly, "She's just as dry as tinder that old place."

"Let me see how you'd do it," Frank said.

He loaded with another parachute flare and fired up and into the wind. In the falling garish light everyone on the dock was lying face down or was on hands and knees with eyes covered.

"God bless you, Captain Frank," came Rupert's deep solemn voice out of the dark when the flare died. "May He in His infinite mercy give you courage to burn Commissioner."

"Where's his wife and children?" Frank asked.

"We get them out. Don't you worry," Rupert said. "No harm of any kind come to anyone innocent."

"Should we burn him?" Frank turned to the others in the cockpit.

"Oh, cut it out," Thomas Hudson said. "For Christ's sake."

"I'm leaving in the morning," Frank said. "As a matter of fact I'm cleared."

"Let's burn him," Fred Wilson said. "Natives seem to favor it."

"Burn him, Captain Frank," Rupert urged. "What do you say?" he asked the others.

"Burn him. Burn him. God give you strength to burn him," said the boys on the dock.

"Nobody want him unburned?" Frank asked them.

"Burn him, Captain Frank. Nobody see it. Nothing ever been heard. Not a word's been said. Burn him."

"Need a few practice shots," Frank said.

"Get off this damned boat if you're going to burn him," Johnny said.

Frank looked at him and shook his head a little so that neither Roger nor the boys on the dock saw it.

"He's ashes now," he said. "Let me have just one more, Rupert, to stiffen my will."

He handed up the cup.

"Captain Frank," Rupert leaned down to speak to him. "This will be the deed of your life."

Up on the dock the boys had started a new song.

> "Captain Frank in the harbor
>   Tonight's the night we got fun."

Then a pause, and pitched higher . . .

> "Captain Frank in the harbor
>   Tonight's the night we got fun."

The second line was sung like a drum bonging. Then they went on:

> "Commissioner called Rupert a dirty black hound
>   Captain Frank fired his flare pistol and burnt him to the ground."

Then they went back to the other old African rhythm four of the men in the launch had heard sung by the Negroes that pulled the ropes on the ferries that crossed the rivers along the coast road between Mombasa, Malindi, and Lamu where, as they pulled in unison, the Negroes sang improvised work songs that described and made fun of the white people they were carrying on the ferry.

"Captain Frank in the harbor
Tonight's the night we got fun.
Captain Frank in the harbor"

Defiant, insultingly, despairingly defiant the minor notes rose. Then the drum's bonging response.

"Tonight's the night we got fun!"

"You see, Captain Frank?" Rupert urged, leaning down into the cockpit. "You got the song already before you even commit the deed."

"I'm getting pretty committed," Frank said to Thomas Hudson. Then, "One more practice shot," he told Rupert.

"Practice makes perfect," Rupert said happily.

"Captain Frank's practicing now for the death," someone said on the dock.

"Captain Frank's wilder than a wild hog," came another voice.

"Captain Frank's a *man*."

"Rupert," Frank said. "Another cup of that, please. Not to encourage me. Just to help my aim."

"God guide you, Captain Frank," Rupert reached down the cup. "Sing the Captain Frank song, boys."

Frank drained the cup.

"The last practice shot," he said and firing just over the cabin cruiser lying astern he bounced the flare off Brown's gas drums and into the water.

"You son of a bitch," Thomas Hudson said to him very quietly.

"Shut up, christer," Frank said to Thomas Hudson. "That was my masterpiece."

Just then, in the cockpit of the other cruiser, a man came out onto the stern wearing pajama trousers with no top and shouted, "Listen, you swine! Stop it, will you? There's a lady trying to sleep down below."

"A lady?" Wilson asked.

"Yes, goddam it, a lady," the man said. "My wife. And you dirty bastards firing those flares to keep her awake and keep anybody from getting any sleep."

"Why don't you give her sleeping pills?" Frank said. "Rupert, send a boy for some sleeping pills."

"Do you know what you do, colonel?" Wilson said. "Why don't you just comport yourself as a good husband should? That'll put her to sleep. She's probably repressed. Maybe she's thwarted. That's what the analyst always tells my wife."

They were very rough boys and Frank was way in the wrong but the man who had been pitching the drunk all day had gotten off to an exceedingly bad start with the approach he had taken. Neither John nor Roger nor Thomas Hudson had said a word. The other two, from the moment the man had come out onto the stern and yelled, "Swine," had worked together like a really fast shortstop and second baseman.

"You filthy swine," the man said. He did not seem to have much of a vocabulary and he looked between thirty-five and forty. It was hard to tell his age closely, even though he had switched on his cockpit lights. He looked much better than Thomas Hudson had expected him to look after hearing the stories all day and Thomas Hudson thought he must have gotten some sleep. Thomas Hudson remembered, then, that he had been sleeping at Bobby's.

"I'd try Nembutal," Frank told him very confidentially. "Unless she's allergic to it."

"I don't see why she's so dissatisfied," Fred Wilson told him. "Why you're quite a fine-looking physical specimen. You really look pretty damned good. I'll bet you're the terror of the Racquet Club. What does it cost you to keep in that wonderful shape? Look at him, Frank. Did you ever see as expensive a looking top of a man as that?"

"You made a mistake though, governor," Frank told him. "You're wearing the wrong end of your pajamas. Frankly I've never seen a man wearing that bottom part before. Do you really wear that to bed?"

"Can't you filthy-mouthed swine let a lady sleep?" the man said.

"Why don't you just go down below," Frank said to him. "You're liable to get in trouble around here using all those epithets. You haven't got your chauffeur here to look after you. Does your chauffeur always take you to school?"

"He doesn't go to school, Frank," Fred Wilson said, putting aside his guitar. "He's a big grown-up boy. He's a businessman. Can't you recognize a big businessman?"

"Are you a businessman, sonny?" Frank asked. "Then you know it's good business for you to run along down into your cabin. There isn't any good business for you up here."

"He's right," Fred Wilson said. "You haven't any future around with us. Just go down to your cabin. You'll get used to the noise."

"You filthy swine," the man said and looked at them all.

"Just take that beautiful body down below, will you?" Wilson said. "I'm sure you'll get the lady to sleep."

"You swine," the man said. "You rotten swine."

"Can't you think up any other names?" Frank said. *"Swine's* getting awfully dull. You better go down below before you catch cold. If I had a wonderful chest like that I wouldn't risk it out here on a windy night like this."

The man looked at them all as though he were memorizing them.

"You'll be able to remember us," Frank told him. "If not I'll remind you any time I see you."

"You filth," the man said and turned and went below.

"Who is he?" Johnny Goodner asked. "I've seen him somewhere."

"I know him and he knows me," Frank said. "He's no good."

"Can't you remember who he is?" Johnny asked.

"He's a jerk," Frank said. "What difference does it make who he is outside of that?"

"None, I guess," Thomas Hudson said. "You two certainly swarmed on him."

"That's what you're supposed to do with a jerk. Swarm on him. We weren't really rude to him."

"I thought you made your lack of sympathy clear," Thomas Hudson said.

"I heard a dog barking," Roger said. "The flares probably scared his dog. Let's cut the flares out. I know you're having fun, Frank. You're getting away with murder and nothing bad's happened. But why terrify the poor bloody dog?"

"That was his wife barking," Frank said cheerily. "Let's shoot one into his cabin and illuminate the whole domestic scene."

"I'm getting the hell out of here," Roger said. "You joke the way I don't like. I don't think jokes with motorcars are funny. I don't think drunken flying is funny. I don't think scaring dogs is funny."

"Nobody's keeping you," Frank said. "Lately you're a pain in the ass to everybody anyway."

"Yes?"

"Sure. You and Tom christing around. Spoiling any fun. All you reformed bastards. You used to have plenty of fun. Now nobody can have any. You and your brand new social conscience."

"So it's social conscience if I think it would be better not to set Brown's dock on fire?"

"Sure. It's just a form of it. You've got it bad. I heard about you on the coast."

"Why don't you take your pistol and go play somewhere else?" Johnny Goodner said to Frank. "We were all having fun till you got so rough."

"So you've got it, too," Frank said.

"Take it a little easy," Roger warned him.

"I'm the only guy here still likes to have any fun," Frank said. "All you big overgrown religious maniacs and social workers and hypocrites—"

"Captain Frank," Rupert leaned down over the edge of the dock.

"Rupert's my only friend," Frank looked up. "Yes, Rupert?"

"Captain Frank, what about Commissioner?"

"We'll burn him, Rupert old boy."

"God bless you, Captain Frank," Rupert said. "Care for any rum?"

"I'm fine, Rupert," Frank told him. "Everybody down now."

"Everybody down," Rupert ordered. "Down flat."

Frank fired over the edge of the dock and the flare lit on the graveled walk just short of the Commissioner's porch and burned there. The boys on the dock groaned.

"Damn," Rupert said. "You nearly made her. Bad luck. Reload, Captain Frank."

The lights went on in the cockpit of the cruiser astern of them and the man was out there again. This time he had a white shirt and white duck trousers on and he wore sneakers. His hair was combed and his face was red with white patches. The nearest man to him in the stern was John, who had his back to him, and next to John was Roger who was just sitting there looking gloomy. There was about three feet of water between the two sterns and the man stood there and pointed his finger at Roger.

"You slob," he said. "You rotten filthy slob."

Roger just looked up at him with a surprised look.

"You mean me, don't you?" Frank called to him. "And it's swine, not slob."

The man ignored him and went on at Roger.

"You big fat slob," the man almost choked. "You phony. You faker. You cheap phony. You rotten writer and lousy painter."

"Who are you talking to and about what?" Roger stood up.

"You. You slob. You phony you. You coward. Oh you slob. You filthy slob."

"You're crazy," Roger said quietly.

"You slob," the man said across the space of water that separated the two boats the same way someone might speak insultingly to an animal in one of those modern zoos where no bars, but only pits, separate the visitors from the beasts. "You phony."

"He means me," Frank said happily. "Don't you know me? I'm the swine."

"I mean you," the man pointed his finger at Roger. "You phony."

"Look," Roger said to him. "You're not talking to me at all. You're just talking to be able to repeat back in New York what you said to me."

He spoke reasonably and patiently as though he really wanted the man to understand and shut up.

"You slob," the man shouted, working himself further and further into this hysteria he had even dressed up for. "You rotten filthy phony."

"You're not talking to me," Roger repeated to him very quietly now and Thomas Hudson saw that he had decided. "So shut up now. If you want to talk to me get up on the dock."

Roger started up for the dock and, oddly enough, the man came climbing up on the dock as fast as you please. He had talked himself into it and worked himself up to it. But he was doing it. The Negroes fell back and then closed in around the two of them leaving plenty of room.

Thomas Hudson didn't know what the man expected to happen when he got up on the dock. No one said anything and there were all those black faces around him and he took a swing at Roger and Roger hit him in the mouth with a left and his mouth started to bleed. He swung at Roger again and Roger hooked him hard to the right eye twice. He grabbed hold of Roger and Roger's sweatshirt tore when he dug the man in the belly hard with his right and then pushed him away and slapped him hard across the face backhand with his open left hand.

None of the Negroes had said a word. They just kept the two men surrounded and gave them plenty of room. Someone, Tom thought it was John's boy Fred, had turned the dock lights on and you could see well.

Roger went after the man and hooked him three times fast to the head high up. The man grabbed him and his sweatshirt tore again as he pushed him away and jabbed him twice in the mouth.

"Cut out those lefts," Frank yelled. "Throw your right and cool the son of a bitch. Cool him."

"Got anything to say to me?" Roger said to the man and hooked him hard on the mouth. The man was bleeding badly from the mouth and the whole right side of his face was coming up and his right eye was almost closed.

The man grabbed Roger and Roger held him inside and steadied him. The man was breathing hard and he hadn't said anything. Roger had a thumb on the inside of the man's two elbows and Tom could see him rubbing the thumbs back and forth over the tendons between the biceps and the forearms.

"Don't you bleed on me, you son of a bitch," Roger said, and brought his left hand up fast and loose and knocked the man's head back and then backhanded him across the face again.

"You can get a new nose now," he said.

"Cool him, Roger. Cool him," Frank pled with him.

"Can't you see what he's doing, you dope?" Fred Wilson said. "He's ruining him."

The man grabbed Roger and Roger held him and pushed him away.

"Hit me," he said. "Come on. Hit me."

The man swung at him and Roger ducked it and grabbed him.

"What's your name?" he said to the man.

The man didn't answer. All he did was breathe as though he were dying with asthma.

Roger was holding the man again with his thumbs pressing in on the inside of his elbows. "You're a strong son of a bitch," he said to the man. "Who the hell ever told you you could fight?"

The man swung at him weakly and Roger grabbed him, pulled him forward, spun him a little, and clubbed him twice on the ear with the base of his right fist.

"You think you've learned not to talk to people?" he asked the man.

"Look at his ear," Rupert said. "Like a bunch of grapes."

Roger was holding the man again with his thumbs pushing in against the tendons at the base of the biceps. Thomas Hudson was watching the man's face. It had not been frightened at the start; just mean as a pig's is; a really mean boar. But it was really completely frightened now. He had probably never heard of fights that no one stopped. Probably he thought in some part of his mind about the stories he had read where men were kicked to death if they went down. He still tried to fight. Each time Roger told him to hit him or pushed him away he tried to throw a punch. He hadn't quit.

Roger pushed him away. The man stood there and looked at him. When Roger wasn't holding him in that way that made him feel absolutely helpless the fear drained away a little and the meanness came back. He stood there frightened, badly hurt, his face destroyed, his mouth bleeding, and that ear looking like an overripe fig as the small individual hemorrhages united into one great swelling inside the skin. As he stood there, Roger's hands off him now, the fear drained and the indestructible meanness welled up.

"Anything to say?" Roger asked him.

"Slob," the man said. As he said it, he pulled his chin in and put his hands up and turned half away in a gesture an incorrigible child might make.

"Now it comes," Rupert shouted. "Now it's going to roll."

But it was nothing dramatic nor scientific. Roger stepped quickly over to where the man stood and raised his left shoulder and dropped his right fist down and swung it up so it smashed against the side of the man's head. He went down on his hands and knees, his forehead resting on the dock. He knelt there a little while with his forehead against the planking and then he went gently over on his side. Roger looked at him and then came over to the edge of the dock and swung down into the cockpit.

The crew of the man's yacht were carrying him on board. They had not intervened in what had happened on the dock and they had picked him up from where he lay on his side on the dock and carried him sagging heavily. Some of the Negroes had helped them lower him down to the stern and take him below. They shut the door after they took him in.

"He ought to have a doctor," Thomas Hudson said.

"He didn't hit hard on the dock," Roger said. "I thought about the dock."

"I don't think that last crack alongside the ear did him a lot of good," Johnny Goodner said.

"You ruined his face," Frank said. "And the ear. I never saw an ear come up so fast. First it was like a bunch of grapes and then it was as full as an orange."

"Bare hands are a bad thing," Roger said. "People don't have any idea what they'll do. I wish I'd never seen him."

"Well, you'll never see him again without being able to recognize him."

"I hope he'll come around," Roger said.

"It was a beautiful fight, Mr. Roger," Fred said.

"Fight, hell," Roger said. "Why the hell did that have to happen?"

"The gentleman certainly brought it on himself," Fred said.

"Cut out worrying, will you?" Frank said to Roger. "I've seen hundreds of guys cooled and that guy is OK."

Up on the dock the boys were drifting away commenting on the fight. There had been something about the way the white man had looked when he was carried aboard that they did not like and all the bravery about burning the Commissioner's house was evaporating.

"Well, good night, Captain Frank," Rupert said.

"Going, Rupert?" Frank asked him.

"Thought we might all go up see what's going on at Mr. Bobby's."

"Good night, Rupert," said Roger. "See you tomorrow."

Roger was feeling very low and his left hand was swollen as big as a grapefruit. His right was puffed too but not as badly. There was nothing else to show he had been in a fight except that the neck of his sweatshirt was ripped open and flapped down on his chest. The man had hit him once high up on his head and there was a small bump there. John put some Mercurochrome on the places where his knuckles were skinned and cut. Roger didn't even look at his hands.

"Let's go up to Bobby's place and see if there's any fun," Frank said.

"Don't worry about anything, Roge," Fred Wilson said and climbed up on the dock. "Only suckers worry."

They went on along the dock carrying their guitar and banjo toward where the light and the singing were coming out of the open door of the Ponce de León.

"Freddy is a pretty good joe," John said to Thomas Hudson.

"He always was," Thomas Hudson said. "But he and Frank are bad together."

Roger did not say anything and Thomas Hudson was worried about him; about him and about other things.

"Don't you think we might turn in?" he said to him.

"I'm still spooked about that character," Roger said.

He was sitting with his back toward the stern, looking glum and holding his left hand in his right.

"Well you don't have to be anymore," John spoke very quietly. "He's walking around now."

"Really?"

"He's coming out now and he's carrying a shotgun."

"I'll be a sad son of a bitch," Roger said. But his voice was happy again. He sat with his back toward the stern and never turned around to look.

The man came out to the stern this time wearing both a pajama top and trousers, but what you saw was the shotgun. Thomas Hudson looked away from it and to his face and his face was very bad. Someone had worked on it and there was gauze and tape over the cheeks and a lot of Mercurochrome had been used. They hadn't been able to do anything about his ear. Thomas Hudson imagined it must have hurt to have anything touch it, and it just stood out looking very taut and swollen and it had become the dominant feature of his face. No one said anything and the man just stood there with his spoiled face and his shotgun. He probably could not see anyone very clearly the way his eyes were puffed tight. He stood there and he did not say anything and neither did anyone else.

Roger turned his head very slowly, saw him, and spoke over his shoulder.

"Go put the gun away and go to bed."

The man stood there with the gun. His swollen lips were working but he did not say anything.

"You're mean enough to shoot a man in the back but you haven't got the guts," Roger spoke over his shoulder very quietly. "Go put the gun away and go to bed."

Roger still sat there with his back toward the man. Then he took what Thomas Hudson thought was an awful chance.

"Doesn't he remind you just a little bit of Lady Macbeth coming out there in his nightclothes?" he asked the three others in the stern.

Thomas Hudson waited for it then. But nothing happened and after a while the man turned and went down into the cabin taking the shotgun with him.

"I feel very, very much better," Roger said. "I could feel that sweat run clean down from my armpit and onto my leg. Let's go home, Tom. Man's OK."

"Not too awfully OK," Johnny said.

"OK enough," Roger said. "What a human being that is."

"Come on, Roger," Thomas Hudson said. "Come on up to my place for a while."

"All right."

They said good night to John and walked up the King's Highway toward the house. There was still plenty of celebrating going on.

"Do you want to go into the Ponce?" Thomas Hudson asked.

"Hell no," Roger said.

"I thought I'd tell Freddy the man's OK."

"You tell him. I'll go on to your house."

When Thomas Hudson got home Roger was lying face down on a bed in the far up-island end of the screen porch. It was dark and you could just barely hear the noise of the celebrating.

"Sleeping?" Thomas Hudson asked him.

"No."

"Would you like a drink?"

"I don't think so. Thanks."

"How's the hand?"

"Just swelled and sore. It's nothing."

"You feeling low again?"

"Yes. I've got it bad."

"The kids will be here in the morning."

"That will be fine."

"You're sure you wouldn't like a drink?"

"No, kid. But you have one."

"I'll have a whisky and soda to go to sleep on."

Thomas Hudson went to the icebox, mixed the drink, and came back out to the screened porch and sat there in the dark with Roger lying on the bed.

"You know, there's an awful lot of real bastards loose," Roger said. "That guy was no good, Tom."

"You taught him something."

"No. I don't think so. I humiliated him and I ruined him a little. But he'll take it out on someone else."

"He brought it on."

"Sure. But I didn't finish it."

"You did everything but kill him."

"That's what I mean. He'll just be worse now."

"I think maybe you taught him a hell of a lesson."

"No. I don't think so. It was the same thing out on the coast."

"What really happened? You haven't told me anything since you got back."

"It was a fight, sort of like this one."

"Who with?"

He named a man who was very high up in what is known as the industry.

"I didn't want any part of it," Roger said. "It was out at the house where I was having some woman trouble and I suppose, technically, I shouldn't have been there. But that night I took it and took it and took it from this character. Much worse than tonight. Finally I just couldn't take it any more and I gave it to him, really gave it to him without thinking about anything, and his head hit wrong on the marble steps going down to the pool. This was all by the pool. He came out of it at the Cedars of Lebanon finally about the third day and so I missed manslaughter. But they had it all set. With the witnesses they had I'd have been lucky to get that."

"So then what?"

"So then, after he's back on the job, I get the real frameroo. The full-sized one. Complete with handles."

"What was it?"

"Everything. In series."

"Want to tell me?"

"No. It wouldn't be useful to you. Just take my word for it that it was a frame. It's so awful nobody mentions it. Haven't you noticed?"

"Sort of."

"So I wasn't feeling so good about tonight. There's a lot of wickeds at large. Really bads. And hitting them is no solution. I think that's one reason why they provoke you." He turned over on the bed and lay face up. "You know evil is a hell of a thing, Tommy. And it's smart as a pig. You know they had something in the old days about good and evil."

"Plenty of people wouldn't classify you as a straight good," Thomas Hudson told him.

"No. Nor do I claim to be. Nor even good nor anywhere near good. I wish I were though. Being against evil doesn't make you good. Tonight I was against it and then I was evil myself. I could feel it coming in just like a tide."

"All fights are bad."

"I know it. But what are you going to do about them?"

"You have to win them when they start."

"Sure. But I was taking pleasure in it from the minute it started."

"You would have taken more pleasure if he could have fought."

"I hope so," Roger said. "Though I don't know now. I just want to destroy them. But when you start taking pleasure in it you are awfully close to the thing you're fighting."

"He was an awful type," Thomas Hudson said.

"He couldn't have been any worse than the last one on the coast. The trouble is, Tommy, there are so many of them. They have them in all countries and they are getting bigger all the time. Times aren't good, Tommy."

"When did you ever see them good?"

"We always had good times."

"Sure. We had good times in all sorts of good places. But the times weren't good."

"I never knew," Roger said. "Everybody claimed they were good and then everybody was busted. I didn't have any money when they all had it. Then when I had some was when things were really bad. But people didn't always seem as goddamned mean and evil though."

"You've been going around with awful people, too."

"I see some good ones once in a while."

"Not very many."

"Sure I do. You don't know all my friends."

"You run with a pretty seedy lot."

"Whose friends were those tonight? Your friends or my friends?"

"Our friends. They're not so bad. They're worthless but they're not really evil."

"No," said Roger. "I guess not. Frank is pretty bad. Bad enough. I don't think he's evil though. But there's a lot of stuff I can't take anymore. And he and Fred eviled up awfully fast."

"I know about good and evil. I'm not trying to misunderstand nor play dumb."

"I don't know much about good because I've always been a failure at it. That evil is my dish. I can recognize that old evil."

"I'm sorry tonight turned out so lousy."

"I'm just feeling low."

"Do you want to turn in? You better sleep here."

"Thanks. I will if you don't mind. But I think I'll go in the library and read for a while. Where are those Australian stories you had the last time I was here?"

"Henry Lawson's?"

"Yes."

"I'll get them."

Thomas Hudson went to bed and when he woke in the night the light was still on in the library.

V

WHEN Thomas Hudson woke there was a light east breeze blowing and out across the flats the sand was bone white under the blue sky and the small high clouds that were traveling with the wind made dark moving patches on the green water. The wheel of the wind charger was turning in the breeze and it was a fine fresh-feeling morning.

Roger was gone and Thomas Hudson breakfasted by himself and read the Mainland paper that had come across yesterday. He had put it away without reading it to save it for breakfast.

"What time the boys coming in?" Joseph asked.

"Around noon."

"They'll be here for lunch though?"

"Yes."

"Mr. Roger was gone when I came," Joseph said. "He didn't have any breakfast."

"Maybe he'll be in now."

"Boy said he see him go off sculling in the dinghy."

After Thomas Hudson had finished breakfast and the paper he went out on the porch on the ocean side and went to work. He worked well and was nearly finished when he heard Roger come in and come up the stairs.

Roger looked over his shoulder and said, "It's going to be good."

"Maybe."

"Where did you see those waterspouts?"

"I never saw these. These are some I'm doing to order. How's your hand?"

"Still puffy."

Roger watched him work and he did not turn around.

"If it wasn't for the hand that would all seem just like a nasty dream."

"Pretty nasty one."

"Do you suppose that guy really did come out with a shotgun?"

"I don't know," Thomas Hudson said. "And I don't care."

"Sorry," Roger said. "Want me to go?"

"No. Stick around. I'm about through. I won't pay any attention to you."

"They got away at first light," Roger said. "I saw them go."

"What were you doing up then?"

"I couldn't sleep after I stopped reading and I wasn't very good company for myself so I went down to the docks and sat around with some of the boys. The Ponce never did close up. I saw Joseph."

"Joseph said you were out sculling."

"Right-hand sculling. Trying to exercise it out. I did too. Feel fine now."

"That's about all I can do now," Thomas Hudson said and started to clean up and put the gear away. "The kids will be just about taking off now." He looked at his watch. "Why don't we just have a quick one?"

"Fine. I could use one."

"It isn't quite twelve."

"I don't think that makes any difference. You're through working and I'm on a vacation. But maybe we better wait till twelve if that's your rule."

"All right."

"I've been keeping that rule too. It's an awful nuisance some mornings when a drink would make you feel all right."

"Let's break it," Thomas Hudson said. "I get awfully excited when I know I'm going to see them," he explained.

"I know."

"Joe," Roger called. "Bring the shaker and rig for martinis."

"Yes *sir*. I got her rigged now."

"What did you rig so early for? Do you think we are rummies?"

"No sir, Mr. Roger. I figured that was what you were saving that empty stomach for."

"Here's to us and the kids," Roger said.

"They ought to have fun this year. You better stay up here too. You can always get away to the shack if they get on your nerves."

"I'll stay up here part of the time if I don't bother you."

"You don't bother me."

"It will be wonderful to have them."

It was too. They were good kids and now they had been at the house for a week. The tuna run was over and there were few boats at the island now and the life was slow and normal again and the weather was early summer.

The boys slept on cots on the screened porch and it is much less lonely sleeping when you can hear children breathing when you wake in the night. The nights were cool from the breeze that came across the banks and when the breeze fell it would be cool from the sea.

The boys had been a little shy when they first came and much neater than they were later. But there was no great neatness problem if you had them rinse the sand from their feet before they came into the house and hang their wet swimming shorts outside and put on dry ones in the house. Joseph aired their pajamas when he made up the cots in the morning and after sunning them folded the pajamas and put them away and there were only the shirts and the sweaters they wore in the evening to be scattered around. That, at least, was how it was in principle. Actually every sort of gear they owned was scattered all over everywhere. Thomas Hudson did not mind it. When a man lives in a house by himself he gets very precise habits and they get to be a pleasure. But it felt good to have some of them broken up. He knew he would have his habits again long after he would no longer have the boys.

Sitting on the sea porch working he could see the biggest one and the middle-sized one and the small one lying on the beach with Roger. They were talking, and digging in the sand, and arguing but he could not hear what they were saying.

The biggest boy was long and dark with Thomas Hudson's neck and shoulders and the long swimmer's legs and big feet. He had a rather Indian face and was a happy boy although in repose his face looked almost tragic.

Thomas Hudson had looked at him when his face had that sad look and asked, "What are you thinking about, Schatz?"

"Fly-tying," the boy would say, his face lighting instantly. It was the eyes and the mouth that made it tragic-looking when he was thinking and, when he spoke, they brought it to life.

The middle boy always reminded Thomas Hudson of an otter. He had the same color hair as an otter's fur and it had almost the same texture as that of an underwater animal and he browned all over in a strange dark gold tan. He always reminded his father of the sort of animal that has a sound and humorous life by itself. Otters and bears are the animals that joke most and bears, of course, are very close to men. This boy would never be wide enough and strong enough to be a bear and he would never be an athlete, nor did he want to be; but he had a lovely small-animal quality and he had a good mind and a life of his own. He was affectionate and he had a sense of justice and was good company. He was also a Cartesian doubter and an avid arguer and he teased well and without meanness although sometimes he teased toughly. He had other qualities no one knew about and the other two boys respected him immensely although they tried to tease him and tear him down on any point where he was vulnerable. Naturally they had rows among themselves and they teased each other with considerable malice, but they were well mannered and respectful with grown-ups.

The smallest boy was fair and was built like a pocket battleship. He was a copy of Thomas Hudson, physically, reduced in scale and widened and shortened. His skin freckled when it tanned and he had a humorous face and was born being very old. He was a devil too, and deviled both his older brothers, and he had a dark side to him that nobody except Thomas Hudson could ever understand. Neither of them thought about this except that they recognized it in each other and knew it was bad and the man respected it and understood the boy's having it. They were very close to each other although Thomas Hudson had never been as much with this boy as with the others. This youngest boy, Andrew, was a precocious excellent athlete and he had been marvelous with horses since he had first ridden. The other boys were very proud of him but they did not want any nonsense from him, either. He was a little unbelievable and anyone could well have doubted his feats except that many people had seen him ride and watched him jump and seen his cold, professional modesty. He was a boy born to be quite wicked who was being very good and he carried his wickedness around with him transmuted into a sort of teasing gaiety. But he was a bad boy and the others knew it and he knew it. He was just being good while his badness grew inside him.

There, below the sea porch, the four of them were lying on the sand with the oldest boy, young Tom, on one side of Roger and the smallest one, Andrew, next to him on the middle side and the middle one, David, stretched out next to Tom on his back with his eyes closed. Thomas Hudson cleaned up his gear and went down to join them.

"Hi, papa," the oldest boy said. "Did you work well?"

"Are you going to swim, papa?" asked the middle boy.

"The water's pretty good, papa," the youngest boy said.

"How are you father?" Roger grinned. "How's the painting business, Mr. Hudson?"

"Painting business is over for the day, gentlemen."

"Oh swell," said David, the middle boy. "Do you think we can go goggle-fishing?"

"Let's go after lunch."

"That's wonderful," the big boy said.

"Won't it maybe be too rough?" Andrew, the youngest boy, asked.

"For you, maybe," his oldest brother, Tom, told him.

"No, Tommy. For anyone."

"They stay in the rocks when it's rough," David said. "They're afraid of the surge the same way we are. I think it makes them seasick too. Papa, don't fish get seasick?"

"Sure," Thomas Hudson said. "Sometimes in the live-well of a smack in rough weather the groupers will get so seasick that they die."

"Didn't I tell you?" David asked his older brother.

"They get sick and they die," young Tom said. "But what proves that it's seasick?"

"I think you could say they were really seasick," Thomas Hudson said. "I don't know whether they would be if they could swim freely, though."

"But don't you see that in the reef they can't swim freely either, papa?" David said. "They have their holes and certain places they move out in. But they have to stay in the holes for fear of bigger fish and the surge bangs them around just the way it would if they were in the well of a smack."

"Not quite as much," young Tom disagreed.

"Maybe not quite as much," David admitted judiciously.

"But enough," Andrew said. He whispered to his father, "If they keep it up, we won't have to go."

"Don't you like it?"

"I like it wonderful but I'm scared of it."

"What scares you?"

"Everything underwater. I'm scared as soon as I let my air out. Tommy can swim wonderfully but he's scared underwater too. David's the only one of us that isn't scared underwater."

"I'm scared lots of times," Thomas Hudson told him.

"Are you really?"

"Everybody is, I think."

"David isn't. No matter where it is. But David's scared now of horses because they threw him so many times."

"Listen, punk," David had heard him. *"How* was I thrown?"

"I don't know. It was so many times I don't remember."

"Well let me tell you. I know how I was thrown so much. When I used to ride Old Paint that year he used to swell himself up when they cinched him and then later the saddle would slip with me."

"I never had that trouble with him," Andrew said smartly.

"Oh, the devil," David said. "Probably he liked you like everybody does. Maybe somebody told him who you were."

"I used to read out loud to him about me out of the papers," Andrew said.

"I'll bet he went off on a dead run then," Thomas Hudson said. "You know what happened to David was that he started to ride that old broken-down quarter horse that got sound on us and there wasn't any place for the horse to run. Horses aren't supposed to go like that across that sort of country."

"I wasn't saying I could have ridden him, papa," Andrew said.

"You better not," David said. Then, "Oh hell, you probably could have. Sure you could have. But honestly, Andy, you don't know how he used to be going before I would spook. I was spooked of the saddle horn. Oh the hell with it. I was spooked."

"Papa, do we actually have to go goggle-fishing?" Andrew asked.

"Not if it's too rough."

"Who decides if it's too rough?"

"I decide."

"Good," Andy said. "It certainly looks too rough to me."

"Papa, have you still got Old Paint out at the ranch?" Andy asked.

"I believe so," Thomas Hudson said. "I rented the ranch, you know."

"Really?"

"Yes. The end of last year."

"But we can still go there, can't we?" David asked quickly.

"Oh sure. We have the big cabin on the beach down by the river."

"The ranch is the best place I was ever at," Andy said. "Outside of here, of course."

"I thought you used to like Rochester best," David teased him. That was where he used to be left with his nurse when she stayed with her family in the summer months when the other boys went west.

"I did, too. Rochester was a wonderful place."

"Do you remember when we came home that fall the time we killed the three grizzlies and you tried to tell him about it, Dave, and what he said?" Thomas Hudson asked.

"No, papa. I can't remember exactly that far back."

"It was in the butler's pantry where you guys ate and you were having children's supper and telling him about it and Anna was saying, 'Oh my gracious, David, that must have been exciting. And what did you do *then?*' and this wicked old man, he must have been about five or six then, spoke up and said, 'Well that's probably very interesting, David, to people who are interested in that sort of thing. But we don't have grizzlies in Rochester.' "

"See, horseman?" David said. "How you were then?"

"All right, papa," Andrew said. "Tell him about when he would read nothing but the funny papers and read funny papers on the trip through the Everglades and wouldn't look at anything after he went to that school the fall we were in New York and got to be a heel."

"I remember it," David said. "Papa doesn't have to tell it."

"You came out of it all right," Thomas Hudson said.

"I had to, I guess. It certainly would have been something pretty bad to have stayed in."

"Tell them about when I was little," young Tom said, rolling over and taking hold of David's ankle. "I'll never get to be as good in real life as the stories about me when I was little."

"I knew you when you were little," Thomas Hudson said. "You were quite a strange character then."

"He was just strange because he lived in strange places," the smallest boy said. "I could have been strange in Paris and Spain and Austria."

"He's strange now, horseman," David said. "He doesn't need any exotic backgrounds."

"What's exotic backgrounds?"

"What you haven't got."

"I'll bet I'll have them, then."

"Shut up and let papa tell," young Tom said. "Tell

them about when you and I used to go around together in Paris."

"You weren't so strange then," Thomas Hudson said. "As a baby you were an awfully sound character. Mother and I used to leave you in the crib that was made out of a clothes basket in that flat where we lived over the sawmill and F. Puss the big cat would curl up in the foot of the basket and wouldn't let anybody come near you. You said your name was G'Ning G'Ning and we used to call you G'Ning G'Ning the Terrible."

"Where did I get a name like that?"

"Off a street car or an autobus I think. The sound the conductor made."

"Couldn't I speak French?"

"Not too well then."

"Tell me about a little later by the time I could speak French."

"Later on I used to wheel you in the carriage, it was a cheap, very light, folding carriage, down the street to the Closerie des Lilas where we'd have breakfast and I'd read the paper and you'd watch everything that went past on the boulevard. Then we'd finish breakfast—"

"What would we have?"

"Brioche and café au lait."

"Me too?"

"You'd just have a taste of coffee in the milk."

"I can remember. Where would we go then?"

"I'd wheel you across the street from the Closerie des Lilas and past the fountain with the bronze horses and the fish and the mermaids and down between the long *allées* of chestnut trees with the French children playing and their nurses on the benches beside the gravel paths—"

"And the École Alsacienne on the left," young Tom said.

"And apartment buildings on the right—"

"And apartment buildings and apartments with glass roofs for studios all along the street that goes down to the left and quite triste from the darkness of the stone because that was the shady side," young Tom said.

"Is it fall or spring or winter?" Thomas Hudson asked.
"Late fall."

"Then you were cold in the face, and your cheeks and
your nose were red and we would go into the Luxembourg
through the iron gate at the upper end and down toward
the lake and around the lake once and then turn to the
right toward the Medici Fountain and the statues and out
of the gate in front of the Odéon and down a couple of
side streets to the Boulevard Saint-Michel—"

"The Boul' Mich'—"

"And down the Boul' Mich' past the Cluny—"

"On our right—"

"That was very dark and gloomy looking and across the
Boulevard Saint-Germain—"

"That was the most exciting street with the most traffic.
It's strange how exciting and dangerous seeming it was
there. And down by the Rue de Rennes it always seemed
perfectly safe—between the Deux Magots and Lipp's
crossing I mean. Why was that, Papa?"

"I don't know, Schatz."

"I wish something would happen beside the names of
streets," Andrew said. "I get tired of the names of streets
in a place I've never been."

"Make something happen, then, papa," young Tom
said. "We can talk about streets when we're alone."

"Nothing much happened then," Thomas Hudson said.
"We would go on down to the Place Saint-Michel and we
would sit on the terrace of the café and Papa would sketch
with a *café crème* on the table and you'd have a beer."

"Did I like beer then?"

"You were a big beer man. But you liked water with a
little red wine in it at meals."

"I remember. *L'eau rougie.*"

"*Exactement,*" Thomas Hudson said. "You were a very
strong *l'eau rougie* man but you liked an occasional *bock.*"

"I can remember in Austria going on a *luge* and our dog
Schnautz and snow."

"Can you remember Christmas there?"

"No. Just you and snow and our dog Schnautz and my
nurse. She was beautiful. And I remember mother on skis

and how beautiful she was. I can remember seeing you and mother coming down skiing through an orchard. I don't know where it was. But I can remember the Jardin du Luxembourg well. I can remember afternoons with the boats on the lake by the fountain in the big garden with the trees. The paths through the trees were all gravelled and men played bowling games off to the left under the trees as we went down toward the Palace and there was a clock high up on the Palace. In the fall the leaves came down and I can remember the trees bare and the leaves on the gravel. I like to remember the fall best."

"Why?" David asked.

"Lots of things. The way everything smelled in the fall and the carnivals and the way the gravel was dry on top when everything was damp and the wind on the lake to sail the boats and the wind in the trees that brought the leaves down. I can remember feeling the pigeons by me warm under the blanket when you killed them just before it was dark and how the feathers were smooth and I would stroke them and hold them close and keep my hands warm going home until the pigeons got cold too."

"Where did you kill the pigeons, papa?" David asked.

"Mostly down by the Medici Fountain just before they shut the gardens. There's a high iron fence all around the gardens and they shut the gates at dark and everyone has to go out. Guards go through warning people and locking up the gates. After the guards went ahead I used to kill the pigeons with a slingshot when they were on the ground by the fountain. They make wonderful slingshots in France."

"Didn't you make your own if you were poor?" Andrew asked.

"Sure. First I had one I made from a forked branch of a sapling I cut down in the Forest of Rambouillet when Tommy's mother and I were on a walking trip there. I whittled it out and we bought the big rubber bands for it at a stationery store on the Place Saint-Michel and made the leather pouch out of leather from an old glove of Tommy's mother."

"What did you shoot in it?"

"Pebbles."

"How close would you have to get?"

"As close as you could so you could pick them up and get them under the blanket as quick as you could."

"I remember the time one came alive," young Tom said. "And I held him quiet and didn't say anything about it all the way home because I wanted to keep him. He was a very big pigeon, almost purple color with a high neck and a wonderful head and white on his wings, and you let me keep him in the kitchen until we could get a cage for him. You tied him by one leg. But that night the big cat killed him and brought him in to my bed. The big cat was so proud and he carried him just as though he were a tiger carrying a native and he jumped up to the bed with him. That was when I had a square bed after the basket. I can't remember the basket. You and mother were gone to the café and the big cat and I were alone and I remember the windows were open and there was a big moon over the sawmill and it was winter and I could smell the sawdust. I remember seeing the big cat coming across the floor with his head high up so the pigeon barely dragged on the floor and then he made one jump and just sailed right up and into the bed with him. I felt awfully that he had killed my pigeon but he was so proud and so happy and he was such a good friend of mine I felt proud and happy, too. I remember he played with the pigeon and then he would push his paws up and down on my chest and purr and then play with the pigeon again. Finally I remember he and I and the pigeon all went to sleep together. I had one hand on the pigeon and he had one paw on the pigeon and then in the night I woke up and he was eating him and purring loud like a tiger."

"That's a lot better than names of streets," Andrew said. "Were you scared, Tommy, when he was eating him?"

"No. The big cat was the best friend I had then. I mean the closest friend. I think he would have liked me to eat the pigeon too."

"You ought to have tried it," Andrew said. "Tell some more about slingshots."

"Mother gave you the other slingshot for Christmas," young Tom said. "She saw it in a gun store and she wanted

to buy you a shotgun but she never had enough money.
She used to look at the shotguns in the window every day
when she went past the store to the Epicerie and one day
she saw the slingshot and she bought it because she was
afraid they would sell it to somebody else and she kept it
hid until Christmas. She had to falsify the accounts so you
wouldn't know about it. She's told me about it lots of
times. I can remember when you got it for Christmas and
you gave me the old one. But I wasn't strong enough to
pull it then."

"Papa, weren't we ever poor?" Andrew asked.

"No. I'd gotten over being poor by the time you guys
were born. We were broke lots of times but never really
poor the way we were with Tom and his mother."

"Tell us some more about in Paris," David said. "What
else did you and Tommy do?"

"What did we do, Schatz?"

"In the fall? We used to buy roasted chestnuts from
a roast chestnut man and I used to keep my hands warm
on them too. We went to the circus and saw the crocodiles
of Le Capitaine Wahl."

"Can you remember that?"

"*Very* well. The Capitaine Wahl wrestled with a croco-
dile (he pronounced it crowcodeel, the crow as in the bird
of that name) and a beautiful girl poked them with a tri-
dent. But the biggest crocodiles wouldn't move. The circus
was beautiful and round and red with gold paint and
smelled of horses. There was a place in back where you
went to drink with Mr. Crosby and the tamer of lions and
his wife."

"Do you remember Mr. Crosby?"

"He never wore a hat nor an overcoat no matter how
cold it was and his little girl had hair that hung down her
back like Alice in Wonderland. In the illustrations I mean.
Mr. Crosby was always very very nervous."

"Who else do you remember?"

"Mr. Joyce."

"What was he like?"

"He was tall and thin and he had a moustache and a
small beard that grew straight up and down on his chin

and he wore thick, thick glasses and walked with his head
held very high. I remember him passing us on the street
and not speaking and you spoke to him and he stopped
and saw us through the glasses like looking out of an
aquarium and he said, 'Ah, Hudson, I was looking for
you,' and we three went to the café and it was cold outside
but we sat in a corner with one of those what do you call
thems?"

"Braziers."

"I thought that was what ladies wore," Andrew said.

"It's an iron can with holes in it they burn coal or charcoal in to heat any place outside like a café terrace where
you sit close to them to keep warm or a race track where
you stand around and get warm from them," young Tom
explained. "At this café where papa and I and Mr. Joyce
used to go they had them all along the outside and you
could be warm and comfortable in the coldest weather."

"I guess you've spent the biggest part of your life in
cafés and saloons and hot spots," the youngest boy said.

"Quite a bit of it," Tom said. "Haven't we, papa?"

"And sound asleep in the car outside while papa has
just a quick one," David said. "Boy, I used to hate that
word *quick one*. I guess a quick one is about the slowest
thing on earth."

"What did Mr. Joyce talk about?" Roger asked young
Tom.

"Gee, Mr. Davis, I can't remember much about that
time. I think it was about Italian writers and about Mr.
Ford. Mr. Joyce couldn't stand Mr. Ford. Mr. Pound had
gotten on his nerves, too. 'Ezra's mad, Hudson,' he said
to papa. I can remember that because I thought *mad* meant
mad like a *mad dog* and I remember sitting there and
watching Mr. Joyce's face, it was sort of red with awfully
smooth skin, cold weather skin, and his glasses that had
one lens even thicker than the other, and thinking of Mr.
Pound with his red hair and his pointed beard and his nice
eyes, with white stuff sort of like lather dripping out of his
mouth. I thought it was terrible Mr. Pound was mad and
I hoped we wouldn't run into him. Then Mr. Joyce said,

'Of course Ford's been mad for years,' and I saw Mr. Ford with his big, pale, funny face and his pale eyes and his mouth with the teeth loose in it and always about half open and that awful lather dripping down *his* jaws too."

"Don't say any more," Andrew said. "I'll dream about it."

"Go on please," David said. "It's like werewolves. Mother locked up the werewolf book because Andrew had such bad dreams."

"Did Mr. Pound ever bite anybody?" Andrew asked.

"No, horseman," David told him. "It's just a way of talking. He means mad out of his head mad. Not hydrophobia mad. Why did he think they were mad?"

"I can't tell you," young Tom said. "I wasn't as young then as when we used to shoot pigeons in the gardens. But I was too young to remember everything and the idea of Mr. Pound and Mr. Ford with that dreadful slaver coming out of their mouths all ready to bite, drove everything out of my head. Did you know Mr. Joyce, Mr. Davis?"

"Yes. He and your father and I were very good friends."

"Papa was much younger than Mr. Joyce."

"Papa was younger than anybody, then."

"Not than me," young Tom said proudly. "I figure I was probably about Mr. Joyce's youngest friend."

"I'll bet he misses you a lot," Andrew said.

"It certainly is a shame he never could have met you," David said to Andrew. "If you hadn't been hanging around Rochester all the time he could have had the privilege."

"Mr. Joyce was a great man," young Tom said. "He wouldn't have wanted to have anything to do with you two punks."

"That's your opinion," Andrew said. "Mr. Joyce and David might have been pals. David writes for the paper at school."

"Papa, tell us some more about when you and Tommy and Tommy's mother were poor. How poor did you ever get?"

"They were pretty poor," Roger said. "I can remember when your father used to make up all young Tom's bottles in the morning and go to the market to buy the best and the cheapest vegetables. I'd meet him coming back from the market when I would be going out for breakfast."

"I was the finest judge of *poireaux* in the sixth arrondissement," Thomas Hudson told the boys.

"What's *poireaux?*"

"Leeks."

"It looks like long, green, quite big onions," young Tom said. "Only it's not bright shiny like onions. It's dull shiny. The leaves are green and the ends are white. You boil it and eat it cold with olive oil and vinegar mixed with salt and pepper. You eat the whole thing, top and all. It's delicious. I believe I've eaten as much of it as maybe anyone in the world."

"What's the sixth whatever it is?" Andrew asked.

"You certainly hold up conversation," David told him.

"If I don't know French I have to ask."

"Paris is divided into twenty arrondissements or city districts. We lived in the sixth."

"Papa, can we skip the arrondissements and you tell us something else?" Andrew asked.

"You can't stand to learn anything, you athlete," David said.

"I want to learn," Andrew said. "But arrondissements is too old for me. You're always telling me things are too old for me. I admit that is too old for me. I can't follow it."

"What's Ty Cobb's lifetime batting average?" David asked him.

"Three sixty-seven."

"That's not too old for you."

"Cut it out, David. Some people like baseball and you like arrondissements."

"I suppose we don't have arrondissements in Rochester."

"Oh cut it out. I just thought papa and Mr. Davis knew things that would be more interesting to everybody than those damn —Oh hell, I can't even remember the name of them."

"You're not supposed to swear when we are around," Thomas Hudson corrected.

"I'm sorry, papa," the small boy said. "I can't help it that I'm so damn young. I'm sorry again. I mean so young."

He was upset and hurt. David could tease him pretty successfully.

"You'll get over being young," Thomas Hudson told him. "I know it's hard not to swear when your feelings get working. Only don't swear in front of grown people. I don't care what you say by yourselves."

"Please, papa. I said I was sorry."

"I know," Thomas Hudson said. "I wasn't bawling you out. I was just explaining. I see you guys so seldom it makes a lot of explaining."

"Not much really, papa," David said.

"No," Thomas Hudson said. "It isn't much."

"Andrew never swears in front of mother," David said.

"Leave me out, David. It's over, isn't it, papa?"

"If you boys want to really know how to swear," young Tom said, "you ought to read Mr. Joyce."

"I can swear as much as I need," David said. "At least for now."

"My friend Mr. Joyce has words and expressions I'd never even heard of. I'll bet nobody could outswear him in any language."

"Then after that he made up a whole new language," Roger said. He was lying on his back on the beach with his eyes closed.

"I can't understand that new language," young Tom said. "I guess I'm not old enough for it. But wait until you boys read *Ulysses*."

"That's not for boys," Thomas Hudson said. "It isn't really. You couldn't understand it and you shouldn't try to. Really. You have to wait till you're older."

"I read it all," young Tom said. "I couldn't understand practically any of it when I first read it, papa, just as you say. But I kept on reading it and now there's part of it I really understand and I can explain it to people. It's certainly made me proud that I was one of Mr. Joyce's friends."

"Was he really a friend of Mr. Joyce, papa?" Andrew asked.

"Mr. Joyce always used to ask about him."

"You're damn right I was a friend of Mr. Joyce," young Tom said. "He was one of the best friends I ever had."

"I don't think you better explain the book much yet," Thomas Hudson said. "Not quite yet. What part is it that you explain?"

"The last part. The part where the lady talks out loud to herself."

"The soliloquy," David said.

"Have you read it?"

"Oh sure," David said. "Tommy read it to me."

"Did he explain it?"

"As well as he could. Some of it's a little old for both of us."

"Where did you get hold of it?"

"In the books at home. I borrowed it and took it to school."

"You what?"

"I used to read passages of it out loud to the boys and tell them how Mr. Joyce was my friend and how much time we used to spend together."

"How did the boys like it?"

"Some of the more devout boys thought it was a little strong."

"Did they find out about it at school?"

"Sure. Didn't you hear, papa? No, I guess that was when you were in Abyssinia. The headmaster was going to expel me but I explained Mr. Joyce was a great writer and a personal friend of mine so finally the headmaster said he'd keep the book and sent it home and I promised I'd consult him before I read anything else to the boys or attempted to explain any classics. First, when he was going to expel me, he thought I had a dirty mind. But I haven't got a dirty mind, papa. That is, not any dirtier than anybody else's."

"Oh yes. He was going to confiscate it but I explained it was a first edition and that Mr. Joyce had written in it for you and that he couldn't confiscate it because it wasn't mine. I think he was very disappointed not to confiscate it."

"When can I read that book by Mr. Joyce, papa?" Andrew asked.

"Not for a long time."

"But Tommy read it."

"Tommy is a friend of Mr. Joyce."

"Boy, I'll say I am," said young Tom. "Papa, we never knew Balzac, did we?"

"No. He was before our time."

"Nor Gautier? I found two swell ones by them at home too. The *Droll Stories* and *Mademoiselle de Maupin*. I don't understand *Mademoiselle de Maupin* at all yet but I am reading it over to try to and it's great. But if they weren't friends of ours I think they would expel me sure if I read them to the boys."

"How are they, Tommy?" David asked.

"Wonderful. You'll like them both."

"Why don't you consult the headmaster as to whether you can read them to the boys?" Roger said. "They're better than what the boys will dig up for themselves."

"No, Mr. Davis. I don't think I'd better. He might get that dirty-mind idea again. Anyway, with the boys it wouldn't be the same as though they were friends of mine like Mr. Joyce. Anyway I don't understand *Mademoiselle de Maupin* well enough to explain it and I wouldn't have the same authority explaining it as when I had Mr. Joyce's friendship to back me up."

"I'd like to have heard that explanation," Roger said.

"Shucks, Mr. Davis. It was very rudimentary. It wouldn't have interested you. You understand that part perfectly well, don't you?"

"Pretty well."

"I wish we would have known Balzac and Gautier, though, as friends the way we knew Mr. Joyce."

"So do I," said Thomas Hudson.

"We knew some good writers, though, didn't we?"

"We certainly did," Thomas Hudson said. It was pleasant and hot on the sand and he felt lazy after working and happy, too. It made him very happy to hear the boys talk.

"Let's go in and swim and then have lunch," Roger said. "It's getting hot."

Thomas Hudson watched them. Swimming slowly, the four of them swam out in the green water, their bodies making shadows over the clear white sand, bodies forging along, shadows projected on the sand by the slight angle of the sun, the brown arms lifting and pushing forward, the hands slicing in, taking hold of the water and pulling it back, legs beating along steadily, heads turning for air, breathing easily and smoothly. Thomas Hudson stood there and watched them swimming out with the wind and he was very fond of the four of them. He thought he ought to paint them swimming, although it would be very difficult. He would try it, though, during the summer.

He was too lazy to swim although he knew he should and finally he walked out feeling the breeze-cooled water fresh and cool on his sun-warmed legs, feeling it cool around his crotch and then, slipping forward into the ocean river, he swam out to meet them as they came in. With his head on the same level theirs were on, it was a different picture, now, changed too because they were swimming against the breeze coming in and the chop was bothering both Andrew and David, who were swimming raggedly. The illusion of them being four sea animals was gone. They had gone out so smoothly and handsomely but now the two younger boys were having difficulty against the wind and the sea. It was not real difficulty. It was just enough to take away any illusion of being at home in the water as they had looked going out. They made two different pictures and perhaps the second was the better one. The five swimmers came out on the beach and walked up to the house.

"That's why I like it better underwater," David said. "You don't have to worry about breathing."

"Why don't you goggle-fish with papa and Tommy this aft," Andrew said to him. "I'll stay ashore with Mr. Davis."

"Don't you want to go, Mr. Davis?"

"I might stay ashore."

"Don't stay in on account of me," Andrew said. "I've

got plenty to do. I just thought maybe you were staying in."

"I think I'll stay in," Roger said. "I may lie around and read."

"Don't let him maneuver you, Mr. Davis. Don't let him charm you."

"I feel like staying in," Roger said.

They were up on the porch now and everyone had changed to dry shorts. Joseph had brought out a bowl of conch salad. All the boys were eating it, and young Tom was drinking a bottle of beer. Thomas Hudson was sitting back in a chair and Roger was standing with the shaker.

"I get sleepy after lunch," he said.

"Well, we'll miss you," young Tom said. "I'd just as soon stay in, too."

"Come on, you stay in, too, Tom," Andrew said. "Let Papa and David go."

"I won't catch you," young Tom told him.

"I don't want you to catch me. There's a Negro boy that will catch me."

"What do you want to be a pitcher for, anyway?" Tommy said. "You'll never be big enough."

"I'll be as big as Dick Rudolph and Dick Kerr."

"Whoever they were," young Tom said.

"What's some jockey's name?" David whispered to Roger.

"Earl Sande."

"You'll be as big as Earl Sande," David told him.

"Oh, go and goggle-fish," Andrew said. "I'm going to be a friend of Mr. Davis like Tom was of Mr. Joyce. Can I, Mr. Davis? Then at school I can say, 'When Mr. Davis and I spent that summer together on that tropical island writing all those vicious stories while my own father was painting those pictures you've all seen of ladies in the nude.' You paint them in the nude, don't you papa?"

"Sometimes. They're quite dark though."

"Oh boy," Andrew said. "I don't care about the color. Tom can have Mr. Joyce."

"You'd be too shy to look at them," David said.

"Maybe I would. But I'd learn."

"A nude by papa would be nothing like that chapter by Mr. Joyce," young Tom said. "It's only because you're a little boy that there seems to be anything extraordinary about a nude at all."

"OK. Just the same I'll take Mr. Davis, with illustrations by papa. Somebody said at school Mr. Davis's stories were truly vicious."

"All right. I'll take Mr. Davis, too. I'm an old, old friend of Mr. Davis."

"And of Mr. Picasso and Mr. Braque and Mr. Miro and Mr. Masson and Mr. Pascin," Thomas Hudson said. "You knew them all."

"And of Mr. Waldo Peirce," young Tom said. "You see, Andy boy, you can't win. You started too late. You can't win. While you were up in Rochester and for years before you were born papa and I were out in the great world. I probably knew most of the greatest painters alive. Many of them were my very good friends."

"I have to start sometime," Andrew said. "And I take Mr. Davis. You don't have to write vicious stories either, Mr. Davis. I'll make all that up the way Tommy does. You just tell me anything awful you ever did and I'll say I was here when it happened."

"The hell I do make things up that way," young Tom said. "Sometimes papa and Mr. Davis refresh my memory for me. But I figured in and took part in a whole epoch in painting and in literature and if I had to I could write my memoirs right now as far as that goes."

"You're getting crazy, Tommy," Andrew said. "You better watch yourself."

"Don't tell him a thing, Mr. Davis," young Tom said. "Make him start from scratch like we did."

"You leave it to me and Mr. Davis," Andrew said. "You stay out of this."

"Tell me about some more of those friends of mine, papa," young Tom said. "I know I knew them and I know we used to be around cafés together but I'd like to know some more definite things about them. The sort of things I know about Mr. Joyce, say."

"Can you remember Mr. Pascin?"

"No. Not really. What was he like?"

"You can't claim him as a friend if you don't even remember him," Andrew said. "Do you think I won't be able to remember what Mr. Davis was like a few years from now?"

"Shut up," young Tom said. "Tell me about him please, papa."

"Mr. Pascin used to make some drawings that could illustrate the parts you like of Mr. Joyce very well."

"Really? Gee, that would be something."

"You used to sit with him at the café and he used to draw pictures of you sometimes on napkins. He was small and very tough and very strange. He used to wear a derby hat most of the time and he was a beautiful painter. He always acted as though he knew a great secret, as though he had just heard it and it amused him. It made him very happy sometimes and sometimes it made him sad. But you could always tell he knew it and it amused him very much."

"What was the secret?"

"Oh drunkenness and drugs and the secret Mr. Joyce knew all about in that last chapter and how to paint beautifully. He could paint more beautifully than anybody then and that was his secret, too, and he didn't care. He thought he didn't care about anything but he did really."

"Was he bad?"

"Oh yes. He was really bad and that was part of his secret. He liked being bad and he didn't have remorse."

"Were he and I good friends?"

"Very. He used to call you The Monster."

"Gee," said young Tom, happily. "The Monster."

"Have we got any pictures of Mr. Pascin's, papa?" David asked.

"A couple."

"Did he ever paint Tommy?"

"No. He used to draw Tommy mostly on napkins and on the marble top of café tables. He called him the horrible, beer-swilling monster of the Left Bank."

"Get that title down, Tom," David said.

"Did Mr. Pascin have a dirty mind?" young Tom asked.

"I believe so."

"Don't you know?"

"I believe you could say he had. I think that was part of his secret."

"But Mr. Joyce didn't."

"No."

"And you haven't."

"No," Thomas Hudson said. "I don't think so."

"Do you have a dirty mind, Mr. Davis?" Tommy asked.

"I don't think so."

"That's good," young Tom said. "I told the headmaster neither papa nor Mr. Joyce had dirty minds and now I can tell him about Mr. Davis if he asks me. He was pretty set on it that I had a dirty mind. But I wasn't worried. There's a boy at school that really has one and you can tell the difference all right. What was Mr. Pascin's first name?"

"Jules."

"How do you spell it?" David asked. Thomas Hudson told him.

"What ever became of Mr. Pascin?" young Tom asked.

"He hanged himself," Thomas Hudson said.

"Oh gee," Andrew said.

"Poor Mr. Pascin," young Tom said in benediction. "I'll pray for him tonight."

"I'm going to pray for Mr. Davis," Andrew said.

"And do it often," Roger said.

VI

THAT night after the boys had gone to bed Thomas Hudson and Roger Davis sat up in the big room talking. It had been too rough to do much goggle-fishing and after supper the boys had gone off with Joseph to go snapper fishing. They had come back tired and happy and said good night and gone to bed. The men had heard them talk a while and then they were asleep.

Andrew was afraid of the dark and the other boys knew it but they never teased him about it.

"Why do you think he's afraid of the dark?" Roger asked.

"I don't know," Thomas Hudson said. "Weren't you?"

"I don't think so."

"I was," Thomas Hudson said. "Is it supposed to mean anything?"

"I don't know," Roger said. "I was afraid of dying and that something would happen to my brother."

"I didn't know you had a brother. Where is he?"

"Dead," Roger said.

"I'm sorry."

"You don't need to be. It was when we were kids."

"Was he older than you?"

"A year younger."

"What was it?"

"A canoe turned over with us."

"How old were you?"

"About twelve."

"Don't talk about it if you don't want to."

"I'm not sure it did me a lot of good," Roger said. "Didn't you know about it really?"

"Never."

"For a long time I thought everybody in the world knew about it. It's strange when you are a boy. The water was too cold and he let go. But what it added up to was that I came back and he didn't."

"Poor bloody Roger."

"No," said Roger. "But it was early to learn about that stuff. And then I loved him very much and I'd always been afraid something would happen to him. The water was cold for me too. But I couldn't say that."

"Where was it?"

"Up in Maine. I don't think my father ever forgave me although he tried to understand it. I've wished it was me every day since. But that's hardly a career."

"What was your brother's name?"

"Dave."

"Hell. Was that why you wouldn't go goggle-fishing today?"

"I guess so. But I'm going every other day. You never work those things out, though."

"You're grown up enough not to talk that way."

"I tried to go down after him. But I couldn't find him," Roger said. "It was too deep and it was really cold."

"David Davis," Thomas Hudson said.

"Yes. In our family the first one is called Roger and the second one David."

"Roge, you did get over it, though."

"No," Roger said. "You never get over it and sooner or later I have to tell it. I'm ashamed of that the way I'm ashamed of the fight on the dock."

"You had nothing to be ashamed of there."

"Yes, I did. I told you once. Let's not go into that."

"All right."

"I'm not going to have any more fights. Ever. You never fight and you can fight as well as I can."

"I can't fight as well as you. But I just made up my mind I wouldn't fight."

"I'm not going to fight and I'm going to be some good and quit writing junk."

"That's the best thing I've heard you say," Thomas Hudson said.

"Do you think I could write something that would be worth a damn?"

"You could try. What did you quit painting for?"

"Because I couldn't kid myself any longer. I can't kid myself any longer on the writing either."

"What are you going to do, practically?"

"Go some place and write a good straight novel as well as I can write it."

"Why don't you stay here and write? You can stay on here after the boys are gone. It's too hot to write in your place."

"I wouldn't bother you too much?"

"No, Roge. I get lonely, too, you know. You can't just

run away from everything all the time. This sounds like a speech. I'll cut it out."

"No. Go on. I need it."

"If you are going to start to work, start here."

"You don't think out West would be better?"

"Any place is good. The thing is not to run from it."

"No. Any place isn't good," Roger objected. "I know that. They're good and then they go bad."

"Sure. But this is a good place now. Maybe it won't always be. But it's fine now. You'd have company when you quit work and so would I. We wouldn't interfere with each other and you could really bite on the nail."

"Do you truly think I could write a novel that would be any good?"

"You never will if you don't try. You told me a hell of a good novel tonight if you wanted to write it. Just start with the canoe"

"And end it how?"

"Make it up after the canoe."

"Hell," Roger said. "I'm so corrupted that if I put in a canoe it would have a beautiful Indian girl in it that young Jones, who is on his way to warn the settlers that Cecil B. de Mille is coming, would drop into, hanging by one hand to a tangle of vines that covers the river while he holds his trusty flintlock, 'Old Betsy,' in the other hand, and the beautiful Indian girl says, 'Jones, it ees you. Now we can make love as our frail craft moves toward the falls that some day weel be Niagara.'"

"No," said Thomas Hudson. "You could just make the canoe and the cold lake and your kid brother——"

"David Davis. Eleven."

"And afterwards. And then make up from there to the end."

"I don't like the end," Roger said.

"I don't think any of us do, really," Thomas Hudson said. "But there's always an end."

"Maybe we better knock off talking," Roger said. "I'm liable to start thinking about the novel. Tommy, why is it fun to paint well and hell to write well? I never painted well. But it was fun even the way I painted."

"I don't know," Thomas Hudson said. "Maybe in paint-ing the tradition and the line are clearer and there are more people helping you. Even when you break from the straight line of great painting, it is always there to help you."

"I think another thing is that better people do it," Roger said. "If I were a good enough guy maybe I could have been a good painter. Maybe I'm just enough of a son of a bitch to be a good writer."

"That's the worst oversimplification I've ever heard."

"I always oversimplify," Roger maintained. "That's one reason I'm no damn good."

"Let's go to bed."

"I'll stay up and read a while," Roger said.

They slept well and Thomas Hudson did not wake when Roger came out to the sleeping porch late in the night. After breakfast the wind was light and there were no clouds in the sky and they organized for a day of under-water fishing.

"You're coming, aren't you, Mr. Davis?" Andrew asked.

"I most certainly am."

"That's good," said Andrew. "I'm glad."

"How do you feel, Andy?" Thomas Hudson asked.

"Scared," said Andrew. "Like always. But I'm not so scared with Mr. Davis going."

"Never be scared, Andy," Roger said. "It's worthless. Your father told me."

"They tell you," Andrew said. "They always tell you. But David's the only young boy I ever knew with any brains that isn't scared."

"Shut up," David said. "You're just a creature of your imagination."

"Mr. Davis and I are always scared," Andrew said. "It's possibly our superior intelligence."

"You're going to be careful, Davy, aren't you?" Thomas Hudson said.

"Naturally."

Andrew looked at Roger and shrugged his shoulders.

VII

Down along the reef where they went for underwater fishing on that day, there was the old iron wreck of a steamer that had broken up and at high tide the rusty iron of her boilers still showed above the sea. Today the wind was in the south and Thomas Hudson anchored in the lee of a patch of reef, not too close in, and Roger and the boys got their masks and spears ready. The spears were very primitive, and of all sorts, and these spears were made according to Thomas Hudson's and the boy's individual ideas.

Joseph had come along to scull the dinghy. He took Andrew in with him and they started for the reef while the others slipped over the side to swim.

"Aren't you coming, papa?" David called up to his father on the flying bridge of his fishing boat. The circle of glass over his eyes, nose, and forehead, with the rubber frame pressed under his nose, into his cheeks, and tight against his forehead, held tight into the flesh by a rubber strap around the back of his head, made him look like one of the characters in those pseudoscientific comic strips.

"I'll come over later on."

"Don't wait too long until everything gets spooked."

"There's plenty of reef. You won't work it all over."

"But I know two holes out beyond the boilers that are wonderful. I found them the day we came alone. They were so untouched and full of fish I left them for when we would all be here."

"I remember. I'll come over in about an hour."

"I'll save them for when you come," David said and started to swim after the others, his right hand holding the six-foot ironwood shaft with the hand-forged, twin-pronged fish grains fitted to the end and made fast with a length of heavy fishing line. His face was down in the water and he was studying the bottom through the glass of his

mask as he swam. He was an undersea boy and now that
he was so brown and that he was swimming with only the
wet back of his head showing he reminded Thomas Hudson
more than ever of an otter.

He watched him swim along, using his left arm and
kicking with his long legs and feet in a slow steady drive
and occasionally, and each time much, much longer than
you thought it would be, lifting his face a little to one side
to breathe. Roger and his oldest boy had swum out with
their masks up on their foreheads and were a long way
ahead. Andrew and Joseph were over the reef in the
dinghy but Andrew had not gone overboard yet. There was
only a light wind and the water over the reef looked light
and creaming, with the reef showing brown and the dark
blue water beyond.

Thomas Hudson went below to the galley where Eddy
was peeling potatoes over a bucket held between his knees.
He was looking out the porthole of the galley toward the
reef.

"Boys oughtn't to scatter," he said. "Ought to keep
close to the dinghy."

"Do you think anything would come in over the reef?"

"Tide's pretty well up. These are spring tides."

"Water's awfully clear," Thomas Hudson said.

"Bad things in the ocean," Eddy said. "This is a tough
ocean around here if they get to smell that fish."

"They haven't got any fish yet."

"They'll get them soon. They want to get those fish right
into that dinghy before any fish smell or any blood smell
trails on that tide."

"I'll swim out."

"No. You holler at them to stay close together and keep
the fish in the dinghy."

Thomas Hudson went up on deck and shouted what
Eddy had said to Roger. He held up his spear and waved
that he had understood.

Eddy came up into the cockpit with the pot full of potatoes in one hand and his knife in the other.

"You take that good rifle, the little good one, and get up
on the topside, Mr. Tom," he said. "I just don't like it. I

don't like boys out there on this tide. We're too close to the real ocean."

"Let's get them in."

"No. Chances are I just get nervous. Bad night last night anyway. I'm fond of them like they're my boys and I worry the hell about them." He put the pot of potatoes down. "Tell you what let's do. Start her up and I'll get the anchor up and we'll run in closer to the reef and anchor. She'll swing clear with this tide and the wind. Let's put her right in."

Thomas Hudson started the big motor and went up to the flying bridge and the topside controls. Ahead, as Eddy got the anchor up, he could see them all in the water now and, as he watched, David came up from underwater with a fish flopping on his spear that he held high in the air and Thomas Hudson heard him shout for the dinghy.

"Put her nose right against the reef," Eddy called from the bow where he was holding the anchor.

Thomas Hudson came up slowly to almost touch the reef, seeing the big brown coral heads, the black sea urchins on the sand, and the purple sea fans swaying toward him with the tide. Eddy heaved the anchor and Thomas Hudson came astern on the engine. The boat swung off and the reef slid away. Eddy paid out line until the rope came taut and Thomas Hudson cut the motor and they swung there.

"Now we can keep an eye on them," Eddy said, standing in the bow. "I can't stand worrying about those kids. Ruins my damn digestion. Bad enough the way it is now."

"I'll stay up here and watch them."

"I'll pass you up the rifle and get the hell back to those potatoes. The boys like potato salad, don't they? The way we fix it?"

"Sure. Roger too. Put in plenty of hard-boiled egg and onion.

"I'll keep the potatoes good and firm. Here's the rifle."

As Thomas Hudson reached for the rifle it was chunky and heavy in its clipped sheep-wool-lined case that he kept saturated with Fiend-oil to keep the sea air from rusting it. He pulled it out by the butt and slid the case under the

decking on the flying bridge. It was a .256 Mannlicher
Shoenauer with the old eighteen-inch barrel they weren't
allowed to sell any more. The stock and forearm were
browned like a walnut nutmeat with oil and rubbing, and
the barrel, rubbed from months of carrying in a saddle
bucket, was oil-slick, without a spot of rust. The cheek
piece of the stock was worn smooth from his own cheek
and when he pulled back the bolt the revolving magazine
was full of heavy bellied cartridges with the long, thin,
pencil-shaped metal-cased bullet with only a tiny exposed
lead tip.

It was really too good a gun to keep on a boat but
Thomas Hudson was so fond of it and it reminded him
of so many things, so many people, and so many places
that he liked to have it with him and he found that, in
the sheepskin case, once the clipped wool was well impregnated with Fiend-oil, the rifle was not harmed at all
by the salt air. A gun is to shoot anyway, he thought,
not to be preserved in a case, and this was a really good
rifle, easy to shoot, easy to teach anyone to shoot with,
and handy on the boat. He had always had more confidence
shooting it, as to being able to place his shots at close
and moderate range, than any other rifle he had ever owned
and it made him happy to pull it out of the case now
and pull back the bolt and shove a shell into the breech.

The boat lay almost steady in the tide and the breeze,
and he slipped the sling over one of the levers of the
topside controls so that the rifle hung there handy, and
lay down on the sunning mattress on the flying bridge.
Lying on his belly to brown his back, he looked out to
where Roger and the boys were spearfishing. They were
all diving, staying down varying lengths of time and coming
up for air to disappear again, occasionally coming up with
fish on the spears. Joseph was sculling from one to
another to take the fish off the spear points and drop them
into the dinghy. He could hear Joseph shouting and laughing and see the bright color of the fish, red or red with
brown speckles or red and yellow or striped yellow as
Joseph took them off the spears or pulled them loose and

tossed them back into the shade under the stern of the dinghy.

"Let me have a drink, Eddy, will you please?" Thomas Hudson called down over the side.

"What's it to be?" Eddie stuck his head out of the forward cockpit. He was wearing his old felt hat and a white shirt and in the bright sun his eyes were bloodshot and Thomas Hudson noticed he had Mercurochrome on his lips.

"What did you do to your mouth?" he asked him.

"Some sort of trouble last night. I just put that on. Does it show bad?"

"It makes you look like some back island whore."

"Oh hell," said Eddy. "I put it on without looking at it in the dark. Just by the feel. Do you want a drink with coconut water? I got some water coconuts."

"Very good."

"Want a Green Isaac's Special?"

"Fine. Make it a Special."

Where Thomas Hudson lay on the mattress his head was in the shade cast by the platform at the forward end of the flying bridge where the controls were and when Eddy came aft with the tall cold drink made of gin, lime juice, green coconut water, and chipped ice with just enough Angostura bitters to give it a rusty, rose color, he held the drink in the shadow so the ice would not melt while he looked out over the sea.

"Boys seem to be doing all right," Eddy said. "We've got fish for dinner already."

"What else will we have?"

"Mashed potatoes with the fish. Got some tomato salad, too. That potato salad to start with."

"Sounds fine. How's that potato salad?"

"It isn't cold yet, Tom."

"Eddy, you like to cook, don't you?"

"Damn right I like to cook. I like going in a boat and I like to cook. What I don't like is rows and fights and trouble."

"You used to be pretty good at trouble, though."

"I always avoided it, Tom. Sometimes you can't avoid it but I always tried to."

"What was it last night?"

"Nothing."

He didn't want to talk about it. He never talked about the old days either when there had been plenty of trouble.

"All right. What else is there to eat? We have to feed them up. They're growing boys."

"I made a cake at the house and brought her and there's a couple of fresh pineapples cold in the ice. I'll slice them up."

"Good. How will we have the fish?"

"Any way you want it. Let's see what the best is of what they get, then cook it how they and you and Roger want it. David just got a good yellowtail. He had another one but he lost it. This one's a big flaggy. He's getting far out, though. He's still got the fish and Joe's the hell over toward Andy with the dinghy."

Thomas Hudson put the drink down in the shade and stood up.

"Jesus Christ," Eddy said. "There it comes!"

Out across the blue water, showing like a brown dinghy sail and slicing through the water with heavy, tail-propelled, lunging thrusts, the high triangular fin was coming in toward the hole at the edge of the reef where the boy with the mask on his face held his fish up out of the water.

"Oh Jesus," Eddy said. "What a son of a bitching hammerhead. Jesus, Tom. Oh Jesus."

Thomas Hudson remembered, afterwards, the main impression he had was the great height of the fin, the way it turned and swung like a hound on a scent, and the way it knifed forward and still seemed to wobble.

He had the .256 up and shot just ahead of the fin. The shot was over and threw a spurt of water and he remembered the barrel was sticky with oil. The fin went right on weaving in.

"Throw him the goddam fish," Eddy yelled to David and jumped off the back of the house down into the cockpit.

Thomas Hudson shot again and was behind with

another spurt of water. He felt sick at his stomach, as though something had hold of him inside and was gripping him there, and he shot again; as carefully and steady as he could; knowing fully what the shot meant; and the spurt of water was ahead of the fin. The fin kept right on with the same awful motion. He had one shot now, no extra shells, and the shark was about thirty yards from the boy, coming in with the same slicing motion. David had the fish of the spear in his hand, the mask was up on his forehead, and he was looking steadily toward the shark coming.

Thomas Hudson was trying to be loose but steady, trying to hold his breath and not to think of anything but the shot; to squeeze and keep just a touch ahead and at the base of the fin which was wobbling more now than it had at the start when he heard the submachine gun start firing from the stern and saw water start to spout all around the fin. Then it clattered again in a short burst and the water jumped in a tighter patch right at the base of the fin. As he shot, the clatter came again, short and tight, and the fin went under and there was a boil in the water and then the biggest hammerhead he had ever seen rose white-bellied out of the sea and began to plane over the water crazily, on his back, throwing water like an aquaplane. His belly was shining an obscene white, his yard-wide mouth like a turned-up grin, the great horns of his head with the eyes on the end, spread wide out as he bounced and slid over the water. Eddy's gun rapping and ripping into the white of his belly making black spots that were red before he turned and went down and Thomas Hudson could see him rolling over and over as he sank.

"Get those goddamned kids in here," he heard Eddy shouting. "I can't stand this sort of thing."

Roger had swum fast toward David, and Joseph was pulling Andy into the dinghy and then sculling out toward the other two.

"Goddam," Eddy said. "Did you ever see such a hammerhead? Thank God they show on the surface when they hook up. Thank God for that. The bastards always get on top. Did you *see* him go?"

"Give me a box of shells," Thomas Hudson said. He was shaky and hollow sick feeling inside. "Come on in here," he shouted. They were swimming alongside of the dinghy and Roger was pushing David up over the gunwale.

"They might as well fish," Eddy said. "Any shark in the ocean will go for *him* now. He'll call the whole ocean up. Did you see him go on his back, Tom, and then that damned roll? Jesus, what a hammerhead. Did you see the kid with the fish ready to throw him? That's my Davy boy. Oh what a old Davy boy."

"They better come in."

"Sure they better. I was just talking. They'll come in. Don't worry they won't come in."

"God, it was a terrible thing. Where did you have that gun?"

"Commissioner made some trouble about me having it ashore so I've been keeping it in the locker under my bunk."

"You certainly can shoot it."

"Hell, who couldn't shoot it with that shark going toward that old Davy boy waiting there quiet with that fish to throw? Looking straight at where the shark was coming. Hell, I don't care if I never see anything else in my goddam life."

They came up over the side out of the dinghy. The kids were wet and very excited and Roger was very shaken. He went over and shook hands with Eddy and Eddy said, "We never should have let them get out like that on this tide."

Roger shook his head and put his arm around Eddy.

"My fault," Eddy said. "I was born here. You're a stranger. It wasn't your fault. I'm the one that's responsible."

"You lived up to your responsibilities all right," Roger said.

"Hell," Eddy said. "Nobody could miss him at that range."

"Could you see him, Dave?" Andrew asked very politely.

"Only his fin till just at the end. Then I could see him before Eddy hit him and he went down and then came out on his back."

Eddy was rubbing him with a towel and Thomas Hudson could see the goose pimples still over his legs and back and shoulders.

"I never saw anything like when he came out of water and started to go on his back," young Tom said. "I never saw anything in the world like that."

"You won't see a lot of things like that," his father told him.

"He must have weighed eleven hundred pounds," Eddy said. "I don't think they make a bigger hammerhead. Jesus, Roger, did you see that fin on him?"

"I saw it," Roger said.

"Do you think we can get him?" David asked.

"Hell no," Eddy said. "He went down rolling over and over to hell knows where. He's down in eighty fathoms and the whole ocean will eat on him. He's calling them up now."

"I wish we could have got him," David said.

"Take it easy, Davy boy. You got the goose flesh on you still."

"Were you very scared, Dave?" Andrew asked.

"Yes," David told him.

"What were you going to do?" Tom asked, very respectfully.

"I was going to throw the fish to him," David said and as Thomas Hudson watched him the little sharp wave of pimples spread over his shoulders. "Then I was going to hit him in the middle of his face with the grains."

"Oh hell," Eddy said and he turned away with the towel. "What do you want to drink, Roger?"

"Have you got any hemlock?" Roger asked him.

"Cut it out, Roger," Thomas Hudson said. "We were all responsible."

"Irresponsible."

"It's over."

"All right."

"I'll make some gin drinks," Eddy said. "Tom had a gin drink when it happened."

"It's still up there."

"It won't be any damn good now," Eddy said. "I'll make you a fresh one."

"You're pretty good, Davy," young Tom told him very proudly. "Wait till I tell the boys about this at school."

"They wouldn't believe it," David said. "Don't tell them if I'm going there."

"Why?" young Tom asked.

"I don't know," David said. Then he started to cry like a little boy. "Oh shit, I couldn't stand it if they didn't believe it."

Thomas Hudson picked him up and held him in his arms with his head against his chest and the other kids turned away and Roger looked away and then Eddy came out with three drinks with his thumb in one of them. Thomas Hudson could tell he'd had another one below.

"What's the matter with you, Davy?" he asked.

"Nothing."

"Good," Eddy said. "That's the way I like to hear you talk, you damn old son of a bitch. Get down and quit blubbering and let your old man drink."

David stood there standing very straight.

"Is it OK to fish that part in low tide?" he asked Eddy.

"Nothing will bother you," Eddy said. "There's morays. But nothing big will come in. They can't make it at low tide."

"Can we go at low tide, papa?"

"If Eddy says so. Eddy's the boss man."

"Hell, Tom," Eddy said, and he was very happy, his Mercurochromed lips were happy and his bloodshot eyes as happy as eyes could be. "Anybody couldn't hit that damned no-good hammerhead with one of those things ought to throw the damn thing away before he'd get in trouble with it."

"You hit him plenty," Thomas Hudson said. "You hit him wonderfully. I wish I could tell you how you hit him."

"You don't have to tell me," Eddy said. "I'll see that

old evil son of a bitch going on his back the rest of my life. Did you ever see anything look more evil?"

They sat there waiting for the lunch and Thomas Hudson was looking out to sea where Joseph had sculled out to where the shark had gone down. Joseph was looking over the side of the dinghy into a water glass.

"Can you see anything?" Thomas Hudson called to him.

"Too deep, Mr. Tom. He went down right over the shelf. He's laying on the bottom now."

"I wish we could have gotten his jaws," young Tom said. "Wouldn't you like to have them all bleached and hanging up, papa?"

"I think they would give me bad dreams," Andrew said. "I'm just as glad we haven't got them."

"They'd be a wonderful trophy," young Tom said. "That would be something to take to school."

"They'd belong to Dave if we had them," Andrew said.

"No. They'd belong to Eddy," young Tom said. "I believe he'd give them to me if I asked him for them."

"He'd give them to Dave," Andrew said.

"I don't think maybe you should go out again so soon, Dave," Thomas Hudson said.

"It won't be till plenty of time after lunch," David said. "We have to wait for the low tide."

"I mean goggle-fish so soon."

"Eddy said it was all right."

"I know. But I'm still pretty spooked."

"But Eddy knows."

"You wouldn't like to just not go as a present to me?"

"Certainly, papa, if you want. But I love it underwater. I guess I love it more than anything. And if Eddy says—"

"OK," said Thomas Hudson. "People aren't supposed to ask for presents anyway."

"Papa, I didn't mean it like that. I won't go if you don't want me to. Only Eddy said—"

"What about a moray? Eddy mentioned morays."

"Papa, there's *always* morays. *You* taught me not to be afraid of morays and how to handle them and how to watch out for them and the kind of holes they live in."

"I know. And I let you go out there where that shark came."

"Papa, we were all out there. Don't make yourself some sort of special guilt about it. I just went too far out and I lost that good yellowtail after I'd speared him and he bloodied the water and that called the shark."

"Didn't he come just like a hound though?" Thomas Hudson said. He was trying to get rid of the emotion. "I've seen them come at really great speed like that before. There was one that used to live off Signal Rock that used to come that way on the smell of a bait. I'm very ashamed I couldn't hit him."

"You were shooting awfully close to him, papa," young Tom said.

"I was doing everything but hit him."

"He wasn't coming for me, papa," David said. "He was coming for the fish."

"He'd have taken you, though," Eddy said. He was setting the table. "Don't ever fool yourself he wouldn't with that fish smell on you and the blood in the water. He'd have hit a horse. He'd have hit anything. Good God, don't talk about it. I'll have to have another drink."

"Eddy," David said. "Will it really be safe on the low tide?"

"Sure. Didn't I tell you so before?"

"You aren't making some sort of a point, are you?" Thomas Hudson asked David. He had stopped looking out across the water and he was all right again. He knew that what David was doing was what he should do no matter why he was doing it and he knew he had been selfish about it.

"Papa, all I mean is that I love it better than anything else and it's such a wonderful day for it and we never know when it might blow—"

"And Eddy says," Thomas Hudson interrupted.

"And Eddy says," David grinned with him.

"Eddy says the hell with all of you. Come on and eat it up now before I throw it the hell overboard." He stood there with the bowl of salad, the platter of browned fish, and the mashed potatoes. "Where's that Joe?"

"He went to look for the shark."

"He's crazy."

When Eddy went below and young Tom was passing the food, Andrew whispered to his father, "Papa, is Eddy a rummy?"

Thomas Hudson was serving the cold, marinated potato salad covered with rough-ground black pepper. He had shown Eddy how to make it the way they used to make it at the Brasserie Lipp in Paris and it was one of the best things Eddy made on the boat.

"Did you see him shoot the shark?"

"I certainly did."

"That isn't the way rummies shoot."

He put some salad on Andrew's plate and took some for himself.

"The only reason I asked is because from where I'm sitting I can see in the galley and I've watched him take about eight drinks out of a bottle since we've been sitting here."

"That's his bottle," Thomas Hudson explained and helped Andrew to some more salad. Andrew was the fastest eater he had ever seen. He said he had learned it at school. "Try and eat a little slower, Andy. Eddy always brings his own bottle on board. Nearly all good cooks drink a little. Some drink quite a lot."

"I know he had eight. Wait. He's taking nine now."

"Damn you, Andrew," David said.

"Cut it out," Thomas Hudson said to both of them.

Young Tom broke in. "Here's a fine wonderful man saves your brother's life and he just takes a drink, or a few drinks, and you call him a rummy. You aren't fit to associate with human beings."

"I didn't call him one. I just asked papa, to know if he is one. I'm not against rummies. I just like to know if a man is or not."

"I'm going to buy Eddy a bottle of whatever it is he drinks with the very first money I get and I'm going to drink it with him," young Tom said grandly.

"What's that?" Eddy's head showed in the companion-way with the old felt hat pushed onto the back of it

showing the white above the sunburnt part of his face
and a cigar sticking out of the corner of his Mercurochromed mouth. "Let me catch you drink anything but
beer I beat the hell out of you. All three of you. Don't
you talk about drinking. Do you want more mashed
potatoes?"

"Please, Eddy," young Tom said and Eddy went below.

"That makes ten," Andrew said, looking down the
companionway.

"Oh shut up, horseman," young Tom said to him.
"Can't you respect a great man?"

"Eat some more fish, David," Thomas Hudson said.

"Which is that big yellowtail?"

"I don't believe he's cooked yet."

"I'll take a yellow grunt then."

"They're awfully sweet."

"I think spearing makes them even better if you eat
them right away because it bleeds them."

"Papa, can I ask Eddy to have a drink with us?" young
Tom asked.

"Sure," Thomas Hudson said.

"He had one. Don't you remember?" Andrew interrupted. "When we first came in he had one. You remember."

"Papa, can I ask him to have another one with us now
and to eat with us?"

"Of course," Thomas Hudson said.

Young Tom went down below and Thomas Hudson
heard him say, "Eddy, papa says would you please make
a drink for yourself and come up and have it with us
and eat with us."

"Hell, Tommy," Eddy said. "I never eat at noon. I just
eat breakfast and at night."

"What about having a drink with us?"

"I had a couple, Tommy."

"Will you take one with me now and let me drink a
bottle of beer with you?"

"Hell yes," said Eddy. Thomas Hudson heard the
icebox open and close. "Here's to you, Tommy."

Thomas Hudson heard the two bottles clink. He looked at Roger but Roger was looking out at the ocean.

"Here's to you, Eddy," he heard young Tom say. "It's a great honor to drink with you."

"Hell, Tommy," Eddy told him. "It's an honor to drink with you. I feel wonderful, Tommy. You see me shoot that old shark?"

"I certainly did, Eddy. Don't you want to eat just a little something with us?"

"No, Tommy. True."

"Would you like me to stay down here with you so you wouldn't have to drink alone?"

"Hell no, Tommy. You aren't getting mixed up on anything, are you? I don't have to drink. I don't have to do anything except cook a little and earn my goddam living. I just feel good, Tommy. Did you see me shoot him? True?"

"Eddy, it was the greatest thing I ever saw. I just asked you if you wanted somebody so as not to be lonesome."

"I never been lonesome in my life," Eddy told him. "I'm happy and I got here what makes me happier."

"Eddy, I'd like to stay with you, anyway."

"No, Tommy. Take this other platter of fish up and go up there where you belong."

"I'd like to come back and stay."

"I ain't sick, Tommy. If I was ever sick I'd be happy to have you sit up with me. I'm just feeling the goddam best I ever felt ever."

"Eddy, are you sure you've got enough of that bottle?"

"Hell yes. If I ever run out I'll borrow some of Roger's and your old man's."

"Well, then, I'll take the fish up," young Tom said. "I'm awfully glad you feel so good, Eddy. I think it's wonderful."

Young Tom brought the platter of yellowtail, yellow and white grunts, and rock hind up into the cockpit. They were scored deep in triangular cuts across their flanks so the white meat showed, and fried crisp and brown, and he started to pass them around the table.

"Eddy said to thank you very much but he'd had a drink," he said. "And he doesn't eat lunch. Is this fish all right?"

"It's excellent," Thomas Hudson told him.

"Please eat," he said to Roger.

"All right," Roger said. "I'll try."

"Haven't you eaten anything, Mr. Davis?" Andrew asked.

"No, Andy. But I'm going to eat now."

VIII

IN the night Thomas Hudson would wake and hear the boys asleep and breathing quietly and in the moonlight he could see them all and see Roger sleeping too. He slept well now and almost without stirring.

Thomas Hudson was happy to have them there and he did not want to think about them ever going away. He had been happy before they came and for a long time he had learned how to live and do his work without ever being more lonely than he could bear; but the boys' coming had broken up all the protective routine of life he had built and now he was used to its being broken. It had been a pleasant routine of working hard; of hours for doing things; places where things were kept and well-cared for; of meals and drinks to look forward to and new books to read and many old books to reread. It was a routine where the daily paper was an event when it arrived, but where it did not come so regularly that its nonarrival was a disappointment. It had many of the inventions that lonely people use to save themselves and even achieve unloneliness with and he had made the rules and kept the customs and used them consciously and unconsciously. But since the boys were here it had come as a great relief not to have to use them.

It would be bad, though, he thought, when he started all that again. He knew very well how it would be. For a part of a day it would be pleasant to have the house neat and to think alone and read without hearing other people talk and look at things without speaking of them and work properly without interruption and then he knew the loneliness would start. The three boys had moved into a big part of him again that, when they moved out, would be empty and it would be very bad for a while.

His life was built solidly on work and on the living by the Gulf Stream and on the island and it would stand up all right. The aids and the habits and the customs were all to handle the loneliness and by now he knew he had opened a whole new country for the loneliness to move into once the boys were gone. There was nothing to do about that, though. That would all come later and if it was coming there was no good derived from any fearing of it now.

The summer, so far, had been a very lucky and good one. Everything had turned out well that could have turned out badly. He did not mean just spectacular things like Roger and the man on the dock, which could have come out very badly; nor David and the shark; but all sorts of small things had come out well. Happiness is often presented as being very dull but, he thought, lying awake, that is because dull people are sometimes very happy and intelligent people can and do go around making themselves and everyone else miserable. He had never found happiness dull. It always seemed more exciting than any other thing and capable of as great intensity as sorrow to those people who were capable of having it. This may not be true but he had believed it to be true for a long time and this summer they had experienced happiness for a month now and, already, in the nights, he was lonely for it before it had ever gone away.

He knew almost what there is to know about living alone and he had known what it is to live with someone that you loved and that loved you. He had always loved his children but he had never before realized how much he

loved them and how bad it was that he did not live
with them. He wished that he had them always and that
he was married to Tom's mother. Then he thought that
was as silly as wishing you had the wealth of the world
to use as intelligently as you could; to be able to draw like
Leonardo or paint as well as Pieter Brueghel; to have an
absolute veto power against all wickedness and be able
to detect it infallibly and always justly when it starts
and stop it with something as simple as pressing a button
and while doing all this to be always healthy and to live
forever and not decay in mind nor body. That was what
he thought tonight would be some good things to have.
But you could not have them any more than you could
have the children; nor that who you loved could be alive
if who you loved was dead or gone out from your life.
Out of all the things you could not have there were
some that you could have and one of those was to know
when you were happy and to enjoy all of it while it was
there and it was good. There were many things that made
it for him when he had it. But just now, in this month,
four people made it something that was as good, in some
ways, as what the one person had once been able to make
and so far there had been no sorrow. There had been no
sorrow at all.

He did not even mind being awake now and remembered how it had been once when he had not been able
to sleep and had lain in the night thinking about how he
had lost the three boys and the fool he had been. He had
thought how he had done things because he could not
help them, or thought he could not help them, and had
moved from one disastrous error of judgment to another
that was worse. Now he accepted that as past and he was
through with remorse. He had been a fool and he did not
like fools. But that was over now and the boys were here
and they loved him and he loved them. He would let it
go at that for now.

They would go away at the end of their stay and he
would have the loneliness again. But it would be only a
stage on the way until they came back. If Roger would
stay and work and keep him company it would be much

easier. But he never knew about Roger nor what he would do. He smiled in the night thinking about Roger. Then he pitied him until he thought how disloyal it was and how Roger would hate pity and he stopped it and, hearing them all breathing quietly, he went to sleep.

But he woke again when the moonlight came on his face and he started to think about Roger and the women he had been in trouble with. He and Roger had both behaved stupidly and badly with women. He did not want to think of his own stupidities so he would think of Roger's.

I won't pity him, he thought, so it is not disloyal. I have been in enough trouble myself so that it is not disloyal to think about Roger's trouble. My own is different because I only really loved one woman and then lost her. I know well enough why. But I am through with thinking about that and it would probably be well not to think about Roger either. But tonight, because of the moonlight which, as always, would not let him sleep, he thought about him and his serious and comic troubles.

He thought about the last girl Roger had been in love with in Paris when they had both lived there and how very handsome and how very false he thought she was when Roger had brought her to the studio. For Roger there was nothing false about her. She was another of his illusions and all his great talent for being faithful was at her service until they were both free to marry. Then, in a month, everything that had always been clear about her to everyone who knew her well was suddenly clear to Roger. It must have been a difficult day when it first happened but the process of seeing her clearly had been going on for some time when Roger had come up to the studio. He had looked at the canvases for a while and spoken critically and very intelligently about them. Then he said, "I told that Ayers I wouldn't marry her."

"Good," Thomas Hudson had said. "Was it a surprise?"

"Not too much. There'd been some talk about it. She's a phony."

"No," Thomas Hudson had said. "How?"

"Right through. Any way you slice her."

"I thought you liked her."

"No. I tried to like her. But I couldn't make it except at the start. I was in love with her."

"What's in love?"

"You ought to know."

"Yes," Thomas Hudson had said. "I ought to know."

"Didn't you like her?"

"No. I couldn't stand her."

"She was your girl. And you didn't ask me."

"I told her. But now I have to make it stick."

"You better pull out."

"No," he said. "Let her pull out."

"I only thought it might be simpler."

"This is my town as much as it is hers."

"I know," Thomas Hudson had said.

"You fought that one out, too, didn't you?" Roger had asked.

"Yes. You can't win on any of them. But you can fight them out. Why don't you just move your *quartier*?"

"I'm all right where I am," Roger had said.

"I remember the formula. *Je me trouve très bien ici et je vous prie de me laisser tranquille.*"

"It starts with *je refuse de recevoir ma femme*," Roger had said. "And you say it to a *huissier*. But this isn't a divorce. It's just breaking up."

"But isn't it going to be hard on you seeing her?"

"No. It's going to cure me. That and hearing her talk."

"What about her?"

"She can figure that out for herself. She's figured plenty out in the last four years."

"Five," Thomas Hudson had said.

"I don't think she was doing so much figuring the first year."

"You'd better clear out," Thomas Hudson had said. "If you don't think she was figuring the first year you'd better go a long way away."

"She writes very powerful letters. Going away would be worse. No. I'm going to stay here and go on the town. I'm going to cure it for keeps."

After he and this girl split up in Paris, Roger was on

the town; really on the town. He joked about it and made fun of himself; but he was very angry inside for having made such a profound fool of himself and he took his talent for being faithful to people, which was the best one he had, next to the ones for painting and writing and his various good human and animal traits, and beat and belabored that talent miserably. He was no good to anyone when he was on the town, especially to himself, and he knew it and hated it and he took pleasure in pulling down the pillars of the temple. It was a very good and strongly built temple and when it is constructed inside yourself it is not so easy to pull down. But he did as good a job as he could.

He had three girls in a row, no one of whom Thomas Hudson could be more than civil to and the only excuse for the last two might have been that they reminded him of the first one. This first one came right after the one he had just broken up with and she was sort of a world low for Roger although she went on to have a very successful career both in and out of bed and got herself a good piece of one of the third or fourth biggest fortunes in America and then married into another. She was named Thanis and Thomas Hudson remembered how Roger could never hear it without wincing and he wouldn't say it; no one ever heard him say the name. He used to call her Bitchy the Great. She was dark with a lovely skin and she looked like a very young, well-groomed, fastidiously vicious member of the Cenci family. She had the morals of a vacuum cleaner and the soul of a pari-mutuel machine, a good figure, and that lovely vicious face, and she only stayed with Roger long enough to get ready for her first good step upwards in life.

She was the first girl that had ever left him and that impressed Roger so that he had two more that looked almost enough like her to be members of the same family. He left both of them, though, really left them, and Thomas Hudson thought that made him feel better; though not a hell of a lot better.

There are probably politer ways and more endearing ways of leaving a girl than simply, with no unpleasantness

and never having been in any row, excusing yourself to go
to the men's room at 21 and never coming back. But, as
Roger said, he did settle the check downstairs and he
loved to think of his last glimpse of her, sitting alone at
the corner table in that décor that suited her so and that
she loved so well.

He planned to leave the other one at the Stork, which
was the place she really loved, but he was afraid Mr.
Billingsley might not like it and he needed to borrow some
money from Mr. Billingsley.

"So where did you leave her?" Thomas Hudson had
asked him.

"At El Morocco. So I could always remember her
sitting there among those zebras. She loved El Morocco
too," he said. "But I think it was the Cub Room that was
graven on her heart."

After that he got mixed up with one of the most deceptive
women Thomas Hudson had ever known. She was a
complete change from his last three Cenci or Park
Avenue Borgia types in looks. She looked really healthy
and had tawny hair and long, good legs, a very good
figure, and an intelligent, lively face. Though it was not
beautiful it was much better-looking than most faces.
And she had beautiful eyes. She was intelligent and very
kindly and charming when you first knew her and she was
a complete rummy. She was not a lush and her alcoholism
had not showed yet. But she was just at it all of the time.
Usually you can tell someone who is really drinking by
their eyes and it always showed in Roger's immediately.
But this girl, Kathleen, had really beautiful tawny eyes that
went with her hair and the little pleasant freckles of health
and good nature around her nose and her cheeks; and
you never saw anything in them of what was going on. She
looked like a girl who was sailing regularly or living some
sort of very healthy outdoor life and she looked like a
girl who was very happy. Instead she was just a girl
who was drinking. She was on a very strange voyage to
somewhere and for a while she took Roger with her.

But he came up to the studio Thomas Hudson had
rented in New York one morning with the back of his

left hand covered with cigarette burns. It looked as though someone had been putting butts out by rubbing them against a tabletop; only the tabletop was the back of his hand.

"That's what she wanted to do last night," he said. "Have you got any iodine? I didn't like to take those things into a drugstore."

"Who's she?"

"Kathleen. The fresh outdoor type."

"You had to participate."

"It seemed to amuse her and we're supposed to amuse them."

"You're burned pretty badly."

"Not really. But I'm going to get out of this town for a while."

"You'll be taking yourself along wherever you go."

"Yes. But I won't be taking a lot of other people I know with me."

"Where are you going to go?"

"Out West for a while."

"Geography isn't any cure for what's the matter with you."

"No. But a healthy life and plenty of work won't hurt. Not drinking may not cure me. But drinking sure as hell isn't helping any now."

"Well, get the hell out then. Do you want to go to the ranch?"

"Do you still own it?"

"Part of it."

"Is it all right if I go out there?"

"Sure," Thomas Hudson had told him. "But it's rugged from now on until spring and spring isn't easy."

"I want it to be rugged," Roger had said. "I'm going to start new again."

"How many times is it now you've started new?"

"Too many," Roger had said. "And you don't have to rub it in."

So now he was going to start new again and how would it turn out this time? How could he think that wasting his talent and writing to order and following a formula that made money could fit him to write well and truly? Everything that a painter did or that a writer wrote was a part of his training and preparation for what he was to do. Roger had thrown away and abused and spent his talent. But perhaps he had enough animal strength and detached intelligence so that he could make another start. Any writer of talent should be able to write one good novel if he were honest, Thomas Hudson thought. But all the time that he should be training for it Roger had been misusing his talent and how could you know if his talent still was there? To say nothing of his métier, he thought. How can anyone think that you can neglect and despise, or have contempt for craftsmanship, however feigned the contempt may be, and then expect it to be at the service of your hands and of your brain when the time comes when you must have it. There is no substitute for it, Thomas Hudson thought. There is no substitute for talent either and you don't have to keep them in a chalice. The one is inside you. It is in your heart and in your head and in every part of you. So is the other, he thought. It is not just a set of tools that you have learned to work with.

It is luckier to be a painter, he thought, because you have more things to work with. We have the advantage of working with our hands and the métier we have mastered is an actual tangible thing. But Roger must start now to use what he has blunted and perverted and cheapened and all of it is in his head. But au fond he has something fine and sound and beautiful. That is a word I would need to be very careful of if I were a writer, he thought. But he has the thing that is the way he is and if he could write the way he fought on the dock it could be cruel but it would be very good. Then if he could think as soundly as he thought after that fight he would be very good.

The moonlight did not shine on the head of Thomas Hudson's bed anymore and gradually he stopped thinking about Roger. Thinking about him doesn't do any good. Either he can do it or he can't. But it would be wonderful if he could do it. I wish that I could help him. Maybe I can, he thought, and then he was asleep.

IX

WHEN the sun woke Thomas Hudson he went down to the beach and swam and then had breakfast before the rest of them were up. Eddy said he did not think they would have much of a breeze and it might even be a calm. He said the gear was all in good shape on the boat and he had a boy out after bait.

Thomas Hudson asked him if he had tested the lines since the boat had not been out for big fish in quite a while and Eddy said he had tested them and taken off all the line that was rotten. He said they were going to have to get some more thirty-six thread line and plenty more twenty-four thread and Thomas Hudson promised to send for it. In the meantime Eddy had spliced enough good line on to replace the discarded line and both the big reels had all they would hold. He had cleaned and sharpened all of the big hooks and checked all the leaders and swivels.

"When did you do all this?"

"I sat up last night splicing," he said. "Then I worked on that new cast net. Couldn't sleep with the goddam moon."

"Does a full moon bother you for sleeping too?"

"Gives me hell," Eddy said.

"Eddy do you think it's really bad for you to sleep with it shining on you?"

"That's what the old heads say. I don't know. Always makes me feel bad, anyway."

"Do you think we'll do anything today?"

"Never know. There's some awfully big fish out there this time of year. Are you going clean up to the Isaacs?"

"The boys want to go up there."

"We ought to get going right after breakfast. I'm not

figuring to cook lunch. I've got conch salad and potato salad and beer and I'll make up sandwiches. We've got a ham that came over on the last run-boat and I've got some lettuce and we can use mustard and that chutney. Mustard doesn't hurt kids, does it?"

"I don't think so."

"We never had it when I was a kid. Say, that chutney's good, too. You ever eat it in a sandwich?"

"No."

"I didn't know what it was for when you first got it and I tried some of it like a marmalade. It's damned good. I use it sometimes on grits."

"Why don't we have some curry pretty soon?"

"I got a leg of lamb coming on the next run-boat. Wait till we eat off it a couple of times—once, I guess, with that young Tom and Andrew eating, and we'll have a curry."

"Fine. What do you want me to do about getting off?"

"Nothing, Tom. Just get them going. Want me to make you a drink? You aren't working today. Might as well have one."

"I'll drink a cold bottle of beer with breakfast."

"Good thing. Cut that damn phlegm."

"Is Joe here yet?"

"No. He went after the boy that's gone for bait. I'll put your breakfast out there."

"No, let me take her."

"No, go on in and drink a cold bottle of beer and read the paper. I've got her all ironed out for you. I'll bring the breakfast."

Breakfast was corned-beef hash, browned, with an egg on top of it, coffee and milk, and a big glass of chilled grapefruit juice. Thomas Hudson skipped the coffee and the grapefruit juice and drank a very cold bottle of Heineken beer with the hash.

"I'll keep the juice cold for the kids," Eddy said. "That's some beer, isn't it, for early in the morning?"

"It would be pretty easy to be a rummy, wouldn't it, Eddy?"

"You'd never make a rummy. You like to work too well."

"Drinking in the morning feels awfully good though."

"You're damned right it does. Especially something like that beer."

"I couldn't do it and work though."

"Well, you're not working today so what's the goddam problem? Drink that one up and I'll get you another."

"No. One's all I want."

They got off by nine o'clock and went down the channel with the tide. Thomas Hudson was steering on the topside and he headed her out over the bar and ran straight out toward where he could see the dark line of the Gulf. The water was so calm and so very clear that they could see the bottom clearly in thirty fathoms, see that sea fans bent with the tide current, still see it, but cloudily, at forty fathoms, and then it deepened and was dark and they were out in the dark water of the stream.

"It looks like a wonderful day, papa," Tom said. "It looks like a good stream."

"It's a fine stream. Look at the little curl of the whirlpools along the edge."

"Isn't this the same water that we have in on the beach in front of the house?"

"Sometimes, Tommy. Now the tide is out and it has pushed the Stream out from in front of the mouth of the harbor. See in there along the beach, where there is no opening, it's made in again."

"It looks almost as blue in there as it is out here. What makes the Gulf water so blue?"

"It's a different density of water. It's an altogether different type of water."

"The depth makes it darker, though."

"Only when you look down into it. Sometimes the plankton in it make it almost purple."

"Why?"

"Because they add red to the blue I think. I know they call the Red Sea red because the plankton make it look really red. They have terrific concentrations of them there."

"Did you like the Red Sea, papa?"

"I loved it. It was awfully hot but you never saw such

wonderful reefs and it's full of fish on the two monsoons. You'd like it, Tom."

"I read two books about it in French by Mr. de Montfried. They were very good. He was in the slave trade. Not the white slave trade. The olden days slave trade. He's a friend of Mr. Davis."

"I know," Thomas Hudson said. "I know him, too."

"Mr. Davis told me that Mr. de Montfried came back to Paris one time from the slave trade and when he would take a lady out anywhere he would have the taxi driver put down the top of the taxi and he would steer the taxi driver wherever he wanted to go by the stars. Say Mr. de Montfried was on the Pont de la Concorde and he wanted to go to the Madeleine. He wouldn't just tell the taxi driver to take him to the Madeleine, or to cross the Place de la Concorde and go up the Rue Royale the way you or I would do it, papa. Mr. de Montfried would steer himself to the Madeleine by the North Star."

"I never heard that one about Mr. de Montfried," Thomas Hudson said. "I heard quite a lot of others."

"It's quite a complicated way to get around in Paris, don't you think? Mr. Davis wanted to go into the slave trade at one time with Mr. de Montfried but there was some sort of a hitch. I don't remember what it was. Yes, now I do. Mr. de Montfried had left the slave trade and gone into the opium trade. That was it."

"Didn't Mr. Davis want to go into the opium trade?"

"No. I remember he said he thought he'd leave the opium trade to Mr. De Quincey and Mr. Cocteau. He said they'd done so well in it that he didn't think it was right to disturb them. That was one of those remarks that I couldn't understand. Papa, you explain anything to me that I ask but it used to slow the conversation up so much to be asking all the time that I would just remember certain things I didn't understand to ask about sometime and that's one of those things."

"You must have quite a backlog of those things."

"I've got hundreds of them. Possibly thousands. But I get rid of a lot of them every year by getting to understand them myself. But some I know I'll have to ask you about. At school this year I may write a list of them for an English composition. I've got some awfully good ones for a composition of that sort."

"Do you like school, Tom?"

"It's just one of those things you have to take. I don't think anyone likes school, do they, that has ever done anything else?"

"I don't know. I hated it."

"Didn't you like art school either?"

"No. I liked to learn to draw but I didn't like the school part."

"I don't really mind it," Tom said. "But after you've spent your life with men like Mr. Joyce and Mr. Pascin and you and Mr. Davis, being with boys seems sort of juvenile."

"You have fun, though, don't you?"

"Oh yes. I have lots of friends and I like any of the sports that aren't built around throwing or catching balls and I study quite hard. But papa, it isn't much of a life."

"That was the way I always felt about it," Thomas Hudson said. "You liven it up as much as you can, though."

"I do. I liven it up all I can and still stay in it. Sometimes it's a pretty close thing, though."

Thomas Hudson looked astern where the wake ran crisply in the calm sea and the two baits from the outriggers were dragging; dipping and leaping in the curl of the waves the wake raised as it cut the calm. David and Andrew sat in the two fishing chairs holding rods. Thomas Hudson saw their backs. Their faces were astern watching the baits. He looked ahead at some bonito jumping, not working and threshing the water, but coming up out and dropping back into the water singly and in pairs, making hardly any disturbance of the surface as they rose, shining in the sun, and returning, heavy heads down, to enter the water almost without splash.

"Fish!" Thomas Hudson heard young Tom shout. "Fish! Fish! There he comes up. Behind you, Dave. Watch him!"

Thomas Hudson saw a huge boil in the water but could not see the fish. David had the rod butt in the gimble and was looking up at the clothespin on the out-rigger line. Thomas Hudson saw the line fall from the outrigger in a long, slow loop that tightened as it hit the water and now was racing out at a slant, slicing the water as it went.

"Hit him, Dave. Hit him hard," Eddy called from the companionway.

"Hit him, Dave. For God's sake hit him," Andrew begged.

"Shut up," David said. "I'm handling him."

He hadn't struck yet and the line was steadily going out at that angle, the rod bowed, the boy holding back on it as the line moved out. Thomas Hudson had throttled the motors down so they were barely turning over.

"Oh for God's sake, hit him," Andrew pleaded. "Or let me hit him."

David just held back on the rod and watched the line moving out at the same steady angle. He had loosened the drag.

"He's a broadbill, papa," he said without looking up. "I saw his sword when he took it."

"Honest to God?" Andrew asked. "Oh boy."

"I think you ought to hit him now," Roger was standing with the boy now. He had the back out of the chair and he was buckling the harness on the reel. "Hit him now, Dave, and really hit him."

"Do you think he's had it long enough?" David asked. "You don't think he's just carrying it in his mouth and swimming with it?"

"I think you better hit him before he spits it out."

David braced his feet, tightened the drag well down with his right hand, and struck back hard against the great weight. He struck again and again bending the rod like a bow. The line moved out steadily. He had made no impression on the fish.

"Hit him again, Dave," Roger said. "Really put it into him."

David struck again with all his strength and the line started zizzing out, the rod bent so that he could hardly hold it.

"Oh God," he said devoutly. "I think I've got it into him."

"Ease up on your drag," Roger told him. "Turn with him, Tom, and watch the line."

"Turn with him and watch the line," Thomas Hudson repeated. "You all right, Dave?"

"I'm wonderful, papa," Dave said. "Oh God, if I can catch this fish."

Thomas Hudson swung the boat around almost on her stern. Dave's line was fading off the reel and Thomas Hudson moved up on the fish.

"Tighten up and get that line in now," Roger said. "Work on him, Dave."

David was lifting and reeling as he lowered, lifting and reeling as he lowered, as regularly as a machine, and was getting back a good quantity of line onto his reel.

"Nobody in our family's ever caught a broadbill," Andrew said.

"Oh keep your mouth off him, please," David said. "Don't put your mouth on him."

"I won't," Andrew said. "I've been doing nothing but pray ever since you hooked him."

"Do you think his mouth will hold?" young Tom whispered to his father, who was holding the wheel and looking down into the stern and watching the slant of the white line in the dark water.

"I hope so. Dave isn't strong enough to be rough with him."

"I'll do anything if we can get him," young Tom said. "Anything. I'll give up anything. I'll promise anything. Get him some water, Andy."

"I've got some," Eddy said. "Stay with him, old Dave boy."

"I don't want him any closer," Roger called up. He was a great fisherman and he and Thomas Hudson understood each other perfectly in a boat.

"I'll put him astern," Thomas Hudson called and swung the boat around very softly and easily so the stern hardly disturbed the calm sea.

The fish was sounding now and Thomas Hudson backed

the boat very slowly to ease the pressure on the line all that he could. But with only a touch of reverse with the stern moving slowly toward the fish the angle was all gone from the line and the rod tip was pointing straight down and the line kept going out in a series of steady jerks, the rod bucking each time in David's hands. Thomas Hudson slipped the boat ahead just a thought so that the boy would not have the line so straight up and down in the water. He knew how it was pulling on his back in that position, but he had to save all the line he could.

"I can't put any more drag on or it will break," David said. "What will he do, Mr. Davis?"

"He'll just keep on going down until you stop him," Roger said. "Or until he stops. Then you've got to try to get him up."

The line kept going out and down, out and down, out and down. The rod was bent so far it looked as though it must break and the line was taut as a tuned cello string and there was not much more of it on the reel.

"What can I do, papa?"

"Nothing. You're doing what there is to do."

"Won't he hit the bottom?" Andrew asked.

"There isn't any bottom," Roger told him.

"You hold him, Davy," Eddy said. "He'll get sick of it and come up."

"These damned straps are killing me," David said. "They cut my shoulders off."

"Do you want me to take him?" Andrew asked.

"No, you fool," David said. "I just said what they were doing to me. I don't care about it."

"See if you can rig him the kidney harness," Thomas Hudson called down to Eddy. "You can tie it on with line if the straps are too long."

Eddy wrapped the broad, quilted pad across the small of the boy's back and fastened the rings on the web straps that ran across it to the reel with heavy line.

"That's much better," David said. "Thank you very much, Eddy."

"Now you can hold him with your back as well as your shoulders," Eddy told him.

"But there isn't going to be any line." David said. "Oh Goddam him, why does he have to keep on sounding?"

"Tom," Eddy called up. "Ease her a little northwest. I think he's moving."

Thomas Hudson turned the wheel and moved her softly, slowly, softly out to sea. There was a big patch of yellow gulf weed ahead with a bird on it and the water was calm and so blue and clear that, as you looked down into it, there were lights in it like the reflections from a prism.

"You see?" Eddy told David. "You're not losing any now."

The boy could not raise the rod; but the line was no longer jerking down into the water. It was as taut as ever and there weren't fifty yards left on the reel. But it was not going out. David was holding him and the boat was on his course. Thomas Hudson could see the just perceptible slant of the white line deep down in the blue water as the boat barely moved, its engines turning so quietly he could not hear them.

"You see, Davy, he went down to where he liked it and now he's moving out to where he wants to go. Pretty soon you'll get some line on him."

The boy's brown back was arched, the rod bent, the line moved slowly through the water, and the boat moved slowly on the surface, and a quarter of a mile below the great fish was swimming. The gull left the patch of weed and flew toward the boat. He flew around Thomas Hudson's head while he steered, then headed off toward another patch of yellow weed on the water.

"Try to get some on him now," Roger told the boy. "If you can hold him you can get some."

"Put her ahead just a touch more," Eddy called to the bridge and Thomas Hudson eased her ahead as softly as he could.

David lifted and lifted, but the rod only bent and the line only tightened. It was as though he were hooked to a moving anchor.

"Never mind," Roger told him. "You'll get it later. How are you, Davy?"

"I'm fine," David said. "With that harness across my back I'm fine."

"Do you think you can stay with him?" Andrew asked.

"Oh shut up," David said. "Eddy, can I have a drink of water?"

"Where'd I put it?" Eddy asked. "I guess I spilled it."

"I'll get one," Andrew went below.

"Can I do anything, Dave?" young Tom asked. "I'm going up so I won't be in the way."

"No, Tom. Goddam it, *why* can't I lift on him?"

"He's an awfully big fish, Dave," Roger told him. "You can't bull him around. You've got to lead him and try to convince him where he has to come."

"You tell me what to do and I'll do it until I die," David said. "I trust you."

"Don't talk about dying," Roger said. "That's no way to talk."

"I mean it," David said. "I mean it really."

Young Tom came back up on the flying bridge with his father. They were looking down at David, bent and harnessed to his fish, with Roger standing by him and Eddy holding the chair. Andrew was putting the glass of water to Dave's mouth. He took some in and spat it out.

"Pour some on my wrists, will you, Andy?" he asked.

"Papa, do you think he can really stay with this fish?" Tom said to his father very softly.

"It's an awful lot of fish for him."

"It scares me," Tom said. "I love David and I don't want any damned fish to kill him."

"Neither do I and neither does Roger and neither does Eddy."

"Well we've got to look after him. If he gets in really bad shape, Mr. Davis ought to take the fish or you take him."

"He's a long way from bad shape yet."

"But you don't know him like we do. He *would* kill himself to get the fish."

"Don't worry, Tom."

"I can't help it," young Tom said. "I'm the one in the family that always worries. I hope I'll get over it."

"I wouldn't worry about this now," Thomas Hudson said.

"But papa, how is a boy like David going to catch a fish like that? He's never caught anything bigger than sailfish and amberjack."

"This fish will get tired. It's the fish that has the hook in his mouth."

"But he's monstrous," Tom said. "And Dave's fastened to him just as much as he is to Dave. It's so wonderful I can't believe it if Dave catches him, but I wish you or Mr. Davis had him.

"Dave's doing all right."

They were getting further out to sea all the time but it was still a flat calm. There were many patches of Gulf weed now, sunburned so that they were yellow on the purple water, and sometimes the slow-moving taut white line ran through a patch of weed and Eddy reached down and cleared any weed that clung to the line. As he leaned over the coaming and pulled the yellow weed off the line and tossed it away, Thomas Hudson saw his wrinkled red brown neck and old felt hat and heard him say to Dave, "He's practically towing the boat, Davy. He's way down there tiring himself and tiring himself all the time."

"He's tiring me, too," David said.

"You got a headache?" Eddy asked.

"No."

"Get a cap for him," Roger said.

"I don't want it, Mr. Davis. I'd rather have some water on my head."

Eddy dipped a bucket of sea water and wet the boy's head carefully with his cupped hand, soaking his head and pushing the hair back out of his eyes.

"You say if you get a headache," he told him.

"I'm fine," David said. "You tell me what to do, Mr. Davis."

"See if you can get any line on him," Roger said.

David tried and tried and tried again but he could not raise the fish an inch.

"All right. Save your strength," Roger told him. Then

to Eddy, "Soak a cap and put it on him. This is a hell of a hot day with the calm."

Eddy dipped a long-visored cap in the bucket of salt water and put it on Dave's head.

"The salt water gets in my eyes, Mr. Davis. Really. I'm sorry."

"I'll wipe it out with some fresh," Eddy said. "Give me a handkerchief, Roger. You go get some ice water, Andy."

While the boy hung there, his legs braced, his body arched against the strain, the boat kept moving slowly out to sea. To the westward a school of either bonito or albacore were troubling the calm of the surface and terns commenced to come flying, calling to each other as they flew. But the school of fish went down and the terns lit on the calm water to wait for the fish to come up again. Eddy had wiped the boy's face and now was dipping the handkerchief in the glass of ice water and laying it across David's neck. Then he cooled his wrists with it and then, with the handkerchief soaked in ice water again, wrung it out while he pressed it against the back of David's neck.

"You say if you have a headache," Eddy told him. "That ain't quitting. That's just sense. This is a hell of a goddam hot sun when it's a calm."

"I'm all right," David told him. "I hurt bad in the shoulders and the arms is all."

"That's natural," Eddy said. "That'll make a man out of you. What we don't want is for you to get no sunstroke nor bust any gut."

"What will he do now, Mr. Davis?" David asked. His voice sounded dry.

"Maybe just what he's doing. Or he might start to circle. Or he may come up."

"It's a damn shame he sounded so deep at the start so we haven't any line to maneuver him with," Thomas Hudson said to Roger.

"Dave stopped him is the main thing," Roger said. "Pretty soon the fish will change his mind. Then we'll work on him. See if you can get any just once, Dave."

David tried but he could not raise him at all.

"He'll come up," Eddy said. "You'll see. All of a sudden there won't be anything to it, Davy. Want to rinse your mouth out?"

David nodded his head. He had reached the breath-saving stage.

"Spit it out," Eddy said. "Swallow just a little." He turned to Roger. "One hour even," he said. "Is your head all right, Davy?"

The boy nodded.

"What do you think, papa?" young Tom said to his father. "Truly?"

"He looks pretty good to me," his father said. "Eddy wouldn't let anything happen to him."

"No, I guess not," Tom agreed. "I wish I could do something useful. I'm going to get Eddy a drink."

"Get me one, too, please."

"Oh good. I'll make one for Mr. Davis, too."

"I don't think he wants one."

"Well I'll ask him."

"Try him once more, Davy," Roger said very quietly, and the boy lifted with all his strength, holding the sides of the spool of the reel with his hands.

"You got an inch," Roger said. "Take it in and see if you can get some more."

Now the real fight began. Before David had only been holding him while the fish moved out to sea and the boat moved with him. But now he had to lift, let the rod straighten with the line he had gained, and then lower the rod slowly while he took the line in by reeling.

"Don't try to do it too fast," Roger told him. "Don't rush yourself. Just keep it steady."

The boy was bending forward and pulling up from the soles of his feet, using all the leverage of his body and all of what weight he had on each lift; then reeling fast with his right hand as he lowered.

"David fishes awfully pretty," young Tom said. "He's fished since he was a little boy but I didn't know he could fish this well. He always makes fun of himself because he can't play games. But look at him now."

"The hell with games," Thomas Hudson said. "What did you say, Roger?"

"Go ahead on him just a touch," Roger called up.

"Ahead on him just a touch," Thomas Hudson repeated and on the next lift, as they nudged slowly forward, David recovered more line.

"Don't you like games either, papa?" Tom asked.

"I used to. Very much. But not anymore."

"I like tennis and fencing," Tom said. "The throw-and-catch ball games are the ones I don't like. That's from being brought up in Europe I guess. I'll bet David could be a fine fencer if he wanted to learn because he has so much brains. But he doesn't want to learn. All he wants to do is read and fish and shoot and tie flies. He shoots better than Andy does in the field. He can tie beautiful flies too. Am I bothering you, papa, talking so much?"

"Of course not, Tom."

He was holding to the rail of the flying bridge and looking aft as his father was and his father put one hand on his shoulder. It was salty from the buckets of sea water the boys had thrown over each other on the stern before the fish struck. The salt was very fine and felt faintly sandy under his hand.

"You see I get so nervous watching David I talk to take my mind off it. I'd rather have David catch that fish than anything on earth."

"He's a hell of a fish. Wait till we see him."

"I saw one one time when I was fishing with you years ago. He hit a big mackerel bait with his sword and he jumped and threw the hook. He was enormous and I used to dream about him. I'll go down and make the drinks."

"There's no hurry," his father told him.

Down in the backless fighting chair, set in its swivel base, David braced his feet against the stern and lifted with his arms, back, withers, and thighs; then lowered and reeled and lifted again. Steadily, an inch, two inches, three inches at a time he was getting more and more line on the reel.

"Is your head all right?" Eddy, who was holding the arms of the chair to steady it, asked him.

David nodded. Eddy put his hand on the top of the boy's head and felt his cap.

"Cap's still wet," he said. "You're giving him hell, Davy. Just like a machine."

"It's easier now than holding him," David said, his voice still dry.

"Sure," Eddy told him. "Something gives now. Other way it was just pulling your back out by the roots."

"Don't work him any faster than you can," Roger said. "You're doing wonderfully, Dave."

"Will we gaff him when he comes up this time?" Andrew asked.

"*Oh keep your mouth off of him, please,*" David said.

"I wasn't trying to mouth him."

"Oh just shut up, Andy, please. I'm sorry."

Andrew came climbing up topside. He had on one of the long-peaked caps but under it his father could see his eyes were wet and the boy turned his head away because his lips trembled.

"You didn't say anything bad," Thomas Hudson told him.

Andrew spoke with his head turned away. "Now if he loses him he'll think I mouthed him," he said bitterly. "All I wanted to do was help get everything ready."

"It's natural for Dave to be nervous," his father told him. "He's trying to be polite."

"I know it," Andrew said. "He's fighting him just as good as Mr. Davis could. I just felt bad he could think that."

"Lots of people are irritable with a big fish. This is the first one Dave's ever had."

"You're always polite and Mr. Davis is always polite."

"We didn't use to be. When we were learning to fish big fish together we used to be excited and rude and sarcastic. We both used to be terrible."

"Truly?"

"Sure. Truly. We used to suffer and act as though everybody was against us. That's the natural way to be. The other's discipline or good sense when you learn. We started to be polite because we found we couldn't catch big fish being rude and excited. And if we did, it wasn't any fun. We were both really awful though; excited and sore and misunderstood and it wasn't any fun. So now we always fight them politely. We talked it over and decided we'd be polite no matter what."

"I'll be polite," Andrew said. "But it's hard sometimes with Dave. Papa, do you think he can *really* get him? That it isn't just like a dream or something?"

"Let's not talk about it."

"Have I said something wrong again?"

"No. Only it always seems bad luck to talk that way. We got it from the old fishermen. I don't know what started it."

"I'll be careful."

"Here's your drink, papa," Tom said, handing it up from below. The glass was wrapped in a triple thickness of paper towel with a rubber band around to hold the paper tight against the glass and keep the ice from melting. "I put lime, bitters, and no sugar in it. Is that how you want it? Or can I change it?"

"That's fine. Did you make it with coconut water?"

"Yes, and I made Eddy a whisky. Mr. Davis didn't want anything. Are you staying up there, Andy?"

"No. I'm coming down."

Tom climbed up and Andrew went down.

Looking back over the stern, Thomas Hudson noticed the line starting to slant up in the water.

"Watch it, Roger," he called. "It looks like he's coming up."

"He's coming up!" Eddy yelled. He had seen the slant in the line too. "Watch your wheel."

Thomas Hudson looked down at the spool of the reel to see how much line there was to maneuver with. It was not yet a quarter full and as he watched it started to whiz off and Thomas Hudson started backing, turning sharp toward the slant of the line, well under way as Eddy yelled, "Back on him, Tom. The son of a bitch is coming up. We ain't got no line to turn."

"Keep your rod up," Roger said to David. "Don't let him get it down." Then to Thomas Hudson, "Back on him all you can, Tom. You're going right. Give her all she'll take."

Then, astern of the boat and off to starboard, the calm of the ocean broke open and the great fish rose out of it, rising, shining dark blue and silver, seeming to come endlessly out of the water, unbelievable as his length and bulk rose out of the sea into the air and seemed to hang there until he fell with a splash that drove the water up high and white.

"Oh, God," David said. "Did you see him?"

"His sword's as long as I am," Andrew said in awe.

"He's so beautiful," Tom said. "He's much better than the one I had in the dream."

"Keep backing on him," Roger said to Thomas Hudson. Then to David, "Try and get some line out of that belly. He came up from way down and there's a big belly of line and you can get some of it."

Thomas Hudson, backing fast onto the fish, had stopped the line going out and now David was lifting, lowering, and reeling, and the line was coming onto the reel in sweeps as fast as he could turn the reel handle.

"Slow her down," Roger said. "We don't want to get over him.

"Son of a bitch'll weigh a thousand pounds," Eddy said. "Get that easy line in, Davy boy."

The ocean was flat and empty where he had jumped but the circle made where the water had been broken was still widening.

"Did you see the water he threw when he jumped, papa?" young Tom asked his father. "It was like the whole sea bursting open."

"Did you see the way he seemed to climb up and up, Tom? Did you ever see such a blue and that wonderful silver on him?"

"His sword is blue too," young Tom said. "The whole back of it is blue. Will he really weigh a thousand pounds, Eddy?" he called down.

"I think he will. Nobody can say. But he'll weigh something awful."

"Get all the line you can, Davy, now while it's cheap," Roger told him. "You're getting it fine."

The boy was working like a machine again, recovering line from the great bulge of line in the water and the boat was backing so slowly that the movement was barely perceptible.

"What will he do now, papa?" Tom asked his father. Thomas Hudson was watching the slant of the line in the water and thinking it would be safer to go ahead just a little but he knew how Roger had suffered with so much line out. The fish had only needed to make one steady rush to strip all the line from the reel and break off and now Roger was taking chances to get a reserve of line. As Thomas Hudson watched the line, he saw that David had the reel nearly half full and that he was still gaining.

"What did you say?" Thomas Hudson asked his boy Tom.

"What do you think he'll do now?"

"Wait a minute, Tom," his father said and called down to Roger. "I'm afraid we're going to get over him, kid."

"Then put her ahead easy," Roger said.

"Ahead easy," Thomas Hudson repeated. David stopped getting in so much line but the fish was in a safer position.

Then the line started to go out again and Roger called up, "Throw her out," and Thomas Hudson threw out the clutches and let the motors idle.

"She's out," he said. Roger was bending over David and the boy was braced and holding back on the rod and the line was slipping steadily away.

"Tighten on him a little bit, Davy," Roger said. "We'll make him work for it."

"I don't want him to break," David said. But he tightened the drag.

"He won't break," Roger told him. "Not with that drag."

The line kept going out but the rod was bent heavier and the boy was braced back holding against the pressure with his bare feet against the wood of the stern. Then the line stopped going out.

"Now you can get some," Roger told the boy. "He's

circling and this is the in-turn. Get back all you can."

The boy lowered and reeled, then lifted; let the rod straighten; lowered and reeled. He was getting line beautifully again.

"Am I doing all right?" he asked.

"You're doing wonderful," Eddy told him. "He's hooked deep, Davy. I could see when he jumped."

Then, while the boy was lifting, the line started to go out again.

"Hell," David said.

"That's OK," Roger told him. "That's what's supposed to happen. He's on the out-turn now. He circled in toward you and you got line. Now he's taking it back."

Steadily, slowly, with David holding him with all the strain the line would take, the fish took out all the line the boy had just recovered and a little more. Then the boy held him.

"All right. Get to work on him," Roger said quietly. "He widened his circle a little bit but he's on the in-swing now."

Thomas Hudson was using the engines only occasionally now to keep the fish astern. He was trying to do everything for the boy that the boat could do and he was trusting the boy and the fight to Roger. As he saw it there was no other thing to do.

On the next circle the fish gained a little line again. On the circle after that he gained too. But the boy still had almost half the line on the reel. He was still working the fish exactly as he should and delivering each time Roger asked him to do something. But he was getting very tired and the sweat and salt water had made salty blotches on his brown back and shoulders.

"Two hours even," Eddy said to Roger. "How's your head, Davy?"

"All right."

"Not ache?"

The boy shook his head.

"You better drink some water this time," Eddy said.

David nodded and drank when Andrew put the glass to his lips.

"How do you feel, Davy, really?" Roger asked him, bending close over him.

"Fine. All except my back and legs and arms." He shut his eyes for an instant and held to the bucking of the rod as the line went out against the heavy drag.

"I don't want to talk," he said.

"You can get some on him now," Roger told him and the boy went back to work.

"David's a saint and a martyr," Tom said to his father. "Boys don't have brothers like David. Do you mind if I talk, papa? I'm awfully nervous about this."

"Go ahead and talk, Tommy. We're both worried."

"He's always been wonderful, you know," Tom said. "He's not a damn genius nor an athlete like Andy. He's just wonderful. I know you love him the most and that's right because he's the best of us and I know this must be good for him or you wouldn't let him do it. But it certainly makes me nervous."

Thomas Hudson put an arm around his shoulder and steered, looking astern with only one hand on the wheel.

"The trouble is, Tommy, what it would do to him if we made him give it up. Roger and Eddy know everything about what they're doing and I know they love him and wouldn't have him do what he can't do."

"But there is no limit with him, papa. Truly. He'll always do what he can't do."

"You trust me and I'll trust Roger and Eddy."

"All right. But I'm going to pray for him now."

"You do," said Thomas Hudson. "Why did you say I loved him the best?"

"You ought to."

"I've loved you the longest."

"Let's not think about me nor you. Let's both of us pray for Davy."

"Good," said Thomas Hudson. "Now look. We hooked him right at noon. There's going to be some shade now. I think we've got some already. I'm going to work her around very softly and put Davy in the shade."

Thomas Hudson called down to Roger. "If it's OK with you, Roge, I'd like to work her around slow and put Dave in the shade. I don't think it will make any difference with the fish the way he's circling and we'll be on his real course."

"Fine," Roger said. "I should have thought of it."

"There hasn't been any shade until now," Thomas Hudson said. He worked the boat around so slowly, just swinging her on her stern, that they lost almost no line by the maneuver. David's head and shoulders were now shaded by the aft part of the house. Eddy was wiping the boy's neck and shoulders with a towel and putting alcohol on his back and on the back of his neck.

"How's that, Dave?" young Tom called down to him.

"Wonderful," David said.

"I feel better about him now," young Tom said. "You know at school somebody said David was my half brother, not my real brother, and I told him we didn't have half brothers in our family. I wish I didn't worry so much though, papa."

"You'll get over it."

"In a family like ours somebody has to worry," young Tom said. "But I never worry about you anymore. It's David now. I guess I better make a couple of more drinks. I can pray while I make them. Do you want one, papa?"

"I'd love one."

"Eddy probably needs one pretty badly," the boy said. "It must be nearly three hours. Eddy's only had one drink in three hours. I've certainly been remiss about things. Why do you suppose Mr. Davis wouldn't take one, papa?"

"I didn't think he would take one while David was going through all that."

"Maybe he will now Dave's in the shade. I'll try him now anyway."

He went below.

"I don't think so, Tommy," Thomas Hudson heard Roger say.

"You haven't had one all day, Mr. Davis," Tom urged.

"Thanks, Tommy," Roger said. "You drink a bottle of beer for me." Then he called up to the wheel. "Put her ahead a little easy, Tom. He's coming better on this tack."

"Ahead a little easy," Thomas Hudson repeated.

The fish was still circling deep, but in the direction the boat was headed now he was shortening the circle. It was the direction he wanted to move in. Now, too, it was easier to see the slant of the line. It was easier to see its true slant much deeper in the dark water with the sun behind the boat and Thomas Hudson felt safer steering with the fish. He thought how fortunate it was that the day was calm for he knew David could never have taken the punishment that he would have had if he were hooked to such a fish in even a moderate sea. Now that David was in the shade and the sea stayed calm he began to feel better about it all.

"Thanks, Tommy," he heard Eddy say and then the boy climbed up with his paper-wrapped glass and Thomas Hudson tasted, took a swallow and felt the cold that had the sharpness of the lime, the aromatic varnishy taste of the Angostura and the gin stiffening the lightness of the ice-cold coconut water.

"Is it all right, papa?" the boy asked. He had a bottle of beer from the icebox that was perspiring cold drops in the sun.

"It's excellent," his father told him. "You put in plenty of gin too."

"I have to," young Tom said. "Because the ice melts so fast. We ought to have some sort of insulated holders for the glasses so the ice wouldn't melt. I'm going to work out something at school. I think I could make them out of cork blocks. Maybe I can make them for you for Christmas."

"Look at Dave now," his father said.

David was working on the fish as though he had just started the fight.

"Look how sort of slab-sided he is," young Tom said. "His chest and his back are all the same. He looks sort of like he was glued together. But he's got the longest arm muscles you could ever see. They're just as long on the back of his arms as on the front. The biceps and the triceps I mean. He's certainly built strangely, papa. He's a strange boy and he's the best damn brother you can have."

Down in the cockpit Eddy had drained his glass and

was wiping David's back with a towel again. Then he wiped his chest and his long arms.

"You all right, Davy?"

David nodded.

"Listen," Eddy told him, "I've seen a grown man, strong, shoulders like a bull, yellow-out and quit on half the work you've put in on that fish already."

David kept on working.

"Big man. Your Dad and Roger both know him. Trained for it. Fishing all the time. Hooked the biggest goddam fish a man ever hooked and yellowed out and quit on him just because he hurt. Fish made him hurt so he quit. You just keep it steady, Davy."

David did not say anything. He was saving his breath and pumping, lowering, raising, and reeling.

"This damn fish is so strong because he's a he," Eddy told him. "If it was a she it would have quit long ago. It would have bust its insides or its heart or burst its roe. In this kind of fish the he is the strongest. In lots of other fish it's the she that is strongest. But not with broadbill. He's awfully strong, Davy. But you'll get him."

The line started to go out again and David shut his eyes a moment, braced his bare feet against the wood, hung back against the rod, and rested.

"That's right, Davy," Eddy said. "Only work when you're working. He's just circling. But the drag makes him work for it and it's tiring him all the time."

Eddy turned his head and looked below and Thomas Hudson knew from the way he squinted his eyes that he was looking at the big brass clock on the cabin wall.

"It's five over three, Roger," he said. "You'e been with him three hours and five minutes, Davy old boy."

They were at the point where David should have started to gain line. But instead the line was going out steadily.

"He's sounding again," Roger said. "Watch yourself, Davy. Can you see the line OK, Tom?"

"I can see it OK," Thomas Hudson told him. It was not yet at a very steep slant and he could see it a long way down in the water from the top of the house.

"He may want to go down to die," Thomas Hudson

told his oldest boy, speaking very low. "That would ruin Dave."

Young Tom shook his head and bit his lips.

"Hold him all you can, Dave," Thomas Hudson heard Roger say. "Tighten up on him and give it all it will take."

The boy tightened up the drag almost to the breaking point of the rod and line and then hung on, bracing himself to take the punishment the best he could, while the line went out and out and down and down.

"When you stop him this time I think you will have whipped him," Roger told David. "Throw her out, Tom."

"She's cut," Thomas Hudson said. "But I think I could save a little backing."

"OK. Try it."

"Backing now," Thomas Hudson said. They saved a little line by backing but not much, and the line was getting terribly straight up and down. There was less on the reel now than at the worst time before.

"You'll have to get out on the stern, Davy," Roger said. "You'll have to loosen the drag up a little to get the butt out."

David loosened the drag.

"Now get the butt into your butt rest. You hold him around the waist, Eddy."

"Oh God, papa," young Tom said. "He's taking it all right to the bottom now."

David was on his knees on the low stern now, the rod bent so that its tip was underwater, its butt in the leather socket of the butt rest that was strapped around his waist. Andrew was holding onto David's feet and Roger knelt beside him watching the line in the water and the little there was on the reel. He shook his head at Thomas Hudson.

There was not twenty yards more on the reel and David was pulled down with half the rod underwater now. Then there was barely fifteen yards on the reel. Now there was not ten yards. Then the line stopped going out. The boy was still bent far over the stern and most of the rod was in the water. But no line was going out.

"Get him back into the chair, Eddy. Easy. Easy,"

Roger said. "When you can, I mean. He's stopped him."

Eddy helped David back into the fighting chair, holding him around the waist so that a sudden lurch by the fish would not pull the boy overboard. Eddy eased him into the chair and David got the rod butt into the gimbel socket and braced with his feet and pulled back on the rod. The fish lifted a little.

"Only pull when you are going to get some line," Roger told David. "Let him pull the rest of the time. Try and rest inside the action except when you are working on him."

"You've got him, Davy," Eddy said. "You're getting it on him all the time. Just take it slow and easy and you'll kill him.

Thomas Hudson eased the boat a little forward to put the fish further astern. There was good shadow now over all the stern. The boat was working steadily further out to sea and no wind troubled the surface.

"Papa," young Tom said to his father. "I was looking at his feet when I made the drinks. They're bleeding."

"He's chafed them pulling against the wood."

"Do you think I could put a pillow there? A cushion for him to pull against?"

"Go down and ask Eddy," Thomas Hudson said. "But don't interrupt Dave."

It was well into the fourth hour of the fight now. The boat was still working out to sea and David, with Roger holding the back of his chair now, was raising the fish steadily. David looked stronger now than he had an hour before but Thomas Hudson could see where his heels showed the blood that had run down from the soles of his feet. It looked varnished in the sun.

"How's your feet, Davy?" Eddy asked.

"They don't hurt," David said. "What hurts is my hands and my arms and my back."

"I could put a cushion under them."

David shook his head.

"I think they'd stick," he said. "They're sticky. They don't hurt. Really."

Young Tom came up to the top side and said, "He's

wearing the bottoms of his feet right off. He's getting his
hands bad too. He's had blisters and now they're all open.
Gee, papa. I don't know."

"It's the same as if he had to paddle against a stiff current, Tommy. Or if he had to keep going up a mountain
or stick with a horse after he was awfully tired."

"I know it. But just watching it and not doing it seems
so sort of awful when it's your brother."

"I know it, Tommy. But there is a time boys have to do
things if they are ever going to be men. That"s where Dave
is now."

"I know it. But when I see his feet and his hands I
don't know, papa."

"If you had the fish would you want Roger or me to
take him away from you?"

"No. I'd want to stay with him till I died. But to see it
with Davy is different."

"We have to think about how he feels," his father told
him. "And what's important to him."

"I know," young Tom said hopelessly. "But to me it's
just Davy. I wish the world wasn't the way it is and that
things didn't have to happen to brothers."

"I do too," Thomas Hudson said. "You're an awfully
good boy, Tommy. But please know I would have stopped
this long ago except that I know that if David catches this
fish he'll have something inside him for all his life and it
will make everything else easier."

Just then Eddy spoke. He had been looking behind him
into the cabin again.

"Four hours even, Roger," he said. "You better take
some water, Davy. How do you feel?"

"Fine," David said.

"I know what I'll do that is practical," young Tom said.
"I'll make a drink for Eddy. Do you want one, papa?"

"No. I'll skip this one," Thomas Hudson said.

Young Tom went below and Thomas Hudson watched
David working slowly, tiredly but steadily; Roger bending
over him and speaking to him in a low voice; Eddy out on
the stern watching the slant of the line in the water. Thomas
Hudson tried to picture how it would be down where the

swordfish was swimming. It was dark of course but probably the fish could see as a horse can see. It would be very cold.

He wondered if the fish was alone or if there could be another fish swimming with him. They had seen no other fish but that did not prove this fish was alone. There might be another with him in the dark and the cold.

Thomas Hudson wondered why the fish had stopped when he had gone so deep the last time. Did the fish reach his maximum possible depth the way a plane reached its ceiling? Or had the pulling against the bend of the rod, the heavy drag on the line, and the resistance of its friction in the water discouraged him so that now he swam quietly in the direction he wished to go? Was he only rising a little, steadily, as David lifted on him; rising docilely to ease the unpleasant tension that held him? Thomas Hudson thought that was probably the way it was and that David might have great trouble with him yet if the fish was still strong.

Young Tom had brought Eddy's own bottle to him and Eddy had taken a long pull out of it and then asked Tom to put it in the bait box to keep it cool. "And handy," he added. "If I see Davy fight this fish much longer it will make a damned rummy out of me."

"I'll bring it any time you want it," Andrew said.

"Don't bring it when I want it," Eddy told him. "Bring it when I ask for it."

The oldest boy had come up with Thomas Hudson and together they watched Eddy bend over David and look carefully into his eyes. Roger was holding the chair and watching the line.

"Now listen, Davy," Eddy told the boy, looking close into his face. "Your hands and your feet don't mean a damn thing. They hurt and they look bad but they are all right. That's the way a fisherman's hands and feet are supposed to get and next time they'll be tougher. But is your bloody head all right?"

"Fine," David said.

"Then God bless you and stay with the son of a bitch because we are going to have him up here soon."

"Davy," Roger spoke to the boy. "Do you want me to take him?"

David shook his head.

"It wouldn't be quitting now," Roger said. "It would just make sense. I could take him or your father could take him."

"Am I doing anything wrong?" David asked bitterly.

"No. You're doing perfectly."

"Then why should I quit on him?"

"He's giving you an awful beating, Davy," Roger said. "I don't want him to hurt you."

"He's the one has the hook in his goddam mouth," David's voice was unsteady. "He isn't giving me a beating. I'm giving him a beating. The son of a bitch."

"Say anything you want, Dave," Roger told him.

"The damn son of a bitch. The big son of a bitch."

"He's crying," Andrew, who had come up topside and was standing with young Tom and his father, said. "He's talking that way to get rid of it."

"Shut up, horseman," young Tom said.

"I don't care if he kills me, the big son of a bitch," David said. "Oh hell. I don't hate him. I love him."

"You shut up now," Eddy said to David. "You save your wind."

He looked at Roger and Roger lifted his shoulders to show he did not know.

"If I see you getting excited like that I'll take him away from you," Eddy said.

"I'm always excited," David said. "Just because I never say it nobody knows. I'm no worse now. It's only the talking."

"Well you shut up now and take it easy," Eddy said. "You stay calm and quiet and we'll go with him forever."

"I'll stay with him," David said. "I'm sorry I called him the names. I don't want to say anything against him. I think he's the finest thing in the world."

"Andy, get me that bottle of pure alcohol," Eddy said. "I'm going to loosen up his arms and shoulders and his legs," he said to Roger. "I don't want to use any more of that ice water for fear I'd cramp him up."

He looked into the cabin and said, "Five and a half even, Roger." He turned to David, "You don't feel too heated up now, do you, Davy?"

The boy shook his head.

"That straight-up-and-down sun in the middle of the day was what I was afraid of," Eddy said. "Nothing going to happen to you now, Davy. Just take it easy and whip this old fish. We want to whip him before dark."

David nodded.

"Papa, did you ever see a fish fight like this one?" young Tom asked.

"Yes," Thomas Hudson told him.

"Very many?"

"I don't know, Tommy. There are some terrible fish in this Gulf. Then there are huge big fish that are easy to catch."

"Why are some easier?"

"I think because they get old and fat. Some I think are almost old enough to die. Then, of course, some of the biggest jump themselves to death."

There had been no boats in sight for a long time and it was getting late in the afternoon and they were a long way out between the island and the great Isaacs light.

"Try him once more, Davy," Roger said.

The boy bent his back, pulled back against his braced feet, and the rod, instead of staying solid, lifted slowly.

"You've got him coming," Roger said. "Get that line on and try him again."

The boy lifted and again recovered line.

"He's coming up," Roger told David. "Keep on him steady and good."

David went to work like a machine, or like a very tired boy performing as a machine.

"This is the time," Roger said. "He's really coming up. Put her ahead just a touch, Tom. We want to take him on the port side if we can."

"Ahead just a touch," Thomas Hudson said.

"Use your own judgment on it," Roger said. "We want to bring him up easy where Eddy can gaff him and we can get a noose over him. I'll handle the leader. Tommy, you come down here to handle the chair and see the line doesn't foul on the rod when I take the leader. Keep the line clear all the time in case I have to turn him loose. Andy, you help Eddy with anything he asks for and give him the noose and the club when he asks for them."

The fish was coming up steadily now and David was not breaking the rhythm of his pumping.

"Tom, you better come down and take the wheel below," Roger called up.

"I was just coming down," Thomas Hudson told him.

"Sorry," he said. "Davy, remember if he runs and I have to turn him loose keep your rod up and everything clear. Slack off your drag as soon as I take hold of the leader."

"Keep her spooled even," Eddy said. "Don't let her jam up now, Davy."

Thomas Hudson swung down from the flying bridge into the cockpit and took the wheel and the controls there. It was not as easy to see into the water as it was on the flying bridge but it was handier in case of any emergency and communication was easier. It was strange to be on the same level as the action after having looked down on it for so many hours, he thought. It was like moving down from a box seat onto the stage or to the ringside or close against the railing of the track. Everyone looked bigger and closer and they were all taller and not foreshortened.

He could see David's bloody hands and lacquered-looking oozing feet and he saw the welts the harness had made across his back and the almost hopeless expression on his face as he turned his head at the last finish of a pull. He looked in the cabin and the brass clock showed that it was ten minutes to six. The sea looked different to him now that he was so close to it, and looking at it from the shade and from David's bent rod, the white line slanted into the dark water and the rod lowered and rose steadily. Eddy knelt on the stern with the gaff in his sun-spotted freckled hands and looked down into the almost purple water trying to see the fish. Thomas Hudson noticed the rope hitches around the haft of the gaff and the rope made fast to the Samson post in the stern and then he looked again at

David's back, his outstretched legs, and his long arms holding the rod.

"Can you see him, Eddy?" Roger asked from where he was holding the chair.

"Not yet. Stay on him, Davy, steady and good."

David kept on his same raising, lowering, and reeling; the reel heavy with line now; bringing in a sweep of line each time he swung it around.

Once the fish held steady for a moment and the rod doubled toward the water and line started to go out.

"No. He can't be," David said.

"He might," Eddy said. "You can't ever know."

But then David lifted slowly, suffering against the weight and, after the first slow lift, the line started to come again as easily and steadily as before.

"He just held for a minute," Eddy said. His old felt hat on the back of his head, he was peering down into the clear, dark purple water.

"There he is," he said.

Thomas Hudson slipped back quickly from the wheel to look over the stern. The fish showed, deep astern, looking tiny and foreshortened in the depth but in the small time Thomas Hudson looked at him he grew steadily in size. It was not as rapidly as a plane grows as it comes in toward you but it was as steady.

Thomas Hudson put his arm on David's shoulder and went back to the wheel. Then he heard Andrew say, "Oh look at him," and this time he could see him from the wheel deep in the water and well astern, showing brown now and grown greatly in length and bulk.

"Keep her just as she is," Roger said without looking back and Thomas Hudson answered, "Just as she is."

"Oh God look at him," young Tom said.

Now he was really huge, bigger than any swordfish Thomas Hudson had ever seen. All the great length of him was purple blue now instead of brown and he was swimming slowly and steadily in the same direction the boat was going; astern of the boat and on David's right.

"Keep him coming all the time, Davy," Roger said. "He's coming in just right."

"Go ahead just a touch," Roger said, watching the fish.

"Ahead just a touch," Thomas Hudson answered.

"Keep it spooled," Eddy told David. Thomas Hudson could see the swivel of the leader now out of water.

"Ahead just a little more," Roger said.

"Going ahead just a little more," Thomas Hudson repeated. He was watching the fish and easing the stern onto the course that he was swimming. He could see the whole great purple length of him now, the great broad sword forward, the slicing dorsal fin set in his wide shoulders, and his huge tail that drove him almost without a motion.

"Just a touch more ahead," Roger said.

"Going ahead a touch more."

David had the leader within reach now.

"Are you ready for him, Eddy?" Roger asked.

"Sure," Eddy said.

"Watch him, Tom," Roger said and leaned over and took hold of the cable leader.

"Slack off on your drag," he said to David and began slowly raising the fish, holding and lifting on the heavy cable to bring him within reach of the gaff.

The fish was coming up looking as long and as broad as a big log in the water. David was watching him and glancing up at his rod tip to make sure it was not fouled. For the first time in six hours he had no strain on his back and his arms and legs and Thomas Hudson saw the muscles in his legs twitching and quivering. Eddy was bending over the side with the gaff and Roger was lifting slowly and steadily.

"He'd go over a thousand," Eddy said. Then he said, very quietly, "Roger, hook's only holding by a thread."

"Can you reach him?" Roger asked.

"Not yet," Eddy said. "Keep him coming easy, easy."

Roger kept lifting on the wire cable and the great fish rose steadily toward the boat.

"It's been cutting," Eddy said. "It's just holding by nothing."

"Can you reach him now?" Roger asked. His tone had not changed.

"Not quite yet," Eddy said as quietly. Roger was lifting as gently and as softly as he could. Then, from lifting, he straightened, all strain gone, holding the slack leader in his two hands.

"No. No. No. Please God, no," young Tom said.

Eddy lunged down into the water with the gaff and then went overboard to try to get the gaff into the fish if he could reach him.

It was no good. The great fish hung there in the depth of water where he was like a huge dark purple bird and then settled slowly. They all watched him go down, getting smaller and smaller until he was out of sight.

Eddy's hat was floating on the calm sea and he was holding onto the gaff handle. The gaff was on the line that was fast to the Samson post in the stern. Roger put his arms around David and Thomas Hudson could see David's shoulders shaking. But he left David to Roger. "Get the ladder out for Eddy to come aboard," he said to young Tom. "Take Davy's rod, Andy. Unhook it."

Roger lifted the boy out of the chair and carried him over to the bunk at the starboard side of the cockpit and laid him down in it. Roger's arms were around David and the boy lay flat on his face on the bunk.

Eddy came on board soaked and dripping, and started to undress. Andrew fished out his hat with the gaff and Thomas Hudson went below to get Eddy a shirt and a pair of dungarees and a shirt and shorts for David. He was surprised that he had no feeling at all except pity and love for David. All other feeling had been drained out of him in the fight.

When he came up David was lying, naked, face-down on the bunk and Roger was rubbing him down with alcohol.

"It hurts across the shoulders and my tail," David said. "Watch out, Mr. Davis, please."

"It's where it's chafed," Eddy told him. "Your father's going to fix your hands and feet with Mercurochrome. That won't hurt."

"Get this shirt on, Davy," Thomas Hudson said. "So you won't get cold. Go get one of the lightest blankets for him, Tom."

Thomas Hudson touched the places where the harness had chafed the boy's back with Mercurochrome and helped him into the shirt.

"I'm all right," David said in a toneless voice. "Can I have a Coke, papa?"

"Sure," Thomas Hudson told him. "Eddy will get you some soup in a little while."

"I'm not hungry," David said. "I couldn't eat yet."

"We'll wait a while," Thomas Hudson said.

"I know how you feel, Dave," Andrew said when he brought the Coke.

"Nobody knows how I feel," David said.

Thomas Hudson gave his oldest boy a compass course to steer back to the island.

"Synchronize your motors at three hundred, Tommy," he said. "We'll be in sight of the light by dark and then I'll give you a correction."

"You check me every once in a while will you please, papa. Do you feel as awful as I do?"

"There's nothing to do about it."

"Eddy certainly tried," young Tom said. "Not everybody would jump in this ocean after a fish."

"Eddy nearly made it," his father told him. "It could have been a hell of a thing with him in the water with a gaff in that fish."

"Eddy would have got out all right," young Tom said. "Are they synchronized all right?"

"Listen for it," his father told him. "Don't just watch the tachometers."

Thomas Hudson went over to the bunk and sat down by David. He was rolled up in the light blanket and Eddy was fixing his hands and Roger his feet.

"Hi, papa," he said and looked at Thomas Hudson and then looked away.

"I'm awfully sorry, Davy," his father said. "You made the best fight on him I ever saw anyone make. Roger or any man ever."

"Thank you very much, papa. Please don't talk about it."

"Can I get you anything, Davy?"

"I'd like another Coke, please," David said.

Thomas Hudson found a cold bottle of Coca-Cola in the ice of the bait box and opened it. He sat by David and the boy drank the Coke with the hand Eddy had fixed.

"I'll have some soup ready right away. It's heating now," Eddy said. "Should I heat some chile, Tom? We've got some conch salad."

"Let's heat some chile," Thomas Hudson said. "We haven't eaten since breakfast. Roger hasn't had a drink all day."

"I had a bottle of beer just now," Roger said.

"Eddy," David said. "What would he really weigh?"

"Over a thousand," Eddy told him.

"Thank you very much for going overboard," David said. "Thank you very much, Eddy."

"Hell," Eddy said. "What else was there to do?"

"Would he really have weighed a thousand, papa?" David asked.

"I'm sure of it," Thomas Hudson answered. "I've never seen a bigger fish, either broadbill or marlin, ever."

The sun had gone down and the boat was driving through the calm sea, the boat alive with the engines, pushing fast through the same water they had moved so slowly through for all those hours.

Andrew was sitting on the edge of the wide bunk now, too.

"Hello, horseman," David said to him.

"If you'd have caught him," Andrew said, "you'd have been probably the most famous young boy in the world."

"I don't want to be famous," David said. "You can be famous."

"We'd have been famous as your brothers," Andrew said. "I mean really."

"I'd have been famous as your friend," Roger told him.

"I'd have been famous because I steered," Thomas Hudson said. "And Eddy because he gaffed him."

"Eddy ought to be famous anyway," Andrew said. "Tommy would be famous because he brought so many drinks. All through the terrific battle Tommy kept them supplied."

"What about the fish? Wouldn't he be famous?" David asked. He was all right, now. Or, at least, he was talking all right.

"He'd be the most famous of all," Andrew said. "He'd be immortal."

"I hope nothing happened to him," David said. "I hope he's all right."

"I know he's all right," Roger told him. "The way he was hooked and the way he fought I know he was all right."

"I'll tell you sometime how it was," David said.

"Tell now," Andy urged him.

"I'm tired now and besides it sounds crazy."

"Tell now. Tell a little bit," Andrew said.

"I don't know whether I better. Should I, papa?"

"Go ahead," Thomas Hudson said.

"Well," David said with his eyes tight shut. "In the worst parts, when I was the tiredest I couldn't tell which was him and which was me."

"I understand," Roger said.

"Then I began to love him more than anything on earth."

"You mean really love him?" Andrew asked.

"Yeah. Really love him."

"Gee," said Andrew. "I can't understand that."

"I loved him so much when I saw him coming up that I couldn't stand it," David said, his eyes still shut. "All I wanted was to see him closer."

"I know," Roger said.

"Now I don't give a shit I lost him," David said. "I don't care about records. I just thought I did. I'm glad that he's all right and that I'm all right. We aren't enemies."

"I'm glad you told us," Thomas Hudson said.

"Thank you very much, Mr. Davis, for what you said when I first lost him," David said with his eyes still shut.

Thomas Hudson never knew what it was that Roger had said to him.

X

THAT night in the heavy calm before the wind rose Thomas Hudson sat in his chair and tried to read. The others were all in bed but he knew he could not sleep and he wanted to read until he was sleepy. He could not read and he thought about the day. He thought about it from the beginning until the end and it seemed as though all of his children except Tom had gone a long way away from him or he had gone away from them.

David had gone with Roger. He wanted David to get everything he could from Roger, who was as beautiful and sound in action as he was unbeautiful and unsound in his life and in his work. David was always a mystery to Thomas Hudson. He was a well-loved mystery. But Roger understood him better than his own father did. He was happy they did understand each other so well but tonight he felt lonely in some way about it.

Then he had not liked the way Andrew had behaved, although he knew Andrew was Andrew and a little boy and that it was unfair to judge him. He had done nothing bad and he had really behaved very well. But there was something about him that you could not trust.

What a miserable, selfish way to be thinking about people that you love, he thought. Why don't you remember the day and not analyze it and tear it to pieces? Go to bed now, he told himself, and make yourself sleep. The hell with anything else. And pick up the rhythm of your life in the morning. You don't have the boys for much longer. See how happy a time you can make for them. I've tried, he said to himself. I've tried truly and for Roger, too. And you have been very happy yourself, he told himself. Yes, of course. But something about today frightened me. Then he told himself: truly, there is something about every day to frighten you. Go on to bed and maybe you'll sleep well. Remember you want them to be happy tomorrow.

A big southwest wind came up in the night and by daylight it was slowing with almost the force of a gale. The palms were bent with it and shutters slammed and papers blew and a surf was piling on the beach.

Roger was gone when Thomas Hudson came down to breakfast alone. The boys were still sleeping and he read his mail that had come from the mainland on the run-boat that brought ice, meat, fresh vegetables, gas, and other supplies once a week. It was blowing so hard he put a coffee cup on a letter to hold it when he laid it down on the table.

"Want me to shut the doors?" Joseph asked.

"No. Only if things start to break."

"Mr. Roger gone walking on the beach," Joseph said. "Headed up toward the end of the island."

Thomas Hudson kept on reading his mail.

"Here's the paper," Joseph said. "I ironed her out."

"Thank you, Joseph."

"Mister Tom, is it true about the fish? What Eddy was telling me?"

"What did he say?"

"About how big he was and having him right up to the gaff."

"It's true."

"God Almighty. If that run-boat hadn't come so I had to stay in to carry ice and groceries I'd have been along. I'd have dove right in after him and gaffed him."

"Eddy dove in," Thomas Hudson said.

"He didn't tell me," Joseph said, subdued.

"I'd like some more coffee, please, Joseph, and another piece of papaw," Thomas Hudson said. He was hungry and the wind gave him even more appetite. "Didn't the run-boat bring any bacon?"

"I believe I can find some," Joseph said. "You're eating good this morning."

"Ask Eddy to come in please."

"Eddy went home to fix his eye."

"What happened to his eye?"

"Somebody balled their fist in it."

Thomas Hudson believed he knew why this might have happened.

"Is he hurt anywhere else?"

"He's beat pretty bad," Joseph said. "On account of people not believing him in different bars. People ain't never going to believe him that story he tells. Certainly is a pity."

"Where'd he fight?"

"Everywhere. Everywhere where they wouldn't believe him. Nobody believe him yet. People took to not believing him late at night that didn't know what it was about even just to get him to fight. He must have fought all the fighting men on the island. Tonight, sure as you eating breakfast, men'll come up from Middle Key just to doubt his word. Couple real bad fighting men down at Middle Key now on that construction."

"Mr. Roger better go out with him," Thomas Hudson said.

"Oh boy," Joseph's face lighted up. "Tonight's the night we got fun."

Thomas Hudson drank the coffee and ate the cold papaw with fresh lime squeezed over it and four more strips of bacon that Joseph brought in.

"I see you were in an eating mood," Joseph said. "When I see you like that, I want to make something out of it."

"I eat plenty."

"Sometimes," Joseph said.

He came in with another cup of coffee and Thomas Hudson took it up to his desk to answer the two letters he needed to get off in the mail boat.

"Go up to Eddy's house and get him to make out the list of what we need to order by the run-boat," he said to Joseph. "Then bring it to me to check. Is there coffee for Mr. Roger?"

"He had his," Joseph said.

Thomas Hudson finished the two letters at the work desk upstairs and Eddy came over with the list of supplies for the next week's run-boat. Eddy looked bad enough.

His eye had not responded to treatment and his mouth and cheeks were swollen. One ear was swollen, too. He had put Mercurochrome on his mouth where it was cut and the bright color made him look very untragic.

"I didn't do any good last night," he said. "I think everything is on here, Tom."

"Why don't you lay off today and go home and take it easy?"

"I feel worse at home," he said. "I'll go to bed early tonight."

"Don't get in any more fights about that," Thomas Hudson said. "It doesn't do any good."

"You're talking to the right man," Eddy said through the scarlet of his split and swollen lips. "I kept waiting for truth and right to win and then somebody new would knock truth and right right on its ass."

"Joseph said you had a lot of them."

"Till somebody took me home," Eddy said. "Big-hearted Benny I guess it was. He and Constable probably saved me from getting hurt."

"You aren't hurt?"

"I hurt but I ain't hurt. Hell, you ought to have been there, Tom."

"I'm glad I wasn't. Did anybody try to really hurt you?"

"I don't think so. They were just proving to me I was wrong. Constable believed me."

"Did he?"

"Yes sir. Him and Bobby. Only people believed me, all right. Constable said any man who hit me first he'd lock him up. Asked me this morning if there was anybody hit me first. I told him yes but I hit *at* them first. It was a bad night for truth and right, Tom. Bad night all right."

"Do you really want to cook lunch?"

"Why not?" Eddy said. "We've got steaks on the run-boat. Real sirloin steak. You ought to see her. I figured to have it with mashed potatoes and gravy and some lima beans. We got that cabbage lettuce and fresh grapefruit for a salad. The boys would like a pie and we got canned loganberries makes a hell of a pie. We got ice cream

from the run-boat to put on top of it. How's that? I want to
feed that goddam David up."

"What did you figure to do when you dove overboard
with the gaff?"

"I was going to get the gaff hook into him right underneath his fin where it would kill him when he came taut
on the rope and then get the hell away from there and
back on board."

"What did he look like underwater?"

"He was as wide as a dinghy, Tom. All purple and his
eye looked as big as your hand is long. It was black and he
was silver underneath and his sword was terrible to see.
He just kept on going down, settling slow, and I couldn't
get down to him because that big haft on the gaff was too
buoyant. I couldn't sink with it. So it wasn't any use."

"Did he look at you?"

"I couldn't tell. He just looked like he was there and
nothing made any difference to him."

"Do you think he was tired?"

"I think he was through. I think he'd decided to give
up."

"We'll never see anything like that again."

"No. Not in our lifetimes. And I know enough now
not to try to make people believe it."

"I'm going to paint a picture of it for David."

"You make it just like it was then. Don't make it comic
like some of those comic ones you paint."

"I'm going to paint it truer than a photograph."

"That's the way I like it when you paint."

"It's going to be awfully hard to paint the underwater
part."

"Will it be like that waterspout picture down at
Bobby's?"

"No. This will be different but I hope it will be better.
I'm going to make sketches for it today."

"I like that waterspout picture," Eddy said. "Bobby,
he's crazy about it and he can make anybody believe there
was that many waterspouts that time when they see the
picture. But this will be a hell of a one to paint with the
fish in the water."

"I think I can do it," Thomas Hudson said.

"You couldn't paint him jumping, too, could you?"

"I think I can."

"Paint him the two of them, Tom. Paint him jumping and then with Roger bringing him up on the leader and Davy in the chair and me on the stern. We can get photographs took of it."

"I'll start the sketches."

"Anything you want to ask me," Eddy said. "I'll be in the kitchen. The boys still asleep?"

"All three of them."

"Hell," Eddy said. "I don't give a damn about anything since that fish. But we've got to have a good meal."

"I wish I had leech for that eye."

"Hell, I don't give a damn about the eye. I can see out of it fine."

"I'm going to let the boys sleep as long as they can."

"Joe, he'll help me when they're up and I'll give them breakfast. If they wake up too late, I won't give them too much so as not to spoil lunch. You didn't see that piece of meat we got?"

"No."

"Goddam she sure costs money but it's beautiful meat, Tom. Nobody on this island has eaten meat like that in their whole lives. I wonder what those beef cattle look like that meat comes from."

"They're built right down close to the ground," Thomas Hudson said. "And they're almost as wide as they are long."

"God, they must be fat," Eddy said. "I'd like to see them alive sometime. Here nobody ever butchers a cow till just before it's going to die from starving. The meat's bitter. People here'd go crazy with meat like that we got. They wouldn't know what it was. Probably make them sick."

"I have to finish these letters," Thomas Hudson said.

"I'm sorry, Tom."

After he finished the mail, answered two other business letters that he had intended to put off until the next week's boat, checking the list of the next week's needs and writing a check for the week's supplies plus the flat ten percent the government charged on all imports from the Mainland, Thomas Hudson walked down to the run-boat that was loading at the government wharf. The captain was taking orders from the islanders for supplies, dry goods, medicines, hardware, spare parts, and all the things that came into the island from the Mainland. The run-boat was loading live crawfish and conches and a deck load of conch shells and empty gasoline and Diesel oil drums and the islanders stood in line in the heavy wind waiting their turn in the cabin.

"Was everything all right, Tom?" Captain Ralph called out the cabin window to Thomas Hudson.

"Hey, get out of this cabin, you boy, and come in your turn," he said to a big Negro in a straw hat. "I had to substitute on a few things. How was the meat?"

"Eddy says it's wonderful."

"Good. Let me have those letters and the list. Blowing a gale outside. I want to get out over the bar on this next tide. Sorry I'm so busy."

"See you next week, Ralph. Don't let me hold you up. Thanks very much, boy."

"I'll try to have everything next week. Need any money?"

"No. I'm all right from last week."

"Got plenty of it here if you want it. OK. Now, you, Lucius, what's your trouble? What you spending money on now?"

Thomas Hudson walked back along the dock where the Negroes were laughing at what the wind was doing to the girls' and the women's cotton dresses and then up the coral road to the Ponce de León.

"Tom," Mr. Bobby said. "Come in and sit down. By God where've you been? We're just swept out and she's officially open. Come on and have the best one of the day."

"It's pretty early."

"Nonsense. That's good imported beer. We've got Dog's Head ale too." He reached into a tub of ice, opened a bottle of Pilsner, and handed it to Thomas

Hudson. "You don't want a glass, do you? Put that down and then decide if you want a drink or not."

"I won't work then."

"Who gives a damn? You work too much as it is. You got a duty to yourself, Tom. Your one and only life. You can't just paint all the time."

"We were in the boat yesterday and I didn't work."

Thomas Hudson was looking at the big canvas of the waterspouts that hung on the wall at the end of the bar. It was a good painting, Thomas Hudson thought. As good as he could do as of today, he thought.

"I got to hang her higher," Bobby said. "Some gentleman got excited last night and tried to climb into the skiff. I told him it would cost him ten thousand dollars if he put his foot through her. Constable told him the same. Constable's got an idea for one he wants you to paint to hang in his home."

"What is it?"

"Constable wouldn't say. Just that he had a very valuable idea he had intention to discuss with you."

Thomas Hudson was looking at the canvas closely. It showed certain signs of wear.

"By God, she sure stands up," Bobby said proudly. "The other night a gentleman let out a shout and threw a full mug of beer at the column of one of the waterspouts trying to break it down. You wouldn't have known she'd ever been hit. Never dented her. Beer run off her like water. By God, Tom, you sure painted her solid."

"She'll only take about so much though."

"By God," said Bobby. "I ain't seen nothing faze her yet. But I'm going to hang her higher just the same. That gentleman last night worried me."

He handed Thomas Hudson another bottle of ice-cold Pilsner.

"Tom, I want to tell you how sorry I am about the fish. I know Eddy since we were boys and I never heard him lie. About anything important, I mean. I mean if you asked him to tell you something true."

"It was a hell of a thing. I'm not going to tell anybody about it."

"That's the right way," Bobby said. "I just wanted you to know how sorry I was. Why don't you finish that beer and have a drink? We don't want to start feeling sad this early. What would make you feel good?"

"I feel good enough. I'm going to work this afternoon and I don't want to get logy."

"Oh well, if I can't break you out maybe somebody will come in that I can. Look at that damn yacht. She must have taken a beating coming across with that shallow draft."

Thomas Hudson looked out the open door and saw the handsome, white, houseboat type craft coming up the channel. She was one of the type that chartered out of a Mainland port to go down through the Florida Keys and on a day such as yesterday, calm and flat, she could have crossed the Gulf Stream without incident. But today she must have taken a beating with her shallow draft and so much superstructure. Thomas Hudson wondered that she had been able to come in over the bar with the sea that was running.

The houseboat ran up the harbor a little further to anchor and Thomas Hudson and Bobby watched her from the doorway, all white and brass and everyone that showed on her in whites.

"Customers," Mr. Bobby said. "Hope they're nice people. We haven't had a full-sized yacht in here since the tuna run was over."

"Who is she?"

"I never seen her before. Pretty boat, all right. Certainly not built for the Gulf, though."

"She probably left at midnight when it was calm and this hit her on the way over."

"That's about it," Bobby said. "Must have been some rolling and some crashing. It's really blowing. Well, we'll see who they are shortly. Tom, let me make you something, boy. You make me nervous not drinking."

"All right. I'll have a gin and tonic."

"No tonic water. Joe took the last case up to the house."

"A whisky sour then."

"With Irish whisky and no sugar," Bobby said. "Three of them. Here comes Roger." Thomas Hudson saw him through the open door.

Roger came in. He was barefooted, wore a faded pair of dungarees, and an old striped fisherman's shirt that was shrunken from washings. You could see the back muscles move under it as he leaned forward and put his arms on the bar. In the dim light of Bobby's, his skin showed very dark and his hair was salt- and sun-streaked.

"They're still sleeping," he said to Thomas Hudson. "Somebody beat up Eddy. Did you see?"

"He was having fights all last night," Bobby told him. "They didn't amount to anything."

"I don't like things to happen to Eddy," Roger said.

"Wasn't anything bad, Roger," Bobby assured him. "He was drinking and fighting people who wouldn't believe him. Nobody did anything wrong to him."

"I feel bad about David," Roger said to Thomas Hudson. "We shouldn't have ever let him do it."

"He's probably all right," Thomas Hudson said. "He was sleeping well. But it was my responsibility. I was the one to call it off."

"No. You trusted me."

"The father has the responsibility," Thomas Hudson said. "And I turned it over to you when I had no right to. It isn't anything to delegate."

"But I took it," Roger said. "I didn't think it was harming him. Neither did Eddy."

"I know," Thomas Hudson said. "I didn't think it was either. I thought something else was at stake."

"So did I," Roger said. "But now I feel selfish and guilty as hell."

"I'm his father," Thomas Hudson said. "It was my fault."

"Damn bad thing about that fish," Bobby said, handing them the whisky sours and taking one himself. "Let's drink to a bigger one."

"No," Roger said. "I don't want to ever see a bigger one."

"What's the matter with you, Roger?" Bobby asked.

"Nothing," Roger said.

"I'm going to paint a couple of pictures of him for David."

"That's wonderful. Do you think you can get it?"

"With luck, maybe. I can see it and I think I know how to do it."

"You can do it all right. You can do anything. I wonder who's on the yacht?"

"Look, Roger, you've been walking your remorse all over the island——"

"Barefooted," he said.

"I just brought mine down here by way of Captain Ralph's run-boat."

"I couldn't walk mine out and I'm certainly not going to try to drink it out," Roger said. "This is a mighty nice drink though, Bobby."

"Yes sir," Bobby said. "I'll make you another one. Get that old remorse on the run."

"I had no business gambling with a kid," Roger said. "Somebody else's boy."

"It depends on what you were gambling for."

"No, it doesn't. You shouldn't gamble with kids."

"I know. I know what I was gambling for. It wasn't a fish, either."

"Sure," Roger said. "But it was the one you didn't need to do it to. The one you didn't need to ever let anything like that happen to."

"He'll be fine when he wakes up. You'll see. He's a very intact boy."

"He's my goddamed hero," Roger said.

"That's a damned sight better than when you used to be your own goddamed hero."

"Isn't it?" Roger said. "He's yours, too."

"I know it," Thomas Hudson said. "He's good for both of us."

"Roger," Mr. Bobby said. "Are you and Tom any sort of kin?"

"Why?"

"I thought you were. You don't look too different."

"Thanks," Thomas Hudson said. "Thank him yourself, Roger."

"Thank you very much, Bobby," Roger said. "Do you really think I look like this combination man and painter?"

"You look like quarter brothers and the boys look like both of you."

"We're no kin," Thomas Hudson said. "We just used to live in the same town and make some of the same mistakes."

"Well, the hell with it," Mister Bobby said. "Drink up and quit all this remorse talk. It don't sound good this time of day in a bar. I got remorse from Negroes, mates on charter boats, cooks off yachts, millionaires and their wives, big rum runners, grocery store people, one-eyed men off turtle boats, sons of bitches, anybody. Don't let's have no morning remorse. A big wind is the time to drink. We're through with remorse. That remorse is old stuff anyway. Since they got the radio everybody just listens to the BBC. There ain't no time and no room for remorse."

"Do you listen to it, Bobby?"

"Just to Big Ben. The rest of it makes me restless."

"Bobby," Roger said. "You're a great and good man."

"Neither. But I'm certainly pleased to see you looking more cheerful."

"I am," said Roger. "What sort of people do you think we'll get off that yacht?"

"Customers," said Bobby. "Let's drink one more so I'll feel like serving them, however they are."

While Bobby was squeezing the limes and making the drinks Roger said to Thomas Hudson, "I didn't mean to be wet about Davy."

"You weren't."

"What I meant was. Oh hell, I'll try to work it out simply. That was a sound crack you made about when I was my own hero."

"I've got no business making cracks."

"You have as far as I'm concerned. The trouble is there hasn't been anything in life that was simple for such a damn long time and I try to make it simple all the time."

"You're going to write straight and simple and good now. That's the start."

"What if I'm not straight and simple and good? Do you think I can write that way?"

"Write how you are but make it straight."

"I've got to try to understand it better, Tom."

"You are. Remember last time I saw you before this summer was in New York with that cigarette-butt bitch."

"She killed herself," Roger said.

"When?"

"While I was up in the hills. Before I went on to the Coast and wrote that picture."

"I'm sorry," Thomas Hudson said.

"She was headed for it all the time," Roger said. "I'm glad I stepped out in time."

"You wouldn't ever do that."

"I don't know," Roger said. "I've seen it look very logical."

"One reason you wouldn't do it is because it would be a hell of an example for the boys. How would Dave feel?"

"He'd probably understand. Anyway when you get into that business that far you don't think much about examples."

"Now you are talking wet."

Bobby pushed over the drinks. "Roger, you talk that kind of stuff you get even me depressed. I'm paid to listen to anything people say. But I don't want to hear my friends talk that way. Roger, you stop it."

"I've stopped it."

"Good," Bobby said. "Drink up. We had a gentleman here from New York lived down at the Inn and he used to come here and drink most of the day. All he used to talk about was how he was going to kill himself. Made everybody nervous half the winter. Constable warned him it was an illegal act. I tried to get Constable to warn him that talking about it was an illegal act. But Constable said he'd have to get an opinion on that from Nassau. After a while people sort of got used to his project and then a lot of the drinkers started siding with him. Especially one day he was talking to Big Harry and he told Big Harry he was thinking of killing himself and he wanted to take somebody with him.

" 'I'm your man,' Big Harry told him. 'I'm who you've been looking for.' So then Big Harry tries to encourage him that they should go to New York City and really pitch one and stay drunk until they couldn't stand it and then jump off of the highest part of the city straight into oblivion. I think Big Harry figured oblivion was some sort of a suburb. Probably an Irish neighborhood.

"Well, the suicide gentleman took kindly to this idea and they'd talk it over every day. Others tried to get in on it and proposed they form an excursion of death seekers and just go as far as Nassau for the preliminaries. But Big Harry, he held out for New York City and finally he confided to the suicide gentleman that he couldn't stand this life no longer and he was ready to go.

"Big Harry, he had to go out for a couple days craw-fishing on a order he had from Captain Ralph and while he was gone the suicide gentleman took to drinking too much. Then he'd take some kind of ammonia from up north that would seem to sober him up and he'd come down to drink here again. But it was accumulating in him some way.

"We all called him Suicides by then so I said to him, 'Suicides, you better lay off or you'll never live to reach oblivion.'

" 'I'm bound for it now,' he says. 'I'm en route. I'm headed for it. Take the money for these drinks. I've made my dread decision.'

" 'Here's your change,' I said to him.

" 'I don't want no change. Keep it for Big Harry so he can have a drink before he joins me.'

"So he goes out in a rush and he dives off of Johnny Black's dock into the channel with the tide going out and it's dark and no moon and nobody sees him any more until he washes up on the point in two days. Everybody looked for him good that night, too. I figured he must have struck his head on some old concrete and went out with the tide. Big Harry come in and he mourned him until the change was all drunk up. It was change from a twenty-dollar bill too. Then Big Harry said to me, 'You know, Bobby, I think old Suicides was crazy.' He was right, too, because when his family sent for him the man who came explained to Commissioner old Suicides had suffered from a thing called Mechanic's Depressive. You never had that, did you, Roger?"

"No," said Roger. "And now I think I never will."

"That's the stuff," Mr. Bobby said. "And don't you ever fool with that old oblivion stuff."

"Fuck oblivion," said Roger.

XI

LUNCH was excellent. the steak was browned outside and striped by the grill. A knife slipped through the outer part and inside the meat was tender and juicy. They all dipped up juice from their plates and put it on the mashed potatoes and the juice made a lake in their creamy whiteness. The lima beans, cooked in butter, were firm; the cabbage lettuce was crisp and cold and the grapefruit was chilly cold.

Everyone was hungry with the wind and Eddy came up and looked in while they were eating. His face looked very bad and he said, "What the hell do you think of meat like that?"

"It's wonderful," young Tom said.

"Chew it good," Eddy said. "Don't waste that eating it fast."

"You can't chew it much or it's gone," young Tom told him.

"Have we got dessert, Eddy?" David asked.

"Sure. Pie and ice cream."

"Oh boy," Andrew said. "Two pieces?"

"Enough to founder you. Ice cream's as hard as a rock."

"What kind of pie?"

"Loganberry pie."

"What kind of ice cream?"

"Coconut."

"Where'd we get it?"

"Run-boat brought it."

They drank iced tea with the meal and Roger and Thomas Hudson had coffee after the dessert.

"Eddy's a wonderful cook," Roger said.

"Some of it's appetite."

"That steak wasn't appetite. Nor that salad. Nor that pie."

"He is a fine cook," Thomas Hudson agreed. "Is the coffee all right?"

"Excellent."

"Papa," young Tom asked, "if the people on the yacht go to Mr. Bobby's can we go down and practice Andy being a rummy on them?"

"Mr. Bobby might not like it. He might get in bad with Constable."

"I'll go down and tell Mr. Bobby and I'll speak to Constable. He's a friend of ours."

"All right. You tell Mr. Bobby and keep a look out for when the yacht people show up. What will we do about Dave?"

"Can't we carry him? He'd look good that way."

"I'll put on Tom's sneakers and walk," David said. "Have you got it worked out, Tommy?"

"We can make it up as we go along," young Tom said. "Can you still turn your eyelids inside out?"

"Oh sure," said David.

"Don't do it now, please," Andrew said. "I don't want to be sick right after lunch."

"For a dime I'd make you throw up now, horseman."

"No please don't. Later on I won't mind."

"Do you want me to go with you?" Roger asked young Tom.

"I'd love it," young Tom said. "We can work it out together."

"Let's go then," Roger said. "Why don't you take a nap, Davy?"

"I might," said David. "I'll read till I go to sleep. What are you going to do, papa?"

"I'm going to work in the lee out on the porch."

"I'll lie out there on the cot and watch you work. Will you mind?"

"No. Make me work better."

"We'll be back," Roger said. "What about you, Andy?"

"I'd like to come and study it. But I think I better not because the people might be there."

"That's smart," young Tom said. "You're smart, horseman."

They went off and Thomas Hudson worked all afternoon. Andy watched for a while and then went out somewhere and David watched and read and did not talk.

Thomas Hudson wanted to paint the leap of the fish first because painting him in the water was going to be much more difficult and he made two sketches, neither of which he liked, and finally a third one that he did like.

"Do you think that gets it, Davy?"

"Gee, papa, it looks wonderful. But water comes up with him when he comes out, doesn't it? I mean not just when he splashed back."

"It must," his father agreed. "Because he has to burst the surface."

"He came up so long. A lot must have come up. I suppose it really drips off him or pours off him if you could see it fast enough. Is he on his way up or on his way down?"

"This is just the sketch. I thought of him as just at the top."

"I know it's just the sketch, papa. You forgive me if I butt in. I don't mean to act as though I knew."

"I like you to tell me."

"You know who'd know would be Eddy. He sees faster than a camera and he remembers. Don't you think Eddy is a great man?"

"Of course he is."

"Practically nobody knows about Eddy. Tommy does, of course. I like Eddy better than anybody except you and Mr. Davis. He cooks just like he loved it and he knows so much and can do anything. Look what he did with the shark and look how he went overboard yesterday after the fish."

"And last night people beating him up because they didn't believe him."

"But, papa, Eddy isn't tragic."

"No. He's happy."

"Even today after he was all beaten up he was happy. And I'm sure he was happy that he went in after him."

"Of course."

"I wish Mr. Davis was happy the way Eddy is."

"Mr. Davis is more complicated than Eddy."

"I know it. But I can remember when he used to be careless happy. I know Mr. Davis very well, papa."

He's pretty happy now. I know he's lost the carelessness though."

"I didn't mean a bad carelessness."

"I didn't, either. But there is some sort of a sureness that he's lost."

"I know it," David said.

"I wish he'd find it. Maybe he'll find it when he writes again. You see Eddy's happy because he does something well and does it every day."

"I guess Mr. Davis can't do his every day the way you do and Eddy does."

"No. And there are other things."

"I know. I know too much for a kid, papa. Tommy knows twenty times as much as I do and knows the damndest things and they don't hurt him. But everything I know hurts me. I don't know why it should, either."

"You mean that you feel it."

"I feel it and it does something to me. It's like a vicarious sin. If there is any such thing."

"I see."

"Papa, you excuse me for talking seriously. I know it itsn't polite. But I like to sometimes because there is so much we don't know and then when we do know, it comes so fast it goes over you like a wave. The way the waves are today."

"You can always ask me anything, Davy."

"I know. Thank you very much. I'll wait, I guess, on some things. There's some I guess you can only learn for yourself probably."

"Do you think we better do this 'rummy' business with Tom and Andy at Bobby's? Remember I got in trouble about the man saying you were always drunk."

"I remember—when he'd seen me drunk on wine twice in three years—but let's not talk about it. This at Mr. Bobby's will be a good alibi in case I ever did drink. If I did it twice with that man I might do it three times. No, I think this is a good thing to do, papa."

"Have you done it lately, the pretend-rummy scene?"

"Tom and I do some pretty good ones. But with Andy they're much better. Andy's sort of a genius on them. He can do horrible ones. Mine are sort of special."

"What have you done lately?" Thomas Hudson went on drawing.

"Did you ever see me do the idiot brother? The mongolian idiot?"

"Never."

"How do you like it now, Davy?" Thomas Hudson showed him the sketch.

"It's fine," David said. "Now I see what you were after. It's when he hangs in the air just before he falls. Can I really have the painting, papa?"

"Sure."

"I'll take care of it."

"There'll be two."

"I'll only take one to school and I'll keep one at home at mother's. Or would you rather keep it here?"

"No. She might like it. Tell me about some others that you did," Thomas Hudson said.

"We used to have some awful ones on trains. Trains are the best because of the sort of people I guess. You don't get those sort of people concentrated almost anywhere except on trains. And then they can't get away."

Thomas Hudson heard Roger talking in the other room

and started to clean up and put away his gear. Young Tom came in and said, "How are you, papa? Did you work well? May I see it?"

Thomas Hudson showed him the two sketches and he said, "I like them both."

"Do you like one better than the other?" David asked him.

"No. They're both fine," he said. Thomas Hudson could see he was in a hurry and that his mind was on something.

"How is it coming?" David asked him.

"It's terrific," young Tom said. "It will be wonderful if we do it right. They're all down there now and we've been working on them all afternoon. We saw Mr. Bobby and Constable before they came. The way it's been so far is that Mr. Davis is sodden and I've been trying to dissuade him."

"You didn't overdo it?"

"Hell no," young Tom said. "You ought to have seen Mr. Davis. Every drink made a difference in him. But only imperceptibly."

"What was he drinking?"

"Tea. Bobby's got it in a rum bottle. He's got a gin bottle fixed with water for Andy."

"How did you try to dissuade Mr. Davis?"

"I pled with him. But so they couldn't hear me. Mr. Bobby's in it, too, but he's using real liquor."

"We better get down there," David said. "Before Mr. Bobby gets too far ahead. How's Mr. Davis feeling?"

"Wonderful. He's a great, great artist, Dave."

"Where's Andy?"

"Downstairs practicing part of it in front of a mirror."

"Is Eddy going to be in it?"

"Eddy and Joseph are both going to be in it."

"They'll never remember."

"They only have one line."

"Eddy can remember one line but I don't know about Joseph."

"He just repeats it after Eddy."

"Is Constable in it?"

"Sure."

"How many of *them* are there?"

"Seven with two girls. One nice-looking and one wonderful. She's sorry for Mr. Davis already."

"Oh boy," said David. "Let's go."

"How're you going to get down there?" young Tom asked David.

"I'll carry him," Thomas Hudson said.

"Please, papa, let me wear sneakers," David said. "Let me wear Tommy's sneakers. I'll walk on the side of my feet and it won't hurt them and it will look good."

"All right. We might as well go. Where's Roger?"

"He's having a quick one with Eddy for his art," young Tom said. "He was at bat a long time on that tea, papa."

The wind was still blowing hard outside when they went into the Ponce de León. The people from the yacht were at the bar drinking rum swizzles. They were a nice-looking lot of people, tanned and dressed in whites, and they were polite and made room at the bar. Two men and a girl were at one end where the slot machine was and three men and the other girl were at the other end nearest the door. It was the lovely-looking girl who was at the slot machine end. But the other girl was awfully nice-looking, too. Roger, Thomas Hudson, and the boys came in straight. David even tried not to limp.

Mr. Bobby looked at Roger and said, "You back?"

Roger nodded hopelessly and Bobby put the rum bottle and a glass on the bar in front of him.

Roger reached for it and didn't say anything.

"You drinking, Hudson?" Bobby said to Thomas Hudson. His face was stern and righteous. Thomas Hudson nodded. "You ought to cut it out," Bobby said. "There's a goddam limit to everything."

"I just want a little rum, Bobby."

"That stuff he's drinking?"

"No. Bacardi."

Mr. Bobby poured a glass and handed it to Thomas Hudson.

"Take it," he said. "Though you know I shouldn't serve you."

Thomas Hudson drank the glass at a gulp and it was warming and inspiring.

"Give me another," Thomas Hudson said.

"In twenty minutes, Hudson," Bobby said. He looked at the clock behind the bar.

By now the people were paying a little attention, but politely.

"What are you drinking, Sport?" Mr. Bobby asked David.

"You know damn well I'm off the stuff," David said to him severely.

"Since when?"

"Since last night you know damn well."

"Excuse me," Mr. Bobby said. He took a quick one himself. "How the hell am I to keep track of you goddam delinquents? All I ask is you get that Hudson out of here when I've got decent trade."

"I'm drinking quietly," Thomas Hudson said.

"You better." Mr. Bobby corked the bottle in front of Roger and put it back on the shelf.

Young Tom nodded to him approvingly and whispered to Roger. Roger lowered his head on his hands. Then he raised his head and pointed to the bottle. Young Tom shook his head. Bobby picked up the bottle, uncorked it, and set it down in front of Roger.

"Drink yourself to death," he said. "I won't lose any sleep."

By now the two groups were watching this pretty closely; but still politely. They were slumming all right but they were polite and they seemed nice people.

Then Roger spoke for the first time.

"Give the little rat a drink," he said to Bobby.

"What will you have, son?" Mr. Bobby asked Andy.

"Gin," Andy said.

Thomas Hudson was careful not to watch the people. But he could feel them.

Bobby put the bottle in front of Andy and set a glass by it. Andy poured the glass full and lifted it to Bobby.

"Here's to you, Mr. Bobby," he said. "The first one all day."

"Drink up," said Bobby. "You come in late."

"Papa had his money," David said. "His birthday money from mother."

Young Tom looked up in his father's face and started to cry. He kept himself from actually crying but it was sad to see and it was not overdone.

Nobody spoke until Andy said, "I'd like another gin, please, Mr. Bobby."

"Pour your own," said Bobby. "You poor unfortunate child." Then he turned to Thomas Hudson. "Hudson," he said. "Have another and get out."

"I can stay as long as I'm quiet," Thomas Hudson said.

"If I know you, you won't be quiet for long," Bobby said, vindictively.

Roger pointed toward the bottle and young Tom hung onto his sleeve. He'd controlled his tears and he was being brave and good.

"Mr. Davis," he said. "You don't have to."

Roger did not say anything and Mr. Bobby put the bottle in front of him again.

"Mr. Davis, you have to write tonight," young Tom said. "You know you promised to write tonight."

"What do you think I'm drinking for?" Roger said to him.

"But, Mr. Davis, you didn't have to drink this much when you wrote *The Storm.*"

"Why don't you shut up?" Roger said to him.

Young Tom was patient and brave and long-suffering.

"I will, Mr. Davis. I only do it because you asked me to. Can't we go back to the house?"

"You're a good kid, Tom," Roger said. "But we're staying here."

"For very long, Mr. Davis?"

"To the goddam end."

"I don't think we need to, Mr. Davis," young Tom said. "Really I don't. And you know if you get so you can't see you won't be able to write."

"I'll dictate," Roger said. "Like Milton."

"I know you dictate beautifully," young Tom said. "But this morning when Miss Phelps tried to take it off the machine it was mostly music."

"I'm writing an opera," Roger said.

"I know you'll write a wonderful opera, Mr. Davis. But don't you think we ought to finish the novel first? You took a big advance on the novel."

"Finish it yourself," Roger said. "You ought to know the plot by now."

"I know the plot, Mr. Davis, and it's a lovely plot but it has that same girl in it that you had die in that other book and people may be confused."

"Dumas did the same thing."

"Don't badger him," Thomas Hudson said to young Tom. "How can he write if you badger him all the time?"

"Mr. Davis, couldn't you just get a really good secretary to write it for you? I've heard that novelists did that."

"No. Too expensive."

"Do you want me to help you, Roger?" Thomas Hudson asked.

"Yes. You can paint it."

"That's wonderful," young Tom said. "Will you truly, papa?"

"I'll paint it in a day," Thomas Hudson said.

"Paint it upside down like Michelangelo," Roger said. "Paint it big enough so King George can read it without his spectacles."

"Are you going to paint it, papa?" David asked.

"Yes."

"Good," David said. "That's the first sensible thing I've heard."

"It won't be too difficult, papa?"

"Hell no. It's probably too simple. Who's the girl?"

"That girl Mr. Davis always has."

"Paint her in half a day," Thomas Hudson said.

"Paint her upside down," Roger said.

"Keep it clean," Thomas Hudson told him.

"Mister Bobby, may I have another slug?" Andy asked.

"How many have you had, son?" Bobby asked him.

"Only two."

"Go ahead," Bobby told him and handed him the bottle. "Listen, Hudson, when are you going to get that picture out of here?"

"Haven't you had any offers on it?"

"No," Bobby said. "And it clutters the place up. Besides it makes me goddam nervous. I want it out of here."

"Pardon me," one of the men from the yacht spoke to Roger. "Is that canvas for sale?"

"Who spoke to you?" Roger looked at him.

"No one," the man said. "You're Roger Davis, aren't you?"

"You're damn right I am."

"If your friend painted that canvas and it is for sale I'd like to discuss the price with him," the man said turning. "You're Thomas Hudson, aren't you?"

"Hudson is the name."

"Is the canvas for sale?"

"No," Thomas Hudson told him. "I'm sorry."

"But the bartender said——"

"He's crazy," Thomas Hudson told him. "He's an awfully good fellow. But he's crazy."

"Mr. Bobby, may I please have another gin?" Andrew asked very politely.

"Certainly, my little man," Bobby said and served it. "Do you know what they ought to do? They ought to put your healthy charming face on the label of those gin bottles instead of that idiotic collection of berries. Hudson, why don't you design a suitable label for a gin bottle that would reproduce the childish charm of young Andy's face?"

"We could launch a brand," Roger said. "They've got Old Tom gin. Why shouldn't we put out Merry Andrew?"

"I'll put up the money," said Bobby. "We can make the gin here on the island. The little lads can bottle it and affix the labels. We can sell it wholesale and in detail."

"It would be a return to craftsmanship," Roger said. "Like William Morris."

"What would we make the gin from, Mr. Bobby?" Andrew asked.

"From bonefish," Bobby said. "And from conches."

The yacht people did not look at Roger or Thomas

Hudson nor at the boys now. They were watching Bobby and they looked worried.

"About that canvas," the one man said.

"What canvas are you referring to, my good man?" Bobby asked him, downing another quick one.

"The very big canvas with the three waterspouts and the man in a dinghy."

"Where?" asked Bobby.

"There," said the man.

"Begging your pardon, sir, I think you've had enough. This is a respectable place. We don't run to waterspouts and men in dinghys here."

"I mean the picture there."

"Don't provoke me, sir. There's no picture there. If there was a painting in here it would be above the bar where paintings belong and it would be a nude reclining full length in a proper shipshape manner."

"I mean that picture there."

"What picture *where?"*

"There."

"I'd be happy to fix you a Bromo Seltzer, sir. Or call you a rickshaw," Bobby said.

"A rickshaw?"

"Yes. A goddam rickshaw if you want it straight to your face. You're a rickshaw. And you've had enough."

"Mr. Bobby?" Andy asked very politely. "Do you think I've had enough?"

"No, my dear boy. Of course not. Serve yourself."

"Thank you, Mr. Bobby," Andy said. "This is four."

"I wish it was a hundred," Bobby said. "You're the pride of my heart."

"What do you say we get out of here, Hal," one of the men said to the man who wanted to buy the picture.

"I'd like to pick up that canvas," the other told him. "If I can get it for a decent price."

"I'd like to get out of here," the first man insisted. "Fun's fun and all that. But watching children drink is a little too much."

"Are you really serving that little boy gin?" the nice-looking blonde girl at the end of the bar toward the door asked Bobby. She was a tall girl with very fair hair and pleasant freckles. They were not redhead freckles but were the sort blondes get when they have skins that tan instead of burn.

"Yes ma'am."

"I think it's shameful," the girl said. "It's disgusting and it's shameful and it's criminal."

Roger avoided looking at the girl and Thomas Hudson kept his eyes down.

"What would you like him to drink, ma'am?" Bobby asked.

"Nothing. He shouldn't have anything to drink."

"Hardly seems fair," Bobby said.

"What do you mean *fair*? Do you think it's fair to poison a child with alcohol?"

"See, papa?" young Tom said. "I thought it was wrong for Andy to drink."

"He's the only one of the three who drinks, ma'am. Since Sport here stopped it," Bobby tried to reason with her. "Do you think it's fair to deprive the only one in a family of three boys of what little pleasure he gets?"

"Fair!" the girl said. "I think you're a monster. And you're another monster," she said to Roger. "And you're another monster, too," she said to Thomas Hudson. "You're all horrible and I hate you."

There were tears in her eyes and she turned her back on the boys and Mr. Bobby and said to the men with her, "Won't any of you *do* anything about it?"

"I think it's a joke," one of the men said to her. "Like that rude waiter they hire at a party. Or like double talk."

"No, it's not a joke. That dreadful man gives him gin. It's horrible and it's tragic."

"Mr. Bobby?" Tom asked. "Is five my limit?"

"For today," Bobby said. "I wouldn't want you to do anything to shock the lady."

"Oh get me out of here," the girl said. "I won't watch it."

She started to cry and two of the men went out with her and Thomas Hudson and Roger and the boys all felt quite bad.

The other girl, the really lovely-looking one, came over. She had a beautiful face and clear brown skin and tawny hair. She wore slacks but she was built wonderfully as far as Thomas Hudson could see and her hair was silky and it swung when she walked. He knew he had seen her before.

"It isn't really gin, is it?" she said to Roger.

"No. Of course not."

"I'll go out and tell her," she said. "She really feels awfully badly."

She went out the door and she smiled at them as she went out. She was a wonderful-looking girl.

"Now it's over, papa," Andy said. "Can we have Cokes?"

"I'd like a beer, papa. If it wouldn't make that lady feel bad," young Tom said.

"I don't think she'd feel badly about a beer," Thomas Hudson said. "Can I buy you a drink?" he asked the man who wanted to buy the picture. "I'm sorry if we were too stupid."

"No. No," the man said. "Very interesting. The whole thing was very interesting to me. Fascinating. I've always been interested in writers and artists. Were you all improvising?"

"Yes," said Thomas Hudson.

"Now about that canvas—"

"It belongs to Mr. Saunders," Thomas Hudson explained to him. "I painted it for him as a present. I don't think he wants to sell it. But it's his and he can do whatever he likes with it."

"I want to keep her," Bobby said. "Don't offer me a lot of money for her because it would just make me feel bad."

"I would really like to have it."

"So would I, goddam it," said Bobby. "And I've got it."

"But Mr. Saunders. That is a valuable canvas to have in a place like this."

Bobby was getting angry.

"Leave me alone, will you?" he said to the man. "We were having a wonderful time. As good a time as I ever had and women have to cry and ball up everything. I know she meant right. But what the hell. Meant right gets you quicker than anything else. My old woman means right and does right and it beats the hell out of me every day. The hell with means right. Now you're here and you think you can take my picture just because you want it."

"But Mr. Saunders, you said yourself you wanted the picture out of here and that it was for sale."

"That was all balls," Bobby said. "That was when we were having fun."

"Then the picture is *not* for sale."

"No. The picture is *not* for sale, rent, nor charter."

"Well," said the man. "Here is my card in case it ever is for sale."

"That's fine," said Bobby. "Tom may have some up at his place he wants to sell. What about it, Tom?"

"I don't think so," Thomas Hudson said.

"I'd like to come up and see them," the man told him.

"I'm not showing anything now," Thomas Hudson answered. "I'll give you the address of the gallery in New York if you'd like it."

"Thank you. Will you write it here?"

The man had a fountain pen with him and he wrote the address on the back of one of his cards and gave another card to Thomas Hudson. Then the man thanked Thomas Hudson again and asked if he might offer him a drink.

"Can you give me any idea about the prices of the larger canvases?"

"No," Thomas Hudson said. "But the dealer will be able to."

"I'll see him as soon as I'm back in town. This canvas is extremely interesting."

"Thank you," Thomas Hudson said.

"You're quite sure it can't be sold."

"Jesus," Bobby said. "Stop it, will you? That's my picture. I had the idea for it and Tom painted it for me."

The man looked as though what he had thought of as "the charades" were beginning again so he smiled with much good fellowship.

"I don't like to be insistent—"

"You're just about as insistent as a goddam loggerhead," Bobby told him. "Come on. Have a drink on me and forget it."

The boys were talking with Roger. "It was pretty good while it lasted, wasn't it, Mr. Davis?" young Tom asked. "I didn't overdo it too badly, did I?"

"It was fine," Roger said. "Dave didn't have much though."

"I was just getting ready to be a monster," David said.

"You'd have killed her, I think," young Tom said. "She was hurt pretty badly already. Were you going to come up as a monster?"

"I had my eyelids inside out and all ready to come up," David told them. "I was bent down fixing myself to come up when we stopped."

"It was bad luck she was such a nice woman," Andy said. "I hadn't started to let it have any effect on me yet. I guess now we won't have any chance to do another one."

"Wasn't Mr. Bobby wonderful?" young Tom asked. "Boy, you were swell, Mr. Bobby."

"Sure was a pity to stop," Bobby said. "And Constable hadn't even come in yet. I was just beginning to get worked up. I know just how those great actors must feel."

The girl came in through the door. As she came in, the wind blew her sweater against her and blew her hair as she turned to Roger.

"She wouldn't come back. But it's all right. She's fine now."

"Will you have a drink with us?" Roger asked her.

"I'd love to."

Roger told her all of their names and she said that she was Audrey Bruce.

"Can I come up and see your pictures?"

"Of course," Thomas Hudson said.

"I'd like to come with Miss Bruce," the man of persistence said.

"Are you her father?" Roger asked him.

"No. But I'm a very old friend."

"You can't come," Roger said. "You have to wait for Very Old Friends Day. Or get a card from the committee."

"Please don't be rude to him," she said to Roger.

"I'm afraid I have been."

"Don't be anymore."

"Fine."

"Let's be pleasant."

"Good."

"I liked Tom's line about that same girl that is in all your books."

"Did you really like it?" young Tom asked her. "It isn't really accurate. I was teasing Mr. Davis."

"I thought it was a little bit accurate."

"You come up to the house," Roger told her.

"Do I bring my friends?"

"No."

"None of them?"

"Do you want them very much?"

"No."

"Good."

"Around what time of day do I come up to the house?"

"Any time," Thomas Hudson said.

"Do I stay for lunch?"

"Naturally," Roger said.

"This sounds like a splendid island," she said. "I'm so glad we're all pleasant."

"David can show you how he was going to be a monster when we called it off," Andy said to her.

"Oh dear," she said. "We'll have absolutely everything."

"How long are you staying?" young Tom asked her.

"I don't know."

"How long is the yacht staying?" Roger asked.

"I don't know."

"What do you know?" Roger asked. "I mean it pleasantly."

"Not very much. What about you?"

"I think you're lovely," Roger said.

"Oh," she said. "Thank you very much."

"Will you stay for a while?"

"I don't know. I might."

"Will you come up to the house now and have a drink instead of having it here?" Roger asked her.

"Let's have one here," she said. "It's awfully nice here."

XII

THE next day the wind had dropped off and Roger and the boys were swimming on the beach and Thomas Hudson was on the upper porch working. Eddy had said he thought it would do David's feet no harm to swim in the salt water if he put a new dressing on them afterwards. So they had all gone in and Thomas Hudson had looked down and watched them from time to time while he painted. He was wondering about Roger and the girl and that distracted him so he stopped thinking about it. He could not help thinking of how much the girl reminded him of young Tom's mother when he had first met her. But so many girls had managed to look in such a way that they reminded him of her, and he went on working. He was sure that he would see this girl in time and he was quite sure they would see much of her. That had been clear enough. Well, she was decorative and she seemed very nice. If she reminded him of Tommy's mother, that was too damn bad. But there was nothing to do about it. He had been through that one enough times before. He kept on working.

This picture would be good he knew. The next one, with the fish in the water, was going to be the really difficult one. Maybe I should have tried it first, he thought. No, it's better to get this one done. I can always work on the other one after they are gone.

"Let me carry you up, Davy," he heard Roger say. "So you won't get dry sand in them."

"All right," David said. "Let me get them both clean here in the ocean first."

Roger carried him up the beach and onto a chair by the doorway that faced the ocean. As they passed under the porch on the way to the chair Thomas Hudson heard David ask, "Do you think she'll turn up, Mr. Davis?"

"I don't know," Roger said. "I hope so."

"Don't you think she's beautiful, Mr. Davis?"

"Lovely."

"She likes us I think. Mr. Davis, what does a girl like that do?"

"I don't know. I didn't ask her."

"Tommy's in love with her. So is Andy."

"Are you?"

"I don't know. I don't get in love with people like they do. Anyway I want to see her some more. Mr. Davis, she isn't a bitch, is she?"

"I don't know. She doesn't look like one. Why?"

"Tommy said he was in love with her but that she was probably just a bitch. Andy said he didn't care if she was a bitch."

"She doesn't look like one," Roger told him.

"Mr. Davis, aren't those men with her a strange quiet lot?"

"They certainly are."

"What do men like that do?"

"We'll ask her when she comes."

"Do you think she'll come?"

"Yes," Roger said. "I wouldn't worry if I were you."

"It's Tommy and Andy that are worried. I'm in love with someone else. You know. I told you."

"I remember. This girl looks like her, too," Roger told him.

"Maybe she saw her in the cinema and tried to look like her," David said.

Thomas Hudson went on working.

Roger was dressing David's feet when she came in sight walking up the beach. She was barefooted and wore a bathing suit with a skirt of the same material over it and she carried a beach bag. Thomas Hudson was glad to see that her legs were as good as her face and as good as her breasts that he had seen under the sweater. Her arms were lovely and all of her was brown. She had no make-up on except for her lips and she had a lovely mouth that he wanted to see with no lipstick on it.

"Hello," she said. "Am I very late?"

"No," Roger told her. "We've been in but I'm going in again."

Roger had moved David's chair out to the edge of the beach and Thomas Hudson watched her as she bent over David's feet and saw the small upturning curls at the nape of her neck as the weight of her hair fell forward. The small curls were silvery in the sun against her brown skin.

"What happened to them?" she asked. "The poor feet."

"I wore them off pulling on a fish," David told her.

"How big was he?"

"We don't know. He pulled out."

"I'm awfully sorry."

"That's all right," David said. "Nobody minds about him anymore."

"Is it all right to swim with them?"

Roger was touching the worn places with Mercurochrome. They looked good and clean but the flesh was a little puckered from the salt water.

"Eddy says it's good for them."

"Who is Eddy?"

"He's our cook."

"And is your cook your doctor, too?"

"He knows about things like that," David explained. "Mr. Davis said it was all right, too."

"Dose Mr. Davis say anything else?" she asked Roger.

"He's glad to see you."

"That's nice. Did you boys have a wild night?"

"Not very," Roger said. "We had a poker game and afterwards I read and went to sleep."

"Who won in the poker game?"

"Andy and Eddy," David said. "What did you do?"

"We played backgammon."

"Did you sleep well?" Roger asked.

"Yes. Did you?"

"Wonderfully," he said.

"Tommy is the only one of us who plays backgammon," David told the girl. "It was taught him by a worthless man who turned out to be a fairy."

"Really? What a sad story."

"The way Tommy tells it, it isn't so sad," David said. "There wasn't anything bad happened."

"I think fairies are all awfully sad," she said. "Poor fairies."

"This was sort of funny though," David said. "Because this worthless man that taught Tommy backgammon was explaining to Tommy what it meant to be a fairy and all about the Greeks and Damon and Pythias and David and Jonathan. You know, sort of like when they tell you about the fish and the roe and the milt and the bees fertilizing the pollen and all that at school and Tommy asked him if he'd ever read a book by Gide. What was it called, Mr. Davis? Not *Corydon*. That other one? With Oscar Wilde in it."

"Si le grain ne meurt," Roger said.

"It's a pretty dreadful book that Tommy took to read the boys in school. They couldn't understand it in French, of course, but Tommy used to translate it. Lots of it is awfully dull but it gets pretty dreadful when Mr. Gide gets to Africa."

"I've read it," the girl said.

"Oh fine," David said. "Then you know the sort of thing I mean. Well this man who'd taught Tommy backgammon and turned out to be a fairy was awfully surprised when Tommy spoke about this book but he was sort of pleased because now he didn't have to go through all the part about the bees and flowers of that business and he said, 'I'm so glad you know,' or something like that and then Tommy said this to him exactly; I memorized it: 'Mr. Edwards, I take only an academic interest in homosexuality. I thank you very much for teaching me backgammon and I must bid you good day.'"

"Tommy had wonderful manners then," David told her. "He'd just come from living in France with papa and he had wonderful manners."

"Did you live in France, too?"

"We all did at different times. But Tommy's the only one who remembers it properly. Tommy has the best memory anyway. He remembers truly, too. Did you ever live in France?"

"For a long time."

"Did you go to school there?"

"Yes. Outside of Paris."

"Wait till you get with Tommy," David said. "He knows Paris and outside of Paris the way I know the reef here or the flats. Probably I don't know them even as well as Tommy knows Paris."

She was sitting down now in the shade of the porch and she was sifting the white sand through her toes.

"Tell me about the reef and the flats," she said.

"It's better if I show them to you," David said. "I'll take you out in a skiff on the flats and we can go goggle-fishing if you like it. That's the only way to know the reef."

"I'd love to go."

"Who's on the yacht?" Roger asked.

"People. You wouldn't like them."

"They seemed very nice."

"Do we have to talk that way?"

"No," Roger said.

"You met the man of persistence. He's the richest and the dullest. Can't we just not talk about them? They're all good and wonderful and dull as hell."

Young Tom came up with Andrew following him. They had been swimming far down the beach and when they had come out and seen the girl by David's chair they had come running on the hard sand and Andrew had been left behind. He came up out of breath.

"You could have waited," he said to young Tom.

"I'm sorry, Andy," young Tom said. Then he said, "Good morning. We waited for you but then we went in."

"I'm sorry I'm late."

"You're not late. We're all going in again."

"I'll stay out," David said. "You all go in now. I've been talking too much anyway?"

"You don't have to worry about undertow," young Tom told her. "It's a long gradual slope."

"What about sharks and barracuda?"

"Sharks only come in at night," Roger told her. "Barracuda never bother you. They'd only hit you if the water was roily or muddy."

"If they just saw a flash of something and didn't know what it was they might strike at it by mistake," David explained. "But they don't bite people in clear water. There's nearly always barracuda around where we swim."

"You can see them float along over the sand right alongside of you," young Tom said. "They're very curious. But they always go away."

"If you had fish, though," David told her, "like goggle-fishing and the fish on a stringer or in a bag, they'd go after the fish and they might hit you by accident because they're so fast."

"Or if you were swimming in a bunch of mullet or a big school of sardines," young Tom said. "They could hit you when they were slashing in after the school fish."

"You swim between Tom and me," Andy said. "Nothing will bother you that way."

The waves were breaking heavily on the beach and the sandpipers and Wilson plover ran twinklingly out onto the hard new-wet sand as the water receded before the next wave broke.

"Do you think we ought to swim when it's this rough and we can't see?"

"Oh, sure," David told her. "Just watch where you walk before you start to swim. It's probably too rough for a sting ray to lie in the sand anyway."

"Mr. Davis and I will look after you," young Tom said.

"I'll look after you," Andy said.

"If you bump into any fish in the surf they're probably little pompanos," David said. "They come in on the high tide to feed on the sand fleas. They're awfully pretty in the water and they're curious and friendly."

"It sounds a little like swimming in an aquarium," she said.

"Andy will teach you how to let the air out of your lungs to stay down deep," David told her. "Tom will show you how not to get in trouble with morays."

"Don't try to scare her, Dave," young Tom said. "We're not big kings of underwater like he is. But just because he's a king of underwater, Miss Bruce—"

"Audrey."

"Audrey," Tom said and stopped.

"What were you saying, Tommy?"

"I don't know," young Tom said. "Let's go in and swim."

Thomas Hudson worked on for a while. Then he went down and sat by David and watched the four of them in the surf. The girl was swimming without a cap and she swam and dove as sleek as a seal. She was as good a swimmer as Roger except for the difference in power. When they came in onto the beach and came walking toward the house on the hard sand, the girl's hair was wet and went straight back from her forehead so there was nothing to trick the shape of her head and Thomas Hudson thought he had never seen a lovelier face nor a finer body. Except one, he thought. Except the one finest and loveliest. Don't think about it, he told himself. Just look at this girl and be glad she's here.

"How was it?" he asked her.

"Wonderful," she smiled at him. "But I didn't see any fish at all," she told David.

"You probably wouldn't in so much surf," David said. "Unless you bumped into them."

She was sitting on the sand with her hands clasped around her knees. Her hair hung, damp, to her shoulders and the two boys sat beside her. Roger lay on the sand in front of her with his forehead on his folded arms. Thomas Hudson opened the screen door and went inside the house and then upstairs to the porch to work on the picture. He thought that was the best thing for him to do.

Below on the sand, where Thomas Hudson no longer watched them, the girl was looking at Roger.

"Are you gloomy?" she asked him.

"No."

"Thoughtful?"

"A little maybe. I don't know."

"On a day like this it's nice not to think at all."

"All right. Let's not think. Is it all right if I watch the waves?"

"The waves are free."

"Do you want to go in again?"

"Later."

"Who taught you to swim?" Roger asked her.

"You did."

Roger raised his head and looked at her.

"Don't you remember the beach at Cap d'Antibes? The little beach. Not Eden Roc. I used to watch you dive at Eden Roc."

"What the hell are you doing here and what's your real name?"

"I came to see you," she said. "And I suppose my name is Audrey Bruce."

"Should we go, Mr. Davis?" young Tom asked.

Roger did not even answer him.

"What your real name?"

"I was Audrey Raeburn."

"And why did you come to see me?"

"Because I wanted to. Was it wrong?"

"I guess not," Roger said. "Who said I was here?"

"A dreadful man I met at a cocktail party in New York. You'd had a fight with him here. He said you were a beachcomber."

"Well it's combed pretty neatly," Roger said looking out to sea.

"He said you were quite a few other things, too. None of them were very complimentary."

"Who were you at Antibes with?"

"With mother and Dick Raeburn. Now do you remember?"

Roger sat up and looked at her. Then he went over and put his arms around her and kissed her.

"I'll be damned," he said.

"Was it all right to come?" she asked.

"You old brat," Roger said. "Is it really you?"

"Do I have to prove it? Couldn't you just believe it?"

"I don't remember any secret marks."

"Do you like me now?"

"I love you now."

"You couldn't expect me to look like a colt forever. Do you remember when you told me I looked like a colt at Auteuil that time and I cried?"

"It was a compliment, too. I said you looked like a colt by Tenniel out of *Alice in Wonderland.*"

"I cried."

"Mr. Davis," Andy said. "And Audrey. We boys are going to go and get some Cokes. Do you want any?"

"No, Andy. You, brat?"

"Yes. I'd love one."

"Come on, Dave."

"No. I want to hear it."

"You are a bastard for a brother sometimes," young Tom said.

"Bring me one, too," David said. "Go right ahead, Mr. Davis, don't mind me at all."

"I don't mind you, Davy," the girl said.

"But where did you go and why are you Audrey Bruce?"

"It's sort of complicated."

"I guess it was."

"Mother married a man named Bruce finally."

"I knew him."

"I liked him."

"I pass," Roger said. "But why the Audrey?"

"It's my middle name. I took it because I didn't like mother's."

"I didn't like mother."

"Neither did I. I liked Dick Raeburn and I liked Bill Bruce and I loved you and I loved Tom Hudson. He didn't recognize me either, did he?"

"I don't know. He's strange and he might not say. I know he thinks you look like Tommy's mother."

"I wish I did."

"You do damned plenty enough."

"Truly you do," David said. "That's something I know about. I'm sorry, Audrey. I ought to shut up and go away."

"You didn't love me and you didn't love Tom."

"Oh yes, I did. You'll never know."

"Where's mother now?"

"She's married to a man named Geoffrey Townsend and lives in London."

"Does she still drug?"

"Of course. And she's beautiful."

"Really?"

"No. She really is. This isn't just filial piety."

"You had a lot of filial piety once."

"I know. I used to pray for everyone. Everything used to break my heart. I used to do First Fridays for mother to give her the grace of a happy death. You don't know how I prayed for you, Roger."

"I wish it would have done more good," Roger said.

"So do I," she said.

"You can't tell, Audrey. You never know when it may," David said. "I don't mean that Mr. Davis needs to be prayed for. I just mean about prayer technically."

"Thanks, Dave," Roger said. "What ever became of Bruce?"

"He died. Don't you remember?"

"No. I remember Dick Raeburn did."

"I imagine you do."

"I do."

Young Tom and Andy came back with the bottles of Coca-Cola and Andy gave a cold bottle to the girl and one to David.

"Thank you," she said. "It's wonderful and cold."

"Audrey," young Tom said. "I remember you now. You used to come to the studio with Mr. Raeburn. You never talked at all. You and I and Papa and Mr. Raeburn used to go to the different circuses and we used to go racing. But you weren't as beautiful then."

"Sure she was," Roger said. "Ask your father."

"I'm sorry about Mr. Raeburn dying," young Tom said. "I remember him dying very well. He was killed by a bobsled that rode high over a turn and went into the crowd. He'd been very ill and Papa and I went to visit him. Then he was better after a while and he went to watch the bob races although he shouldn't have. We weren't there when he was killed. I'm sorry if talking about it upsets you, Audrey."

"He was a nice man," Audrey said. "It doesn't upset me, Tommy. It was a long time ago."

"Did you know either of us boys?" Andy asked her.

"How could she, horseman? We weren't born yet," David said.

"How was I to know?" Andy asked. "I can't remember anything about France and I don't think you remember much."

"I don't pretend to. Tommy remembers France for all of us. Later on I'll remember this island. And I can remember every picture papa ever painted that I've seen."

"Can you remember the racing ones?" Audrey asked.

"Every one I've seen."

"I was in some of them," Audrey said. "At Longchamps and at Auteuil and St. Cloud. It's always the back of my head."

"I can remember the back of your head then," young Tom said. "And your hair was down to your waist and I was two steps above you to see better. It was a hazy day the way it is in the fall when it's blue smoky looking and we were in the upper stand right opposite the water jump and on our left was the bullfinch and the stone wall. The finish was on the side closer to us and the water jump was on the inner course of the track. I was always above and behind you to see better except when we were down at the track."

"I thought you were a funny little boy then."

"I guess I was. And you never talked. Maybe because I was so young. But wasn't Auteuil a beautiful track though?"

"Wonderful. I was there last year."

"Maybe we can go this year, Tommy," David said. "Did you use to go to the races with her, too, Mr. Davis?"

"No," Roger said. "I was just her swimming teacher."

"You were my hero."

"Wasn't papa ever your hero?" Andrew asked.

"Of course he was. But I couldn't let him be my hero as much as I wanted because he was married. When he and Tommy's mother were divorced I wrote him a letter. It was very powerful and I was ready to take Tommy's mother's place in any way I could. But I never sent it because he married Davy's and Andy's mother."

"Things are certainly complicated," young Tom said.

"Tell us some more about Paris," David said. "We ought to learn all we can if we're going there now."

"Do you remember when we'd be down on the rail, Audrey, and how after the horses came over the last obstacle they would be coming straight down toward us and the way they would look coming bigger and bigger and the noise they would make on the turf when they would go past?"

"And how cold it used to be and how we would get close to the big braziers to get warm and eat the sandwiches from the bar?"

"I loved it in the fall," young Tom said. "We used to ride back home in a carriage, an open one, do you remember? Out of the Bois and then along the river with it just getting dark and the burning leaves smell and the tugs towing barges on the river."

"Do you really remember it that well? You were an awfully small boy."

"I remember every bridge on the river from Suresnes to Charenton," Tommy told her.

"You can't."

"I can't name them. But I've got them in my head."

"I don't believe you can remember them all. And part of the river's ugly and many of the bridges are."

"I know it. But I was there a long time after I knew you, and papa and I used to walk the whole river. The ugly parts and the beautiful parts and I've fished a lot of it with different friends of mine."

"You really fished in the Seine?"

"Of course."

"Did papa fish it, too?"

"Not so much. He used to fish sometimes at Charenton. But he wanted to walk when he finished work and so we would walk until I got too tired and then get a bus back some way. After we had some money we used to take taxis or horsecabs."

"You must have had money when we were going to the races."

"I think we did that year," Tommy said. "I can't remember that. Sometimes we had money and sometimes we didn't."

"We always had money," Audrey said. "Mother never married anyone who didn't have lots of money."

"Are you rich, Audrey?" Tommy asked.

"No," the girl said. "My father spent his money and lost his money after he married mother and none of my stepfathers ever made any provision for me."

"You don't have to have money," Andrew said to her.

"Why don't you live with us?" young Tom asked her. "You'd be fine with us."

"It sounds lovely. But I have to make a living."

"We're going to Paris," Andrew said. "You come along. It will be wonderful. You and I can go and see all the arrondissements together."

"I'll have to think it over," the girl said.

"Do you want me to make you a drink to help you decide?" David said. "That's what they always do in Mr. Davis's books."

"Don't ply me with liquor."

"That's an old white slaver's trick," young Tom said. "Then the next thing they know they're in Buenos Aires."

"They must give them something awfully strong," David said. "That's a long trip."

"I don't think there's anything much stronger than the way Mr. Davis makes martinis," Andrew said. "Make her a martini, please, Mr. Davis."

"Do you want one, Audrey?" Andrew asked.

"Yes. If it's not too long before lunch."

Roger got up to make them and young Tom came over and sat by her. Andrew was sitting at her feet.

"I don't think you ought to take it, Audrey," he said. "It's the first step. Remember *ce n'est que le premier pas qui conte.*"

Up on the porch Thomas Hudson kept on painting. He could not keep from hearing their talk but he had not looked down at them since they had come in from swimming. He was having a difficult time staying in the carapace of work that he had built for his protection and he thought, if I don't work now I may lose it. Then he thought that there would be time to work when they were all gone. But he knew he must keep on working now or he would lose the security he had built for himself with work. I will do exactly as much as I would have done if they were not here, he thought. Then I will clear up and go down and the hell with thinking of Raeburn or of the old days or of anything. But as he worked he felt a loneliness coming into him already. It was next week when they would leave. Work, he told himself. Get it right and keep your habits because you are going to need them.

When he had finished work and gone down to join them, Thomas Hudson was still thinking about the painting and he said "Hi" to the girl and then looked away from her. Then he looked back.

"I couldn't help hearing it," he said. "Or overhearing it. I'm glad we're old friends."

"So am I. Did you know?"

"Maybe," he said. "Let's get lunch. Are you dry, Audrey?"

"I'll change in the shower," she said. "I have a shirt and the skirt to this."

"Tell Joseph and Eddy that we're ready," Thomas Hudson said to young Tom. "I'll show you the shower, Audrey."

Roger went into the house.

"I thought I shouldn't be here under false pretenses," Audrey said.

"You weren't."

"Don't you think I could be any good for him?"

"You might. What he needs is to work well to save his soul. I don't know anything about souls. But he misplaced his the first time he went out to the Coast."

"But he's going to write a novel now. A great novel."

"Where did you hear that?"

"It was in one of the columns. Cholly Knickerbocker, I think."

"Oh," Thomas Hudson said. "Then it must be true."

"Don't you truly think I might be good for him?"

"You might."

"There are some complications."

"There always are."

"Should I tell you now?"

"No," Thomas Hudson said. "You better get dressed and comb your hair and get up there. He might meet some other woman while he was waiting."

"You weren't like this in the old days. I thought you were the kindest man I ever knew."

"I'm awfully sorry, Audrey. And I'm glad you're here."

"We are old friends, aren't we?"

"Sure," he said. "Change and fix yourself up and get up there."

He looked away from the girl and she shut the door of the shower. He did not know what made him feel as he did. But the happiness of the summer began to drain out of him as when the tide changes on the flats and the ebb begins in the channel that opens out to sea. He watched the sea and the line of beach and he noticed that the tide had changed and the shore birds were working busily well down the slope of new wet sand. The breakers were diminishing as they receded. He looked a long way up along the shore and then went into the house.

XIII

THEY had a fine time the last few days. It was as good as any of the time before and there was no pre-going sadness. The yacht left and Audrey took a room over the Ponce de León. But she stayed at the house and slept on a cot on the sleeping porch at the far end of the house and used the guest room.

She did not say anything again about being in love with Roger. All Roger said to Thomas Hudson about her was, "She's married to some sort of a son of a bitch."

"You couldn't expect her to wait all her life for you, could you?"

"At least he's a son of a bitch."

"Aren't they always? You'll find he has his nice side."

"He's rich."

"That's probably his nice side," Thomas Hudson said. "They're always married to some son of a bitch and he always has some tremendously nice side."

"All right," Roger said. "Let's not talk about it."

"You're going to do the book, aren't you?"

"Sure. That's what she wants me to do."

"Is that why you're going to do it?"

"Shove it, Tom," Roger told him.

"Do you want to use the Cuba House? It's only a shack. But you'd be away from people."

"No. I want to go West."

"The Coast?"

"No. Not the Coast. Could I stay at the ranch for a while?"

"There's only the one cabin that's on the far beach. I rented the rest."

"That would be fine."

The girl and Roger took long walks on the beach and swam together and with the boys. The boys went bonefishing and took Audrey bone-fishing and goggle-fishing on the reef. Thomas Hudson worked hard and all the time he was working and the boys were out on the flats he had the good feeling that they would be home soon and they would be having supper or dinner together. He was worried when they were goggle-fishing but he knew Roger and Eddy would make them be careful. One time they all went trolling for a full day up to the furthest light at the end of the bank and had a wonderful day with bonito and dolphin and three big wahoo. He painted a canvas of a wahoo with his strange flattened head and his stripes around his long speed-built body for Andy, who had caught the biggest one. He painted him against a background of the big spider-legged lighthouse with the summer clouds and the green of the banks.

Then one day the old Sikorsky amphibian circled the house once and then landed in the bay and they rowed the three boys out to her in the dinghy. Joseph sculled out in another dinghy with their bags. Young Tom said, "Goodbye, papa. It certainly was a swell summer."

David said, "Goodbye, papa. It certainly was wonderful. Don't worry about anything. We'll be careful."

Andrew said, "Goodbye, papa. Thanks for a wonderful, wonderful summer and for the trip to Paris."

They climbed up into the cockpit door and all waved from the door to Audrey, who was standing on the dock, and called, "Goodbye! Goodbye, Audrey."

Roger was helping them up and they said, "Goodbye, Mr. Davis. Goodbye, papa." Then very loud and carrying over the water, "Goodbye, Audrey!"

Then the door closed and locked and they were faces through the small glass panes and then they were water-splashed faces as the old coffee mills revved up. Thomas Hudson pulled away from the rush of spray and the ancient, ugly plane taxied out and took off into the little breeze there was and then circled once and straightened course, steady, ugly, and slow across the Gulf.

Thomas Hudson knew Roger and Audrey would be leaving and as the run-boat was coming the next day he asked Roger when he was going.

"Tomorrow, old Tom," Roger said.

"With Wilson?"

"Yes. I asked him to come back."

"I just wanted to know about ordering on the run-boat."

So the next day they left the same way. Thomas Hudson kissed the girl goodbye and she kissed him. She had cried when the boys left and she cried that day and held him close and hard.

"Take good care of him and take good care of you."

"I'm going to try. You've been awful good to us, Tom."

"Nonsense."

"I'll write," Roger said. "Is there anything you want me to do out there?"

"Have fun. You might let me know how things are."

"I will. This one will write, too."

So they were gone, too, and Thomas Hudson stopped in at Bobby's on the way home.

"Going to be goddam lonely," Bobby said.

"Yes," Thomas Hudson said. "It's going to be goddam lonely."

XIV

THOMAS HUDSON was unhappy as soon as the boys were gone. But he thought that was normal lonesomeness for them and he just kept on working. The end of a man's own world does not come as it does in one of the great paintings Mr. Bobby had outlined. It comes with one of the island boys bringing a radio message up the road from the local post office and saying, "Please sign on the detachable part of the envelope. We're sorry, Mr. Tom."

He gave the boy a shilling. But the boy looked at it and put it down on the table.

"I don't care for a tip, Mr. Tom," the boy said and went out.

He read it. Then he put it in his pocket and went out the door and sat on the porch by the sea. He took the radio form out and read it again. YOUR SONS DAVID AND ANDREW KILLED WITH THEIR MOTHER IN MOTOR ACCIDENT NEAR BIARRITZ ATTENDING TO EVERYTHING PENDING YOUR ARRIVAL DEEPEST SYMPATHY. It was signed by the Paris branch of his New York bank.

Eddy came out. He had heard about it from Joseph who had heard about it from one of the boys at the radio shack.

Eddy sat down by him and said, "Shit, Tom, how can such things happen?"

"I don't know," said Thomas Hudson. "I guess they hit something or something ran into them."

"I'll bet Davy wasn't driving," Eddy said.

"I'll bet so too. But it doesn't matter any more."

Thomas Hudson looked out at the flatness of the blue sea and the darker blue of the Gulf. The sun was low and soon it would be behind the clouds.

"Do you think their mother was driving?"

"Probably. Maybe they had a chauffeur. What difference does it make?"

"Do you think it could have been Andy?"

"Could be. His mother might let him."

"He's conceited enough," Eddy said.

"He was," said Thomas Hudson. "I don't think he's conceited now."

The sun was going down and there were clouds in front of it.

"We'll get a wire to Wilkinson on their next radio schedule to come over early and for him to call up and save me space on a plane to New York."

"What do you want me to do while you're away?"

"Just look after things. I'll leave you some checks for each month. If there are any blows, get plenty of good help with the boat and the house."

"I'll do everything," Eddy said. "But I don't give a shit about anything any more."

"I don't either," said Thomas Hudson.

"We've got young Tom."

"For the time being," Thomas Hudson said and for the first time he looked straight down the long and perfect perspective of the blankness ahead.

"You'll make it all right," Eddy said.

"Sure. When didn't I ever make it?"

"You can stay in Paris a while and then go to the Cuba house and young Tom can keep you company. You can paint good over there and it will be like a change."

"Sure," said Thomas Hudson.

"You can travel and that'll be good. Go on those big boats like I always wanted to go on. Travel on all of them. Let them take you anywhere they go."

"Sure."

"Shit," said Eddy. "What the fuck they kill that Davy for?"

"Let's leave it alone, Eddy," Thomas Hudson said. "It's way past things we know about."

"Fuck everything," Eddy said and pushed his hat back on his head.

"We'll play it out the way we can," Thomas Hudson told him. But now he knew he did not have much interest in the game.

XV

ON the eastward crossing on the *Île de France* Thomas Hudson learned that hell was not necessarily as it was described by Dante or any other of the great hell-describers, but could be a comfortable, pleasant, and well-loved ship taking you toward a country that you had always sailed for with anticipation. It had many circles and they were not fixed as in those of the great Florentine egotist. He had gone aboard the ship early, thinking of it, he now knew, as a refuge from the city where he had feared meeting people who would speak to him about what had happened. He thought that on the ship he could come to some terms with his sorrow, not knowing, yet, that there are no terms to be made with sorrow. It can be cured by death and it can be blunted or anesthetized by various things. Time is supposed to cure it, too. But if it is cured by anything less than death, the chances are that it was not true sorrow.

One of the things that blunts it temporarily through blunting everything else is drinking and another thing that can keep the mind away from it is work. Thomas Hudson knew about both these remedies. But he also knew the drinking would destroy the capacity for producing satisfying work and he had built his life on work for so long now that he kept that as the one thing that he must not lose.

But since he knew he could not work now for some time he planned to drink and read and exercise until he was tired enough to sleep. He had slept on the plane. But he had not slept in New York.

Now he was in his stateroom, which had a sitting room connected with it, and the porters had left his bags and the big package of magazines and newspapers he had bought. He had thought they would be the easiest thing to start with. He gave his ticket to the room steward and asked him for a bottle of Perrier water and some ice. When they came, he took out a fifth of good Scotch from one of his bags and opened it and made himself a drink. Then he cut the string around the big bundle of magazines and papers and spread them on the table. The magazines looked fresh and virginal compared with the way they looked when they arrived at the island. He took up *The New Yorker*. At the island he had always saved it for the evenings and it had been a long time since he had seen a *New Yorker* of the week of publication or one that had not been folded. He sat in the deep comfortable chair and drank his drink and learned that you cannot read *The New Yorker* when people that you love have just died. He tried *Time* and he could read it all right, including "Milestones," where the two boys were dead complete with their ages; their mother's age, not quite accurate; her marital status, and the statement that she had divorced him in 1933.

Newsweek had the same facts. But reading the short item Thomas Hudson had the odd sensation that the man who wrote it was sorry that the boys were dead.

He made himself another drink and thought how much better the Perrier was than anything else you could put in whisky and then he read both *Time* and *Newsweek* through. What the hell do you suppose she was doing at Biarritz? he thought. At least she could have gone to St. Jean-de-Luz.

From that he knew that the whisky was doing some good.

Give them up now, he told himself. Just remember how

they were and write them off. You have to do it sooner or later. Do it now.

Read some more, he said. Just then the ship started to move. It was moving very slowly and he did not look out of the window of the sitting room. He sat in the comfortable chair and read through the pile of papers and magazines and drank the Scotch and Perrier.

You haven't any problem at all, he told himself. You've given them up and they're gone. You should not have loved them so damn much in the first place. You shouldn't have loved them and you shouldn't have loved their mother. Listen to the whisky talking, he said to himself. What a solvent of our problems. *The solvent alchemist that in a trice our leaden gold into shit transmutes*. That doesn't even scan. *Our leaden gold to shit transmutes* is better.

I wonder where Roger is with that girl, he thought. The bank will know where Tommy is. I know where I am. I'm in here with a bottle of Old Parr. Tomorrow I'll sweat this all out in the gym. I'll use the heat box. I'll ride on one of those bicycles that goes nowhere and on a mechanical horse. That's what I need. A good ride on a mechanical horse. Then I'll get a good rubdown. Then I'll meet somebody in the bar and I'll talk about other things. It's only six days. Six days is easy.

He went to sleep that night and when he woke in the night he heard the movement of the ship through the sea and at first, smelling the sea, he thought that he was at home in the house on the island and that he had wakened from a bad dream. Then he knew it was not a bad dream and he smelled the heavy grease on the edges of the open window. He switched the light on and drank some of the Perrier water. He was very thirsty.

There was a tray with some sandwiches and fruit on the table where the steward had left them the night before and there was still ice in the bucket that held the Perrier.

He knew he should eat something and he looked at the clock on the wall. It was three-twenty in the morning. The sea air was cool and he ate a sandwich and two apples and then took some ice out of the bucket and made himself a drink. The Old Parr was about gone but he had another bottle and now, in the cool of the early morning, he sat in the comfortable chair and drank and read *The New Yorker*. He found that he could read it now and he found that he enjoyed drinking in the night.

For years he had kept an absolute rule about not drinking in the night and never drinking before he had done his work except on non-working days. But now, as he woke in the night, he felt the simple happiness of breaking training. It was the first return of any purely animal happiness or capacity for happiness that he had experienced since the cable had come.

The New Yorker was very good, he thought. And it's evidently a magazine you can read on the fourth day after something happens. Not on the first or the second or the third. But on the fourth. That was useful to know. After *The New Yorker* he read *The Ring* and then he read everything that was readable in *The Atlantic Monthly* and some that was not. Then he made his third drink and read *Harper's*. You see, he said to himself, there's nothing to it.

Part II

CUBA

CUBA

AFTER they were all gone he lay on the fiber matting on the floor and listened to the wind. It was blowing a gale from the northwest and he spread blankets on the floor, piled pillows to brace against the stuffed chairback he placed against the leg of the living-room table, and wearing a long, peaked cap to shade his eyes, read his mail in the good light from the big reading lamp that stood on the table. His cat lay on his chest and he pulled a light blanket over them both and opened and read the letters and drank from a glass of whisky and water that he replaced on the floor between sips. His hand found the glass when he wanted it.

The cat was purring, but he could not hear him because he had a silent purr, and he would hold a letter in one hand and touch the cat's throat with the finger of his other hand.

"You have a throat mike, Boise," he said. "Do you love me?"

The cat kneaded his chest softly with the claws just catching in the wool of the man's heavy blue jersey and he felt the cat's long, lovingly spread weight and the purring under his fingers.

"She's a bitch, Boise," he told the cat and opened another letter.

The cat put his head under the man's chin and rubbed it there.

"They'll scratch the hell out of you, Boise," the man said and stroked the cat's head with the stubble of his chin. "Womens don't like them. It's a shame you don't drink, Boy. You do damned near everything else."

The cat had originally been named after the cruiser *Boise* but now, for a long time, the man had called him Boy for short.

He read the second letter through without comment and reached out and took a drink of the whisky and water.

"Well," he said. "We aren't getting anywhere. I'll tell you, Boy. You read the letters and I'll lie on your chest and purr. How would you like that?"

The cat put his head up to rub against the man's chin and the man rubbed against it pushing his beard stubble down between the cat's ears and along the back of his head and between his shoulder blades while he opened the third letter.

"Did you worry about us, Boise, when the blow came up?" he asked. "I wish you could have seen us come into the mouth of the harbor with the sea breaking over the Morro. You'd have been spooked, Boy. We came in in a bloody, huge, breaking sea like a damn surfboard."

The cat lay, contentedly, breathing in rhythm with the man. He was a big cat, long and loving, the man thought, and poor from much night hunting.

"Did you do any good while I was away, Boy?" He had laid the letter down and was stroking the cat under the blanket. "Did you get many?" The cat rolled on his side and offered his stomach to be caressed the way he had done when he was a kitten, in the time when he had been happy. The man put his arms around him and held him tight against his chest, the big cat on his side, his head under the man's chin. Under the pressure of the man's arms he turned suddenly and lay flat against the man, his claws dug into the sweater, his body pressed tight. He was not purring now.

"I'm sorry, Boy," the man said. "I'm awfully sorry. Let

me read this other damned letter. There's nothing we can do. You don't know anything to do—do you?"

The cat lay against him, heavy and unpurring and desperate. The man stroked him and read the letter. "Just take it easy, Boy," he said. "There isn't any solution. If I ever find any solution I'll tell you."

By the time he had finished the third and longest letter the big black and white cat was asleep. He was asleep in the position of the Sphinx, but with his head lowered in the man's chest.

I'm awfully glad, the man thought. I ought to undress and take a bath and go to bed properly but there will be no hot water and I wouldn't sleep in a bed tonight. Too much movement. The bed would throw me. Probably won't sleep here either with that old beast on me.

"Boy," he said. "I'm going to lift you off so I can lie on my side."

He lifted the heavy limp weight of the cat, that came alive suddenly in his hands, and then was limp again, and laid him by his side, then turned over to rest on his right elbow. The cat lay along his back. He had resented it while he was being moved but now he was asleep again, curled up against the man. The man took the three letters and read them through for the second time. He decided not to read the papers and reached up and put the light out and lay on his side, feeling the touch of the cat's body against his buttocks. He lay with his two arms around a pillow and his head on another pillow. Outside the wind was blowing hard and the floor of the room still had some of the motion of the flying bridge. He had been on the bridge nineteen hours before they had come in.

He lay there and tried to sleep, but he could not. His eyes were very tired and he did not want the light on, nor to read, so he lay there and waited for morning. Through the blankets he could feel the matting, made to the measure of the big room, that had been brought from Samoa on a cruiser six months before Pearl. It covered all the tiled floor of the room, but where the French doors opened onto the patio it had been bent back and buckled by the movement of the doors and he could feel the wind get under it and billow it as the wind came in under the gap below the door frames. He thought this wind would blow from the northwest at least another day, then go into the north and finally blow itself out from the northeast. That was the way it moved in winter but it might stay in the northeast for several days, blowing hard, before it settled into the *brisa* which was the local name for the northeast trade wind. Blowing at gale force out of the northeast against the Gulf Stream it made a very heavy sea, one of the heaviest he had ever seen anywhere, and he knew no Kraut would surface in it. So, he thought, we will be ashore at least four days. Then they will be up for sure.

He thought about this last trip and how the blow had caught them sixty miles down the coast and thirty offshore and the punishing trip in when he had decided to come into Havana rather than Bahía Honda. He had punished her all right. He had punished her plenty and there were several things he would have to check. It probably would have been better to put in at Bahía Honda. But they had been in there too much lately. He had been out twelve days, too, expecting to be out not more than ten. He was low on certain things and he could not be at all sure of the duration of this blow; so he had made the decision to come into Havana and had taken the beating. In the morning he would bathe, shave, clean up, and go in and make his report to the Naval Attaché. They might have wanted him to stay down the coast. But he knew nothing would surface in this weather; it was impossible for them to. That was all there was to it, really. If he was right on that, the rest of it would be OK although things were not always that simple. They certainly were not.

The floor hardened against his right hip and his thigh and right shoulder, so he lay on his back now and rested against the muscles of his shoulders, drawing his knees up under the blanket and letting his heels push against the blanket. This took some of the tiredness out of his body and he put his left hand on the sleeping cat and stroked him.

"You relax awfully well, Boy, and you sleep good,"

he said to the cat. "I guess it isn't too bad, then."

He thought of letting some of the other cats out so he would have them to talk to and for company now that Boise was asleep. But he decided against it. It would hurt Boise and make him jealous. Boise had been outside the house waiting for them when they had driven up in the station wagon. He had been terribly excited and had been underfoot during the unloading, greeting everyone and slipping in and out each time a door was opened. He had probably waited outside every night since they left. From the time he had orders to go, the cat knew it. Certainly he could not tell about orders; but he knew the first symptoms of preparation, and, as they proceeded through the various phases to the final disorder of the people sleeping in the house (he always had them sleep in by midnight when leaving before daylight), the cat became steadily more upset and nervous until, finally when they loaded to leave, he was desperate and they had to be careful to lock him in so that he would not follow down the drive, into the village, and out onto the highway.

One time on the Central Highway he had seen a cat that had been hit by a car and the cat, fresh hit and dead, looked exactly like Boy. His back was black and his throat, chest, and forefeet were white and there was the black mask across his face. He knew it couldn't be Boy because it was at least six miles from the farm; but it had made him feel sick inside and he had stopped the car and gone back and lifted the cat and made sure it was not Boy and then laid him by the side of the road so nothing else would run over him. The cat was in good condition, so he knew he was someone's cat, and he left him by the road so they would find him and know about him rather than have to worry about him. Otherwise he would have taken the cat into the car and had him buried at the farm.

That evening, coming back to the farm, the body of the cat was gone from where he had left him so he thought that his people must have found him. That night, when he had sat in the big chair reading, with Boise by his side in the chair, he had thought that he did not know what he would do if Boise should be killed. He thought, from his actions and his desperations, that the cat felt the same way about the man.

He sweats them out worse than I do. Why do you do it, Boy? If you would take them easier you would be much better off. I take them as easy as I can, he said to himself. I really do. But Boise can't.

At sea he thought about Boise and his strange habits and his desperate, hopeless love. He remembered him the first time he had seen him when he was a kitten playing with his reflection on the glass top of the cigar counter of the bar at Cojímar that was built out on the rocks overlooking the harbor. They had come down to the bar on a bright Christmas morning. There were a few drunks there left over from the celebration of the night before, but the wind was blowing freshly from the east through the open restaurant and the bar, and the light was so bright and the air felt so new and cool that it was no morning for drunks.

"Shut the doors against that wind," one of them said to the proprietor.

"No," the proprietor said. "I like it. Go and find a lee somewhere else if it's too fresh."

"We pay to be comfortable," one of the leftovers from the night's drinking said.

"No. You pay for what you drink. Find another place to be comfortable."

He looked out across the open terrace of the bar at the sea, dark blue and with whitecaps, with the fishing boats crisscrossing it sailing and trolling for dolphin. There were half a dozen fishermen at the bar and two tables of them sitting on the terrace. They were fishermen who had done well the day before, or who believed the good weather and the current would hold and were taking a chance and staying in for Christmas. None of them that the man, whose name was Thomas Hudson, knew ever went to church even on Christmas and none of them dressed, consciously, as fishermen. They were the most unfishermanlike fishermen he had ever known and they were among the very best. They wore old straw hats, or were bareheaded. They wore old clothes and were sometimes barefooted and sometimes they wore shoes. You could tell a fisherman from a countryman, or *guajiro,* because the countrymen wore formalized pleated shirts, wide hats, tight trousers, and riding boots when they came to town and nearly all of them carried machetes, while the fishermen wore the remnants of any old clothes they had and were cheerful, self-confident men. The country men were reserved and shy unless they were drinking. The only way you could tell a fisherman, surely, was by his hands. The hands of the old men were gnarled and brown, spotted with sun blotches, and the palms and fingers were deep cut and scarred by the handlines. The young men's hands were not gnarled; but most of them had the sun blotches and they were all deeply scarred and the hair on the hands and arms of all but the very darkest men was bleached by the sun and the salt.

Thomas Hudson remembered how on this Christmas morning, the first Christmas of the war, the proprietor of the bar had asked him, "Do you want some shrimps?" and brought a big plate piled with fresh cooked prawns and put it on the bar while he sliced a yellow lime and spread the slices on a saucer. The prawns were huge and pink and their antennae hung down over the edge of the bar for more than a foot and he had picked one up and spread the long whiskers to their full width and remarked that they were longer than those of a Japanese admiral.

Thomas Hudson broke the head off the Japanese admiral prawn and then split open the belly of the shell with his thumbs and shucked the prawn out and it was so fresh and silky feeling under his teeth, and had such a flavor, cooked in sea water with fresh lime juice and whole black peppercorns, that he thought he had never eaten a better one; not even in Málaga nor in Tarragona nor in Valencia. It was then that the kitten came over to him, scampering down the bar, to rub against his hand and beg a prawn.

"They're too big for you, cotsie," he said. But he snipped off a piece of one with his thumb and finger and gave it to the kitten who ran with it back to the tobacco counter to eat it quickly and savagely.

Thomas Hudson looked at the kitten, with his handsome black and white markings, his white chest and forelegs and the black, like a formal mask across his eyes and forehead, eating the prawn and growling, and asked the proprietor who he belonged to.

"You if you want him."

"I have two at the house. Persians."

"Two is nothing. Take this one. Give them a little Cojímar blood."

"Papa, can't we have him?" asked the one of his sons, that he did not think about any more, who had come up from the steps of the terrace where he had been watching the fishing boats come in, seeing the men unstep their masts, unload their coiled lines, and throw their fish ashore. "Please, papa, can't we have him? He's a beautiful cat."

"Do you think he'd be happy away from the sea?"

"Certainly, papa. He'll be miserable here in a little while. Haven't you seen how miserable the cats are in the streets? And they were probably just like him once."

"Take him," the proprietor said. "He'll be happy on a farm."

"Listen, Tomás," one of the fishermen who had been listening to the conversation from the table said. "If you want cats I can get an Angora, a genuine Angora, from Guanabacoa. A true Tiger Angora."

"Male?"

"As much as you," the fisherman said. At the table they all laughed.

Nearly all Spanish joking had that same base. "But with fur on them," the fisherman tried for another laugh and got it.

"Papa, can we please have this cat?" the boy asked. "This cat is a male."

"Are you sure?"

"I know, papa. I know."

"That's what you said about both the Persians."

"Persians are different, papa. I was wrong on the

Persians and I admit it. But I know now, papa. Now I really know."

"Listen, Tomás. Do you want the Angora Tiger from Guanabacoa?" the fisherman asked.

"What is he? A witchcraft cat?"

"Witchcraft nothing. This cat never even heard of Saint Barbara. This cat is more of a Christian than you are."

"Es muy posible," another fisherman said and they all laughed.

"What does this famous beast cost?" Thomas Hudson asked.

"Nothing. He's a gift. A genuine Angora Tiger. He's a Christmas gift."

"Come on up to the bar and have a drink and describe him to me."

The fisherman came up to the bar. He wore hornrimmed glasses and a clean, faded, blue shirt that looked as though it would not stand another washing. It was lacy thin in back between the shoulders and the fabric was beginning to rip. He had on faded khaki trousers and was barefoot on Christmas. His face and hands were burned a dark wood color and he put his scarred hands on the bar and said to the proprietor, "Whisky with ginger ale."

"Ginger ale makes me sick," Thomas Hudson said. "Let me have one with mineral water."

"It's very good for me," the fisherman said. "I like Canada Dry. Otherwise I don't like the taste of the whisky. Listen, Tomás. This is a serious cat."

"Papa," the boy said, "before you and this gentleman start drinking, can we have this cat?"

He had tied a shrimp husk on the end of a piece of white cotton string and was playing with the kitten, who was standing on his hind legs, as a rampant lion does in heraldry, boxing with the lure the boy swung at him.

"Do you want him?"

"You know I want him."

"You can have him."

"Thank you very much, papa. I'm going to take him out to the car to gentle him."

Thomas Hudson watched the boy cross the road with

the kitten in his arms and get into the front seat with him. The top of the car was down and from the bar he watched the boy, his brown hair flattened by the wind, sitting in the convertible in the bright sunlight. He could not see the kitten because the boy was holding him on the seat, sitting low on the seat out of the wind, stroking the kitten.

Now the boy was gone and the kitten had grown into an old cat and had outlived the boy. The way he and Boise felt now, he thought, neither one wanted to outlive the other. I don't know how many people and animals have been in love before, he thought. It probably is a very comic situation. But I don't find it comic at all.

No, he thought, I do not find it comic any more than it is comic for a boy's cat to outlive him. Many things about it are certainly ridiculous, as Boise was when he growled and then made that sudden tragic cry and stiffened his whole length against the man. Sometimes, the servants said, he would not eat for several days after the man was gone but his hunger always drove him to it. Although there were days when he tried to live by his hunting and would not come in with the other cats, he always came in finally and he would leap out of the room over the backs of the other crowding cats when the door was opened by the servant that brought the tray of ground meat and then leap back in over all the other cats as they milled around the boy who had brought the food. He always ate very quickly and then wanted to leave the cat room as soon as he had finished. There was no cat that he cared for in any way.

For a long time now the man thought that Boise had regarded himself as a human being. He did not drink with the man as a bear would but he ate everything the man ate especially all of those things cats would not touch. Thomas Hudson remembered the summer before when they had been eating breakfast together and he had offered Boise a slice of fresh, chilled mango. Boise had eaten it with delight and he had mango every morning as long as Thomas Hudson was ashore and the mango season lasted. He had to hold the slices for him so he could get them into his mouth since they were too slippery for the cat to pick off the plate and he thought he must rig some sort of a rack, like a toast rack, so the cat could take them without having to hurry.

Then when the alligator pear trees, the big, dark green *aguacates* with their fruit only a little darker and shinier than the foliage, had come into bearing this time when he had been ashore in September for overhaul, preparing to go down to Haiti, he had offered Boise a spoonful out of the shell, the hollow where the seed had been, filled with oil and vinegar dressing, and the cat had eaten it and then afterwards at each meal, he had eaten half an *aguacate*.

"Why don't you climb up in the trees and get them for yourself?" Thomas Hudson had asked the cat as they walked together over the hills of the property. But Boise, of course, had not answered.

He had found Boy up in an alligator pear tree one evening when he had gone out in the dusk to walk and see the flight of blackbirds going in toward Havana where they flew each night from all the countryside to the south and east, converging in long flights to roost, noisily, in the Spanish laurel trees of the Prado. Thomas Hudson liked to watch the blackbirds come flying over the hills and to see the first bats come out in the evening and the very small owls coming out for their night flying when the sun went down into the sea beyond Havana and the lights began to come on over the hills. On that night he had missed Boise, who nearly always walked with him, and he had taken Big Goats, one of Boise's sons, a big-shouldered, heavy-necked, wide-faced, tremendous-whiskered, black, fighting cat for the walk. Goats never hunted. He was a fighter and a stud cat and that kept him occupied. But he was cheerful, except where his work was concerned, and he liked to walk especially if Thomas Hudson would stop every now and then and push him hard with his foot so that he would lie flat on his side. Thomas Hudson would then stroke the cat's belly with his foot. It was difficult to stroke Goats too hard or too roughly, and he would as soon be stroked with a shoe on as barefoot.

Thomas Hudson had just reached down and patted him—he liked to be patted as strongly as you would pat a big dog—when he looked up and saw Boise well up in the alligator pear tree. Goats looked up and saw him too.

"What are you doing, you old bastard?" Thomas Hudson called to him "Have you finally started to eat them on the tree?"

Boise looked down at them and saw Goats.

"Come on down and we'll take a walk," Thomas Hudson told him. "I'll give you *aguacate* for supper."

Boise looked at Goats and said nothing.

"You look awfully handsome in those dark green leaves. Stay up if you want."

Boise looked away from them and Thomas Hudson and the big black cat went on through the trees.

"Do you think he's crazy, Goats?" the man asked. Then to please the cat he said, "Do you remember the night we couldn't find the medicine?"

Medicine was a magic word with Goats and as soon as he heard it, he lay on his side to be stroked.

"Remember the medicine?" the man asked him and the big cat writhed in his hardy rough delight.

Medicine had become a magic word with him one night when the man had been drunk, really drunk, and Boise would not sleep with him. Princessa would not sleep with him when he was drunk, nor would Willy. No one would sleep with him when he was drunk except Friendless, which was Big Goats' early name, and Friendless's Brother, who was really his sister, and who was an unfortunate cat who had many sorrows and occasional ecstasies. Goats liked him drunk better than sober or, perhaps, it was because only when Thomas Hudson was drunk that Goats got to sleep with him that made it seem that way. But on this night Thomas Hudson had been ashore about four days when he got really drunk. It had started at noon at the Floridita and he had drunk first with Cuban politicians that had dropped in, nervous for a quick one; with sugar planters and rice planters; with Cuban government functionaries, drinking through their lunch hour; with second and third secretaries of Embassy, shepherding someone to the Floridita; with the inescapable FBI men, pleasant and all trying to look so average, clean-cut-young-American that they stood out as clearly as though they had worn a bureau shoulder patch on their white linen or seersucker suits. He had drunk double frozen daiquiris, the great ones that Constante made, that had no taste of alcohol and felt, as you drank them, the way downhill glacier skiing feels running through powder snow and, after the sixth and eighth, felt like downhill glacier skiing feels when you are running unroped. Some Navy that he knew came in and he drank with them and then with some of the then-called Hooligan Navy or Coast Guard. This was getting too near to shop, which he was drinking away from, so he went down to the far end of the bar where the old respectable whores were, the fine old whores that every resident drinker at the Floridita had slept with sometime in the last twenty years, and sat on a stool with them and had a club sandwich and drank more double frozens.

When he had come back to the farm that night he was very drunk and none of the cats would sleep with him but Goats, who was not allergic to the basic rum smell, had no prejudice against drunkenness, and revelled in the rich whore smell, as full-bodied as a fine Christmas fruit-cake. They slept heavily together, Goats purring loudly whenever he woke, and finally Thomas Hudson, waking and remembering how much he had drunk, said to Goats, "We've got to take the medicine."

Goats loved the sound of the word, which symbolized all this rich life he was sharing, and purred stronger than ever.

"Where is the medicine, Goats?" Thomas Hudson had asked. He turned on the reading light by the bed but it was dead. In the storm that had kept him ashore, wires had blown down or been shorted and not yet repaired and there was no electricity. He felt on the night table by the bed for the big double Seconal capsule, the last one that he had, that would put him to sleep again and let him wake in the morning without a hangover. He knocked it off the table as he reached in the darkness and he couldn't find it. He felt all over the floor carefully and he couldn't find it. He had no matches by the bed because he was not smoking and the flashlight battery had been overused by the servants while he was away and was dead.

"Goats," he had said. "We have to find the medicine."

He had got out of bed and Goats came down on the floor, too, and they hunted for the medicine. Goats went under the bed, not knowing what he was hunting, but doing all he could, and Thomas Hudson said to him, "The medicine, Goats. Find the medicine."

Goats made whimpery cries under the bed and ranged all of the area. Finally he came out, purring, and Thomas Hudson, feeling over the floor, touched the capsule. It was dusty and cobwebby under his fingers. Goats had found it.

"You found the medicine," he had told Goats. "You wonder cat." After he had washed off the capsule in the palm of his hand with some water from the carafe by the bed and then swallowed it with a drink of water he lay, feeling it take hold slowly, and praised Goats, and the big cat purred at the praise and always afterwards medicine was a magic word to him.

At sea he used to think about Goats as well as Boise. But there was nothing tragic about Goats. Although he had been through some truly bad times he was absolutely entire and, even when he had been beaten in some of his most terrible fights, he was never pitiful. Even when he had not been able to walk up to the house and lay under the mango tree below the terrace panting and soaked wet with sweat so you saw how big his shoulders were and how narrow and thin his flanks, lying there, too dead to move, trying to get the air into his lungs, he was never pitiful. He had the wide head of a lion and he was as unbeaten. Goats was fond of the man, and Thomas Hudson was fond of him and respected and loved him. But there was no question of Goats being in love with him or he in love with Goats as there had come to be with Boise.

Boise had simply become worse and worse. The night he and Goats had found Boise up in the *aguacate* tree, Boy had stayed out late and not come in when the man had gone to bed. He was sleeping in the big bed then in the bedroom at the far end of the house where there were big windows on all three sides of the room and the breeze blew through at night. When he woke he listened to the noises of the night birds and he was awake and listening when he heard Boise leap up onto the window ledge. Boise was a very silent cat. But he called to the man as soon as he was on the window ledge and Thomas Hudson went to the screen and opened it. Boise leaped in. He had two fruit rats in his mouth.

In the moonlight that came in through the window, throwing the shadow of the trunk of the *ceiba* tree across the wide, white bed, Boise had played with the fruit rats. Leaping and turning, batting them along the floor, and then carrying one away to crouch and rush the other, he had played as wildly as when he was a kitten. Then he had carried them into the bathroom and after that Thomas Hudson had felt his weight as he jumped up on the bed.

"So you weren't eating mangoes out of trees?" the man had asked him. Boise rubbed his head against him.

"So you were hunting and looking after the property? My old cat and Brother Boise. Aren't you going to eat them now you have them?"

Boise had only rubbed his head against the man and purred with his silent purr and then, because he was tired from the hunt, he had gone to sleep. But he had slept restlessly and in the morning he had shown no interest in the dead fruit rats at all.

Now it was getting daylight and Thomas Hudson, who had not been able to sleep, watched the light come and the gray trunks of the royal palms show in the gray of the first light. First he saw only the trunks and the outline of their tops. Then, as the light was stronger, he could see the tops of the palms blowing in the gale and then, as the sun began to come up behind the hills, the palm trunks were whitish gray and their blowing branches a bright green and the grass of the hills was brown from the winter drought and the limestone tops of the far hills made them look as though they were crested with snow.

He got up from the floor and put on moccasins and
an old mackinaw coat and, leaving Boise sleeping curled
up on the blanket, walked through the living room into
the dining room and out through it to the kitchen. The
kitchen was in the north end of one wing of the house
and the wind was wild outside, blowing the bare branches
of the *flamboyán* tree against the walls and the windows.
There was nothing to eat in the icebox and the screened-in
kitchen safe was empty of everything but condiments, a
can of American coffee, a tin of Lipton's tea, and a tin of
peanut oil for cooking. The Chinaman, who cooked,
bought each day's supply of food in the market. They were
not expecting Thomas Hudson back and the Chinaman
had undoubtedly gone to the market already to buy the
day's food for the servants. When one of the boys comes,
Thomas Hudson thought, I'll send him into town for
some fruit and eggs.

He boiled some water and made himself a pot of tea
and took it and a cup and saucer back to the living room.
The sun was up now and the room was bright and he sat
in the big chair and drank the hot tea and looked at the
pictures on the walls in the fresh, bright winter sunlight.
Maybe I ought to change some of them, he thought. The
best ones are in my bedroom and I'm never in my bedroom
any more.

From the big chair, the living room looked huge after
being on the boat. He did not know how long the room
was. He had known, when he had ordered the matting,
but he had forgotten. However long it was, it seemed
three times as long this morning. That was one of the
things about being fresh ashore; that and that there was
nothing in the icebox. The motion of the boat in the big
confused sea the northwester had built up, blowing a gale
across the heavy current, was all gone now. It was as far
away from him now as the sea itself was. He could see
the sea, looking through the open doors of the white
room and out of the windows across the tree clumped
hills cut by the highway, the farther bare hills that were
the old fortifications of the town, the harbor, and the
white of the town beyond. But the sea was only the blue

beyond the far white spread of the town. It was as distant now as all things that were past and he meant to keep it that way, now that the motion was gone, until it was time to go out onto it again.

The Krauts can have it for the next four days, he thought. I wonder if the fish hang close under them and play around them when they are submerged in weather like this. I wonder how far down the motion goes. There are fish in these waters at any depth that they submerge to. The fish are probably very interested. Some of the submarine bottoms must be pretty foul and the fish would certainly fool around them. They are probably not foul much though on the schedules they run. The fish would be around them anyway. He thought a moment of the sea and how it would really be offshore today with the hills of blue water with the white blowing from their crests and then he put it away from him.

The cat, asleep on the blanket, woke as the man reached over and stroked him. He yawned and stretched his front legs, then curled up again.

"I never had a girl that waked when I did," the man said. "And now I haven't even got a cat that does. Go on and sleep, Boy. It's a damned lie, anyway. I had a girl that woke when I did and even woke before I did. You never knew her, you've never known a woman that was any damn good. You had bad luck, Boise. The hell with it.

"You know what? We ought to have a good woman, Boy. We could both be in love with her. If you could support her you could have her. I've never seen one that could live on fruit rats very long, though."

The tea had dulled his hunger for a moment but now he was very hungry again. At sea he would have eaten a big breakfast an hour ago and probably had a mug of tea an hour before that. It had been too rough to cook on the run in and he had eaten a couple of corned beef sandwiches with thick slices of raw onion on them on the flying bridge. But he was very hungry now and he was irritated that there was nothing in the kitchen. I must buy some canned stuff and keep it here for coming in, he thought. But I'll have to get a cupboard with a lock to be sure they do not use it up and I hate to lock up food in a house.

Finally he poured himself a Scotch whisky and water and sat in the chair and read the accumulated daily papers and felt the drink soothe the hunger and ease the nervousness of being home. You can drink today if you want, he told himself. Once you've checked in. If it's this cold, there won't be many people at the Floridita. It will be good to be there again, though. He did not know whether to eat there or up at the Pacifico. It will be cold at the Pacifico, too, he thought. But I'll have a sweater and a coat and there is a table in the lee of the wall by the bar that will be out of the wind.

"I wish you liked to travel, Boy," he told the cat. "We could have a fine day in town."

Boise did not like to travel. He was terrified that it meant being taken to the vet's. He was still frightened of the veterinary surgeons. Goats would have made a good car cat, he thought. Probably would have been a hell of a boat cat, too, except for the spraying. I ought to let them all out. I wish I could have brought them some sort of a present. I'll get catnip in town if there is any and get Goats and Willy and Boy drunk tonight on it. There still should be some catnip in the shelf of drawers of the cat room if it hasn't gotten too dry and lost its force. It lost its force very quickly in the tropics and the catnip that you raised in the garden had no force at all. I wish we noncats had something that was as harmless as catnip that would have as much effect, he thought. Why don't we have something like that we can get drunk on?

The cats were very odd about catnip. Boise, Willy, Goats, Friendless's Brother, Littless, Furhouse, and Taskforce were all addicts. Princessa, which was the name the servants had given Baby, the blue Persian, would never touch catnip; neither would Uncle Woolfie, the gray Persian. With Uncle Woolfie, who was as stupid as he was beautiful, it could have been stupidity or insularity. Uncle Woolfie would never try anything new and would sniff cautiously at any new food until the other cats had taken it all and he was left with nothing. But Princessa, who was the grandmother of all the cats and was intelligent, delicate, high-principled, aristocratic, and most loving, was afraid of the odor of catnip and fled from it as though it were a vice. Princessa was such a delicate and aristocratic cat, smoke gray, with golden eyes and beautiful manners, and such a great dignity that her periods of being in heat were like an introduction to, and explanation and finally exposition of, all the scandals of royal houses. Since he had seen Princessa in heat, not the first tragic time, but after she was grown and beautiful, and so suddenly changed from all her dignity and poise into wantonness, Thomas Hudson knew that he did not want to die without having made love to a princess as lovely as Princessa.

She must be as grave and as delicate and as beautiful as Princessa before they were in love and made the love and then be as shameless and as wanton in their bed as Princessa was. He dreamed about this princess sometimes in the nights and nothing that could ever happen could be any better than the dreams were but he wanted it actually and truly and he was quite sure he would have it if there were any such princess.

The trouble was that the only princess that he had ever made love to outside of Italian princesses, who did not count, was quite a plain girl with thickish ankles and not very good legs. She had a lovely northern skin, though, and shining well-brushed hair and he liked her face and her eyes and he liked her and her hand felt good in his hand when they stood by the rail going through the Canal coming up onto the lights of Ismailia. They liked each other very much and they were already close to being in love; close enough so that she had to be careful about the tone of their voices when they were with other people; and close enough so that, now, when they were holding each other's hands in the dark against the rail he could feel what there was between them with no doubt about it at all. Feeling this and being sure, he had spoken to her about it and had asked her something since they made a great thing about being completely frank with each other about everything.

"I would like to very much," she said. "As you know. But I cannot. As you know."

"But there is some way," Thomas Hudson had said. "There's always some way."

"You mean in a lifeboat?" she said. "I wouldn't want it in a lifeboat."

"Look," he said and he put his hand on her breast and felt it rise, alive, against his fingers.

"That is nice," she interrupted. "There are two of them you know."

"I know."

"That's very nice," she said. "You know I love you, Hudson. I just found out today."

"How?"

"Oh I just found out. It wasn't terribly difficult. Didn't you find out anything?"

"I didn't have to find out anything," he lied.

"That's good," she said. "But the lifeboat is no good. Your cabin is no good. My cabin is no good."

"We could go to the Baron's cabin."

"There's someone always in the Baron's cabin. The wicked Baron. Isn't it nice to have a wicked Baron just as in olden times?"

"Yes," he said. "But I could make sure there would be no one there."

"No. That's no good. Just love me very hard now just the way you are. Feel that you love me all you can and do what you are doing."

He did and then he did something else.

"No," she said. "Don't do that. I couldn't stand that?"

She did something then and said, "Can you stand that?"

"Yes."

"Good. I'll hold there very good. No. Don't kiss me. If you kiss me here on deck then we might as well have done everything else."

"Why don't we do everything else?"

"Where, Hudson? Where? Tell me in this life about where?"

"I'll tell you about why."

"I know all about why. Where is the problem."

"I love you very much."

"Oh yes. I love you, too. And no good will come of it, except we love each other which is good."

He did something then and she said, "Please. If you do that I have to go."

"Let's sit down."

"No. Let's stand up just as we are here."

"Do you like what you are doing?"

"Yes. I love it. Do you mind?"

"No. But it doesn't go on forever."

"All right," she said and she turned her head and kissed him quickly and then looked out again across the desert they were sliding by in the night. It was winter and the night was cool and they stood close together looking straight out. "You can do it, then. A mink coat is good for something finally in the tropics. You won't before me?"

"No."

"You promise?"

"Yes."

"Oh Hudson. Please. Please now."

"You?"

"Oh yes. Any time with you. Now. Now. Oh yes. Now."

"Really now?"

"Oh yes. Believe me now."

Afterwards they stood there and the lights were much closer and the bank of the canal and the distance beyond was still sliding by.

"Now are you ashamed of me?" she asked.

"No. I love you very much."

"But it's bad for you and I was selfish."

"No. I don't think it is bad for me. And you're not selfish."

"Don't think it was a waste. It wasn't a waste. Truly not for me."

"Then it wasn't a waste. Kiss me, will you?"

"No. I can't. Just hold your hand against me tight."

Later she said, "You don't mind how fond I am of him?"

"No. He's very proud."

"Let me tell you a secret."

She told him a secret that did not come to him as a great surprise.

"Is that very wicked?"

"No," he said. "That's jolly."

"Oh Hudson," she said. "I love you very much. Please go and make yourself comfortable in every way and then come back to me here. Should we have a bottle of champagne at the Ritz?"

"That would be lovely. What about your husband?"

"He's still playing bridge. I can see him through the window. After he finishes he will look for us and join us."

So they had gone to the Ritz which was at the stern of the ship and had a bottle of Perrier-Jouet Brut 1915 and then another one and after a while the Prince had joined them. The Prince was very nice and Hudson liked him. They had been hunting in East Africa, as he had been, and he had met them at the Muthaiga Club and at Torr's in Nairobi and they had taken the same boat from Mombasa. The ship was a round-the-world cruise ship which made a stop at Mombasa en route for Suez, the Mediterranean, and eventually Southampton. It was a super luxury ship where all the cabins were private suites. It had been sold out for the world cruise as ships were in those years but some of the passengers had left the ship in India and one of those men who know about everything had told Thomas Hudson in the Muthaiga Club that the ship was coming in with several vacancies and that passage on her might be had quite reasonably. He had told the Prince and Princess, who had not enjoyed flying out to Kenya in those times when the Handley Pages were so slow and the flight so long and tiresome, and they had been delighted with the idea of the trip and the rates.

"We'll have such a jolly trip and you're a wonderful chap to have found out about it," the Prince had said. "I'll ring them up about it in the morning."

It had been a jolly trip, too, with the Indian Ocean blue and the ship coming out slowly from the new harbor and then Africa was behind them, and the old white town with the great trees and all the green behind it, then the sea breaking on the long reef as they passed and then the ship gained speed and was in the open ocean and flying fish were splitting out of the water and ahead of the ship. Africa dropped to a long blue line behind them and a steward was beating on a gong and he and the Prince and the Princess and the Baron, who was an old friend and lived out there and was really wicked, were having a dry martini in the bar.

"Pay no attention to that gong and we'll lunch in the Ritz," the Baron said. "Do you agree?"

He had not slept with the princess on the ship although by the time they had reached Haifa they had done so many other things that they had both reached a sort of ecstasy of desperation that was so intense that they should have been required by law to sleep with each other until they could not stand it another time simply for the relief of their nerves, if for no other reason. Instead, from Haifa they made a motor trip to Damascus. On the way up, Thomas Hudson sat in the front seat with the chauffeur and the two of them sat in back. Thomas Hudson saw a small part of the Holy Land and a small part of the T. E. Lawrence country and many cold hills and much desert on the way up, and on the way back they sat in the back and the Prince sat in front with the chauffeur. Thomas Hudson saw the back of the Prince's head and the back of the chauffeur's head on the return trip and he remembered now that the road from Damascus to Haifa, where the ship was anchored in the harbor, runs down a river. There is a steep gorge in the river but it is very small as it would be on a small-scale relief map and in the gorge there is an island. He remembered the island better than anything on the trip.

The trip to Damascus did not help much and when they had left Haifa and the ship was headed out across the Mediterranean and they were up on the boat deck, that was cold now with a northeast wind, that was making a sea that the ship was beginning to buck slowly, she said to him, "We have to do something."

"Do you like understatement?"

"No. I want to go to bed and stay in it for a week."

"A week doesn't sound very long."

"A month then. But we have to do it right away and right away we can't."

"We can go down to the Baron's cabin."

"No. I do not want to do it until we can do it really without worrying."

"How do you feel now?"

"As though I were going crazy and were already quite a way there . . ."

"In Paris we can make love in a bed."

"But how do I get away? I have no experience of how to get away."

"You go shopping."

"But I have to go shopping with someone."

"You can go shopping with someone. Have you no one you can trust?"

"Oh yes. But I so much did not want to ever have to do that."

"Don't do it then."

"No. I must. I know I must. But that does not make it better."

"Were you never unfaithful to him before?"

"No. And I thought I never would be. But now it is all that I want to do. But it hurts me that anyone should know."

"We'll figure out something."

"Please put your arm around me and hold me very close against you," she said. "Please let us not talk, nor think, nor worry. Please just hold your arm tight and love me very much because I ache now everywhere."

After a while he said to her, "Look, whenever you do this it is going to be as bad for you as now. You don't want to be unfaithful and you don't want anyone to know. But it will be like that whenever it happens."

"I want to do it. But I don't want to hurt him. I have to do it. It's not in my hands any more."

"Then do it. Now."

"But it's terribly dangerous now."

"Do you think there is anyone on this ship that sees us and hears us and knows us that thinks we have not slept together? Do you think the things we have done are any different from that?"

"Oh, of course they are different. There is all the difference. We couldn't have a baby from what we have done."

"You're wonderful," he had said. "You really are."

"But if we have a baby I'll be glad. He wants a baby very much and we never have one. I'll sleep with him right away and he'll never know it is ours."

"I wouldn't sleep with him *right* away."

"No I suppose not. But the next night."

"How long since you slept with him?"

"Oh I sleep with him every night. I have to, Hudson. I get so excited I have to. I think that's one reason he plays bridge until so late now. He'd like me to be asleep when he comes in. I think he is getting a little tired since we have been in love."

"Is this the first time you have ever been in love since you married him?"

"No. I am sorry. But it is not. I have been in love several times. But I have never been unfaithful to him or even considered it. He is so good and nice and such a good husband and I like him so much and he loves me and is always kind to me."

"I think we had better go down to the Ritz and have some champagne," Thomas Hudson had said. His feelings were becoming very mixed.

The Ritz was deserted and a waiter brought them the wine at one of the tables against the wall. They kept the Perrier-Jouet Brut (1915) on ice all of the time now and simply asked, "The same wine, Mr. Hudson?"

They raised their glasses to each other and the Princess said, "I love this wine. Don't you?"

"Very much."

"What are you thinking about?"

"You."

"Naturally. All I think about is you. But what about me?"

"I was thinking we should go down to my cabin now. We talk too much and fool around too much and do nothing. What time have you?"

"Ten after eleven."

"What time have you?" he called to the wine steward.

"Eleven-fifteen, sir." The steward looked at the clock inside the bar.

When the steward was out of earshot, he asked, "How late will he play bridge?"

"He said he would play late and for me not to stay awake for him."

"We'll finish the wine and go to the cabin. I have some there."

"But Hudson, it is very dangerous."

"It will always be dangerous," Thomas Hudson had said. "But not doing it is getting to be a damned sight more dangerous."

That night he made love to her three times and when he took her to her cabin, she had said that he shouldn't and he had said it would look much sounder if he did, the Prince was still playing bridge. Thomas Hudson had gone back to the Ritz, where the bar was still open, and ordered another bottle of the same wine and read the papers that had come aboard at Haifa. He realized that it was the first time he had had time to read the papers in a long time and he felt very relaxed and very happy to be reading the papers. When the bridge game broke up and the Prince came by and looked into the Ritz, Thomas Hudson asked him to have a glass of wine before he went to bed and he liked the Prince more than ever and felt a strong kinship with him.

He and the Baron had got off the ship at Marseilles. Most of the others were going on for the rest of the cruise, which finished at Southampton. In Marseilles he and the Baron were sitting at a sidewalk restaurant in the Vieux Port eating *moules marinés* and drinking a carafe of *vin rosé*. Thomas Hudson was very hungry and he remembered that he had been hungry most of the time ever since they had left Haifa.

He was damned hungry now, too, he thought. Where the hell were those servants? At least one should have shown up. It was blowing colder than ever outside. It reminded him of the cold day there on the steep street in Marseilles that ran down to the port, sitting at the café table with their coat collars up eating the *moules* out of the thin black shells you lifted from the hot, peppery milk broth with hot melted butter floating in it, drinking the wine from Tavel that tasted the way Provence looked, and watching the wind blow the skirts of the fisherwomen, the cruise passengers and the ill-dressed whores of the port as they climbed the steep cobbled street with the mistral lashing at them.

"You have been a very naughty boy," the Baron had said. "Very naughty indeed."

"Do you want some more *moules?*"

"No. I want something solid."

"Shouldn't we have a *bouillabaisse,* too?"

"Two soups?"

"I'm hungry. And we won't be here again for a long time."

"I should think you might be hungry. Good. We'll have a *bouillabaisse* and then a good *Châteaubriand* very rare. I'll build you up, you bastard."

"What are you going to do?"

"The question is what are you going to do. Do you love her?"

"No."

"That's much better. It is better for you to leave now. Much better."

"I promised to spend some time with them for the fishing."

"If it were the shooting it might be worthwhile," the Baron had said. "The fishing is very cold and very unpleasant and she has no business to make a fool of her husband."

"He must know about it."

"He does not. He knows she is in love with you. That is all. You are a gentleman so whatever you do is all right. But she has no business to make a fool of her husband. You wouldn't marry her, would you?"

"No."

"She couldn't marry you anyway and there is no need

that he should be made unhappy unless you are in love with her."

"I'm not. I know that now."

"Then I think you should get out."

"I'm quite sure that I should."

"I'm so glad that you agree. Now tell me truly, how is she?"

"She's very well."

"Don't be silly. I knew her mother. You should have known her mother."

"I'm sorry I didn't."

"You should be. I don't know how you got yourself mixed up with such good dull people. You don't need her for your painting or anything like that, do you?"

"No. That's not the way it's done. I like her very much. I still like her. But I'm not in love with her and it's getting very complicated."

"I'm so glad that you agree. Now where do you think that you will go?"

"We've just come from Africa."

"Exactly. Why don't you go to Cuba for a while or the Bahamas? I could join you if I get hold of any money at home."

"Do you think you will get any money at home?"

"No."

"I think I will stay in Paris for a while. I've been away from town for a long time."

"Paris isn't town. London is town."

"I'd like to see what's going on in Paris."

"I can tell you what's going on."

"No. I mean I want to see the pictures and some people and go to the Six-Day and Auteuil and Enghien and Le Tremblay. Why don't you stay?"

"I don't like racing and I can't afford to gamble."

And why go on with that? he thought now. The Baron was dead and the Krauts had Paris and the Princess did not have a baby. There would be no blood of his in any royal house, he thought, unless he had a nosebleed sometime in Buckingham Palace, which seemed extremely un-

likely. If one of those boys did not come in twenty minutes, he decided, he would go down into the village and
get some eggs and some bread. It is a hell of a thing to be
hungry in your own house, he thought. But I'm too
damned tired to go down there.

Just then he heard someone in the kitchen and he
pushed the buzzer that was set in the underside of the big
table and heard it burr twice in the kitchen.

The second houseboy came in with his faintly fairy, half
Saint Sebastian, sly, crafty, and long-suffering look and
said, "You rang?"

"What the hell do you think I did? Where is Mario?"

"He went for the mail."

"How are all the cats?"

"Very well. Without news. Big Goats fought with El
Gordo. But we treated the wounds."

"Boise looks thin."

"He goes out much at night."

"How is Princessa?"

"She was a little sad. But she eats well now."

"Did you have difficulty getting meat?"

"We got it from Cotorro."

"How are the dogs?"

"All of them are well. Negrita is with puppies again."

"Couldn't you keep her shut up?"

"We tried but she escaped."

"Has anything else happened?"

"Nothing. How was the voyage?"

"Without incident."

As he talked, irritated and short as always with this boy
who he had let go twice but had taken back each time
when his father had come and pled for him, Mario, the
first houseboy, came in carrying the papers and the mail.
He was smiling and his brown face was gay and kind and
loving.

"How was the voyage?"

"A little rough at the end."

"*Figúrate.* Imagine it. It's a big norther. Have you
eaten?"

"There's nothing to eat."

"I brought eggs and the milk and bread. *Tú*," he said to the second houseboy. "Go in and prepare the caballero's breakfast. How do you want the eggs?"

"As usual."

"Los huevos como siempre," Mario said. "Was Boise there to meet you?"

"Yes."

"He has suffered very much this time. More than ever."

"And the others?"

"Only one bad fight between Goats and Fats." He used the English names proudly. "The Princessa was a little sad. But it was nothing."

"¿Y tú?"

"Me?" He smiled shyly and very pleased. "Very well. Thank you very much."

"And the family?"

"All very well, thank you. Papa is working again."

"I am glad."

"He is, too. Did none of the other gentlemen sleep here?"

"No. They all went into town."

"They must be tired."

"They are."

"There were calls from various friends. I have them all written down. I hope you can recognize them. I can do nothing with the English names."

"Write them as they sound."

"But they do not sound the same to me as to you."

"Did the Colonel call?"

"No sir."

"Bring me a whisky with mineral water," Thomas Hudson said. "And bring milk for the cats, please."

"In the dining room or here?"

"The whisky here. The milk for the cats in the dining room."

"Instantly," Mario said. He went to the kitchen and came back with a whisky and mineral water. "I think it is strong enough," he said.

Should I shave now or wait until after breakfast? Thomas Hudson thought. I ought to shave. That's what

I ordered the whisky for, to get me through the shaving. All right, go in and shave then. The hell with it, he thought. No. Go in and do it. It's good for your damned morale and you have to go into town after breakfast.

Shaving, he sipped the drink halfway through lathering, after lathering, and during the process of relathering, and changing blades three times in getting the two-week stubble off his cheeks, chin, and throat. The cat walked around and watched him while he shaved and rubbed against his legs. Then suddenly he bounded out of the room and Thomas Hudson knew he had heard the milk bowls being put down on the tiled floor of the dining room. He had not heard the click himself nor had he heard any calling. But Boise had heard it.

Thomas Hudson finished shaving and poured his right hand full of the wonderful ninety-degree pure alcohol that was as cheap in Cuba as miserable rubbing alcohol in the States and doused it over his face, feeling its cold bite take away the soreness from the shaving.

I don't use sugar, nor smoke tobacco, he thought, but by God I get my pleasure out of what they distill in this country.

The lower parts of the bathroom windows were painted over because the stone paved patio ran all around the house, but the upper halves of the windows were of clear glass and he could see the branches of the palm trees whipping in the wind. She's blowing even heavier than I thought. There would almost be time to haul out. But you can't tell. It all depends on what she does when she goes into the northeast. It certainly had been fun not to think about the sea for the last few hours. Let's keep it up, he thought. Let's not think about the sea nor what is on it or under it, or anything connected with it. Let's not even make a list of what we will not think of about it. Let's not think of it at all. Let's just have the sea in being and leave it at that. And the other things, he thought. We won't think about them either.

"Where would the señor like to have breakfast?" Mario asked.

"Any place away from the *puta* sea."

"In the living room or in the señor's bedroom?"

"In the bedroom. Pull out the wicker chair and put the breakfast on a table by it."

He drank the hot tea and ate a fried egg and some toast with orange marmalade.

"Is there no fruit?"

"Only bananas."

"Bring some."

"Are they not bad with alcohol?"

"That is superstition."

"But while you were away a man died in the village from eating bananas when he was drinking rum."

"How do you know he wasn't just a banana-eating rummy who died from rum?"

"No, señor. This man died very suddenly from drinking a small amount of rum after eating a large quantity of bananas. They were his own bananas from his garden. He lived on the hill behind the village and worked for the route number seven of the buses."

"May he rest in peace," Thomas Hudson said. "Bring me a few bananas."

Mario brought the bananas, small, yellow, ripe, from the tree in the garden. They were hardly bigger, peeled, than a man's fingers and they were delicious. Thomas Hudson ate five of them.

"Observe me for symptoms," he said. "And bring the Princessa to eat the other egg."

"I gave her an egg to celebrate your return," the boy said. "I also gave an egg to Boise and to Willy."

"What about Goats?"

"The gardener said it was not good for Goats to eat much until his wounds are healed. His wounds were severe."

"What sort of a fight was it?"

"It was very serious. They fought for nearly a mile. We lost them in the thorn brush beyond the garden. They fought with no noise at all; the way they fight now. I don't know who won. Big Goats came in first and we took care of his wounds. He came to the patio and lay beside the cistern. He couldn't jump to the top of it. Fats came in an hour later and we cared for his wounds."

"Do you remember how loving they were when they were brothers?"

"Of course. But I am afraid now that Fats will kill Goats. He must weigh nearly a pound more."

"Goats is a great fighting cat."

"Yes, señor. But figure out for yourself what a full pound means."

"I don't think it can mean as much in cats as it does in fighting cocks. You think of everything in terms of fighting chickens. It doesn't mean much in men unless one man must weaken himself to make the weight. Jack Dempsey weighed only 185 pounds when he won the championship of the world. Willard weighed 230. Goats and Fats are both big cats."

"The way they fight, a pound is a terrible advantage," Mario said. "If they were being fought for money, no one would give away a pound. They would not give away ounces."

"Bring me some more bananas."

"Please, señor."

"You really believe that nonsense?"

"It's not nonsense, señor."

"Then bring me another whisky and mineral water."

"If you order me to."

"I ask you to."

"If you ask, it is an order."

"Then bring it."

The boy brought in the whisky with ice and cold, charged mineral water and Thomas Hudson took it and said, "Observe me for symptoms." But the worried look on the boy's dark face made him tire of the teasing and he said, "Truly, I know it will not make me sick."

"The señor knows what he is doing. But it was my duty to protest."

"That's all right. You've protested. Has Pedro come yet?"

"No, señor."

"When he comes tell him to have the Cadillac ready to go to town at once."

Now you take a bath, Thomas Hudson said to himself. Then you dress for Havana. Then you ride into town to see the Colonel. What the hell is wrong with you? Plenty is wrong with me, he thought. Plenty. The land of plenty. The sea of plenty. The air of plenty.

He sat in a wicker chair with his feet up on the extension that pulled out from under the seat and looked at the pictures on the wall of his bedroom. At the head of the bed, the cheap bed with the no-good mattress that had been bought as an economy because he never slept in it except in case of quarrels, there was Juan Gris's *Guitar Player. Nostalgia hecha hombre,* he thought in Spanish. People did not know that you died of it. Across the room, above the bookcase, was Paul Klee's *Monument in Arbeit.* He didn't love it as he loved the *Guitar Player* but he loved to look at it and he remembered how corrupt it had seemed when he first bought it in Berlin. The color was as indecent as the plates in his father's medical books that showed the different types of chancres and venereal ulcers, and how frightened of it his wife had been until she had learned to accept its corruption and only see it as a painting. He knew no more about it now than when he first saw it in Flechtheim's Gallery in the house by the river that wonderful cold fall in Berlin when they had been so happy. But it was a good picture and he liked to look at it.

Above the other bookcase was one of Masson's forests. This was Ville d'Avray and he loved it the way he loved the *Guitar Player.* That was the great thing about pictures; you could love them with no hopelessness at all. You could love them without sorrow and the good ones made you happy because they had done what you always tried to do. So it was done and it was all right, even if you failed to do it.

Boise came into the room and jumped up onto his lap. He jumped beautifully and could leap, without effort showing, to the top of the high chest of drawers in the big bedroom. Now, having leaped moderately and neatly, he settled down on Thomas Hudson's lap and made loving pushes with his forepaws.

"I'm looking at the pictures, Boy. You'd be better off if you liked pictures."

Who knows though but he may get as much from leaping and from night hunting as I get from the pictures, Thomas Hudson thought. It is a damned shame he can't see them though. You can't tell. He might have frightful taste in pictures.

"I wonder who you'd like, Boy. Probably the Dutch period when they painted such wonderful still lifes of fish and oysters and game. Hey, lay off me there. This is the day time. You're not supposed to do that sort of thing in the day time."

Boise continued with his lovemaking and Thomas Hudson pushed him onto his side to quiet him.

"You have to observe a few decencies, Boy," he said. "I haven't even gone out to see the other cats, to please you."

Boise was happy and Thomas Hudson felt the purr in his throat with his fingers.

"I have to bathe, Boy. You spend half your time doing that. But you do it with your own tongue. That's when you won't pay any attention to me. When you wash yourself you're just like a damned businessman at his office. That's business. That's not to be interrupted. Well, I have to bathe now. But instead I sit here drinking in the morning like a damned rummy. That's one of the differences between us. You couldn't steer eighteen hours either. I can, though. Twelve anytime. Eighteen when I have to. Nineteen yesterday and this morning. But I can't jump and I can't hunt at night like you. We do some pretty damn fancy hunting at night though. But you've got your radar in your whiskers. And a pigeon probably has his Huff Duff in that incrustation above his beak. Anyway, all homing pigeons have the incrustation. What sort of ultrahigh frequencies have you got, Boy?"

Boise lay there heavy and solid and long, purring silently and very happy.

"What does your search receiver say, Boy? What's your

pulse width? What's your pulse repetition frequency? I've got a magnetron built in. But don't tell anybody. But with the consequent higher resolution attained by the UHF, enemy whores can be detected at a greater distance. It's microwave, Boy, and you're purring it right now."

So that's how you kept your resolution not to think about it until we get going again. It wasn't the sea you wanted to forget. You know you love the sea and would not be anywhere else. Go on out to the porch and look at her. She is not cruel or callous nor any of that *Quatsch*. She is just there and the wind moves her and the current moves her and they fight on her surface but down below none of it matters. Be thankful that you are going out on her again and thank her for being your home. She is your home. Don't talk nor think nonsense about her. She is not your trouble. You're making a little more sense, he told himself. Although you don't make too damned much ashore. All right, he told himself. I have to make so much sense at sea that I don't want to make any ashore.

Ashore is a lovely place, he thought. Today we would see just how lovely it could be. After I see the goddamned Colonel, he thought. Well I always enjoy seeing him because it builds up my morale. Let's not go into the Colonel, he thought. That's one of those things we are going to skip while we have a lovely day. I will go to see him. But I won't go into him. Enough has gone into him already that will never get out. And enough has gone out of him that they will never get back in. So I thought you weren't going to go into him. I'm not. I'm just going in to see him and report.

He finished the drink, lifted the cat off his lap, stood up and looked at the three paintings, and then went in and took a shower. The water heater had only been on since the boys came in the morning and there was not much hot water. But he soaped himself clean, scrubbed his head, and finished off with cold water. He dressed in white flannel shirt, dark tie, flannel slacks, wool socks and his ten-year-old English brogues, a cashmere pullover sweater, and an old tweed jacket. He rang for Mario.

"Is Pedro here?"

"Yes, señor. He has the car outside."

"Make me a Tom Collins with coconut water and bitters to take. Put it in one of the cork holders."

"Yes, señor. Don't you want a coat?"

"I'll take a coat to wear back if it gets cold."

"Will you be back for lunch?"

"No. Nor for dinner."

"Do you want to see any of the cats before you go? They are all out in the lee of the wind in the sun."

"No. I will see them tonight. I want to bring them a present."

"I go to make the drink. It will take a moment for the coconut."

Now why in hell wouldn't you go to see the cats? he asked himself. I don't know, he answered. That one I did not understand at all. That was a new one.

Boise was following him, a little worried at this going away, but not panicky since there was no baggage and no packing. "Maybe I did it for you, Boy," Thomas Hudson said. "Don't you worry. I'll be back sometime tonight or in the morning. With my ashes dragged, I hope. Properly, I hope. Then maybe we will make a little better sense around here. *Vámonos a limpiar la escopeta.*"

He came out of the long, bright living room that still seemed enormous and down the stone steps into the even greater brightness of the Cuban winter morning. The dogs played around his legs and the sad pointer came up grovelling and wagging his lowered head.

"You poor miserable beast," he said to the pointer. He patted him and the dog fawned on him. The other mongrel dogs were gay and prancing in the excitement of the cold and the wind. There were some dead branches broken off the *ceiba* tree that grew out of the patio and they lay on the steps where they had fallen in the wind. The chauffeur came from behind the car, shivering exaggeratedly, and said, "Good morning, Mr. Hudson. How was the voyage?"

"Good enough. How are the cars?"

"All in perfect shape."

"I'll bet," Thomas Hudson said in English. Then to Mario, who came out of the house and down the steps to the car carrying the tall dark, rusty-colored drink, wrapped round with a sheet of moulded cork that came to within a half-inch of the rim of the glass, "Get a sweater for Pedro. One of those that buttons in front. From Mr. Tom's clothes. See that the steps are cleaned of this trash."

Thomas Hudson handed the drink to the chauffeur to hold and stooped to pet the dogs. Boise was sitting on the steps, watching them with contempt. There was Negrita, a small black bitch going gray with age, her tail curled over her back, her tiny feet and delicate legs almost sparkling as she played, her muzzle as sharp as a fox terrier and her eyes loving and intelligent.

He had seen her one night in a bar following some people out and asked what breed of dog she was.

"Cuban," the waiter said. "She's been here four days. She follows everyone out but they always shut the doors of their cars on her."

They had taken her home to the Finca and for two years she had not been in heat and Thomas Hudson had thought she was too old to breed. Then, one day, he had to break her loose from a police dog and after that she had police dog pups, pups from a pit bull, pointer pups, and a wonderful unknown pup that was bright red and looked as though his father might have been an Irish setter except that he had the chest and shoulders of a pit bull and a tail that curled up over his back like Negrita's.

Now her sons were all around her and she was pregnant again.

"Who did she breed with?" Thomas Hudson asked the chauffeur.

"I don't know."

Mario, who came out with the sweater and gave it to the chauffeur, who took off his frayed uniform coat to put it on, said, "The father is the fighting dog in the village."

"Well, goodbye, dogs," Thomas Hudson said. "So long, Boy," he said to the cat who came bounding down through the dogs to the car. Thomas Hudson, sitting in the car now, holding the cork-wrapped drink, leaned out of the window and touched the cat who rose on his hind legs to push his head against his fingers. "Don't worry, Boy. I'll be back."

"Poor Boise," Mario said. He picked him up and held him in his arms and the cat looked after the car as it turned, circling the flower bed, and went down the uneven gully-washed driveway until it was hidden by the hill slope and the tall mango trees. Then Mario took the cat into the house and put him down and the cat jumped up onto the window sill and continued to look out at where the driveway disappeared under the hill.

Mario stroked him but the cat did not relax.

"Poor Boise," the tall Negro boy said. "Poor, poor Boise."

In the car Thomas Hudson and the chauffeur went down the driveway and the chauffeur jumped out and unchained the gate and then climbed back in and drove the car through. A Negro boy was coming up the street and he called to him to close the gate and the boy grinned and nodded his head.

"He is a younger brother of Mario."

"I know," Thomas Hudson said.

They rolled through the squalor of the village side street and turned onto the central highway. They passed the houses of the village, the two grocery stores open onto the street with their bars and rows of bottles flanked by shelves of canned goods, and then were past the last bar and the huge Spanish laurel tree whose branches spread all the way across the road and were rolling downhill on the old stone highway. The highway ran downhill for three miles with big old trees on either side. There were nurseries, small farms, large farms with their decrepit Spanish colonial houses that were being cut up into subdivisions, their old hilly pastures being cut by streets that ended at grassy hillsides, the grass brown from the drought. The only green now on the land, in this country of so many greens, was along the watercourses where the royal palms grew tall and gray, their green tops slanted by the wind. This was a dry norther, dry, hard, and cold. The Straits of Florida had been chilled by the other northers that had come before it and there was no fog and no rain with this wind.

Thomas Hudson took a sip of the ice-cold drink that tasted of the fresh green lime juice mixed with the tasteless coconut water that was still so much more full-bodied than any charged water, strong with the real Gordon's gin that made it alive to his tongue and rewarding to swallow, and all of it tautened by the bitters that gave it color. It tastes as good as a drawing sail feels, he thought. It is a hell of a good drink.

The cork glass-holder kept the ice from melting and weakening the drink and he held it fondly in his hand and looked at the country as they drove into town.

"Why don't you coast down here and save gas?"

"I will if you say," the chauffeur answered. "But this is government gas."

"Coast for the practice," Thomas Hudson said. "Then you will know how to do it when it is our gas and not the government's."

They were down on the flat now where flower-growers' fields ran off the left and on the right were the houses of the basket-weavers.

"I must get a basket-weaver to come up and mend the big mat in the living room where it is worn."

"Sí, señor."

"Do you know one?"

"Sí, señor."

The chauffeur, whom Thomas Hudson disliked very much for his general misinformation and stupidity, his conceit, his lack of understanding of motors, and his atrocious care of the cars and general laziness, was being very short and formal because of the reprimand about coasting. With all his faults he was a splendid driver, that is, he was an excellent car handler with beautiful reflexes in the illogical and neurotic Cuban traffic. Also he knew too much about their operations to be fired.

"Are you warm enough with the sweater?"

"Sí, señor."

The hell with you, Thomas Hudson thought. You keep that up and I'll ream you out good.

"Was it very cold in your house last night?"

"It was terrible. It was *horroroso*. You can't imagine it, Mr. Hudson."

Peace had been made and they were now crossing the bridge, where the trunk of the girl who had once been cut into six pieces by her policeman lover and the pieces wrapped in brown paper and scattered along the Central Highway, had been found. The river was dry now. But on that evening it had been running with water and cars had been lined up for half a mile in the rain while their drivers stared at the historic spot.

The next morning the papers published photographs of the torso on their front pages and one news story pointed out that the girl was undoubtedly a North American tourist since no one of that age living in the tropics could be so undeveloped physically. How they had already arrived at her exact age Thomas Hudson never knew since the head was not discovered until some time later in the fishing port of Batabano. But the torso, as shown in the front pages, did fall rather short of the best fragments of Greek sculpture. She was not an American tourist, though; and it turned out that she had developed whatever attractions she had in the tropics. But for a while Thomas Hudson had to give up doing any road work in the country outside the Finca because anybody seen running or even hurrying, was in danger of being pursued by the populace crying, "There he goes! That's him! That's the man who chopped her up!"

Now they were over the bridge and going up the hill into Luyano where there was a view, off to the left, of El Cerro that always reminded Thomas Hudson of Toledo. Not El Greco's Toledo. But a part of Toledo itself seen from a side hill. They were coming up on it now as the car climbed the last of the hill and he saw it again clearly and it was Toledo all right, just for a moment, and then the hill dipped and Cuba was close on either side.

This was the part he did not like on the road into town. This was really the part he carried the drink for. I drink against poverty, dirt, four-hundred-year-old dust, the nose-snot of children, cracked palm fronds, roofs made from hammered tins, the shuffle of untreated syphilis, sewage in the old beds of brooks, lice on the bare necks of infested poultry, scale on the backs of old men's necks, the smell of old women, and the full-blast radio, he thought. It is a hell of a thing to do. I ought to look at it closely and do something about it. Instead you have your drink the way they carried smelling salts in the old days. No. Not quite that, he thought. Sort of a combination of that and the way they drank in Hogarth's *Gin Lane*. You're drinking against going in to see the Colonel, too, he thought. You're always drinking against something or for something now, he thought. The hell you are. Lots of times you are just drinking. You are going to do quite a lot of it today.

He took a long sip of the drink and felt it clean and cold and fresh-tasting in his mouth. This was the worst part of the road where the street car line ran and the traffic was bumper to bumper on the level crossing of the railroad when the gates were down. Ahead now beyond the lines of stalled cars and trucks was the hill with the castle of Atarés where they had shot Colonel Crittenden and the others when that expedition failed down at Bahía Honda forty years before he was born and where they had shot one hundred and twenty-two American volunteers against that hill. Beyond, the smoke blew straight across the sky from the tall chimneys of the Havana Electric Company and the highway ran on the old cobblestones under the viaduct, parallel to the upper end of the harbor where the water was as black and greasy as the pumpings from the bottoms of the tanks of an oil tanker. The gates came up and they moved again and now they were in the lee of the norther and the wooden-hulled ships of the pitiful and grotesque wartime merchant marine lay against the creosoted pilings of the wooden docks and the scum of the harbor lay along their sides blacker than the creosote of the pilings and foul as an uncleaned sewer.

He recognized various craft that he knew. One, an old barque, had been big enough for a sub to bother with and the sub had shelled her. She was loaded with timber and was coming in for a cargo of sugar. Thomas Hudson could still see where she had been hit, although she was repaired now, and he remembered the live Chinamen and the dead Chinamen on her deck when they had come alongside her at sea. I thought you weren't going to think about the sea today.

I have to look at it, he said to himself. Those that are on it are a damned sight better off than those that live in what we have just been riding through. This harbor that has been fouled for three or four hundred years isn't the sea anyway. And this harbor isn't bad out by the mouth. Nor even so bad over by the Casablanca side. You've known good nights in this harbor and you know it.

"Look at that," he said. The chauffeur, seeing him looking, started to stop the car. But he told him to go on. "Keep going to the Embassy," he said.

He had looked at the old couple that lived in the board and palm frond lean-to they had built against the wall that separated the railway track from a tract of ground where the electric company stored coal they unloaded from the harbor. The wall was black with coal dust from the coal that was hauled overhead on the unloader and it was less than four feet from the roadbed of the railway. The lean-to was built at a steep slant and there was barely room for two people to lie down in it. The couple who lived in it were sitting in the entrance cooking coffee in a tin can. They were Negroes, filthy, scaly with age and dirt, wearing clothing made from old sugar sacks, and they were very old. He could not see the dog.

"¿Y el perro?" he asked the chauffeur.

"Since a long time I haven't seen him."

They had passed these people now for several years. At one time the girl, whose letters he had read last night, had exclaimed about the shame of it each time they passed the lean-to.

"Why don't you do something about it, then?" he had asked her. "Why do you always say things are so terrible and write so well about how terrible they are and never do anything about it?"

This made the girl angry and she had stopped the car, gotten out, gone over to the lean-to and given the old woman twenty dollars and told her this was to help her find a better place to live and to buy something to eat.

"*Si, señorita,*" the old woman said. "You are very amiable."

The next time they came by the couple were living in the same place and they waved happily. They had bought a dog. It was a white dog too, small and curly, probably not bred originally, Thomas Hudson thought, for the coal dust trade.

"What do you think has become of the dog?" Thomas Hudson asked the chauffeur.

"It probably died. They have nothing to eat."

"We must get them another dog," Thomas Hudson said.

Past the lean-to, which was now well behind them, they passed on the left the mud colored plastered walls of the headquarters of the general staff of the Cuban army. A Cuban soldier with some white blood stood indolently but proudly in his khakis faded from his wife's washings, his campaign hat much neater than General Stillwell's, his Springfield at the most comfortable angle across the ill-covered bones of his shoulder. He looked at the car absently. Thomas Hudson could see he was cold in the norther. I suppose he could warm up by walking his post, Thomas Hudson thought. But if he stays in that exact position and does not waste any energy the sun should be on him soon and that will warm him. He must not have been in the army very long to be so thin, he thought. By spring, if we still come by here in the spring, I probably will not recognize him. That Springfield must be awfully heavy for him. It is a shame he cannot stand guard with a light plastic gun the way bullfighters now use a wooden sword in their work with the *muleta* so their wrists will not tire.

"What about the division that General Benítez was going to lead into battle in Europe?" he asked the chauffeur. "Has that division left yet?"

"*Todavía no,*" the chauffeur said. "Not yet. But the general is practicing learning to ride a motorcycle. He practices early in the morning along the Malecon."

"It must be a motorized division then," Thomas Hudson said. "What are those packages that the soldiers and officers are carrying as they come out of the Estado Mayor?"

"Rice," the chauffeur said. "There was a cargo of rice came in."

"Is it difficult to get now?"

"Impossible. It's in the clouds."

"Do you eat badly now?"

"Very badly."

"Why? You eat at the house. I pay for everything, no matter how far the price goes up."

"I mean when I eat at home."

"When do you eat at home?"

"Sundays."

"I'll have to buy you a dog," Thomas Hudson said.

"We have a dog," the chauffeur said. "A really beautiful and intelligent dog. He loves me more than anything in the world. I cannot move a foot that he does not want to come with me. But, Mr. Hudson, you cannot realize nor appreciate, you who have everything, what this war means in suffering to the people of Cuba."

"There must be much hunger."

"You cannot realize it."

No, I can't, Thomas Hudson thought. I can't realize it at all. I can't realize why there should ever be any hunger in this country ever. And you, you son of a bitch for the way you look after the motors of cars, you ought to be shot, not fed. I would shoot you with the greatest of pleasure. But he said, "I will see what I can do about getting you some rice for your house."

"Thank you very much. You cannot conceive of how hard life is now for us Cubans."

"It must be really bad," Thomas Hudson said. "It is a shame I cannot take you to sea for a rest and a vacation."

"It must be very difficult at sea, too."

"I believe it is," Thomas Hudson said. "Sometimes, even on a day such as today, I believe it is."

"We all have our crosses to bear."

"I would like to take my cross and stick it up the *culo* of a lot of people I know."

"It is necessary to take things with calm and patience, Mr. Hudson."

"Muchas gracias," said Thomas Hudson.

They had turned into San Isidro street below the main railway station and opposite the entrance to the old P. and O. docks where the ships from Miami and Key West used to dock and where the Pan American airways had its terminal when they were still flying the old clippers. It was abandoned now that the P. and O. boats had been taken over by the Navy and Pan American was flying DC-2's and DC-3's to the Rancho Boyeros airport and the Coast Guard and the Cuban navy had their sub chasers tied up where the clippers used to land.

Thomas Hudson remembered this part of Havana best from the old days. The part that he loved now had then been just the road to Matanzas; an ugly stretch of town, the castle of Atarés, a suburb whose name he did not know, and then a brick road with towns strung along it. You sped through them so that you did not remember one from another. Then he had known every bar and dive around this part of town and San Isidro had been the great whorehouse street of the waterfront. It was dead now, with not a house functioning on it, and had been dead ever since they closed it and shipped all the whores back to Europe. That great shipment had been the reverse of how Villefranche used to be when the American ships on the Mediterranean station would leave and all the girls would be waving. When the French ship left Havana with the girls aboard, all the waterfront was crowded and it was not only men that were saying goodbye, waving from the shore, the docks, and the sea wall of the harbor. There were girls in the chartered launches and the bumboats that circled the ship and ran alongside her as she went out the channel. It was very sad, he remembered, although many people thought it was very funny. Why whores should be funny he had never understood. The shipment was supposed to be very comic, though. But many people were sad after the ship had gone and San Isidro street had never recovered. The name still moved him, he thought, although it was a dull enough street

now and you hardly ever saw a white man or woman
on it except for truck drivers and delivery cart pushers.
There were gay streets in Havana where only Negroes
lived and there were some very tough streets and tough
quarters, such as Jesús y María, which was just a short
distance away. But this part of town was just as sad as it
had been ever since the whores had gone.

Now the car had come out onto the waterfront itself
where the ferry that ran across to Regla docked and
where the coastwise sailing ships tied up. The harbor was
brown and rough, but the sea that was running did not
make whitecaps. The water was too brown. But it was
fresh and clear brown-looking after the black foulness of
the inner parts of the bay. Looking across it, he saw the
calm of the bay that lay in the lee of the hills above
Casablanca where the fishing smacks were anchored, where
the gray gunboats of the Cuban navy lay, and where he
knew his own ship was anchored, although he could not
see her from here. Across the bay he saw the ancient
yellow church and the sprawl of the houses of Regla,
pink, green, and yellow houses, and the storage tanks
and the refinery chimneys of Belot and behind them
the gray hills toward Cojímar.

"Do you see the ship?" the chauffeur asked.

"Not from here."

Here they were to the windward of the smoking chimneys of the Electric Company and the morning was as
bright and clean and the air as clear and new-washed
as on the hills of the farm. Everyone moving about the
docks looked cold in the norther.

"Let's go to the Floridita first," Thomas Hudson said
to the chauffeur.

"We are only four blocks from the Embassy here."

"Yes. But I said I wished to go to the Floridita first."

"As you wish."

They rode straight up into town and were out of the
wind and, passing the warehouses and stores, Thomas
Hudson smelled the odor of stored flour in sacks and
flour dust, the smell of newly opened packing cases, the
smell of roasting coffee that was a stronger sensation

than a drink in the morning, and the lovely smell of the tobacco that came strongest just before the car turned to the right toward the Floridita. This was one of the streets he loved but he did not like to walk along it in daylight because the sidewalks were too narrow and there was too much traffic and at night when there was no traffic they were not roasting the coffee and the windows of the storehouses were closed so you could not smell the tobacco.

"It is closed," the chauffeur said. The iron shutters were still down on both sides of the café.

"I thought it would be. Go on down Obispo now to the Embassy."

This was the street he had walked down a thousand times in the daytime and in the night. He did not like to ride down it because it was over so quickly but he could not justify himself delaying in reporting any longer and he drank the last of his drink and looked at the cars ahead, the people on the sidewalk, and the crossing traffic on the north and south streets, and saved the street for later when he could walk it. The car stopped in front of the Embassy and Consulate building and he went in.

Inside you were supposed to fill out your name and address and the object of your visit at a table where a sad clerk with plucked eyebrows and a moustache across the extreme lower part of his upper lip looked up and pushed the paper toward him. He did not look at it and went into the elevator. The clerk shrugged his shoulders and smoothed his eyebrows. Perhaps he had emphasized them a little too much. Still they were cleaner and neater that way than wooly and bushy and they did go with his moustache. He had, he believed, the narrowest moustache it was possible to achieve and still have a moustache. Not even Errol Flynn had a narrower one, not even Pincho Gutiérrez, not even Jorge Negrete. Still that son of a bitch Hudson had no right to walk in like that and ignore him.

"What sort of *maricones* have you on the door now?" Thomas Hudson asked the elevator operator.

"That's not a *maricón*. That's nothing."

"How's everything here?"

"Good. Fine. The same as always."

He got off at the fourth floor and walked down the hall. He went in the middle door of the three and asked the Marine warrant officer at the desk if the Colonel was in.

"He flew down to Guantánamo this morning."

"When will he be back?"

"He said he might go to Haiti."

"Is there anything for me?"

"Nothing with me."

"Did he leave any message for me?"

"He said to tell you to stick around."

"How was he feeling?"

"Awful."

"How did he look?"

"Terrible."

"Was he plugged at me?"

"I don't think so. He just said to tell you to stick around."

"Is there anything I ought to know?"

"I don't know. Is there?"

"Cut it out."

"Okay. I suppose you had it pretty dusty. But you weren't working for him in this office. You get out to sea. I don't give a goddam—"

"Take it easy."

"Are you staying out in the country?"

"Yes. But I'm going to be in town today and tonight."

"He won't be back today or tonight. I'll call you out in the country when he comes in."

"You're sure he's not plugged at me?"

"I know he's not plugged at you. What's the matter? Have you got a bad conscience?"

"No. Is anybody else plugged at me?"

"As far as I know not even the Admiral is plugged at you. Go on out and get drunk for me."

"I'm going to get drunk for myself first."

"Get drunk for me, too."

"What's the matter? You're drunk every night, aren't you?"

"That's not enough. How did Henderson do?"

"All right. Why?"

"Nothing."

"Why?"

"Nothing. I just asked you. You have any complaints?"

"We don't make complaints."

"What a man. What a leader."

"We formulate charges."

"You can't. You're a civilian."

"Go to hell."

"I don't have to. I'm there now."

"You call me as soon as he gets in. And make my compliments to the Colonel and tell the Colonel I checked in."

"Yes sir."

"What's the sir for?"

"Politeness."

"Goodbye, Mr. Hollins."

"Goodbye, Mr. Hudson. Listen. Keep your people where you can find them in a hurry."

"Thank you very much, Mr. Hollins."

Down the hall a Lieutenant Commander that he knew came out of the code room. His face was brown from golf and from the beach at Jaimanitas. He looked healthy and his unhappiness did not show. He was young and a very good Far East man. Thomas Hudson had known him when he had had the motor car agency in Manila and a branch agency in Hong Kong. He spoke Tagalog and good Cantonese. Naturally he also spoke Spanish. So he was in Havana.

"Hi, Tommy," he said. "When did you get into town?"

"Last night."

"How were the roads?"

"Moderately dusty."

"You'll turn the goddamned car over some time."

"I'm a careful driver."

"You always were," the Lieutenant Commander, whose

name was Fred Archer, said. He put his arm around
Thomas Hudson's shoulders. "Let me feel of you."

"Why?"

"You cheer me up. It cheers me up when I feel of you."

"Have you been over to eat at the Pacífico?"

"Not for a couple of weeks. Should we go?"

"Anytime."

"I can't make lunch but we can eat there tonight. Do
you have anything for tonight?"

"No. Just afterwards."

"Me afterwards, too. Where shall I meet you? The
Floridita?"

"Come on up there when the shop shuts."

"Good. I have to come back here afterwards. So we
can't get too drunk."

"Don't tell me you bastards work nights now."

"I do," Archer said. "It isn't a popular move."

"I'm awfully glad to see you, Mr. Freddy," Thomas
Hudson said. "You make me feel cheerful, too."

"You don't have to feel cheerful," Fred Archer said.
"You've got it."

"You mean I've had it."

"You've had it. And you've rehad it. And you've rehad
it doubled."

"Not in spades."

"Spades won't be any use to you, brother. And you've
still got it."

"Write it out for me sometime, Freddy. I'd like to
be able to read it early in the mornings."

"You got a head in her yet?"

"No. Where the head was is about thirty-five thousand
dollars worth of junk I signed for."

"I know. I saw it in the safe. What you signed."

"They're goddamned careless then."

"You can say that again."

"Is everybody careless?"

"No. And things are a lot better. Really, Tommy."

"Good," said Thomas Hudson. "That's the thought for
today."

"Don't you want to come in? There's some new guys you'd like. Two really nice guys. One of them really beat up."

"No. Do they know anything about the business?"

"No. Of course not. They just know you're out there and they'd like to meet you. You'd like them. Nice guys."

"Let's meet them another time," Thomas Hudson said.

"Okay, chief," Archer said. "I'll come up to your place when the joint closes."

"The Floridita."

"That's what I meant."

"I'm getting stupid."

"It's just sheepherder's madness," Archer said. "Do you want me to bring any of these characters?"

"No. Not unless you want to very much. Some of my mob may be around."

"I should think you bastards wouldn't want to see each other ashore."

"Sometimes they get sort of lonesome."

"What they ought to do is net them all and lock them up."

"They'd get out."

"Go on," Archer said. "You're late at the place."

Fred Archer went in the door opposite the code room and Thomas Hudson walked down the hall and walked down the stairs instead of taking the elevator. Outside it was so bright the glare hurt his eyes and it was still blowing heavily from the north-northwest.

He got into the car and told the chauffeur to go up O'Reilly to the Floridita. Before the car circled the Plaza in front of the Embassy building and the Ayuntamiento and turned into O'Reilly he saw the size of the waves in the mouth of the harbor and the heavy rise and fall of the channel buoy. In the mouth of the harbor the sea was very wild and confused and clear green water was breaking over the rock at the base of the Morro, the tops of the seas blowing white in the sun.

It looks wonderful, he said to himself. It not only looks wonderful; it is wonderful. I'm going to have a drink on it. Christ, he thought, I wish I were as solid as Freddy

Archer thinks I am. Hell, I am as solid. I always go and I always want to go. What the hell more do they want? For you to eat Torpex for breakfast? Or stick it under your armpits like tobacco? That would be a hell of a good way to get jaundice, he thought. What do you suppose made you think of that? Are you getting spooky, Hudson? I am not, he said. I have certain unavoidable reactions. Many of them have not been classified. Especially not by me. I would just like to be as solid as Freddy thinks instead of being human. I think you have more fun as a human being even though it is much more painful. It is goddamned painful right about now. It would be nice to be like they think, though. All right now. Don't think about that either. If you don't think about it, it doesn't exist. The hell it doesn't. But that's the system I'm going on, he thought.

The Floridita was open now and he bought the two papers that were out, *Crisol* and *Alerta,* and took them to the bar with him. He took his seat on a tall bar stool at the extreme left of the bar. His back was against the wall toward the street and his left was covered by the wall behind the bar. He ordered a double frozen daiquiri with no sugar from Pedrico, who smiled his smile which was almost like the rictus on a dead man who has died from a suddenly broken back, and yet was a true and legitimate smile, and started to read *Crisol.* The fighting was in Italy now. He did not know the country where the Fifth Army was fighting but he knew the country on the other side where the Eighth Army was and he was thinking about it when Ignacio Natera Revello came into the bar and stood beside him.

Pedrico set out a bottle of Victoria Vat, a glass with large chunks of ice in it, and a bottle of Canada Dry soda in front of Ignacio Natera Revello and he made a highball hurriedly and then turned toward Thomas Hudson, looking at him through his green-tinted, hornrimmed glasses and feigning to have just seen him.

Ignacio Natera Revello was tall and thin, dressed in a white linen countryman's shirt, white trousers, black silk socks, well-shined, old brown English brogues, and he had a red face, a yellow, toothbrushy moustache and nearsighted, bloodshot eyes that the green glasses protected. His hair was sandy and brushed stiffly down. Seeing his eagerness for the highball, you might think it was his first of the day. It was not.

"Your ambassador is making an ass of himself," he said to Thomas Hudson.

"I'll be a sad son of a bitch," Thomas Hudson said.

"No. No. Be serious. Let me tell you. Now this is absolutely between you and me."

"Drink up. I don't want to hear about it."

"Well, you should hear about it. And you should do something about it."

"Aren't you cold?" Thomas Hudson asked him. "In that shirt and the light trousers?"

"I'm never cold."

You're never sober either, Thomas Hudson thought. You start to drink in that little bar by the house and by the time you come here for the first one of the day you're potted. You probably didn't even notice the weather when you dressed. Yes, he thought. And what about yourself? What time of day did you take your first drink this morning and how many have you had before this first one? Don't you cast the first stone at any rummies. It's not rummies, he thought. I don't mind him being a rummy. It is just that he is a damned bore. You don't have to pity bores and you do not have to be kind to them. Come on, he said. You're going to have fun today. Relax and enjoy it.

"I'll roll you for this one," he said.

"Very well," said Ignacio. "You roll."

He rolled three kings in one, stood on them, naturally, and won.

That was pleasant. It couldn't make the drink taste any better. But it was a pleasant feeling to roll three kings in one and he enjoyed winning from Ignacio Natera Revello because he was a snob and a bore and winning from him gave him some useful significance.

"Now we'll roll for this one," Ignacio Natera Revello said. He's the type of snob and bore, that you always think of by all his three names, Thomas Hudson thought, just as you think of him as a snob and a bore. It's probably like people who put III after their names. Thomas Hudson the third. Thomas Hudson the turd.

"You're not Ignacio Natera Revello the third are you by any chance?"

"Of course not. You know my father's name very well."

"That's right. Of course I do."

"You know both my brothers' names. You know my grandfather's name. Don't be silly."

"I'll try not to be," Thomas Hudson said. "I'll try quite hard."

"Do," Ignacio Natera Revello said. "It will be good for you."

Concentrating, working the leather cup in his best form, doing his hardest and best work of the morning, he rolled four jacks all day.

"My poor dear friend," Thomas Hudson said. He shook the dice in the heavy leather cup and loved the sound of them. "Such kind good dice. Such rich-feeling and laudable dice," he said.

"Go on and throw them and don't be silly."

Thomas Hudson rolled out three kings and a pair of tens on the slightly dampened bar.

"Want to bet?"

"We have a bet," Ignacio Natera Revello said. "The second round of drinks."

Thomas Hudson shook the dice lovingly again and rolled a queen and a jack.

"Want to bet now?"

"The odds are still greatly in your favor."

"OK. I'll just take the drinks then."

He rolled a king and an ace, feeling them come out of the shaker solidly and proudly.

"You lucky sod."

"Another double frozen daiquiri without sugar and whatever Ignacio wants," Thomas Hudson said. He was beginning to feel fond of Ignacio.

"Look, Ignacio," he said. "I never heard of anyone looking at the world through green-colored glasses. Rose colored, yes. Green colored, no. Doesn't it give everything a sort of grassy look? Don't you feel as though you were on the turf? Do you never feel as though you had been turned out to pasture?"

"This is the most restful tint for the eyes. It's been proven by the greatest optometrists."

"Do you run around much with the greatest optometrists? They must be a pretty wild bunch."

"I don't know any optometrists personally except my own. But he is familiar with the findings of the others. He is the best in New York."

"I want to know the best in London."

"I know the best optometrist in London. But the very best is in New York. I'll be glad to give you a card to him."

"Let's roll for this one."

"Very well. You roll back to me."

Thomas Hudson picked up the leather cup and felt the heavy confident weight of the big Floridita dice. He barely stirred them in order not to irritate their kindness and generosity and rolled out three kings, a ten, and a queen.

"Three kings in one. The *clásico*."

"You *are* a bastard," Ignacio Natera Revello said and rolled an ace, two queens, and two jacks.

"Another double frozen daiquiri absolutely without sugar and whatever Don Ignacio wishes," Thomas Hudson said to Pedrico. Pedrico made his smile and the drink. He set down the mixer before Thomas Hudson with at least another full daiquiri in the bottom of it.

"I could do that to you all day," Thomas Hudson said to Ignacio.

"The horrible thing is that I'm afraid you could."

"The dice love me."

"It's good something does."

Thomas Hudson felt the faint prickle go over his scalp that he had felt many times in the last month.

"How do you mean that, Ignacio?" he asked very politely.

"I mean that *I* certainly don't, with you taking all my money."

"Oh," said Thomas Hudson. "Here's to your good health."

"I hope you die," Ignacio Natera Revello said.

Thomas Hudson felt the prickle go over his scalp again. He reached his left hand against the bar where Ignacio Natera Revello could not see it and tapped softly three times with the ends of his fingers.

"That's nice of you," he said. "Do you want to roll for another round?"

"No," the other said. "I've lost quite enough money to you for one day."

"You haven't lost any money. Only drinks."

"I pay my bar bill here."

"Ignacio," Thomas Hudson said. "That's the third slightly edgy thing you've said."

"Well, I am edgy. If you'd had someone be as damned rude to you as your bloody ambassador was to me."

"I still don't want to hear about it."

"There you are. And you call me edgy. Look, Thomas. We're good friends. I've known you and your boy Tom for years. By the way how is he?"

"He's dead."

"I'm so sorry. I didn't know."

"That's all right," Thomas Hudson said. "I'll buy you a drink."

"I'm so very sorry. Please know how terribly sorry I am. How was he killed?"

"I don't know yet," Thomas Hudson said. "I'll let you know when I know."

"Where was it?"

"I don't know that. I know where he was flying but I don't know anything else."

"Did he get into London and see any of our friends?"

"Oh yes. He'd been in town several times and to White's each time and he'd seen whoever was around."

"Well, that's a comfort in a way."

"A what?"

"I mean it's nice to know he saw our friends."

"Certainly. I'm sure he had a good time. He always had an awfully good time."

"Should we drink to him?"

"Shit, no," Thomas Hudson said. He could feel it all coming up; everything he had not thought about; all the grief he had put away and walled out and never even thought of on the trip nor all this morning. "Let's not."

"I think it is the thing to do," Ignacio Natera Revello said. "I think it is eminently proper and the thing to do. But I must buy the drink."

"All right. We'll drink to him."

"What was his rank?"

"Flight lieutenant."

"He'd probably have been a wing commander by now or at least squadron leader."

"Let's skip his rank."

"Just as you wish," Ignacio Natera Revello said. "To my dear friend and your son Tom Hudson. *Dulce es morire pro patria.*"

"In the pig's asshole," Thomas Hudson said.

"What's the matter. Was my Latin faulty?"

"I wouldn't know, Ignacio."

"But your Latin was excellent. I know from people who were at school with you."

"My Latin is very beat up," Thomas Hudson said. "Along with my Greek, my English, my head, and my heart. All I know how to speak now is frozen daiquiri. *¿Tú hablas frozen daiquiri tú?*"

"I think we might show a little more respect to Tom."

"Tom was a pretty good joker."

"He certainly was. He had one of the finest and most delicate senses of humor I've ever known. And he was one of the best-looking boys and with the most beautiful manners. And a damned fine athlete. He was tops as an athlete."

"That's right. He threw the discus 142 feet. He played fullback on offense and left tackle on defense. He played a good game of tennis and he was a first-rate wing shot and a good fly fisherman."

"He was a splendid athlete and a fine sportsman. I think of him as one of the very finest."

"There's only one thing really wrong with him."

"What's that?"

"He's dead."

"Now don't be morbid, Tommy. You must think of Tom as he was. Of his gaiety and his radiance and his wonderful promise. There's no sense being morbid."

"None at all," Thomas Hudson said. "Let's not be morbid."

"I'm glad you agree. It's been splendid to have a chance to talk about him. It's been terrible to have the news. But I know you will bear up just as I will, even though it is a thousand times worse for you being his father. What was he flying?"

"Spitfires."

"Spitties. I shall think of him then in a Spitty."

"That's a lot of bother to go to."

"No, no it isn't. I've seen them in the cinema. I've several books on the RAF and we get the publications of the British Information Bureau. They have excellent stuff, you know. I know exactly how he would have looked. Probably wearing one of those Mae Wests and with his chute and his flying togs and his big boots. I can picture him exactly. Now I have to be getting home to lunch. Will you come with me? I know Lutecia would love to have you."

"No. I have to meet a man here. Thanks very much."

"Goodbye, old boy," Ignacio Natera Revello said. "I know you'll take this thing the way you should."

"You were kind to help me."

"No, I wasn't kind at all. I loved Tom. As you did. As we all did."

"Thanks for all the drinks."

"I'll get them back from you another day."

He went out. From beyond him, down the bar, one of the men from the boat moved up to Hudson. He was a dark boy, with short, clipped, curly black hair, and a left eye that had a slightly droopy lid; the eye was artificial but this did not show since the government had presented him with four different eyes, bloodshot, slightly bloodshot, almost clear, and clear. He was wearing slightly bloodshot, and he was already a little drunk.

"Hi, Tom. When did you get in town?"

"Yesterday," then speaking slowly and almost without moving his lips, "Take it easy. Don't be a fucking comedian."

"I'm not. I'm just getting drunk. They cut me open they find security written on my liver. I'm the security king. You know that. Listen, Tom, I was standing up next to the phony Englishman and I couldn't help but hear. Did your boy Tommy get killed?"

"Yeah."

"Oh shit," the boy said. "Oh shit."

"I don't want to talk about it."

"Of course not. But when did you hear?"

"Before the last trip."

"Oh shit."

"What are you doing today?"

"I'm going to eat over at the Basque Bar with a couple of characters and then we're all going to get laid."

"Where are you going to have lunch tomorrow?"

"At the Basque Bar."

"Ask Paco to call me up from lunch tomorrow, will you?"

"Sure. Out at the house?"

"Yes. At the house."

"Do you want to come around with us and get laid? We're going up to Henry's Sin House?"

"I might come around."

"Henry's hunting girls now. He's been hunting girls ever since breakfast. He's been laid a couple of times already. But he's trying to beat the two tomatoes we had. We got them at the Kursaal and they look pretty bad in the daylight. We couldn't find a goddam thing. This town's really gone to hell. He's got the two tomatoes up at the sin house just in case and he's out hunting girls with Honest Lil. They've got a car."

"Were they doing any good?"

"I don't think so. Henry wants that little girl. The little one he sees all the time at the Fronton. Honest Lil can't get her because she's afraid of him because he's so big. She said she could get her for me. But she can't get her for Henry because she's spooked of his size and his weight and things she's heard. But Henry doesn't want anything else now because the two tomatoes topped him off. So now it's this little girl and he's in love with her. Just like that. In love with her. He's probably forgotten about it now and is banging the tomatoes again right now. He's got to eat, though, and we're going to meet at the Basque Bar."

"Make him eat," Thomas Hudson said.

"You can't make him do anything. *You* can. But I can't. But I'll beg him to eat. I'll plead with him to eat. I'll set him an example by eating."

"Get Paco to make him eat."

"Wouldn't you think he would be hungry after that?"

"Wouldn't you?"

Just then the biggest man that Thomas Hudson knew, and the most cheerful and with the widest shoulders and the best manners came in through the door of the bar with a smile on his face, which was beading with sweat even on the cold day. His hand was out in greeting. He was so big he made everyone at the bar look stunted and he had a lovely smile. He was dressed in old blue trousers, a Cuban countryman's shirt, and rope-soled shoes. "Tom," he said. "You bastard. We've been in search of the lovelies."

His handsome face, as soon as he was out of the wind, sweated even more.

"Pedrico. I'll have one of those, too. The double size. Or larger if you make them. Imagine seeing you here, Tom. And I've forgotten. Here's Honest Lil. Come over here, my beauty."

Honest Lil had come in the other door. She looked her best when sitting at the far end of the bar when you saw only her lovely dark face and the grossness that had come over her body was hidden by the polished wood of the bar. Now, coming toward the bar from the door, there was no hiding her body, so she propelled it, swaying, to the bar as rapidly as she could without visibly hurrying and got up onto the stool Thomas Hudson had occupied.

This moved him one stool to the right and gave her the covered left flank.

"Hello, Tom," she said and kissed Thomas Hudson. "Henry is terrible."

"I'm not at all terrible, my beauty," Henry told her.

"You're terrible," she told him. "Every time I see you, you are more terrible. Thomas, you protect me from him."

"What's he being terrible about?"

"He wants a little tiny girl that he is crazy for and the little tiny girl can't go with him. But she wouldn't go anyway because she is frightened of him because he is so big and weighs two hundred and thirty pounds."

Henry Wood blushed, sweat visibly, and took a big sip of his drink.

"Two hundred and twenty-five," he said.

"What did I tell you?" the dark boy said. "Isn't that exactly what I told you?"

"Just what business is it of yours to be telling anyone anything?" Henry asked him.

"Two tramps. Two tomatoes. Two broken-down waterfront broads. Two cunts with but a single thought: the rent. We lay them. We trade cunts and re-lay them. It's strictly from wet decks. I say one friendly understanding word now and I am not a gentleman."

"They weren't really awfully good, were they?" Henry said, blushing again.

"Awfully good? We ought to have poured gasoline on them and set them on fire."

"How horrible," Honest Lil said.

"Listen, lady," the dark boy said. "I *am* horrible."

"Willie," Henry said. "Do you want the key to Sin House and go over and see if everything is all right?"

"I do not," the dark boy said. "I have a key to Sin House as you have evidently forgotten and I do not want to go over there and see if everything is all right. The only way everything is all right there is whenever you or I kick those cunts into the street."

"But suppose we can't get anything else?"

"We have got to get something else. Lillian, why don't you get off that stool and onto that telephone. Forget that little dwarf. Get that gnome out of your mind, Henry. You keep on with things like that and you'll be psycho. I know. I've been psycho."

"You're psycho now," Thomas Hudson told him.

"Maybe I am, Tom. You should know. But I don't fuck gnomes." (He pronounced the word *Guhnomays*.) "If Henry has to have a guhnomay that's his business. But I don't believe he has to have one any more than he has to have one-armed women or one-legged women. Let him forget the goddam guhnomay and get Lillian there onto the telephone."

"I'll take any good girls we can get," Henry said. "I hope you're not mixed up, Willie?"

"We don't want good girls," Willie said. "You start on that, right away you'll get psycho in a different way. Am I right, Tommy? Good girls is the most dangerous thing of all. Besides they will get you either on a contributing to delinquency or on a rape or attempted rape. Out with that good girls stuff. We want whores. Nice, clean, attractive, interesting, inexpensive whores. That can fuck. Lillian, what is keeping you away from that telephone?"

"One thing is that a man is using it and another is waiting by the cigar counter for him to finish," Honest Lil said. "You're a bad boy, Willie."

"I'm a horrible boy," Willie said. "I'm the worst goddam boy you'll ever know. But I'd like us to get better organized than we are now."

"We're going to have a drink or so," Henry said. "Then I'm sure Lillian will find someone that she knows. Won't you, my beauty?"

"Of course," Honest Lil said in Spanish. "Why couldn't I? But I want to telephone from a telephone in a booth. Not from here. It isn't proper to call from here and it isn't fitting."

"A delay," Willie said. "All right. I accept it. Just another delay. Let's drink then."

"What the hell have you been doing?" Thomas Hudson asked.

"Tommy, I love you," Willie said. "What the hell have you been doing yourself?"

"I had a few with Ignacio Natera Revello."

"That sounds like an Italian cruiser," Willie said. "Wasn't there an Italian cruiser named that?"

"I don't think so."

"It sounds like it, anyway."

"Let me see the tabs," Henry said. "How many were there, Tom?"

"Ignacio took them. I won them from him rolling."

"How many were there really?" Henry asked.

"I think four."

"What did you drink before that?"

"A Tom Collins coming in."

"And at home?"

"Plenty."

"You're just a damned rummy," Willie said. "Pedrico, three more double frozen daiquiris and whatever the lady wants."

"Un highbalito con agua mineral," Honest Lil said. "Tommy, come and sit with me at the other end of the bar. They don't like me to sit at this end of the bar."

"The hell with them," Willie said. "Great friends like us that never see each other and then we can't have a drink with you at this end of the bar. The hell with that."

"I'm sure you're all right here, beauty," Henry said. Then he saw two planter friends of his farther down the bar and went to speak to them without waiting for his drink.

"He's off now," Willie said. "He'll forget about the guhnomay now."

"He's very distrait," Honest Lil said. "He's awfully distrait."

"It's the life we lead," Willie said. "Just the ceaseless pursuit of pleasure for pleasure's sake. Goddammit, we ought to pursue pleasure seriously."

"Tom's not distrait," Honest Lil said. "Tom is sad."

"Cut out that shit," Willie said to her. "What are you pissed off about? First somebody is distrait. Then somebody is sad. Before that I'm horrible. So what? Where does a cunt like you get off criticizing people all the time? Don't you know you're supposed to be gay?"

Honest Lil began to cry, real tears, bigger and wetter than any in the movies. She could always cry real tears any time she wanted to or needed to or was hurt.

"That cunt cries bigger tears than mother used to make," Willie said.

"Willie, you shouldn't call me that."

"Cut it out, Willie," Thomas Hudson said.

"Willie, you are a cruel wicked boy and I hate you," Honest Lil said. "I don't know why men like Thomas Hudson and Henry go around with you. You are wicked and you talk vile."

"You're a lady," Willie said. "You shouldn't says things like that. Vile is a bad word. It's like spit on the end of your cigar."

Thomas Hudson put his hand on the boy's shoulder.

"Drink up, Willie. Nobody's feeling too good."

"Henry's feeling good. I could tell him what you told me and then he'd feel awful."

"You asked me."

"That isn't what I mean. Why don't you split your goddam grief? Why did you keep that by yourself the last two weeks?"

"Grief doesn't split."

"A grief hoarder," Willie said. "I never thought you'd be a goddamned grief hoarder."

"I don't need any of this, Willie," Thomas Hudson said to him. "Thank you very much, though. You don't have to work on me."

"OK. Hoard it. But it'll do you no damn good. I tell you I was brought up on the goddamned stuff."

"So was I," Thomas Hudson said. "No shit."

"Were you really? Then maybe your own system's best. You were getting to look pretty screwy, though."

"That's just from drinking and being tired and not relaxed yet."

"You hear from your woman?"

"Sure. Three letters."

"How's that going?"

"Couldn't be worse."

"Well," Willie said. "There we are. You might as well hoard it so as to have something."

"I've got something."

"Sure. Your cat Boise loves you. I know that. I've seen that. How is the screwy old bastard?"

"Just as screwy."

"He beats the shit out of me," Willie said. "He does."

"He certainly sweats things out."

"Doesn't he, though? If I suffered like that cat does I'd be nuts. What are you drinking, Thomas?"

"Another one of those."

Willie put his arm around Honest Lil's ample waist. "Listen, Lilly," he said. "You're a good girl. I didn't mean to get you sore. It was my fault. I was feeling emotional."

"You won't talk that way any more?"

"No. Not unless I get emotional."

"Here's yours," Thomas Hudson said to him. "Here's to you, you son of a bitch."

"Now you're talking," Willie said. "Now you've got the old pecker pointed north. We ought to have that cat Boise here. He'd be proud of you. See what I meant by sharing it?"

"Yes," Thomas Hudson said. "I see."

"All right," Willie said. "We'll drop it. Put out your can, here comes the garbage man. Look at that damn Henry. Get a load of him. What do you suppose makes him sweat like that on a cold day like today?"

"Girls," Honest Lil said. "He is obsessed with them."

"Obsessed," Willie said. "You bore a hole in his head anywhere you want with a half-inch bit and women would run out. Obsessed. Why don't you get a word that would fit it?"

"Obsessed is a strong word in Spanish anyway."

"Obsessed? Obsessed is nothing. If I get time this afternoon I'll think up the word."

"Tom, come down to the other end of the bar where we can talk and I can be comfortable. Will you buy me a sandwich? I've been out all morning with Henry."

"I'm going to the Basque Bar," Willie said. "Bring him over there, Lil."

"All right," Honest Lil said. "Or I'll send him."

She made her stately progress to the far end of the bar, speaking to many of the men she passed and smiling at others. Everyone treated her with respect. Nearly everyone she' spoke to had loved her at some time in the last twenty-five years. Thomas Hudson went down to the far end of the bar, taking his bar checks with him, as soon as Honest Lil had seated herself and smiled at him. She had a beautiful smile and wonderful dark eyes and lovely black hair. When it would begin to show white at the roots along the line of her forehead and along the line of her part, she would ask Thomas Hudson for money to have it fixed and when she came back from having it dyed it was as glossy and natural-looking and lovely as a young girl's hair. She had a skin that was as smooth as olive-colored ivory, if there were olive-covered ivory, with a slightly smoky roselike cast. Actually, the color always reminded Thomas Hudson of well-seasoned *mahagua* lumber when it is freshly cut, then simply sanded smooth and waxed lightly. Nowhere else had he ever seen that smoky almost greenish color. But the *mahagua* did not have the rose tint. The rose tint was just the color that she used but it was almost as smooth as a Chinese girl's. There was this lovely face looking down the bar at him, lovelier all the time as he came closer. Then he was beside her and there was the big body and the rose color was artificial now and there was no mystery about any of it, although it was still a lovely face.

"You look beautiful, Honest," he said to her.

"Oh, Tom, I am so big now. I am ashamed."

He put his hand on her great haunches and said, "You're a nice big."

"I'm ashamed to walk down the bar."

"You do it beautifully. Like a ship."

"How is our friend?"

"He's fine."

"When am I going to see him?"

"Any time. Now?"

"Oh no. Tom, what was Willie talking about? The part I couldn't understand?"

"He was just being crazy."

"No, he wasn't. It was about you and a sorrow. Was it about you and your señora."

"No. Fuck my señora."

"I wish you could. But you can't when she is away."

"Yeah. I found that out."

"What is the sorrow, then?"

"Nothing. Just a sorrow."

"Tell me about it. Please."

"There's nothing to tell."

"You can tell me, you know. Henry tells me about his sorrows and cries in the night. Willie tells me dreadful things. They are not sorrows, so much as terrible things. You can tell me. Everyone tells me. Only you don't tell me."

"Telling never did me any good. Telling is worse for me than not telling."

"Tom, Willie says such bad things. Doesn't he know it hurts me to hear such words? Doesn't he know I've never used those words and have never done a piglike thing nor a perverted thing?"

"That's why we call you Honest Lil."

"If I could be rich doing perverted things and be poor doing normal things, I would be poor."

"I know. What about the sandwich?"

"I'm not hungry just yet."

"Do you want another drink?"

"Yes. Please, Tom. Tell me. Willie said there was a cat in love with you. That isn't true, is it?"

"Yes. It's true."

"I think it's dreadful."

"No. It's not. I'm in love with the cat, too."

"That's terrible to say. Don't tease me, Tom, please. Willie teased me and made me cry."

"I love the cat," Thomas Hudson said.

"I don't want to hear about it. Tom, when will you take me out to the bar of the crazies?"

"One of these days."

"Do the crazies really come there just like ordinary people come here to meet and have drinks?"

"That's right. The only difference is they wear shirts and trousers made out of sugar sacks."

"Did you really play on the ball team of the crazies against the lepers?"

"Sure. I was the best knuckle-ball pitcher the crazies ever had."

"How did you get to know them?"

"I just stopped there one time on the way back from Rancho Boyeros and liked the place."

"Will you really take me out to the bar of the crazies?"

"Sure. If you won't be scared."

"I'll be scared. But I won't be too scared if I'm with you. That's why I want to go out there. To be scared."

"There's some wonderful crazies out there. You'll like them."

"My first husband was a crazy. But he was the difficult kind."

"Do you think Willie is crazy?"

"Oh no. He just has a difficult character."

"He's suffered very much."

"Who hasn't? Willie presumes on his suffering."

"I don't think so. I know about it. I promise you."

"Let's talk about something else, then. Do you see that man down there at the bar talking to Henry?"

"Yes."

"All he likes in bed are piglike things."

"Poor man."

"He's not poor. He's rich. But all he cares for is *porquerías*."

"Didn't you ever like *porquerías*?"

"Never. You can ask anyone. And I've never done anything with girls in my life."

"Honest Lil," Thomas Hudson said.

"Wouldn't you rather have me that way? You don't like *porquerías*. You like to make love and be happy and go to sleep. I know you."

"Todo el mundo me conoce."

"No, they don't. They have all sorts of different ideas about you. But I know you."

He was drinking another of the frozen daiquiris with no sugar in it and as he lifted it, heavy and the glass frost-rimmed, he looked at the clear part below the frappéd top and it reminded him of the sea. The frappéd part of the drink was like the wake of a ship and the clear part was the way the water looked when the bow cut it when you were in shallow water over marl bottom. That was almost the exact color.

"I wish they had a drink the color of sea water when you have a depth of eight hundred fathoms and there is a dead calm with the sun straight up and down and the sea full of plankton," he said.

"What?"

"Nothing. Let's drink this shallow water drink."

"Tom, what's the matter? Do you have some problem?"

"No."

"You're awfully sad and you're a little bit old today."

"It's the norther."

"But you always used to say a norther gave you pep and cheered you up. How many times have we made love because there was a norther?"

"Plenty."

"You always liked a norther and you bought me this coat to wear when we have them."

"It's a pretty coat, too."

"I could have sold it half a dozen times," Honest Lil said. "More people were crazy for this coat than you can imagine."

"This is a fine norther for it."

"Be happy, Tom. You always get happy when you drink. Drink that drink and have another one."

"If I drink it too fast it hurts across the front of my forehead."

"Well just drink slow and steady, then. I'm going to have another *highbalito*."

She made it herself from the bottle Serafin had left in front of her on the bar and Thomas Hudson looked at it and said, "That's a fresh water drink. That is the color of the water in the Firehole River before it joins the Gibbon to become the Madison. If you put a little more whisky in it you could make it the color of a stream that comes out of a cedar swamp to flow into the Bear River at a place called Wab-Me-Me."

"Wab-Me-Me is funny," she said. "What does it mean?"

"I don't know," he said. "It is an Indian place-name. I ought to know what it means but I've forgotten. It's Ojibway."

"Tell me about Indians," Honest Lil said. "I like to hear about the Indians even more than about the crazies."

"There are quite a few Indians down the coast. They are sea Indians and they fish and dry the fish and are charcoal burners."

"I don't want to hear about Cuban Indians. They're all *mulatos.*"

"No, they're not. Some are real Indians. But they may have captured them in the early days and brought them over from Yucatan."

"I don't like *yucatecos.*"

"I do. Very much."

"Tell me about Wabmimi. Is it in the Far West?"

"No, it's up north. In the part that's near Canada."

"I know Canada. I came into Montreal up the river once on a Princess ship. But it was raining and we could see nothing and we left that same evening for New York on the train."

"Did it rain all the time on the river?"

"All the time. And outside, before we came into the river there was fog and part of the time it snowed. You can have Canada. Tell me about Wabmimi."

"It was just a village where there was a sawmill on the river and the train ran through it. There were always great piles of sawdust beside the railroad tracks. They had booms across the river to hold the logs and they were almost solid across the river. The river was covered with logs a long way above the town. One time I had been fishing and I wanted to cross the river and I crawled across on the logs. One rolled with me and I went into the water.

When I came up it was all logs above me and I could not get through between them. It was dark under them and all I could feel with my hands was their bark. I could not spread two of them apart to get up to the air."

"What did you do?"

"I drowned."

"Oh," she said. "Don't say it. Tell me quick what you did?"

"I thought very hard and I knew I had to get through very quickly. I felt carefully around the bottom of a log until I came to where it was pushed against another log. Then I put my two hands together and pushed up and the logs spread apart just a little. Then I got my hands through and then my forearms and elbows through and then I spread the two logs apart with my elbows until I got my head up and I had an arm over each log. I loved each log very much and I lay there like that a long time between them. That water was brown from the logs in it. The water that's like your drink was in a little stream that flowed into that river."

"I don't think I could ever have come up between the logs."

"I didn't think I could for a long time."

"How long were you underwater?"

"I don't know. I know I rested a long time with my arms on the logs before I tried to do anything else."

"I like that story. But it will make me have bad dreams. Tell me something happy, Tom."

"All right," he said. "Let me think."

"No. Tell one right away without thinking."

"All right," Thomas Hudson said. "When young Tom was a little baby—"

"*¡Qué muchacho más guapo!*" Honest Lil interrupted. "*¿Qué noticias tienes de él?*"

"*Muy buenas.*"

"*Me alegro,*" said Honest Lil, tears coming into her eyes at the thought of young Tom the flyer. "*Siempre tengo su fotografía en uniforme con el sagrado corazón de Jesús arriba de la fotografía y al lado la virgen del Cobre.*"

"You have great faith in the Virgen del Cobre?"

"Absolutely blind faith."

"You must keep it."

"And she is looking after Tom day and night."

"Good," said Thomas Hudson. "Serafín, another of these big ones, please. Do you want the happy story?"

"Yes, please," Honest Lil said. "Please tell me the happy story. I feel sad again."

"Pues el happy story es muy sencillo," Thomas Hudson said. "The first time we ever took Tom to Europe, he was only three months old and it was a very old, small, and slow liner and the sea was rough most of the time. The ship smelled of bilge and oil and the grease on the brass of portholes and of the lavabos and the disinfectant they used that was in big pink cakes in the pissoirs—"

"Pues, this isn't a very happy story."

"Sí, mujer. You're wrong as hell. This is a happy story, *muy* happy. I go on. The ship also smelled of baths you had to take at regular hours or be looked down on by the bath steward and of the smell of hot salt water coming out of the brass nozzles of the bath fixtures and of the wet wooden grate on the floor and of the starched jacket of the bath steward. It also smelled of cheap English ship cooking which is a discouraging smell and of the dead butts of Woodbines, Players, and Gold Flakes in the smoking room and wherever they were dropped. It did not have one good smell, and as you know the English, both men and women, all have a peculiar odor, even to themselves, much as we have to Negroes, and so they have to bathe very often. An Englishman never smells sweet as a cow's breath does and a pipe-smoking Englishman does not conceal his odor. He only adds something to it. Their tweeds smell good and so does the leather of their boots and all their saddlery smells good. But there is no saddlery on a ship and the tweeds are impregnated with the dead pipe smell. The only way you could get a good smell on that ship was when your nose was deep in a tall glass of dry sparkling cider from Devon. This smelled wonderful and I kept my nose in it as much as I could afford. Maybe more."

"Pues, it is a little more happy now."

"Here is the happy part. Our cabin was so low, just above the water line, that the port had to be kept closed all the time and you saw the sea racing by and then you saw it solid green as the sea went past the porthole. We had built a barricade with trunks and suitcases roped together so that Tom could not fall out of the berth and when his mother and I would come down to see how he was, every time we ever came, if he was awake, he was laughing."

"Did he really laugh when he was three months old?"

"He laughed all the time. I never heard him cry when he was a baby."

"¡Qué muchacho más lindo más guapo!"

"Yes," Thomas Hudson said. "Very high-class muchacho. Want me to tell you another happy story about him?"

"Why did you leave his lovely mother?"

"A very strange combination of circumstances. Do you want another happy story?"

"Yes. But without so many smells in it."

"This frozen daiquiri, so well beaten as it is, looks like the sea where the wave falls away from the bow of a ship when she is doing thirty knots. How do you think frozen daiquiris would be if they were phosphorescent?"

"You could put phosphorus in them. But I don't think it would be healthy. Sometimes people in Cuba commit suicide by eating phosphorus from the heads of matches."

"And drinking *tinte rapido.* What is rapid ink?"

"It is a dye to make shoes black. But most often girls who have been crossed in love or when their fiancés have not kept their promises and done the things to them and then gone, away without marrying, commit suicide by pouring alcohol on themselves and setting themselves on fire. That is the classic way."

"I know," Thomas Hudson said. *"Auto da fé."*

"It's very certain," Honest Lil said. "They nearly always die. The burns are on the head first and usually all over the body. Rapid ink is more of a gesture. Iodine is *au fond* a gesture, too."

"What are you two ghouls talking about?" Serafín the barman asked.

"Suicides."

"Hay mucho," Serafín said "Especially among the poor. I don't remember a rich Cuban committing suicide. Do you?"

"Yes," Honest Lil said. "I know of several cases—good people, too."

"You would," Serafín said.

"Señor Tomás, do you want something to eat with those drinks? *¿Un poco de pescado? ¿Puerco frito?* Any cold meats?"

"Sí," Thomas Hudson said. "Whatever there is."

Serafín put a plate of bits of pork, fried brown and crisped, and a plate of red snapper fried in batter so that it wore a yellow crust over the pink-red skin and the white sweet fish inside. He was a tall boy, naturally rough spoken, and he walked roughly from the wooden shoes he wore against the wet and the spillage behind the bar.

"Do you want cold meats?"

"No. This is enough."

"Take anything they will give you, Tom," Honest Lil said. "You know this place."

The bar had a reputation for never buying a drink. But actually it gave an uncounted number of plates of hot free lunch each day; not only the fried fish and pork, but plates of little hot meat fritters and sandwiches of French-fried bread with toasted cheese and ham. The bartenders also mixed the daiquiris in a huge shaker and there was always at least a drink and a half left in the shaker after the drinks were poured.

"Are you less sad now?" Honest Lil asked.

"Yes."

"Tell me, Tom. What are you sad about?"

"El mundo entero."

"Who isn't sad about the whole world? It goes worse all the time. But you can't spend your time being sad about that."

"There isn't any law against it."

"There doesn't have to be a law against things for them to be wrong."

Ethical discussions with Honest Lil are not what I need, Thomas Hudson thought. What do you need, you bastard? You needed to get drunk which you are probably doing even though it does not seem so to you. There is no way for you to get what you need and you will never have what you want again. But there are various palliative measures you should take. Go ahead. Take one.

"Voy a tomar otro de estos grandes sin azúcar," he said to Serafín.

"En seguida, Don Tomás," Serafín said. "Are you going to try to beat the record?"

"No. I'm just drinking with calmness."

"You were drinking with calmness when you set the record," Serafín said. "With calmness and fortitude from morning until night. And you walked out on your own feet."

"The hell with the record."

"You've got a chance to break it," Serafín told him. "Drinking as you are now and eating a little as you go along, you have an excellent chance."

"Tom, try to break the record," Honest Lil said. "I'm here as a witness."

"He doesn't need any witness," Serafín said. "I'm the witness. When I go off I'll give the count to Constante. You're further along right now than you were the day you set the record."

"The hell with the record."

"You're in good form. You're drinking well and steady and they're not having any effect on you."

"Fuck the record."

"All right. *Como usted quiere.* I'm keeping count just in case you change your mind."

"He'll keep count all right," Honest Lil said. "He has the duplicate tickets."

"What do you want, woman? Do you want a real record or a phony record?"

"Neither. I want a *highbalito* with *agua mineral.*"

"Como siempre," Serafín said.

"I drink brandy, too."

"I don't want to be here when you drink brandy."

"Tom, did you know I fell down trying to get onto a streetcar and was nearly killed?"

"Poor Honest Lil," Serafín said. "A dangerous and adventurous life."

"Better than yours standing all day in wooden shoes behind a bar and serving rummies."

"That's my trade," Serafín said. "It's a privilege to serve such distinguished rummies as you."

Henry Wood came over. He stood, tall and sweating and newly excited by a change of plans. There was nothing that pleased him, Thomas Hudson thought, like a sudden change of plans.

"We're going over to Alfred's Sin House," he said. "Do you want to come, Tom?"

"Willie's waiting for you at the Bar Basque."

"I don't believe we really want Willie on this one."

"You ought to tell him, then."

"I'll call him up. Don't you want to come? This is going to be very good."

"You ought to eat something."

"I'll eat a good big dinner. How are you doing.?"

"I'm doing fine," Thomas Hudson said. "Really fine."

"Are you going to try for the record?"

"No."

"Will I see you tonight?"

"I don't think so."

"I'll come out and sleep at the house if you like."

"No. Have fun. But eat something."

"I'll eat an excellent dinner. Word of honor."

"Be sure and call Willie."

"I'll call Willie. You can be quite sure."

"Where's Alfred's Sin House?"

"It's an absolutely beautiful place. It overlooks the harbor and it's well furnished and really delightful."

"I mean what is the address."

"I don't know but I'll tell Willie."

"You don't think Willie will be hurt?"

"I can't help it if he is, Tom. I really can't ask Willie on this. You know how fond I am of Willie. But there are things I simply can't ask him on. You know that as well as I do."

"All right. But call him up."

"Word of honor I'll call him. And word of honor I'll eat a first-rate dinner."

He smiled, patted Honest Lil on the shoulder, and was gone. He moved very beautifully for such a big man.

"What about the girls at his place?" Thomas Hudson asked Honest Lil.

"They're gone by now," Honest Lil said. "There's nothing to eat there. And I don't think there is much to drink. Do you want to go around there or would you rather come to my place?"

"Your place," Thomas Hudson said. "But later on."

"Tell me another happy story."

"All right. What about?"

"Serafín," Lil said. "Give Tomás another double frozen without sugar. *Tengo todavía mi highbalito.*" Then to Thomas Hudson, "About the happiest time you remember. And not with smells."

"It has to have smells," Thomas Hudson said. He watched Henry Wood across the square getting into the sport car of the very rich sugar planter named Alfred. Henry Wood was too big for the car. He was too big for almost anything, he thought. But he knew three or four things he was not too big for. No, he said to himself. This is your day off. Take your day off.

"What do you want the story to be about?"

"What I asked you."

He watched Serafín pour the drink from the shaker into the tall glass and saw the top of it curl over the edge and onto the bar. Serafín pushed the base of the glass into the slit in a cardboard protector and Thomas Hudson lifted it, heavy and cold above the thin stem he held in his fingers, and took a long sip and held it in his mouth, cold against his tongue and teeth, before he swallowed it.

"All right," he said. "The happiest day I ever had was any day when I woke in the morning when I was a boy and I did not have to go to school or to work. In the morning I was always hungry when I woke and I could smell the dew in the grass and hear the wind in the high branches of the hemlock trees, if there was a wind, and if there was no wind I could hear the quietness of the forest and the calmness of the lake and I would listen for the first noises of morning. Sometimes the first noise would be a kingfisher flying over the water that was so calm it mirrored his reflection and he made a clattering cry as he flew. Sometimes it would be a squirrel chittering in one of the trees outside the house, his tail jerking each time he made a noise. Often it would be the plover calling on the hillside. But whenever I woke and heard the first morning noises and felt hungry and knew I would not have to go to school nor have to work, I was happier than I have ever been."

"Even than with women?"

"I've been very happy with women. Desperately happy. Unbearably happy. So happy that I could not believe it; that it was like being drunk or crazy. But never as happy as with my children when we were all happy together or the way I was early in the morning."

"But how could you be as happy by yourself as with someone?"

"This is all silly. You asked me to tell you whatever came in my mind."

"No, I didn't. I said to tell me a happy story about the happiest time you remember. That wasn't a story. You just woke up and were happy. Tell me a real story."

"What about?"

"Put some love in it."

"What kind of love? Sacred or profane?"

"No. Just good love with fun."

"I know a good story about that."

"Tell it to me then. Do you want another drink?"

"Not till I finish this one. All right. At this time I was in Hong Kong which is a very wonderful city where I was very happy and had a crazy life. There is a beautiful bay and on the mainland side of the bay is the city of Kowloon. Hong Kong itself is on a hilly island that is beautifully wooded and there are winding roads up to the top of the hills and houses built high up in the hills and the city is at the base of the hills facing Kowloon. You go back and forth by fast, modern ferryboats. This Kowloon is a fine city and you would like it very much. It is clean and well laid-out and the forest comes to the edge of the city and there is very fine wood pigeon shooting just outside of the compound of the Women's Prison. We used to shoot the pigeons, which were large and handsome with lovely purple shading feathers on their necks, and a strong swift way of flying, when they would come in to roost just at twilight in a huge laurel tree that grew just outside the white-washed wall of the prison compound. Sometimes I would take a high incomer, coming very fast with the wind behind him, directly overhead and the pigeon would fall inside the compound of the prison and you would hear the women shouting and squealing with delight as they fought over the bird and then squealing and shrieking as the Sikh guard drove them off and retrieved the bird which he then brought dutifully out to us through the sentry's gate of the prison.

"The mainland around Kowloon was called the New Territories and it was hilly and forested and there were many wood pigeons, and in the evening you could hear them calling to each other. There were often women and children digging the earth from the side of the roads and putting it into baskets. When they saw you with a shotgun, they ran and hid in the woods. I found out that they dug the earth because it had wolfram, the ore of tungsten, in it. This was very saleable then."

"Es un poco pesada esta historia."

"No, Honest Lil. It isn't really a dull story. Wait and see. Wolfram itself is *pesado*. But it is a very strange business. Where it exists it is the easiest thing there is to mine. You simply dig up the dirt and haul it away. Or you pick up the stones and carry them off. There are whole villages in Extremadura in Spain that are built of rock that has very high grade wolfram ore and the stone fences of the peasant's field are all made of this ore. Yet the peasants are very poor. At this time it was so valuable that we were using DC-2's, transport planes such as fly from here to

Miami, to fly it over from a field at Nam Yung in Free China to Kai Tak airport at Kowloon. From there it was shipped to the States. It was considered very scarce and of vital importance in our preparations for war since it was needed for hardening steel, yet anyone could go out and dig up as much of it in the hills of the New Territories as he or she could carry on a flat basket balanced on the head to the big shed where it was bought clandestinely. I found this out when I was hunting wood pigeons and I brought it to the attention of people purchasing wolfram in the interior. No one was very interested and I kept bringing it to the attention of people of higher rank until one day a very high officer who was not at all interested that wolfram was there free to be dug up in the New Territories said to me, 'But after all, old boy, the Nam Yung set-up *is* functioning you know.' But when we shot in the evenings outside the women's prison and would see an old Douglas twin-motor plane come in over the hills and slide down toward the airfield, and you knew it was loaded with sacked wolfram and had just flown over the Jap lines, it was strange to know that many of the women in the women's prison were there for having been caught digging wolfram illicitly."

"*Sí, es raro,*" Honest Lil said. "But when does the love come in?"

"Any time you want it," Thomas Hudson said. "But you'll like it better if you know the sort of place it happened in.

"There are many islands and bays around Hong Kong and the water is clear and beautiful. The New Territories was really a wooded and hilly peninsula that extended out from the mainland and the island Hong Kong was built on is in the great, blue, deep bay that runs from the South China Sea all the way up to Canton. In the winter the climate was much as it is today when there is a norther blowing, with rain and blustery weather and it was cool for sleeping.

"I would wake in the mornings and even if it were raining I would walk to the fish market. Their fish are almost the same as ours and the basic food fish is the red grouper.

But they had very fat and shining pompano and huge prawns, the biggest I have ever seen. The fish market was wonderful in the early morning when the fish were brought in shining and fresh caught and there were quite a few fish I did not know, but not many and there were also wild ducks for sale that had been trapped. You could see pintails, teal, widgeon, both males and females in winter plumage, and there were wild ducks that I had never seen with plumage as delicate and complicated as our wood ducks. I would look at them and their unbelievable plumage and their beautiful eyes and see the shining, fat, new-caught fish and the beautiful vegetables all manured in the truck gardens by human excrement, they called it 'night-soil' there, and the vegetables were as beautiful as snakes. I went to the market every morning, and every morning it was a delight.

"Then in the mornings there were always people being carried through the streets to be buried, with the mourners dressed in white and a band playing gay tunes. The tune they played oftenest for funeral processions that year was 'Happy Days Are Here Again.' During a day you were almost never out of sound of it, for people were dying in great numbers and there were said to be four hundred millionaires living on the Island besides whatever millionaires were living in Kowloon."

"¿Millonarios chinos?"

"Mostly Chinese millionaires. But millionaires of all sorts. I knew many millionaires myself and we used to have lunch together at the great Chinese restaurants. They had several restaurants that are as great as any in the world and the Cantonese cooking is superb. My best friends that year were ten millionaires, all of whom I knew only by their first two initials, H.M., M.Y., T.V., H.J., and so on. All important Chinese were known in this way. Also three Chinese generals, one of whom came from Whitechapel in London and was a truly splendid man, an inspector of police; about six pilots for the Chinese National Aviation Company, who were making fabulous money and earning all of it and more; a policeman; a partially insane Australian; a number of British officers and— But I will not bore you with the rest of them. I had more friends, close and intimate friends, in Hong Kong than I ever had before or since."

"*¿Cuándo viene el amor?*"

"I am trying to think what *amor* to put in first. All right. Here comes some *amor.*"

"Make it good because I'm already a little tired by China."

"You wouldn't have been. You would have been in love with it as I was."

"Why didn't you stay there, then?"

"You couldn't stay there because the Japs were going to come in and take it at any time."

"*Todo está jodido por la guerra.*"

"Yes," said Thomas Hudson. "I agree." He had never heard Honest Lil use such a strong word and he was surprised.

"*Me cansan con la guerra.*"

"Me, too," said Thomas Hudson. "I'm very tired of it. But I'm never tired of thinking about Hong Kong."

"Tell me about it then. It is *bastante interestante.* I just wanted to hear about love."

"Actually everything was so interesting that there was not much time for love."

"Who did you make love to first?"

"I made love to a very tall and beautiful Chinese girl who was very European and emancipated but would not go to the hotel to sleep with me because she said everybody would know about it and who would not let me sleep at her house because she said the servants would know about it. Her police dog already knew about it. He used to make it very difficult."

"So where did you make love?"

"The way you do when you are children; in any place I could persuade her to and especially in vehicles and conveyances."

"It must have been very bad for our friend, Mister X."

"It was."

"Was that all the love you made? Didn't you ever sleep a night together?"

"Never."

"Poor Tom. Was she worth all that trouble?"

"I don't know. I think so. I should have rented a house instead of staying on at the hotel."

"You should have rented a Sin House the way everyone does here."

"I don't like a Sin House."

"I know. But after all if you wanted the girl."

"The problem was solved another way. You're not bored?"

"No, Tom, please. Not now. How was the problem solved?"

"One night I had dinner with the girl and then we rode in a boat for a long time and that was wonderful but uncomfortable. She had skin that was wonderful to touch and all the preliminaries of making love made her very excited and her lips were thin but they were very heavy with love. Then we went from the boat to her house and the police dog was there and there was the problem of not waking anyone and finally I went to the hotel alone and I didn't feel good about any of it and I was tired of arguing and I knew she was right but I thought what the hell is the use of being so damned emancipated if you can't go to bed. I thought if we are going to be emancipated, let's free the sheets. Anyway I was feeling gloomy and *frustrado*—"

"I've never seen you *frustrado*. You must be funny *frustrado*."

"I'm not. I'm just mean and that night I felt mean and disgusted."

"Go on with the story."

"Well, I got my key at the desk very *frustrado* and the hell with everything. It was a very big and rich and richly gloomy hotel and I rode up in the elevator to what I knew was my big and rich and gloomy and lonely room and no beautiful tall Chinese girl in it. So I walked down the corridor and unlocked the massive door of my gigantic gloomy room and then I saw what was there."

"What was it?"

"Three absolutely beautiful Chinese girls, so beautiful they made my beautiful Chinese girl that I couldn't get to bed seem like a schoolteacher. They were so beautiful you couldn't stand it and none of them spoke any English."

"Where were they from?"

"One of my millionaires sent them. One of them had a note for me on very thick paper in a parchment envelope. All it said was, 'Love from C.W.' "

"What did you do?"

"I didn't know their own customs so I shook hands with them and I kissed each one of them and then I told them that I thought the best way for all to get acquainted was to all take a shower."

"How did you tell them?"

"In English."

"Did they understand?"

"I made them understand correctly."

"Then what did you do?"

"I was very embarrassed because I had never made love with three girls. Two girls is fun even though *you* do not like it. It's not twice as good as one girl but it is different, and it is fun anyway when you are drunk. But three girls is a lot of girls and I was embarrassed. So I asked them if they wanted a drink and they didn't. So I had a drink and we sat on the bed, which was fortunately, a very big bed, although they were all very small, and then I turned the lights out."

"Was it fun?"

"It was wonderful. It was wonderful to be in bed with a Chinese girl who was just as smooth as the girl I knew, and much smoother, and who was both shy and shameless and not emancipated at all, and then multiply that by three, and have it in the dark. I had never held three girls in my arms before. But you can do it. They had been trained and they knew many things I did not know and it was all in the dark and I did not want ever to go to sleep. But I did finally and when I woke in the morning they were all asleep and as beautiful as they had looked when I first came in the room. They were the most beautiful girls I ever saw."

"More beautiful than I was when you first knew me twenty-five years ago?"

"No, Lil. *No puede ser*. They were Chinese girls and you know how beautiful a Chinese girl can be. And I loved Chinese girls anyway."

"No es pervertido."

"No, it certainly isn't a perversion."

"But three."

"Three is several. And love was made to be made with one, I grant you."

"Anyway, I'm glad you had them. Don't think I'm jealous. You didn't seek it out and besides it was a present. I hate the police dog woman who wouldn't go to bed. But, Tom, didn't you feel hollow in the morning?"

"Of such hollowness you can't imagine. Really hollow. And I felt debauched from the top of my head to between my toes and my back was dead and the root of my spine ached."

"So you had a drink."

"So I had a drink and I felt a little better and very happy."

"So what did you do?"

"I looked at them all asleep and I wished I could take a picture of them. They would have made a wonderful picture asleep and I was so damned hungry and hollow feeling and I looked out through the curtains at the weather outside. It was raining. So I thought that was fine and we would stay in bed all day. But I had to have some breakfast and I had to figure out about breakfast for them. So I took a shower with the door shut and then dressed very quietly and went out, closing the door so it made no noise at all. Downstairs I had breakfast in the early morning dining room of the hotel and I had a big breakfast of kippers, rolls and marmalade, and some mushrooms and bacon. All very good. I drank a big pot of tea and had a double whisky and soda with breakfast and still felt hollow inside. I read the Hong Kong morning English paper and wondered how late they slept. Finally I went out to the front door of the hotel and looked outside and it was still raining hard. I went to the bar but it was not yet open. They had brought me my drink at breakfast from the service bar. Then I couldn't wait any longer and I went back up to the room and unlocked the door. They were all gone."

"How terrible."

"That's what I thought."

"So what did you do? You had a drink I suppose."

"Yes. I had a drink and then I went in and washed myself again very good with much soap and water and then I commenced to have double remorse."

"*¿Un doble remordimiento?*"

"No. Two remorses. Remorse because I had slept with three girls. And remorse because they were gone."

"I remember when you used to have remorse after you stayed with me. But you got over it."

"I know. I always get over everything. I was always a man of big remorses. But this morning in the hotel was gigantic double remorse."

"So you took another drink."

"How did you guess it? And I called up my millionaire. But he wasn't at his home. Nor in his office."

"He must have been in his Sin House."

"Undoubtedly. Where the girls had gone to join him and to tell him about the night."

"But where did they get three such beautiful girls? You couldn't get three really beautiful girls in all of Havana now. I know the trouble I had trying to get something even decent for Henry and Willie this morning. Though, naturally, it is a bad time of day."

"Oh, in Hong Kong the millionaires had scouts all through the country. All over China. It was just like the Brooklyn Dodgers' baseball team looking for ballplayers. As soon as a beautiful girl was located in any town or village their agents bought her and she was shipped in and trained and groomed and cared for."

"But how did they look so beautiful in the morning if they had coiffures *muy estilizado* such as Chinese women wear? The more *estilizado* the hairdress, the worse they would look in the morning after a night like that."

"They didn't have such coiffures. They wore their hair shoulder length the way American girls did that year and the way many still do. It was curled, too, very softly. That was the way C.W. liked them. He had been in America and, naturally, he had seen the cinema."

"Did you never have them again?"

"Only one at a time. C.W. would send me over one at a time as a present. But he never sent all three. They were new and naturally he wanted them for himself. And, too, he said he did not want to do anything that was bad for my morals."

"He sounds like a fine man. What happened to him?"

"I believe he was shot."

"Poor man. That was a nice story though and very delicate for a story like that. You seem more cheerful, too."

I guess I am, Thomas Hudson thought. Well, that is what I set out to be. Or was it?

"Look, Lil," he said. "Don't you think we've drunk maybe just about enough of these?"

"How do you feel?"

"Better."

"Make Tomás another double frozen without sugar. I'm getting a little drunk. I don't want anything."

I do feel better, Thomas Hudson thought. That is the funny part. You always feel better and you always get over your remorse. There's only one thing you don't get over and that is death.

"You ever been dead?" he said to Lil.

"Of course not."

"Yo tampoco."

"Why did you say that? You scare me when you talk like that."

"I don't mean to scare you, honey. I don't want to scare anybody ever."

"I like it when you call me honey."

This isn't getting anywhere, Thomas Hudson thought. Isn't there anything else you could do that would produce the same effect rather than sit with beat-up old Honest Lil in La Floridita at the old tarts' end of the bar and get drunk? If you only have four days couldn't you employ them better? Where?, he thought. At Alfred's Sin House? You're doing all right where you are. The drinking couldn't be any better, nor as good, anywhere in the world and you're down to the drinking now, kid, and you better get just as far in it as you can. That's what you've got now and you better like it and like it on all frequencies. You know you always liked it and you loved it and it's what you have now, so you better love it.

"I love it," he said out loud.

"What?"

"Drinking. Not just drinking. Drinking these double frozens without sugar. If you drank that many with sugar it would make you sick."

"Ya lo creo. And if anybody else drank that many without sugar they'd be dead."

"Maybe I'll be dead."

"No, you won't. You'll just break the record and then we'll go to my place and you'll go to sleep and the worst thing that will happen is if you snore."

"Did I snore last time?"

"Horrores. And you called me by about ten different names in the night."

"I'm sorry."

"No. I thought it was funny. I learned two or three things I didn't know. Don't your other girls ever get upset when you call them by so many different names?"

"I haven't any other girls. Just a wife."

"I try hard to like her and think well of her but it is very difficult. Naturally I never let anyone speak against her."

"I'll speak against her."

"No. Don't. That is vulgar. I hate two things. Men when they cry. I know they have to cry. But I don't like it. And I hate to hear them speak against their wives. Yet they nearly all do. So don't you do it, because we are having such a lovely time."

"Good. The hell with her. We won't speak about her."

"Please, Tom. You know I think she is very beautiful. She is. Really. *Pero no es mujer para ti.* But let us not speak against her."

"Right."

"Tell me another happy story. It doesn't even have to have love in it if it makes you happy to tell it."

"I don't think I know any happy stories."

"Don't be like that. You know thousands. Take another drink and tell me a happy story."

"Why don't you do some of the work?"

"What work?"

"The goddamned morale building."

"Tú tienes la moral muy baja."

"Sure. I'm well aware of it. But why don't you tell a few stories to build it up?"

"You have to do it yourself. You know that. I'll do anything else you want me to. You know that."

"OK," Thomas Hudson said. "You really want another happy story?"

"Please. There's your drink. One more happy story and one more drink and you'll feel good."

"You guarantee it?"

"No," she said and she began to cry again as she looked up at him, crying easily and naturally as water wells up in a spring. "Tom, why can't you tell me what's the matter? I'm afraid to ask now. Is that it?"

"That's it," Thomas Hudson said. Then she began to cry hard and he had to put his arm around her and try to comfort her with all of the people there at the bar. She was not crying beautifully now. She was crying straight and destructively.

"Oh my poor Tom," she said. "Oh my poor Tom."

"Pull yourself together, *mujer,* and drink a brandy. Now we are going to be cheerful."

"Oh, I don't want to be cheerful now. I'll never be cheerful again."

"Look," Thomas Hudson said. "You see how much good it does to tell people things?"

"I'll be cheerful," she said. "Just give me a minute. I'll go out to the ladies and I'll be all right."

You damned well better be, Thomas Hudson thought. Because I'm feeling really bad and if you don't quit crying, or if you talk about it, I'll pull the hell out of here. And if I pull the hell out of here where the hell else have I got to go? He was aware of the limitations, and no one's Sin House was the answer.

"Give me another double frozen daiquiri without sugar. *No sé lo que pasa con esta mujer.*"

"She cries like a sprinkling can," the barman said. "They ought to have her instead of the aqueduct."

"How's the aqueduct coming?" Thomas Hudson asked.

The man next to him on his left at the bar, a short, cheerful-faced man with a broken nose whose face he knew well but whose name and whose politics escaped him said, "Those *cabrones*. They can always get money for water since water is the one great necessity. Everything else is necessary. But water there is no substitute for and you cannot do without some water. So they can always get money to bring water. So there will never be a proper aqueduct."

"I'm not sure I follow you completely."

"*Sí, hombre.* They can always get money for an aqueduct because an aqueduct is absolutely necessary. Therefore they cannot afford an aqueduct. Would you kill the goose that lays the golden aqueduct?"

"Why not build the aqueduct and make some money out of it and find another *truco?*"

"There's no trick like water. You can always get money for the promise to produce water. No politician would destroy a *truco* like that by building an adequate aqueduct. Aspirant politicians occasionally shoot one another in the lowest levels of politics. But no politician would so strike at the true basis of political economy. Let me propose a toast to the Custom House, a lottery racket, the free numbers racket, the fixed price of sugar, and the eternal lack of an aqueduct."

"*Prosit,*" Thomas Hudson said.

"You're not German, are you?"

"No. American."

"Then let us drink to Roosevelt, Churchill, Batista, and the lack of an aqueduct."

"To Stalin."

"Certainly. To Stalin, Central Hershey, marijuana, and the lack of an aqueduct."

"To Adolphe Luque."

"To Adolph Luque, to Adolf Hitler, to Philadelphia, to

Gene Tunney, to Key West, and to the lack of an aqueduct."

Honest Lil came in to the bar from the ladies room while they were talking. She had repaired her face and she was not crying but you could see she had been hit.

"Do you know this gentleman?" Thomas Hudson said to her, introducing his new friend, or his old friend newly found.

"Only in bed," the gentleman said.

"Cállate," Honest Lil said. "He's a politician," she explained to Thomas Hudson. *"Muy hambriento en este momento."*

"Thirsty," the politician corrected. "And at your orders," he said to Thomas Hudson. "What will you have?"

"A double frozen daiquiri without sugar. Should we roll for them?"

"No. Let me buy them. I have unlimited credit here."

"He's a good man," Honest Lil said to Thomas Hudson in a whisper while the other was attracting the attention of the nearest barman. "A politician. But very honest and very cheerful."

The man put his arm around Lil. "You're thinner every day, *mi vida,"* he said. "We must belong to the same political party."

"To the aqueduct," Thomas Hudson said.

"My God, no. What are you trying to do? Take the bread out of our mouths and put water in?"

"Let's drink to when the *puta guerra* will finish," Lil said.

"Drink."

"To the black market," the man said. "To the cement shortage. To those who control the supply of black beans."

"Drink," Thomas Hudson said and added, "To rice."

"To rice," the politician said. "Drink."

"Do you feel better?" Honest Lil asked.

"Sure."

He looked at her and saw she was going to start to cry again.

"You cry again," he said, "and I'll break your jaw."

There was a lithographed poster behind the bar of a

politician in white suit and the slogan *"Un Alcalde Mejor,"* a better mayor. It was a big poster and the better mayor stared straight into the eyes of every drinker.

"To *Un Alcalde Peor,"* the politican said. "To A Worse Mayor."

"Will you run?" Thomas Hudson asked him.

"Absolutely."

"That's wonderful," Honest Lil said. "Let's draw up our platform."

"It isn't difficult," the candidate said. *"Un Alcalde Peor.* We've got a winning slogan. What do we need a platform for?"

"We ought to have a platform," Lil said. "Don't you think so, Tomás?"

"I think so. What about Down with the Rural Schools?"

"Down," said the candidate.

"Menos guaguas y peores," Honest Lil suggested.

"Good. Fewer and worse buses."

"Why not do away with transport entirely?" suggested the candidate. *"Es más sencillo."*

"Okay," Thomas Hudson said. *"Cero transporte."*

"Short and noble," the candidate said. "And it shows we are impartial. But we could elaborate it. What about *Cero transporte aéreo, terrestre, y marítimo?"*

"Wonderful. We're getting a real platform. How do we stand on leprosy?"

"Por una lepra más grande para Cuba," said the candidate.

"Por el cáncer cubano," Thomas Hudson said.

"Por una tuberculosis ampliada, adecuada, y permanente para Cuba y los cubanos," said the candidate. "That's a little bit long but it will sound good on the radio. Where do we stand on syphilis, my coreligionists?"

"Por una sífilis criolla cien por cien."

"Good," said the candidate. "Down with *Penicilina* and other tricks of *Yanqui* Imperialism."

"Down," said Thomas Hudson.

"It seems to me as though we ought to drink something," Honest Lil said. "How does it seem to you, *correligionarios?"*

"A magnificent idea," said the candidate. "Who but you could have had an idea like that?"

"You," Honest Lil said.

"Attack my credit," the candidate said. "Let's see how my credit stands up under really heavy fire. Bar-chap, bar-fellow, boy: the same all around. And for this political associate of mine: without sugar."

"That's an idea for a slogan," Honest Lil said. "Cuba's Sugar for Cubans."

"Down with the Colossus of the North," Thomas Hudson said.

"Down," repeated the others.

"We need more domestic slogans, more municipal slogans. We shouldn't get too much into the international field while we are fighting a war and are still allies."

"Still I think we ought to Down the Colossus of the North," Thomas Hudson said. "It's really an ideal time while the Colossus is fighting a global war. I think we ought to down him."

"We'll down him after I'm elected."

"To *Un Alcalde Peor*," Thomas Hudson said.

"To All of Us. To the party," the Alcalde Peor said. He raised his glass.

"We must remember the circumstances of the founding of the party and write out the manifesto. What's the date anyway?"

"The twentieth. More or less."

"The twentieth of what?"

"The twentieth more or less of February. *El grito de La Floridita.*"

"It's a solemn moment," Thomas Hudson said. "Can you write, Honest Lil? Can you perpetuate all this?"

"I can write. But I can't write right now."

"There are a few more problems we have to take a stand on," the Alcalde Peor said. "Listen, Colossus of the North, why don't you buy this round? You've seen how valiant my credit is and how he stands up to the attack. But there's no need to kill the poor bird when we know he's losing. Come on, Colossus."

"Don't call me Colossus. We're against the damn Colossus."

"All right, governor. What do you do, anyway?"

"I'm a scientist."

"Sobre todo en la cama," Honest Lil said. "He made extensive studies in China."

"Well, whatever you are, buy this one," the Alcalde Peor said. "And let's get on with the platform."

"What about the Home?"

"A sacred subject. The Home enjoys equal dignity with religion. We must be careful and subtle. What about this: *Abajo los padres de familias?"*

"It has dignity. But why not just: Down with the Home?"

"Abajo el Home. It's a beautiful sentiment but many might confuse it with *béisbol."*

"What about Little Children?"

"Suffer them to come unto me once they are of electoral age," said the Alcalde Peor.

"What about divorce?" Thomas Hudson asked.

"Another touchy problem," the Alcalde Peor said. *"Bastante espinoso.* How do you feel about divorce?"

"Perhaps we shouldn't take up divorce. It conflicts with our campaign in favor of the Home."

"All right, let's drop it. Now let me see——"

"You can't," Honest Lil said. "You're cockeyed."

"Don't criticize me, woman," the Alcalde Peor told her. "One thing we must do."

"What?"

"Orinar."

"I agree," Thomas Hudson heard himself saying. "It is basic."

"As basic as the lack of the aqueduct. It is founded on water."

"It's founded on alcohol."

"Only a small percentage in comparison with the water. Water is the basic thing. You are a scientist. What percentage of water are we composed of?"

"Eighty-seven and three-tenths," said Thomas Hudson, taking a chance and knowing he was wrong.

"Exactly," said the Alcalde Peor. "Should we go while we can still move?"

In the men's room a calm and noble Negro was reading a Rosicrucian pamphlet. He was working on the weekly lesson of the course he was taking. Thomas Hudson greeted him with dignity and his greeting was returned in kind.

"Quite a chilly day, sir," the attendant with the religious literature observed.

"It is indeed chilly," Thomas Hudson said. "How are your studies progressing?"

"Very well, sir. As well as can be expected."

"I'm delighted," Thomas Hudson said. Then to the Alcalde Peor, who was having certain difficulties, "I belonged to a club in London once where half the members were trying to urinate and the other half were trying to stop."

"Very good," said the Alcalde Peor, completing his chore, "What did they call it, *El Club Mundial?*"

"No. As a matter of fact, I've forgotten the name of it."

"You've forgotten the name of your club?"

"Yes. Why not?"

"I think we better go get another one. How much does this urination cost?"

"Whatever you wish, sir."

"Let me get them," Thomas Hudson said. "I love to buy them. It's like flowers."

"Could it have been the Royal Automobile Club?" the Negro asked, standing proffering a towel.

"It could not have been."

"I'm sorry, sir," the student of Rusicrucian said. "I know that's one of the biggest clubs in London."

"That's right," Thomas Hudson said. "One of the biggest. Now buy yourself something very handsome with this." He gave him a dollar.

"Why did you give him a peso?" the Alcalde Peor asked him as they were outside the door and back to the noise of the bar, the restaurant, and the traffic on the street outside.

"I have no real use for it."

"Hombre," the Alcalde Peor said. "Are you feeling all right? Do you feel OK?"

"Quite," said Thomas Hudson. "I'm quite OK, thank you very much."

"How was the trip?" Honest Lil asked from her stool at the bar. Thomas Hudson looked at her and saw her again for the first time. She looked considerably darker and much wider.

"It was a nice trip," he said. "You always meet interesting people when you travel."

Honest Lil put her hand on his thigh and squeezed it and he was looking down the bar, away from Honest Lil, past the Panama hats, the Cuban faces, and the moving dice cups of the drinkers and out the open door into the bright light of the square, when he saw the car pull up and the doorman opened the rear door, his cap in his hand, and she got out.

It was her. No one else got out of a car that way, practically and easily and beautifully and at the same time as though she were doing the street a great favor when she stepped on it. Everyone had tried to look like her for many years and some came quite close. But when you saw her, all the people that looked like her were only imitations. She was in uniform now and she smiled at the doorman and asked him a question and he answered happily and nodded his head and she started across the sidewalk and into the bar. There was another woman in uniform behind her.

Thomas Hudson stood up and he felt as though his chest was being constricted so that he could not breathe. She had seen him and she was walking down the gap between the people at the bar and the tables toward him. The other woman was following behind her.

"Excuse me," he said to Honest Lil and to the Alcalde Peor. "I have to see a friend."

They met halfway down the free corridor between the bar and the tables and he was holding her in his arms. They were both holding hard and tight as people can hold and he was kissing her hard and well and she was kissing him and feeling both his arms with her hands.

"Oh you. You. You," she said.

"You devil," he said. "How did you get here?"

"From Camagüey, of course."

People were looking at them and he picked her off her feet and held her tight against him and kissed her once more then put her down and took her hand and started for a table in the corner.

"We can't do that here," he said. "We'll get arrested."

"Let's get arrested," she said. "This is Ginny. She's my secretary."

"Hi, Ginny," Thomas Hudson said. "Let's get this mad woman behind that table."

Ginny was a nice, ugly girl. They were both wearing the same uniform; officers' blouses without insignia, shirts and ties, skirts, stockings, and brogues. They had overseas caps and a patch on their left shoulders he had not seen before.

"Take your cap off, devil."

"I'm not supposed to."

"Take it off."

"All right."

She took it off and lifted her face and shook her hair loose and moved her head back and looked at him and he saw the high forehead, the magic rolling line of the hair that was the same silvery ripe-wheat color as always, the high cheekbones with the hollows just below them, the hollows that could always break your heart, the slightly flattened nose, and the mouth he had just left that was disarranged by the kissing, and the lovely chin and throat line.

"How do I look?"

"You know."

"Did you ever kiss anybody in these clothes before? Or scratch yourself on army buttons?"

"No."

"Do you love me?"

"I always love you."

"No. Do you love me right now. This minute."

"Yes," he said and his throat ached.

"That's good," she said. "It would be pretty awful for you if you didn't."

"How long are you here for?"

"Just today."

"Let me kiss you."

"You said we'd be arrested."

"We can wait. What do you want to drink?"

"Do they have good champagne?"

"Yes. But there's an awfully good local drink."

"There must be. About how many of them have you had?"

"I don't know. About a dozen."

"You only look tight around the eyes. Are you in love with anyone?"

"No. You?"

"We'll have to see. Where is your bitch of a wife?"

"In the Pacific."

"I wish she was. About a thousand fathoms deep. Oh, Tommy, Tommy, Tommy, Tommy, Tommy."

"Are you in love with anyone?"

"I'm afraid so."

"You bastard."

"Isn't it terrible? The first time I ever meet you since I went away and you're not in love with anyone and I'm in love with someone."

"You went away?"

"That's my story."

"Is he nice?"

"He's nice, this one, like children are nice. I'm very necessary to him."

"Where is he?"

"That's a military secret."

"Is that where you're going?"

"Yes."

"What are you?"

"We're USO."

"Is that the same as OSS?"

"No, goofy. Don't pretend to be stupid and don't be

stuffy just because I love someone. You never consult me when you fall in love with people."

"How much do you love him?"

"I didn't say I loved him. I said I was in love with him. I won't even be in love with him today if you don't want. I'm only here for a day. I don't want not to be polite."

"Go to hell," he said.

"How would it be if I took the car and went to the hotel?" Ginny asked.

"No, Ginny. We're going to have some champagne first. Do you have a car?" she asked Thomas Hudson.

"Yeah. Outside on the square."

"Can we drive out to your place?"

"Of course. We can eat and then go out. Or I can pick up something for us to eat out there."

"Weren't we lucky that we could get here?"

"Yes," Thomas Hudson said. "How did you know anyone was here?"

"A boy at the field at Camagüey told me you might be here. If we didn't find you, we were going to see Havana."

"We can see Havana."

"No," she said. "Ginny can see it. Do you know anybody who could take Ginny out?"

"Sure."

"We have to get back to Camagüey tonight."

"What time does your plane leave?"

"Six o'clock, I think."

"We'll fix everything up," Thomas Hudson said.

A man came over to the table. He was a local boy.

"Pardon me," he said. "May I have your autograph?"

"Of course."

He gave her a card with the picture of the bar on it with Constante standing behind it making a cocktail and she signed with the overlarge theatrical writing Thomas Hudson knew so well.

"It's not for my little daughter or my son who is in school," the man said. "It's for me."

"Good," she said and smiled at him. "You were very nice to ask me."

"I've seen all of your pictures," the man said. "I think you are the most beautiful woman in the world."

"That's wonderful," she said. "Please keep on thinking that."

"Would you let me buy you a drink?"

"I'm drinking with a friend."

"I know him," the radio announcer said. "I've known him for many years. May I sit down, Tom? There is an extra lady here."

"This is Mr. Rodríguez," Thomas Hudson said. "What's your last name, Ginny?"

"Watson."

"Miss Watson."

"I'm delighted to know you, Miss Watson," the radio announcer said. He was a good-looking man, dark and tanned with pleasant eyes, a nice smile, and the big good hands of a ball player. He had been both a gambler and a ball player and he had some of the good looks of the modern gambler left.

"Could you all three have lunch with me?" he asked. "It is nearly lunchtime now."

"Mr. Hudson and I have to make a trip into the country," she said.

"I'd love to have lunch with you," Ginny said. "I think you're wonderful."

"Is he all right?" she asked Thomas Hudson.

"He's a fine man. As good as you'll find in town."

"Thank you very much, Tom," the man said. "You are sure you won't all eat with me?"

"We really have to go," she said. "We're late now. Then I'll see you at the hotel, Ginny. Thank you so much, Mr. Rodríguez."

"You really are the most beautiful woman in the world," Mr. Rodríguez said. "If I hadn't always known it, I know it now."

"Please keep on thinking so," she said and then they were out in the street.

"Well," she said. "That wasn't too bad. Ginny likes him, too, and he's nice."

"He *is* nice," Thomas Hudson said and the chauffeur opened the door of the car for them.

"You're nice," she said. "I wish you hadn't had quite so many drinks. That's why I skipped the champagne. Who was your dark friend at the end of the bar?"

"Just my dark friend at the end of the bar."

"Do you need a drink? We could stop somewhere and get one."

"No. Do you?"

"You know I never do. I'd like some wine though."

"I have wine out at the house."

"That's wonderful. Now you can kiss me. They won't arrest us now."

"*¿Adondé vamos?*" the chauffeur asked looking straight ahead.

"*A la finca,*" Thomas Hudson said.

"Oh, Tommy, Tommy, Tommy," she said. "Go right ahead. It doesn't make any difference if he sees us, does it?"

"No. It makes no difference. You can cut his tongue out if you like."

"No, I don't want to. Nor nothing brutal ever. But you were nice to offer it."

"It wouldn't be a bad idea. How are you? You old love-house of always."

"I'm the same."

"Really the same?"

"The same as one always is. I'm yours in this town."

"Until the plane leaves."

"Exactly," she said and changed her position for the better in the car. "Look," she said. "We've left the shining part and it's dirty and smoky. When didn't we do that?"

"Sometimes."

"Yes," she said. "Sometimes."

Then they looked at the dirty and the smoky and her quick eyes and lovely intelligence saw everything instantly that had taken him so many years to see.

"Now it gets better," she said. She had never told him a lie in his life and he had tried to never lie to her. But he had been quite unsuccessful.

"Do you still love me?" she asked. "Tell me true without adornments."

"Yes. You ought to know."

"I know," she said, holding him to prove it if it could prove it.

"Who is the man now?"

"Let's not talk about him. You wouldn't care for him."

"Maybe not," he said and held her so close that it was as though something must break if both were truly serious. It was their old game and she broke and the break was clean.

"You don't have breasts," she said. "And you always win."

"I don't have a face to break your heart. Nor what you have and the long lovely legs."

"You have something else."

"Yes," he said. "Last night with a pillow and a cat making love."

"I'll make up for the cat. How far is it now?"

"Eleven minutes."

"That's too far the way things are now."

"Should I take it from him and drive it in eight?"

"No, please, and remember everything I taught you about patience."

"That was the most intelligent and stupid lesson I learned. Reteach it to me a little now."

"Do I have to?"

"No. It is only eight minutes now."

"Will it be a nice place and will the bed be big?"

"We will have to see," Thomas Hudson said. "Are you starting to have your old doubts already?"

"No," she said. "I want a big, big bed. To forget all about the army."

"There is a big bed," he said. "Maybe not as big as the army."

"You don't have to be rough," she said. "All the beautiful ones end up showing pictures of their wives. You should know the Airbornes."

"I'm glad I don't. We're a little waterlogged. But we were never waterborne nor said so."

"Can you tell me anything about it?" she asked him, her hand now soundly in his pocket.

"No."

"You never would and I love you for it. But I get curious and people ask me and I worry."

"Just be curious," he said. "And never worry. Don't you remember that curiosity killed a cat? I've got a cat and he's curious enough." He thought of Boise. Then he said, "But worry kills big businessmen right in their prime. Do I have to worry about you?"

"Only as an actress. Then not too much. Now it's only two minutes more. It's nice country now and I like it. Can we have lunch in bed?"

"Can we go to sleep then, too?"

"Yes. It's not a sin, if we don't miss the plane."

The car climbed steeply now on the old stone-paved road with the big trees on either side.

"Have you anything to miss?"

"You," he said.

"I mean duty."

"Did I look as though I were on duty?"

"You might be. You're a wonderful actor. The worst I ever saw. I love you, my dear crazy," she said. "I've seen you play all your great roles. The one I loved you the best in was when you were playing the Faithful Husband and you were doing it so wonderfully and there was a big spot of natural juices showed on your trousers and every time you looked at me it was bigger. That was in the Ritz, I think."

"That was where I played the Faithful Husband best," he said. "Like Garrick at the Old Bailey."

"You're a little confused," she said. "I think you played it best on the *Normandie*."

"When they burned her I didn't give a damn about anything for six days."

"That's not your record."

"No," he said.

They were stopped at the gate now and the chauffeur was unlocking it.

"Do we really live here?"

"Yes. Up the hill. I'm sorry the drive's in such bad shape."

The car climbed it through the mango trees and the unflowering *flamboyanes,* turned past the cattle sheds and on up the circular drive to the house. He opened the door of the car and she stepped out as though conferring a warm and generous favor to the ground.

She looked at the house and could see the open windows of the bedroom. They were big windows and in some way it reminded her of the *Normandie.*

"I'll miss the plane," she said. "Why can't I be ill? All the other women are ill."

"I know two good doctors that will swear you are."

"Wonderful," she said, going up the stairs. "We won't have to ask them to dinner, will we?"

"No," he said, opening the door, "I'll call them up and send the chauffeur for the certificates."

"I am ill," she said. "I've decided. Let the troops entertain themselves for once."

"You'll go."

"No. I'm going to entertain you. Have you been entertained properly lately?"

"No."

"Me either, or is it neither?"

"I don't know," he said and held her close and looked in her eyes and then away. He opened the door to the big bedroom. "It's neither," he said reflectively.

The windows were open and the wind was in the room. But it was pleasant now with the sun.

"It *is* like the *Normandie.* Did you make it like the *Normandie* for me?"

"Of course, darling," he lied. "What did you think?"

"You're a worse liar than I am."

"I'm not even faster."

"Let's not lie. Let's pretend you made it for me."

"I made it for you," he said. "Only it looked like someone else."

"Is that as hard as you can hold anyone?"

"Without breaking them." Then he said, "Without lying down."

"Who is against lying down?"

"Not me," he said and picked her up and carried her to the bed.

"Let me drop the jalousie. I don't mind your entertaining the troops. But we have a radio that entertains the kitchen. They don't need us."

"Now," she said.

"Yes."

"Now remember everything I ever taught you."

"Aren't I?"

"Now and then."

"Then," he said. "Where did we know him?"

"We met him. Don't you remember?"

"Look, let's not remember anything and let's not talk and let's not talk and let's not talk."

Afterwards she said, "People used to get hungry even on the *Normandie*."

"I'll ring for the steward."

"But this steward doesn't know us."

"He will."

"No. Let's go out and see the house. What have you painted?"

"What all nothing."

"Don't you have time?"

"What do you think?"

"But couldn't you when you're ashore?"

"What do you mean ashore?"

"Tom," she said. They were in the living room now in the big old chairs and she had taken her shoes off to feel the matting on the floor. She sat curled in the chair and she had brushed her hair to please him, and because of what she knew it did to him, and she sat so it swung like a heavy silken load when her head moved.

"Damn you," he said. "Darling," he added.

"You damned me enough," she said.

"Let's not talk about it."

"Why did you marry her, Tom?"

"Because you were in love."

"It wasn't a very good reason."

"Nobody ever said it was. Especially not me. But I

don't have to make my errors and repent of them and then discuss them, do I?"

"If I want you to."

The big black and white cat- had come in and he rubbed against her leg.

"He's got us mixed up," Thomas Hudson said. "Or maybe he's getting good sense."

"It couldn't be—?"

"Sure. Of course. Boy," he called.

The cat came over to him and jumped into his lap. It did not matter which one it was.

"We might as well both love her, Boy. Take a good look at her. You'll never see any more womens like that."

"Is he the one you sleep with?"

"Yes. Is there any reason why I shouldn't?"

"None. I like him better than the man I sleep with now and he's just about as sad."

"Do we have to talk about him?"

"No. And you don't have to pretend you haven't been at sea when your eyes are burned and there are white slit marks in the corners of them and your hair is as sun-streaked as though you used something on it—"

"And I walk with a rolling gait and carry a parrot on my shoulder and hit people with my wooden leg. Look, darling, I go to sea occasionally because I am a painter of marine life for the Museum of Natural History. Not even war must interfere with our studies."

"They are sacred," she said. "I'll remember that lie and stick with it. Tom, you truly don't care for her at all?"

"Not at all."

"You still love me?"

"Didn't I give any signs of it?"

"It could have been a role. The one of the always faithful lover no matter what whores I find you with. Thee hasn't been faithful to me, Cynara, in thy fashion."

"I always told you that you were too literate for your own good. I was through with that poem when I was nineteen."

"Yes, and I always told you that if you would paint and

work at it as you should, instead of making fantasies and falling in love with other people—"

"Marrying them, you mean."

"No. Marrying them is bad enough. But you fall in love with them and then I don't respect you."

"That's that old lovely one I remember. 'And then I don't respect you.' I'll buy that one at any price you put on it and take it out of circulation."

"I respect you. And you don't love her, do you?"

"I love you and respect you and I don't love her."

"That's wonderful. I'm so glad I'm so ill and that I missed the plane."

"I really do respect you, you know, and I respect every damned fool thing you do or did."

"And you treat me wonderfully and keep all your promises."

"What was the last one?"

"I don't know. If it was a promise you broke it."

"Would you want to skip it, beauty?"

"I'd like to have skipped it."

"Maybe we could. We skipped most things."

"No. That's untrue. There's visible evidence on that. But you think making love to a woman is enough. You never think about her wanting to be proud of you. Nor about small tendernesses."

"Nor about being a baby like the men you love and care for."

"Couldn't you be more needing and make me necessary and not be so damned give it and take it and take it away I'm not hungry."

"What did we come out here for? Moral lectures?"

"We came out here because I love you and I want you to be worthy of yourself."

"And of you and God and all other abstractions. I'm not even an abstract painter. You'd have asked Toulouse-Lautrec to keep away from brothels and Gauguin not to get the syphilis and Baudelaire to get home early. I'm not as good as they were but the hell with you."

"I never was like that."

"Sure you were. Along with your work. Your goddam hours of work."

"I would have given it up."

"Sure, I know you would. And sung in night clubs and I could be the bouncer. Do you remember when we planned that?"

"What have you heard from Tom?"

"He's fine," the man said and felt the strange prickling go over his skin.

"He hasn't written me in three weeks. You'd think he'd write his mother. He always was so good about writing."

"You know how it is with kids in a war. Or maybe they're holding up all mail. Sometimes they do."

"Do you remember when he couldn't speak any English?"

"And he had his gang at Gstaad? And up in the Engadine and at Zug?"

"Do you have any new pictures of him?"

"Only that one you have."

"Could we have a drink? What do you drink here?"

"Anything you want. I'll go and find the boy. The wine is in the cellar."

"Please don't be gone long."

"That's a funny thing to say to each other."

"Please don't be gone long," she repeated. "Did you hear it? And I never asked you to get in early. That wasn't the trouble and you know it."

"I know it," he said. "And I won't be gone long."

"Maybe the boy could make something to eat, too."

"Maybe he could," Thomas Hudson said. Then to the cat, "You stay with her, Boise."

Now, he thought. Why did I say that? Why did I lie? Why did I do that breaking it gently thing? Did I want to keep my grief for myself, as Willie said? Am I that sort of guy?

Well, you did it, he thought. How did you tell a mother that her boy is dead when you've just made love to her again? How do you tell yourself your boy is dead? You used to know all the answers. Answer me that.

There aren't any answers. You should know that by now. There aren't any answers at all.

"Tom," her voice called. "I'm lonely and the cat isn't you, even though he thinks he is."

"Put him on the floor. The boy's gone to the village and I'm getting ice."

"I don't care about the drink."

"Neither do I," he said and came back into the room walking on the tiled floor until he felt the matting. He looked at her and she was still there.

"You don't want to talk about him," she said.

"No."

"Why? I think it's better."

"He looks too much like you."

"That isn't it," she said. "Tell me. Is he dead?"

"Sure."

"Please hold me tight. I *am* ill now." He felt her shaking and he knelt by the chair and held her and felt her tremble. Then she said, "And poor you. Poor, poor you."

After a time she said, "I'm sorry for everything I ever did or said."

"Me, too."

"Poor you and poor me."

"Poor everybody," he said and did not add, "Poor Tom."

"What can you tell me?"

"Nothing. Just that."

"I suppose we'll learn how to take it."

"Maybe."

"I wish I could break down but I'm just hollow sick."

"I know."

"Does it happen to everybody?"

"I suppose so. Anyway it can only happen to us once."

"And now it's like in a house of the dead."

"I'm sorry I didn't tell you when I saw you."

"That's all right," she said. "You always put things off. I'm not sorry."

"I wanted you so damned much and I was selfish and stupid."

"You weren't selfish. We always loved each other. We only made mistakes."

"I made the worst ones."

"No. We both made them. Let's not fight any more ever, though." Something was happening to her and then finally she cried and said, "Oh, Tommy, all of a sudden I just can't stand it."

"I know," he said. "My sweet good lovely beauty. I can't stand it either."

"We were so young and stupid and we were both beautiful and Tommy was so damned beautiful—"

"Like his mother."

"And now there'll never be any visible evidence."

"My poor dearest love."

"And what will we do?"

"You do what you're doing and I'll do what I'm doing."

"Couldn't we be together for a while?"

"Only if this wind keeps up."

"Then let it blow. Do you think making love is wicked?"

"I don't think Tom would disapprove."

"No. Surely no."

"Do you remember skiing with him on your shoulders and how we'd sing coming down through the orchard behind the inn in the dusk?"

"I remember everything."

"So do I," she said. "And why were we so stupid?"

"We were rivals as well as lovers."

"I know it and we shouldn't have been. But you don't love anyone else, do you? Now that that's all we have?"

"No. Truly."

"I don't either really. Do you think we could take each other back?"

"I don't know whether it would work. We could try it."

"How long will the war be?"

"Ask the man who owns one."

"Will it be years?"

"A couple, anyway."

"Are you liable to be killed too?"

"Very."

"That's not good."

"And if I'm not?"

"I don't know. Now Tom's gone we wouldn't start being bitter and bad again?"

"I could try not to. I'm not bitter and I've learned how to handle the bad. Really."

"What? With whores?"

"I guess so. But I wouldn't need them if we were together."

"You always did put things so prettily."

"See? Let's not start it."

"No. Not in the house of the dead."

"You said that once."

"I know," she said. "I'm sorry. But I don't know how to put it any other way and mean the same thing. It's started to get numb already."

"It will get number," he said. "Numb is as bad as at the start. But it will get number."

"Will you tell me every bad thing you know about it so mine will get numb quicker?"

"Sure," he said. "Christ, I love you."

"You always did," she said. "Now tell me."

He was sitting at her feet and he did not look at her. He looked at Boise the cat, who was lying in a patch of sunlight on the matting. "He was shot down by a flak ship in a routine sweep off Abbeville."

"Did he bail out?"

"No. The kite burned. He must have been hit."

"I hope he was," she said. "I hope so much he was."

"It's almost sure he was. He had time to bail out."

"You're telling me the truth? His chute didn't burn?"

"No," he lied, thinking that was enough for today.

"Who did you hear it from?"

He told her the name of the man. "Then it's true," she said. "I don't have a son any more and neither do you. I suppose we can learn about that. Do you know anything else?"

"No," he told her, as truly as possible.

"And we just go on?"

"That's it."

"With what?"

"With nothing," he said.

"Couldn't I stay here and be with you?"

"I don't think it would be any good because I have to go out as soon as the weather is possible. You never talk and you bury anything I tell you. So bury that."

"But I could be with you until then and I could wait until you're back."

"That's no good," he said. "I never know when we'll be back and it would be worse for you not working. Stay if you want until we go."

"Good," she said. "I'll stay until you go and we'll think of Tom all we want. And we'll make love as soon as you think it's right."

"Tommy never had anything to do with that room."

"No. And I'll exorcise anyone who ever did."

"Now we really should eat something and drink a glass of wine."

"A bottle," she said. "Wasn't Tom a lovely boy? And so funny and good."

"What are you made of?"

"What you love," she said. "And steel added."

"I don't know what's become of the house boys," Thomas Hudson told her. "They didn't expect me back today. But one boy is supposed to be on the telephone. I'll get the wine. It's cold now."

He opened the bottle and poured two glasses. It was the good wine he saved for coming-homes, after he had cooled out, and it bubbled small and neat and faithfully.

"Here's to us and all our mistakes and all our losses and the gains we'll make."

"Made," he said.

"Made," she said. Then she said, "The one thing you were always faithful to was good wine."

"Admirable of me, wasn't it?"

"I'm sorry I said it about the drinking this morning."

"Those things are good for me. It's funny, but they are."

"You mean what you were drinking? Or the criticism?"

"What I was drinking. The tall frozen ones."

"Maybe they are. And I don't make any criticism now

except that it is awfully hard to get something to eat in this house."

"Be patient. You've told me that enough times."

"I'm patient," she said. "I'm just hungry. I know now why people eat at wakes and before funerals."

"Be as rough with it as is good for you."

"Don't worry. I'll be. Are we going to go on saying we're sorry for everything? I said it once."

"Listen, you," he said. "I've had this thing three weeks longer than you and maybe I'm in a different phase."

"You'd have a different and more interesting phase," she said. "I know you. Why don't you just get back to your whores?"

"Wouldn't you like to stop it?"

"No. It makes me feel better."

"Who was it said, 'Mary, pity women'?"

"Some man," she said. "Some bastard of a man."

"Do you want to hear the whole poem?"

"No. And I'm tired of you already and you knowing it three weeks earlier and all that. Just because I'm a non-combatant and you're in something so secret you have to sleep with a cat so you won't talk—"

"And you still don't see why we broke up?"

"We broke up because I got tired of you. You've always loved me and you couldn't help it and you can't help it now."

"That's true."

The house boy was standing in the dining room. He had unavoidably seen and heard quarrels in the living room before and they made his brown face perspire with unhappiness. He loved his master and the cats and dogs and he admired the beautiful women respectfully and it made him feel terrible when there were quarrels. He thought that he had never seen such a beautiful woman and the caballero was quarreling with her and she was saying angry things to the caballero.

"Señor," he said. "Pardon me. May I speak to you in the kitchen?"

"Excuse me please, darling."

"I suppose it's something mysterious," she said and poured her glass full of wine.

"Señor," the boy said. "The Lieutenant spoke in *castellano* and he said for to come in immediately repeat immediately. He said you would know where and that it was a business matter. I did not wish to call on our phone and I called from the village. Then they told me you were here."

"Good," said Thomas Hudson. "Thank you very much. Please fry some eggs for the señorita and me and tell the chauffeur to have the car ready."

"Yes sir," the boy said.

"What was it, Tom?" she asked. "Is it bad?"

"I have to go to work."

"But you said you wouldn't have to with this wind."

"I know it. But it's out of my hands."

"Do you want me to stay here?"

"You can stay and read Tom's letters if you like and the chauffeur will take you to your plane."

"All right."

"You can take the letters with you, too, if you want and any pictures or anything you see. Go through my desk."

"You *are* changed."

"Maybe a little," he said.

"Go out to the studio and look at any of the stuff," he said. "There are some good ones from before we started this project. Take anything you like. There's a good one of you."

"I'll take it," she said. "You're awfully good when you're good."

"Read the letters from her if you like. Some of them are museum pieces. Take any along that are comic enough."

"You sound as though I travelled with a trunk."

"You can read them and then drop them out of the john in the plane."

"All right."

"I'll try to get back before you go. But don't count on

it. If I have to use the chauffeur I'll send a taxi to take you to the hotel or the airport."

"Good."

"The boy will look after you. He can do any pressing for you and you can use any clothes of mine or anything you find around."

"Good. Will you try to love me, Tom, and not let anything like that last one ruin it?"

"Sure. They don't mean anything and you pointed out I couldn't help it."

"Try and not be able to help it."

"It's out of my hands. Take any books you want or anything you find around the joint and give my eggs or one anyway to Boise. He likes them cut up small. I better shove. There's been a time lag on this already."

"Goodbye, Tom," she said.

"Goodbye, devil, and take good care. This is probably nothing anyway."

He was gone out the door. But the cat had slipped through it with him and was looking up at him.

"It's all right, Boise," he said. "I'll be back before we shove."

"Where do we go?" the driver asked him.

"Town."

I can't believe there's any business with this heavy sea. But maybe they found something. Maybe one is in trouble somewhere. Christ, I hope we make it this time. I want to remember to make out one of those pocket wills and leave her the joint. Must remember to get it witnessed at the Embassy and leave it in the safe. She certainly took it awfully well. But then it hasn't really hit her yet. I wish I could help her when it hits her. I wish I could be some real good to her. Maybe I can if we get by this one and the next one and the next one.

Let's get by this one first. I wonder if she'll take the stuff. I hope she will and that she'll remember to give Boise the egg. He gets hungry when the weather's cold.

The boys won't be hard to find and she can take another beating before we haul her out. One more anyway. One for sure. We'll gamble on it. There are spares for nearly

everything. What's one more beating if we get to close?
It would have been nice to have stayed in. Maybe it
would have been. The hell it would have been.

Get it straight. Your boy you lose. Love you lose. Honor
has been gone for a long time. Duty you do..

Sure and what's your duty? What I said I'd do. And all
the other things you said you'd do?

In the bedroom of the farmhouse, now, the room that
looked like the *Normandie,* she was lying on the bed with
the cat named Boise beside her. She had not been able to
eat the eggs and the champagne had no taste. She had cut
up all the eggs for Boise and pulled open one desk drawer
and seen the boy's handwriting on the blue envelopes
and the censor stamp and then she had gone over and lain
face down on the bed.

"Both of them," she said to the cat, who was happy
from the eggs and from the smell of the woman who lay
beside him.

"Both of them," she said. "Boise, tell me. What are we
going to do about it?"

The cat purred imperceptibly.

"You don't know either," she said. "And neither does
anyone else."

Part III

AT SEA

AT SEA

I

THERE was a long white beach with coconut palms behind it. The reef lay across the entrance to the harbor and the heavy east wind made the sea break on it so that the entrance was easy to see once you had opened it up. There was no one on the beach and the sand was so white that it hurt his eyes to look at it.

The man on the flying bridge studied the shore. There were no shacks where the shacks should have been and there were no boats anchored in the lagoon that he could see.

"You've been in here before," he said to his mate.

"Yes."

"Weren't the shacks over there?"

"They were over there and it shows a village on the chart."

"They sure as hell aren't here now," the man said. "Can you make out any boats up in the mangroves?"

"There's nothing that I can see."

"I'm going to take her in and anchor," the man said. "I know this cut. It's about eight times as deep as it looks."

He looked down into the green water and saw the size of the shadow of his ship on the bottom.

"There's good holding ground east from where the village used to be," his mate said.

"I know. Break out the starboard anchor and stand by. I'm going to lay off there. With this wind blowing day and night there will be no insects."

"No sir."

They anchored and the boat, not big enough to be called a ship except in the mind of the man who was her master, lay with her bow into the wind with the waves breaking white and green on the reef.

The man on the bridge watched that she swung well and held solidly. Then he looked ashore and cut his motors. He continued to look at the shore and he could not figure it out at all.

"Take three men in and have a look," he said. "I'm going to lie down a while. Remember you're scientists."

When they were scientists no weapons showed and they wore machetes and wide straw hats such as Bahaman spongers wear. These the crew referred to as *"sombreros científicos."* The larger they were the more scientific they were considered.

"Someone has stolen my scientific hat," a heavy-shouldered Basque with thick eyebrows that came together over his nose said. "Give me a bag of frags for science's sake."

"Take my scientific hat," another Basque said. "It's twice as scientific as yours."

"What a scientific hat," the widest of the Basques said. "I feel like Einstein in this one. Thomas, can we take specimens?"

"No," the man said. "Antonio knows what I want him to do. You keep your damned scientific eyes open."

"I'll look for water."

"It's behind where the village was," the man said. "See how it is. We had probably better fill."

"H_2O," the Basque said. "That scientific stuff. Hey, you worthless scientist. You hat stealer. Give us four five-gallon jugs so we won't waste the trip."

The other Basque put four wicker-covered jugs in the dinghy.

The man heard them talking. "Don't hit me in the back with that damned scientific oar."

"I do it only for science."

"Fornicate science and his brother."

"Science's sister."

"*Penicilina* is her name."

The man watched them rowing toward the too white beach. I should have gone in, he thought. But I was up all night and I've steered twelve hours. Antonio can size it up as well as I can. But I wonder what the hell has happened.

He looked once at the reef and then at the shore and at the current of clean water running against the side and making little eddies in the lee. Then he shut his eyes and turned on his side and went to sleep.

He woke as the dinghy came alongside and he knew it was something bad when he saw their faces. His mate was sweating as he always did with trouble or bad news. He was a dry man and he did not sweat easily.

"Somebody burned the shacks," he said. "Somebody tried to put them out and there are bodies in the ashes. You can't smell them from here because of the wind."

"How many bodies?"

"We counted nine. There could be more."

"Men or women?"

"Both."

"Are there any tracks?"

"Nothing. It's rained since. Heavy rain. The sand is still pitted with it."

The wide-shouldered Basque whose name was Ara said, "They've been dead a week anyway. Birds haven't worked on them but the land crabs are working on them."

"How do you know they have been dead a week?"

"No one can say exactly," Ara said. "But they have been dead about a week. From the land crab trails the rain was about three days ago."

"How was the water?"

"It looked all right."

"Did you bring it?"

"Yes."

"I don't see why they would have poisoned the water," Ara said. "It smelled good so I tasted it and brought it."

"You shouldn't have tasted it."

"It smelled good and there was no reason to believe it was poisoned."

"Who killed the people?"

"Anybody."

"Didn't you check?"

"No. We came to tell you. You are the skipper."

"All right," said Thomas Hudson. He went below and buckled on his revolver. There was a sheath knife on the other side of the belt, the side that rode high, and the weight of the gun was on his leg. He stopped in the galley and took a spoon and put it in his pocket.

"Ara, you and Henry come ashore. Willie come in with the dinghy and then see if you can get some conches. Let Peters sleep." To his mate he said, "Check the engines, please, and all tanks."

The water was clear and lovely over the white sand bottom and he could see every ridge and wrinkle in the sand. As they waded ashore when the dinghy grounded on a ridge of sand he felt small fish playing around his toes and looked down and saw they were tiny pompano. Maybe they are not true pompano, he thought. But they look exactly like them and they are most friendly.

"Henry," he said when they were ashore. "You take the windward beach and walk it all the way up to the mangroves. Watch for tracks or anything else. Meet me here. Ara, you take the other beach and do the same."

He did not have to ask where the bodies were. He saw the tracks that led to them and heard the rattle of the land crabs in the dry bush. He looked out at his ship and the line of the breakers and Willie in the stern of the skiff with a water glass looking over the side for conches while the skiff drifted.

Since I have to do it I might as well get it over with, he thought. But this day was built for something else. It is strange how they had such a rain here where there was no need for it and we had nothing. How long is it now that we have seen the rains go by on either side and never had a drop?

The wind was blowing heavily and had blown now, day

and night, for more than fifty days. It had become a part of the man and it did not make him nervous. It fortified him and gave him strength and he hoped that it would never stop.

We wait always for something that does not come, he thought. But it is easier waiting with the wind than in a calm or with the capriciousness and malignancy of squalls. There is always water somewhere. Let it stay dry. We can always find it. There is water on all these keys if you know how to look for it.

Now, he thought to himself. Go in and get it over with.

The wind helped him to get it over with. As he crouched under the scorched sea-grape bushes and sifted the sand in double handfuls the wind blew the scent of what was just ahead of him away. He found nothing in the sand and he was puzzled but he looked in all the sand to windward of the burned shacks before he moved in. He had hoped to find what he looked for the easier way. But there was nothing.

Then, with the wind at his back, so that he turned and gulped it and then held his breath again he went to work with his knife probing into the charred deliquescence that the land crabs were feeding on. He touched a sudden hardness that rolled against a bone and dug it out with the spoon. He laid it on the sand with the spoon and probed and dug and found three more in the pile. Then he turned into the wind and cleaned the knife and the spoon in the sand. He took the four bullets in a handful of sand and with the knife and the spoon in his left hand made his way back through the brush.

A big land crab, obscenely white, reared back and lifted his claws at him.

"You on the way in, boy?" the man said to him. "I'm on the way out."

The crab stood his ground with his claws raised high and the points open sharply.

"You're getting pretty big for yourself," the man said. He put his knife slowly in its sheath and the spoon in his pocket. Then he shifted the handful of sand with the four bullets in it to his left hand. He wiped his right hand on his shorts carefully. Then he drew the sweat-darkened, well-oiled .357 Magnum.

"You still have a chance," he said to the land crab. "Nobody blames you. You're having your pleasure and doing your duty."

The crab did not move and his claws were held high. He was a big crab, nearly a foot across, and the man shot him between his eyes and the crab disintegrated.

"Those damn .357's are hard to get now because draft-dodging FBI's have to use them to hunt down draft-dodgers," the man said. "But a man has to fire a shot sometime or he doesn't know how he is shooting."

Poor old crab, he thought. All he was practicing was his trade. But he ought to have shuffled along.

He came out onto the beach and saw where his ship was riding and the steady line of the surf and Willie anchored now and diving for conches. He cleaned his knife properly and scrubbed the spoon and washed it and then washed the four bullets. He held them in his hand and looked at them as a man who was panning for gold, expecting only flakes, would look at four nuggets in his pan. The four bullets had black noses. Now the meat was out of them, the short twist rifling showed clearly. They were 9mm standard issue for the Schmeisser machine pistol.

They made the man very happy.

They picked up all the hulls, he thought. But they left these as plain as calling cards. Now I must try to think it out. We know two things. They left nobody on the Cay and the boats are gone. Go on from there, boy. You're supposed to be able to think.

But he did not think. Instead he lay back on the sand with his pistol pulled over so it lay between his legs and he watched the sculpture that the wind and sand had made of a piece of driftwood. It was gray and sanded and it was embedded in the white, floury sand. It looked as though it were in an exhibition. It should be in the Salon d'Automne.

He heard the breaking roar of the seas on the reef and he thought, I would like to paint this. He lay and looked at the sky which had nothing but east wind in it and the four bullets were in the buttoned-down change pocket of his shorts. He knew they were the rest of his life. But he did not wish to think about them now nor make all the practical thinking that he must make. I will enjoy the gray wood, he thought. Now we know that we have our enemies and that they cannot escape. Neither can we. But there is no necessity to think about it until Ara and Henry are back. Ara will find something. There is something to be found and he is not a fool. A beach tells many lies but somewhere the truth is always written. He felt the bullets in his change pocket and then he elbowed his way back to where the sand was drier and even whiter, if there could be a comparison in such whiteness, and he lay with his head against the gray piece of driftwood and his pistol between his legs.

"How long have you been my girl?" he said to the pistol.

"Don't answer," he said to the pistol. "Lie there good and I will see you kill something better than land crabs when the time comes."

II

HE was lying there looking out at the line of the surf and he had it pretty well thought out by the time he saw Ara and Henry coming down the beach. He saw them and then looked away from them and out to sea again. He had tried not to think about it and to relax but it had been impossible. Now he would relax until they came and he would think of nothing but the sea on the reef. But there was not time. They came too fast.

"What did you find?" he asked Ara who sat down by the gray driftwood. Henry sat beside him.

"I found one. A young man. Dead."

"He was a German all right," Henry said. "He only

had on shorts and he had very long hair, blond and sun-
streaked, and he was face down in the sand."

"Where was he shot?"

"At the base of the spine and in the back of the neck,"
Ara said. "*Rematado*. Here are the bullets. I washed
them."

"Yes," said Thomas Hudson. "I have four like them."

"They're 9mm Luger aren't they?" Henry asked. "It's
the same caliber as our .38's."

"These with the black ends are for the machine pistol,"
Thomas Hudson said. "Thanks for digging them out,
doctor."

"At your orders," Ara said. "The neck one had gone
clean through and I found it in the sand. Henry cut out
the other one."

"I didn't mind it," Henry said. "The wind and the
sun had sort of dried him. It was like cutting into a pie.
He wasn't like those in there. Why did they kill him, Tom?"

"I don't know."

"What do you think?" Ara asked. "Did they come in
here to make repairs?"

"No. They've lost their boat."

"Yes," Ara said. "They took the boats."

"Why was the sailor killed?" Henry asked. "You forgive
me if I don't sound too intelligent, Tom. But you know
how much I want to do what I can and I'm so happy we
have contact."

"We haven't contact," Thomas Hudson said. "But
Christ we've got a lovely scent."

"Breast high?" Henry asked hopefully.

"Don't mention that word to me."

"But Tom, who killed the sailor and why?"

"Family trouble," Thomas Hudson said. "Did you ever
see a man shot in the base of the spine for kindness?
Afterwards whoever did it was kind and shot him in the
neck."

"Maybe there were two," said Ara.

"Did you find the hulls?"

"No," Ara said. "I looked where they would be. Even

if it was a machine pistol it would not have thrown them further than I looked."

"It could be the same methodical bastard that picked up the other ones."

"Where would they go?" Ara asked. "Where would they make for with the boats?"

"They have to go south," Thomas said. "You know damned well they can't go north."

"And we?"

"I'm trying to think in their heads," Thomas Hudson said. "I haven't many facts to go on."

"You have the deads and the boats gone," Henry said. "You can think it out, Tom."

"And one known weapon and where did they lose their undersea boat and how many are they? Stir that and add we couldn't raise Guantánamo last night and add how many keys there are south of here plus when we have to fill our tanks. Add Peters and serve."

"It will be all right, Tom."

"Sure," Thomas Hudson said. "All right and all wrong are identical twins in this business."

"You're confident we will get them though, aren't you?"

"Of course," Thomas Hudson said. "Now go and flag Willie in and let Antonio get started on his conches. We will have chowder. Ara, you load all the water you can in the next three hours. Tell Antonio to go ahead on the motors. I want to get out of here before dark. Was there nothing on the island? No pigs nor any fowl?"

"Nothing," Ara told him. "They took everything."

"Well, they will have to eat them. They have no feed for them and no ice. They are Germans so they are capable and they can get turtle in these months. I think we will find them at Lobos. It is logical they should take Lobos. Have Willie fill the ice-well with conches and we will take only enough water to the next key."

He stopped and reconsidered, "No, I'm sorry. I was wrong. Fill water until sundown and I will take her out at moonrise. We lose three hours but we save six later on."

"Did you taste the water?" Ara asked.

"Yes," he said. "It was clean and good. You were quite right."

"Thank you," Ara said. "I will go now to call in Willie. He has been diving many."

"Tom," Henry asked. "Do you want me to stay with you or to carry water or what?"

"Carry water until you are too tired and then get some sleep. I want you on the bridge with me tonight."

"Can I bring you a shirt or a sweater?" Henry asked.

"Bring me a shirt and one of the very light blankets," Thomas Hudson said. "I can sleep now in the sun and the sand is dry. But later on it will be cool with the wind."

"Isn't the sand wonderful? I've never known such dry or powdery sand."

"The wind has beaten it for many years."

"Will we get them, Tommy?"

"Of course," Thomas Hudson said. "There is no doubt of it at all."

"Please forgive me if I am ever stupid," Henry said.

"You were forgiven when you were born," Thomas Hudson said. "You are a very brave boy, Henry, and I am fond of you and trust you. You're not stupid either."

"You truly think we will have a fight?"

"I know it. Do not think about that. Think about details. Think about all the things you should do and how we should be a happy ship until we fight. I'll think about the fight."

"I will go and do my duty as well as I can," Henry said. "I wish we could practice the fight so I could do my part better."

Thomas Hudson said, "You'll do it all right. I do not see any way that we can miss it."

"It's been so very long," Henry said.

"But everything is long," Thomas Hudson told him. "And pursuit is the longest."

"Get some sleep," Henry said. "You never sleep any more."

"I'll sleep," Thomas Hudson said.

"Where do you suppose they lost their own boat, Tom?" Ara asked.

"They got these boats here and they did away with these people a week ago, say. So they must be the one that Camagüey claimed. But they got somewhere close to here before they lost her. They didn't sail any rubber boats into that wind."

"Then they must have lost her east of here."

"Naturally. And they were damned well in the clear when they lost her," Thomas Hudson said.

"It was still a long way home," Henry said.

"It is going to be a longer way home now," Ara said.

"They're funny people," Thomas Hudson said. "They're all brave and some of them are so damned admirable. Then they have mean ones like this."

"We better go and do our work," Ara said. "We can talk tonight on watch to keep awake. You get some rest, Tom."

"Get some sleep," Henry said.

"Rest is as good as sleep."

"No it isn't," Ara said. "You need sleep, Tom."

"I'll try to get some," Thomas Hudson said. But when they were gone he could not sleep.

What did they have to do this rotten thing here for? he thought. We will get them anyway. All these people would have done was tell us how many they were and how they were armed. I suppose that was worth killing for, from their standpoint. Especially if they thought of these people as Negroes. But all that shows something about them. To have killed like that they must have some plan and they must have some hope of being picked up. Also there must have been dissension about the plan or they would not have done this murdering here of the sailor. That could be an execution for anything, though. He might have let her go down when she could have been kept up to make the try to get home.

Where does that bring us? he thought. You can't bank on that. It is only a possibility. But if it was true it would mean she went down in sight of land and fast. That would mean they would not have much stuff. Maybe the boy did not do it and was falsely accused.

You don't know how many boats they have because there could be a boat or two boats from here out turtling. There is nothing to do but think around it and check your keys.

But suppose they have crossed the Old Bahama channel and hit the Cuban coast? Sure, he thought. Why didn't you think of that before? That's the best thing for them to do.

If they do that they can make for home on a Spanish boat out of Havana. There is a screening at Kingston. But that is an easier chance to take and you know plenty of people have beaten it. That damned Peters with his radio out. FCC, he thought. Frankly Can't Communicate. Then we got the beauty big one and it was too much radio for him. I don't know how he has fucked it. But he couldn't get Guantánamo last night on our call hour and if he doesn't get her tonight we are on our own. The hell with it, he thought. There are worse places to be than on your own. Get some sleep now, he said to himself. There is nothing you can do now that is sounder than that.

He moved his shoulders against the sand and went to sleep with the roaring of the surf on the reef.

III

WHILE Thomas Hudson was asleep he dreamed that his son Tom was not dead and that the other boys were all right and that the war was over. He dreamed that Tom's mother was sleeping with him and she was sleeping on top of him as she liked to do sometimes. He felt all of this and the tangibility of her legs against his legs and her body against his and her breasts against his chest and her mouth was playing against his mouth. Her hair hung down and

lay heavy and silky on his eyes and on his cheeks and he
turned his lips away from her searching ones and took the
hair in his mouth and held it. Then with one hand he
moistened the .357 Magnum and slipped it easily and
sound asleep where it should be. Then he lay under her
weight with her silken hair over his face like a curtain and
moved slowly and rhythmically.

That was when Henry put the light blanket over him
and Thomas Hudson said, asleep, "Thank you for being
so moist and lovely and for pressing on me so hard. Thank
you for coming back so quickly and for not being too
thin."

"The poor son of a bitch," Henry said and covered him
carefully. He went away carrying two wicker five-gallon
demijohns on his shoulders.

"I thought you wanted me thin, Tom," the woman said
in the dream. "You said I felt like a young goat when I
was thin and that nothing felt better than a young goat."

"You," he said. "Who's going to make love to who?"

"Both of us," she said. "Unless you want it differently."

"You make love to me. I'm tired."

"You're just lazy. Let me take the pistol off and put it
by your leg. The pistol's in the way of everything."

"Lay it by the bed," he said. "And make everything the
way it should be."

Then it was all the way it should be and she said,
"Should I be you or you be me?"

"You have first choice."

"I'll be you."

"I can't be you. But I can try."

"It's fun. You try it. Don't try to save yourself at all.
Try to lose everything and take everything too."

"All right."

"Are you doing it?"

"Yes," he said. "It's wonderful."

"Do you know now what we have?"

"Yes," he said. "Yes I know. It's easy to give up."

"Will you give up everything? Are you glad I brought
back the boys and that I come and be a devil in the night?"

"Yes. I'm glad of everything and will you swing your hair across my face and give me your mouth please and hold me so tight it kills me?"

"Of course. And you'll do it for me?"

When he woke he touched the blanket and he did not know, for an instant, that it was a dream. Then he lay on his side and felt the pistol holster between his legs and how it was really and all the hollownesses in him were twice as hollow and there was a new one from the dream. He saw it was still light and he saw the dinghy carrying water to his ship and he saw the white pounding of the surf on the reef. He turned on his side and tucked the blanket around himself and slept on his arms. He was asleep when they came to wake him and he had not dreamed at all this time.

IV

He steered all that night and he had Ara on the flying bridge with him until midnight and then Henry. They were running with a heavy beam sea and steering was like riding a horse downhill, he thought. It is all downhill and sometimes it is across the side of a hill. The sea is many hills and in here it is a broken country like the badlands.

"Talk to me," he said to Ara.

"What about, Tom?"

"Anything."

"Peters couldn't raise Guantánamo again. He has ruined it. The new big one."

"I know," Thomas Hudson said and tried to roll her as little as he could, riding the side of the hill. "He's burnt out something that he can't repair."

"He's listening," Ara said. "Willie is keeping him awake."

"Who's keeping Willie awake?"

"He's awake good," Ara said. "He doesn't sleep any better than you."

"How about you?"

"I'm good for all night if you want. Don't you want me to steer?"

"No. I haven't anything else to do."

"Tom, how badly do you feel?"

"I don't know. How badly can you feel?"

"It's useless," Ara said. "Would you like the wineskin?"

"No. Bring me up a bottle of cold tea and check on Peters and Willie. Check on everything."

Ara went down and Thomas Hudson was alone with the night and the sea and he still rode it like a horse going downhill too fast across broken country.

Henry came up with the bottle of cold tea.

"How are we, Tom?" he asked.

"We're perfect."

"Peters has the Miami police department on the old radio. All the prowl cars. Willie wants to talk to them. But I told him he couldn't."

"Correct."

"On the UHF, Peters has something squirting in German but he says it is way up with the wolf packs."

"He couldn't hear it then."

"It's a very funny night, Tom."

"It's not that funny."

"I don't know. I'm just telling you. Give me the course and let me take her and you go down."

"Has Peters logged it?"

"Of course."

"Tell Juan to give me a fix and have Peters log it. When was the son of a bitch squirting?"

"When I came up."

"Tell Juan to get the fix and log it right away."

"Yes, Tom."

"How are all the comic characters?"

"Sleeping. Gil, too."

"Get the rag out and have Peters log the fix."

"Do you want it?"

"I know too damn well where we are."

"Yes, Tom," Henry said. "Take it easy if you can."

Henry came up but Thomas Hudson did not feel like talking and Henry stood by him on the flying bridge and braced himself against the roll. After an hour he said, "There's a light, Tom. Off our starboard bow about twenty degrees."

"That's right."

When he was abeam of it he changed the course and the sea was astern.

"Now she is headed home to pasture," he said to Henry. "We're in the channel now. Wake Juan and get him up here and really keep your eyes open. You were late on the light."

"I'm sorry, Tom. I'll get Juan. Wouldn't you like a four-man watch?"

"Not until just before daylight," Thomas Hudson said. "I'll give you the word."

They might have cut across the banks, Thomas Hudson was thinking. But I don't think they would. They wouldn't want to cross at night and in daytime the banks wouldn't look good to deep-water sailors. They'd make their turn where I did. Then they would edge across comfortably the way we are going to do and they would probably hit for the highest part of the Cuban coast that showed. They don't want to get into any port so they will run with the wind. They will keep outside of Confites because they know there is a radio station there. But they have to get food and they have to get water. Actually they would do best to try to get as close to Havana as they could to land somewhere around Bacuranao and then infiltrate in from there. I'll send a signal from Confites. I won't ask him what to do. That will hold us up if he's away. I'll tell him what it is and what I'm doing. He can make his own dispositions. Guantánamo can make theirs and Camagüey can make theirs and La Fe theirs and the FBI theirs and maybe something will happen in a week.

Hell, he thought. I'll get them this week. They've got to stop for water and to cook what they have before the animals starve and rot. There's a good chance they will run only at nights and lay up daytimes. That would be logical. That's what I would do if I were them. Try to think like an intelligent German sailor with the problems this undersea boat commander has.

He has problems all right, Thomas Hudson thought. And the worst problem he has is us and he doesn't even know about us. We don't look dangerous to him. We look good to him.

Don't take it in any bloodthirsty way, he thought. Nothing of this is going to bring back anything. Use your head and be glad to have something to do and good people to do it with.

"Juan," he said. "What do you see, boy?"

"All bloody ocean."

"You other gentlemen see anything?"

"Bloody nothing," Gil said.

"My bloody belly sees coffee. But it doesn't come any closer," Ara said.

"I see land," Henry said. He had seen it that instant, a low square smudge as though a man's thumb had daubed weak ink against the lightening sky.

"That's behind Romano," Thomas Hudson said. "Thank you, Henry. Now you characters go down for coffee and send up four other desperate men to see strange and amusing things."

"Do you want coffee, Tom?" Ara asked.

"No. I'll take tea when it's made."

"We've only been on watch a couple of hours," Gil said. "We don't need to go off, Tom."

"Go on down and get coffee and give the other desperate men a chance for glory."

"Tom, didn't you say you thought they were at Lobos?"

"Yes. But I changed my mind."

The others had gone down and four were coming up.

"Gentlemen," Thomas Hudson said. "Split the four quadrants up amongst you. Is there coffee below?"

"Plenty," his mate said. "And tea. The engines are good and she didn't make any more water than you would expect in the cross sea."

"How is Peters?"

"He drank his own whisky in the night. The one with the little lamb on it. But he stayed awake. Willie kept him awake and drank his whisky," his mate said.

"We have to fill gas at Confites and take on anything else there is."

"They can load fast and I can kill a pig and scald and scrape him," his mate said. "I'll give them a quarter at the radio station to help me and I can butcher him while you are running. You get some sleep while we load. Would you like me to steer?"

"No. I only have to send three signals at Confites and you load and I will sleep. Then we will pursue."

"Toward home?"

"Of course. They may avoid us for a time. But they cannot escape us. Later we will talk about it. How are they?"

"You know them. We will talk about it later. Steer in a little more, Tom. With the countercurrent you'll shorten it."

"Did you lose much with rolling?"

"Nothing that matters. It was a bitch of a beam sea," his mate said.

"*Ya lo creo,*" said Thomas Hudson. "I believe it."

"There should only be the people of this one undersea boat around here. She must surely be the one they claimed sunk. Now they are off La Guayra and above Kingston and on all the petrol lanes. Also they are with the wolf packs."

"Also they are here sometimes."

"Yes, for our sins."

"And for theirs."

"On this thing we will pursue well and intelligently."

"Let us get it started," Thomas Hudson said.

"There has been no delay."

"It goes slowly for me."

"Yes," his mate said. "But get some sleep in Confites and I promise everything will go faster than you could hope."

V

THOMAS HUDSON saw the high lookout post on the sandy key and the tall signalling mast. They were painted white and were the first things that showed. Then he saw the stumpy radio masts and the high cocked wreck of the ship that lay on the rocks and obscured the view of the radio shack. The key was not handsome from his side.

The sun was behind him and it was easy to find the first big pass through the reef and then, skirting the shoals and the coral heads, to come up on the leeward shelter. There was a sandy half-moon of beach and the island was covered with dry grass on this side and was rocky and flat on its windward end. The water was clear and green over the sand and Thomas Hudson came in close to the center of the beach and anchored with his bow almost against the shore. The sun was up and the Cuban flag was flying over the radio shack and the out-buildings. The signalling mast was bare in the wind. There was no one in sight and the Cuban flag, new and brightly clean, was snapping in the wind.

"Maybe they had a relief," Thomas Hudson said. "The old flag was pretty worn when we left."

He looked and saw his drums of gas where he had left them and the marks of digging in the sand where his blocks of ice should be buried. The sand was high like new-made graves and over the island sooty terns were flying in the wind. They nested in the rocks up at the windward end and a few nested in the grass of the lee. They were flying now, falling off with the wind, cutting sharply into it, and dipping down toward the grass and the rocks. They were all calling, sadly and desperately.

Must be somebody out getting eggs for breakfast,

Thomas Hudson thought. Just then he smelled ham frying in the galley and he went astern and called down that he would take his breakfast on the bridge. He studied the island carefully. They might be here, he thought. They could have taken this.

But when a man in shorts came down the path that ran from the radio shack to the beach, it was the Lieutenant. He was very brown and cheerful and he had not cut his hair in three months and he called out, "How was your trip?"

"Good," said Thomas Hudson. "Will you come aboard for a beer?"

"Later," the Lieutenant said. "They brought your ice and supplies and some beer two days ago. We buried the ice. The other things are at the house."

"What news do you have?"

"The aviation were supposed to have sunk a submarine off Guinchos ten days ago. But that was before you left."

"Yes," Thomas Hudson said. "That was two weeks ago. Is that the same one?"

"Yes."

"Any other news?"

"Another submarine was supposed to have shot down a blimp off Cayo Sal day before yesterday."

"Is that confirmed?"

"We heard so. Then there was your pig."

"Yes?"

"The same day of the blimp they brought a pig for you with your supplies and he swam out to sea the next morning and was drowned. We had fed him, too."

"*¡Qué puerco más suicido!*" Thomas Hudson said.

The Lieutenant laughed. He had a very cheerful brown face and he was not stupid. He was acting because it amused him. He had orders to do anything he could for Hudson and to ask him nothing. Thomas Hudson had orders to use any facilities the station could give and tell nothing to anyone.

"Any more news?" he asked. "Have you seen any Bahaman sponging or turtle boats?"

"What would they be doing here when they have all the turtle and sponge over there? But there were two Bahaman turtle boats came by here this week. They turned off the point and tacked to come in. But they ran for Cayo Cruz instead."

"I wonder what they were doing here?"

"I don't know. You cruise those waters for scientific purposes. Why should turtle boats leave the best turtling grounds to come here?"

"How many men could you see?"

"We could only see the men at the tiller. The boats had palm branches spread over the deck. They were built up like a shack. It could be to give shade for the turtles."

"Were the helmsmen white or black?"

"White and sunburned."

"Could you make out any numbers or names on the boats?"

"No. They were too far away. I put the key in a state of defense that night and the next day and night and there was nothing."

"When did they go by?"

"The day before your ice and groceries and your suicidal pig arrived. Eleven days after the sub was reported sunk by your aviation. Three days before you arrived here. Are they friends of yours?"

"You signalled them, of course?"

"Naturally. And I have heard nothing."

"Can you send three messages for me?"

"Of course. Send them in as soon as they are ready."

"I will start to load gas and ice and put the supplies aboard. Was there anything in them you can use?"

"I don't know. There is a list. I signed for it but I could not read it in English."

"Didn't they send any chickens or turkeys?"

"Yes," the Lieutenant said. "I was saving them for a surprise."

"We'll split them," Thomas Hudson said. "We'll split the beer, too."

"Let my people help you load the gas and ice."

"Good. Thank you very much. I would like to be gone in two hours."

"I understand. Our relief has been put off another month."

"Again?"

"Again."

"How do your people take it?"

"They're all here on a disciplinary basis."

"Thank you very much for your help. The whole world of science is grateful."

"Guantánamo, too?"

"Guantánamo, the Athens of science."

"I think they may have holed up somewhere."

"So do I," said Thomas Hudson.

"The shelters were of coconut palm and they were still green."

"Tell me anything else."

"I don't know anything else. Send in the messages. I don't want to come on board to take up any of your time or be a nuisance."

"If anything perishable comes out while I am gone, use it before it spoils."

"Thank you. I'm sorry your pig committed such suicide."

"Thank you," said Thomas Hudson. "We all have our small problems."

"I'll tell the men not to come on board but only to help load at the stern and help alongside."

"Thank you," Thomas Hudson said. "Can you remember anything more about the turtle boats?"

"They were typical. One was almost exactly the same as the other. They looked as though they had been built by the same builder. They turned the point of the reef and made to tack in here. Then they ran before the wind for Cayo Cruz."

"Inside the reef?"

"Inside until they were out of sight."

"And the sub off Cayo Sal?"

"Stayed on the surface and shot it out with the blimp."

"I'd stay in a state of defense if I were you."

"I am," the Lieutenant said. "That's why you haven't seen anybody."

"I saw the birds moving."

"The poor birds," the Lieutenant said.

VI

THEY were running to the westward inside the reef with the wind astern. The tanks had been filled, the ice stowed, and below one watch was picking and cleaning chickens. The other was cleaning weapons. The canvas that shielded the flying bridge to waist height was laced on and the two long boards that announced in twelve-inch block letters the scientific mission of the boat were in place. Looking over the side watching the depth of water Thomas Hudson saw the patches of chicken feathers floating out onto the following sea.

"Take her in just as close as we can get without hitting any of those sandbars," he told Ara. "You know this coast."

"I know it's no good," Ara said. "Where are we going to anchor?"

"I want to check up at the head of Cayo Cruz."

"We can check there but I don't think it will be much use. You don't think they would stay there, do you?"

"No. But there might be fishermen in there who would have seen them. Or charcoal burners."

"I wish this wind would fail," Ara said. "I'd like to have a couple of days of flat calm."

"It's squally over Romano."

"I know. But this wind blows through here like through a pass in the mountains. We'll never catch them if this wind keeps up."

"We've been right so far," Thomas Hudson said. "And maybe we'll get some luck. They could have taken Lobos and used the radio there to call up that other sub to take them off."

"That shows they didn't know the other sub was there."

"Must be. They move a lot in ten days."

"When they want to," Ara said. "Let's stop thinking, Tom. It gives me a headache. I'd rather handle gas drums. You think and tell me where you want me to steer."

"Just as she goes and watch for that no-good Minerva. Keep well inside of that and outside the sandspits."

"Good."

Do you suppose she lost her radio when she got smacked? Thomas Hudson thought. She must have had an emergency radio that she could have used. But Peters never picked her up on the UHF after she was smacked. Still, that doesn't necessarily prove anything. Nothing proves anything except that those two boats were seen on the course we are on three days ago. Did I ask him if they had their dinghys on deck? No, I forgot to. But they must have because he said they were ordinary Bahaman turtling boats except for the shelters they had rigged with the palm branches.

How many people? You don't know. Any wounded? You don't know. How armed? All you know is a machine pistol. Their course? We are on it until now.

Maybe we will find something between Cayo Cruz and Mégano, he thought. What you'll probably find is lots of willets and iguana tracks in the sand toward the water hole.

Well, it keeps your mind off things. What things? There aren't any things any more. Oh yes, there are. There is this ship and the people on her and the sea and the bastards you are hunting. Afterwards you will see your animals and go into town and get drunk as you can and your ashes dragged and then get ready to go out and do it again.

Maybe this time you will get these characters. You did

not destroy their undersea boat but you were faintly instrumental in its destruction. If you can round up the crew, it will be extremely useful.

Then why don't you care anything about anything? he asked himself. Why don't you think of them as murderers and have the righteous feelings that you should have? Why do you just pound and pound on after it like a riderless horse that is still in the race? Because we are all murderers, he told himself. We all are on both sides, if we are any good, and no good will come of any of it.

But you have to do it. Sure, he said. But I don't have to be proud of it. I only have to do it well. I didn't hire out to like it. You did not even hire out, he told himself. That makes it even worse.

"Let me take her, Ara," he said.

Ara gave him the wheel.

"Keep a good lookout to starboard. But don't let the sun blind you."

"I'll get my glasses. Look, Tom. Why don't you let me steer and get a good four-man lookout up here? You're tired and you didn't rest at all at the key."

"We don't need a four-man lookout in here. Later on we will."

"But you're tired."

"I'm not sleepy. Look, if they run nights along here close in to shore they are going to get in trouble. Then they will have to lay up to make repairs and we will find them."

"That's no reason for you never to rest, Tom."

"I'm not doing it to show off," Thomas Hudson said.

"No one has ever thought so."

"How do you feel about these bastards?"

"Only that we will catch them and kill what is necessary and bring the others in."

"What about the massacre?"

"I don't say we would have done the same thing. But they thought it was necessary. They did not do it for pleasure," Ara said.

"And their dead man?"

"Henry has wanted to kill Peters several times. I have wanted to kill him myself sometimes."

"Yes," Thomas Hudson agreed. "It is not an uncommon feeling."

"I don't think of any of these things and so I don't worry. Why don't you not worry, and read when you relax the way you always did?"

"I'm going to sleep tonight. After we anchor I'll read and then sleep. We've gained four days on them, though it does not show. Now we must search carefully."

"We will get them or we will drive them into other people's hands," Ara said. "What difference does it make? We have our pride but we have another pride people know nothing of."

"That is what I had forgotten," Thomas Hudson said.

"It is a pride without vanity," Ara continued. "Failure is its brother and shit is its sister and death is its wife."

"It must be a big pride."

"It is," Ara said. "You must not forget it, Tom, and you must not destroy yourself. Everyone in the ship has that pride, including Peters. Although I do not like Peters."

"Thanks for telling me," Thomas Hudson said. "I feel fuck-all discouraged about things sometimes."

"Tom," Ara said. "All a man has is pride. Sometimes you have it so much it is a sin. We have all done things for pride that we knew were impossible. We didn't care. But a man must implement his pride with intelligence and care. Now that you have ceased to be careful of yourself I must ask you to be, please. For us and for the ship."

"Who is us?"

"All of us."

"OK," Thomas Hudson said. "Ask for your dark glasses."

"Tom, please understand."

"I understand. Thanks very much. I'll eat a hearty supper and sleep like a child."

Ara did not think it was funny and he always thought funny things were funny.

"You try it, Tom," he said.

VII

THEY anchored in the lee of Cayo Cruz in the sandy bight between the two keys.

"We'll put out another anchor to lay here," Thomas Hudson called to his mate. "I don't like this bottom."

The mate shrugged his shoulders and bent down to the second anchor and Thomas Hudson eased her ahead against the tide, watching the grass from the banks riding by in the current. He came astern until his second anchor was well dug in. The boat lay with her bow into the wind and the tide running past her. There was much wind even in this lee and he knew that when the tide changed she would swing broadside to the swell.

"The hell with it," he said. "Let her roll."

But his mate had lowered the dinghy already and they were running out a stern anchor. Thomas Hudson watched them drop the little Danforth where it would hold her into the wind when the tide came aflood.

"Why don't you put out a couple more?" he called. "Then maybe we could sell her for a goddam spider."

The mate grinned at him.

"Get the outboard on her. I'm going in."

"No, Tom," his mate said. "Let Ara and Willie go in. I'll take them in and another party to Mégano. Do you want them to take the *niños*?"

"No. Be scientists."

I'm accepting a lot of handling, he thought. That must mean I really do need some rest. The thing is I am neither tired nor sleepy.

"Antonio," he said.

"Yes," said his mate.

"I'll take the air mattress and two cushions and a big drink."

"What kind of drink?"

"Gin and coconut water with Angostura and lime."

"A *Tomini?*" his mate said, pleased that he was drinking again.

"Double quantity."

Henry threw the air mattress up and climbed after it with a book and a magazine.

"You're out of the wind here," he said. "Do you want me to open any of this canvas for ventilation?"

"Since when did I rate all this?"

"Tom, we talked of it and we all agreed that you need some rest. You've been driving yourself past what a man can stand. You are past it now."

"Shit," said Thomas Hudson.

"Maybe," said Henry. "I said I thought you were OK and could go quite a lot more and hold the pace. But the others were worried and they convinced me. You can deconvince me. But take it easy now, Tom."

"I never felt better. I just don't give a damn."

"That's what it's about. You won't come down off the bridge. You want to stand all the watches steering. And you don't give a damn about anything."

"OK," said Thomas Hudson. "I get the picture. But I still command."

"I didn't mean it in any bad way, truly."

"Forget it," Thomas Hudson said. "I'm resting. You know how to search a key, don't you?"

"I should."

"See what there is on Mégano."

"That's mine. Willie and Ara have gone in already. I'm just waiting with the other party for Antonio to come back with the dinghy."

"How is Peters?"

"He's been working hard on the big radio all afternoon. He thinks he has it fixed OK."

"That would be wonderful. If I'm asleep, wake me as soon as you get back."

"Yes, Tom." Henry reached down and took something that was handed to him. It was a big glass full of ice and a rusty-colored liquid and it was wrapped in a double thickness of paper towel held fast by a rubber band.

"A double *Tomini*," Henry said. "Drink it and read and go to sleep. You can put the glass in one of the big frag slots."

Thomas Hudson took a long sip.

"I like it," he said.

"You used to. Everything will be fine, Tom."

"Everything we can do damn well better be."

"Just get a good rest."

"I will."

Henry went down and Thomas Hudson heard the hum of the outboard coming in. It stopped and there was talking and then he heard the hum of it going away. He waited a little, listening. Then he took the drink and threw it high over the side and let the wind take it astern. He settled the glass in the hole it fitted best in the triple rack and lay face down on the rubber mattress with his two arms around it.

I think they had wounded under the shelters, he thought. Of course it could be to conceal many people. But I do not believe that. They would have come in here the first night. I should have gone ashore. I will from now on. But Ara and Henry could not be better and Willie is very good. I must try to be very good. Try hard tonight, he told himself. And chase hard and good and with no mistakes and do not overrun them.

VIII

He felt a hand on his shoulder. It was Ara and he said, "We got one, Tom. Willie and I."

Thomas Hudson swung down and Ara was with him. The German lay on the stern wrapped in a blanket. His head was on two cushions. Peters was sitting on the deck beside him with a glass of water.

"Look what we got," he said.

The German was thin and there was a blond beard on his chin and on his sunken cheeks. His hair was long and uncombed and in the late afternoon light, with the sun almost down, he looked like a saint.

"He can't talk," Ara said. "Willie and I tried him. You better keep to windward of him, too."

"I smelled it coming down," Thomas Hudson said. "Ask him if he wants anything," he said to Peters.

The radio operator spoke to him in German and the German looked toward him but he did not speak nor move his head. Thomas Hudson heard the humming of the outboard motor, and looked across the bight at the dinghy coming out of the sunset. It was loaded down to the water line. He looked down at the German again.

"Ask him how many they are. Tell him we must know how many they are. Tell him this is important."

Peters spoke to the German softly and it seemed to Thomas Hudson almost lovingly.

The German said three words with great effort.

"He says nothing is important," Peters said.

"Tell him he is wrong. I have to know. Ask him if he wants morphine."

The German looked at Thomas Hudson kindly and said three words.

"He says it doesn't hurt anymore," Peters said. He spoke rapidly in German and again Thomas Hudson caught the loving tone; or, perhaps it was only the loving sound of the language.

"Shut up, Peters," Thomas Hudson said. "Translate only and exactly what I say. Did you hear me?"

"Yes, sir," Peters said.

"Tell him I can make him tell."

Peters spoke to the German and he turned his eyes toward Thomas Hudson. They were old eyes now but they were in a young man's face gone old as driftwood and nearly as gray.

"Nein," the German said slowly.

"He says no," Peters translated.

"Yeah, I got that part of it," Thomas Hudson said. "Get him some warm soup, Willie, and bring some cognac. Peters, ask him if he wouldn't like some morphine really if he doesn't have to talk. Tell him we have plenty."

Peters translated and the German looked toward Thomas Hudson and smiled a thin, northern smile.

He spoke almost inaudibly to Peters.

"He says thank you but he doesn't need it and it's better to save it."

Then he said something softly to Peters who translated, "He says he could have used it last week."

"Tell him I admire him," Thomas Hudson said.

Antonio, his mate, was alongside in the dinghy with Henry and the rest of the Mégano party.

"Come aboard easy," Thomas Hudson said to them. "Keep away from the stern. We got a Kraut dying on the stern that I want to have die easy. What did you find?"

"Nothing," Henry said. "Absolutely nothing."

"Peters," Thomas Hudson said. "Talk to him all you want. You might get something. I'm going forward with Ara and Willie to get a drink."

Below, he said, "How's your soup, Willie?"

"The first one I put my hands on was clam broth," Willie said. "It's about hot enough."

"Why didn't you give him oxtail or mulligatawny?" Thomas Hudson said. "They're more deadly in his condition. Where the hell is the chicken?"

"I didn't want to give him the chicken. That's Henry's."

"Quite right, too," Henry said. "Why should we coddle him?"

"I don't think we really are. When I ordered it I thought some soup and a drink might help him talk. But he isn't going to talk. Give me a gin, will you, Ara?"

"They made a shelter for him, Tom, and he had a good bed made from branches and plenty of water and food in a crock. They tried to make him comfortable and they ditched the sand for drainage. There were many good tracks from the beach and I would say they were eight or ten. Not more. Willie and I were very careful carrying him. Both his wounds are gangrenous and the gangrene is very high toward the right thigh. Perhaps we should not have brought him but instead have come for you and Peters to question him in his shelter. If so, it is my fault."

"Did he have a weapon?"

"No. Nor any identification."

"Give me my drink," Thomas Hudson said. "When would you say the branches for the shelter were cut?"

"Not later than yesterday morning, I would say. But I could not be sure."

"Did he speak at all?"

"No. He looked as though made of wood when he saw us with the pistols. He looked afraid of Willie once. When he saw his eye, I think. Then he smiled when we lifted him."

"To show he could," Willie said.

"Then he went away," Ara said. "How long do you think it will take him to die, Tom?"

"I don't know."

"Well, let's go out and take the drinks," Henry said. "I don't trust Peters."

"Let's drink the clam broth up," Willie said. "I'm hungry. I can heat him a can of Henry's chicken if he says it is OK."

"If it will help to make him talk," Henry said. "Of course."

"It probably won't," Willie said. "But it's kind of shitty to give him clam broth the way he is. Take him out the cognac, Henry. Maybe he really likes that, like you and me."

"Don't bother him," Thomas Hudson said. "He's a good Kraut."

"Sure," Willie said. "They're all good Krauts when they fold up."

"He hasn't folded up," Thomas Hudson said. "He's just dying."

"With much style," Ara said.

"You getting to be a Kraut-lover, too?" Willie asked him. "That makes you and Peters."

"Shut up, Willie," Thomas Hudson said.

"What's the matter with you?" Willie said to Thomas Hudson. "You're just the exhausted leader of a little group of earnest Kraut-lovers."

"Come up forward, Willie," Thomas Hudson said. "Ara, take the soup astern when it is warm. The rest of you go watch the Kraut die, if you want. But don't crowd him."

Antonio started to follow as Thomas Hudson and Willie went forward but Thomas Hudson shook his head at him and the big man went back to the galley.

They were in the forward cockpit and it was almost dark. Thomas Hudson could just see Willie's face. It looked better in this light and he was on the side of the good eye. Thomas Hudson looked at Willie and then at his two anchor lines and at a tree he could still see on the beach. It's a tricky sandy bottom, he thought; and he said, "All right, Willie. Say the rest of it."

"You," Willie said. "Flogging yourself to death up there because your kid is dead. Don't you know everybody's kids die?"

"I know it. What else?"

"That fucking Peters and a fucking Kraut stinking up the fantail and what kind of a ship is it where the cook is the mate?"

"How does he cook?"

"He cooks wonderful and he knows more about small-boat handling than all of us put together, including you."

"Much more."

"Shit, Tom. I'm not blowing my top. I got no goddam top to blow. I'm used to doing things a different way. I like it on the ship and I like everybody except that half-cunt Peters. Only you quit flogging yourself."

"I'm not really," Thomas Hudson said. "I don't think about anything except work."

"You're so noble you ought to be stuffed and crucified," Willie said. "Think about cunt."

"We're headed toward it."

"That's the way to talk."

"Willie, are you OK now?"

"Sure. Why the hell wouldn't I be? That Kraut got me, I guess. They had him fixed up nice like we wouldn't fix up anybody. Or maybe we would if we had time. But they took time. They don't know how close we are. But they got to know somebody's chasing. Everybody's after them now. But they fixed him up just as nice as anybody could be fixed in the condition he was."

"Sure," Thomas Hudson said. "They fixed up those people back on the key nice, too."

"Yeah," said Willie. "Isn't that the hell of it?"

Just then Peters came in. He always held himself as a Marine even when he was not at his best and he was proudest of the real discipline without the formalities of discipline which was the rule of the ship. He was the one who took the greatest advantage of it. Now he stopped, came to attention, saluted, which showed he was drunk, and said, "Tom, I mean, sir. He is dead."

"Who's dead?"

"The prisoner, sir."

"OK," Thomas Hudson said. "Get your generator going and see if you can get Guantánamo."

They ought to have something for us, he thought.

"Did the prisoner talk?" he asked Peters.

"No sir."

"Willie," he asked. "How do you feel?"

"Fine."

"Get some flashbulbs and take two, in profile of the face, lying on the stern. Take the blanket off and his shorts off and take one full-length lying as he is across the stern. Shoot one full-face of his head and one full-face lying down."

"Yes sir," Willie said.

Thomas Hudson went up on the flying bridge. He heard

the motor of the generator start and saw the sudden flashes of the bulbs. ONI, up where they evaluate, won't believe we even have this much of a Kraut, he thought. There isn't any proof. Somebody will claim it is a stiff they pushed out that we picked up. I should have photographed him sooner. The hell with them. Maybe we will get the others tomorrow.

Ara came up.

"Tom, who do you want to have take him ashore and bury him?"

"Who worked the least today?"

"Everybody has worked hard. I'll take Gil in and we will do it. We can bury him in the sand just above high water."

"Maybe a little higher."

"I'll send Willie up and you tell him how you want the board lettered. I have a board from a box in stores."

"Send Willie up."

"Do we sew him up?"

"No. Just wrap him in his own blanket. Send Willie up."

"What was it that you wanted?" Willie asked.

"Letter the board, 'Unknown German Sailor' and put the date underneath."

"OK, Tom. Do you want me to go in with the burial detail?"

"No. Ara and Gil are going in. Letter the board and take it easy and have a drink."

"As soon as Peters gets Guantánamo, I'll send it up. Don't you want to come down?"

"No. I'm taking it easy up here."

"What's it like on the bridge of a big ship like this, full of responsibility and horseshit?"

"Just about the same as lettering that board."

When the signal came from Guantánamo it read, decoded, CONTINUE SEARCHING CAREFULLY WESTWARD.

That's us, said Thomas Hudson to himself. He lay down and was asleep immediately and Henry covered him with a light blanket.

IX

AN hour before daylight he was below and had checked his glass. It was four-tenths lower and he woke his mate and showed it to him.

The mate looked at him and nodded.

"You saw the squalls over Romano yesterday," he whispered. "She is going into the south."

"Make me some tea, will you, please," Thomas Hudson asked.

"I have some cold in a bottle on the ice."

He went astern and found a mop and a bucket and scrubbed the deck of the stern. It had been scrubbed before but he scrubbed it again and rinsed the mop. Then he took his bottle of cold tea up on the flying bridge and waited for it to get light.

Before it was light his mate got in the stern anchor and then with Ara brought in the starboard anchor and they and Gil hoisted the dinghy aboard. Then his mate pumped the bilges and checked his motors.

He put his head up and said, "Any time."

"Why did she make that much water?"

"Just a stuffing box. I tightened it a little. But I'd rather she made a little water than run hot."

"All right. Send up Ara and Henry. We'll get going."

They got in the anchor and he turned to Ara. "Show me the tree again."

Ara pointed it out just above the line of beach they were leaving and Thomas Hudson made a small pencilled cross on the chart.

"Peters never did get Guantánamo again?"

"No. He burned out once more."

"Well, we are behind them and they have other people ahead of them and we've got orders."

"Do you think the wind will really go into the south, Tom?" Henry asked.

"The glass shows it will. We can tell better when it starts to get up."

"It fell off to almost nothing about four o'clock."

"Did the sand flies hit you?"

"Only at daylight."

"You might as well go down and Flit them all out. There's no sense our carrying them around with us."

It was a lovely day and looking back at the bight where they had anchored and at the beach and the scrub trees of Cayo Cruz that they both knew so well, Thomas Hudson and Ara saw the high, piled clouds over the land. Cayo Romano rose so that it was like the mainland and the clouds were high above it with their promise of south wind or calm and land squalls.

"What would you think if you were a German, Ara?" Thomas Hudson asked. "What would you think if you saw that and knew that you were going to lose your wind?"

"I'd try to get inside," Ara said. "I think that's what I'd do."

"You'd need a guide for inside."

"I'd get me a guide," Ara said.

"Where would you get him?"

"From fishermen up at Antón or inside at Romano. Or at Coco. There must be fishermen salting fish along there now. There might even be a live-well boat at Antón."

"We'll try Antón," Thomas Hudson said. "It's nice to wake up in the morning and steer with the sun behind you."

"If you always steered with the sun behind you and on a day like this, what a place the ocean would be."

The day was like true summer and in the morning the squalls had not yet built. The day was all gentle promise and the sea lay smooth and clear. They could see bottom clearly until they ran out of soundings, and then far out and just where it should be was the Minerva with the sea breaking restfully on its coral rocks. It was the swell that was left from the two months of unremitting heavy trade wind. But it broke gently and kindly and with a passive regularity.

It is as though she were saying we are all friends now and there will never be any trouble nor any wildness again, Thomas Hudson thought. Why is she so dishonest? A river can be treacherous and cruel and kind and friendly. A stream can be completely friendly and you can trust it all your life if you do not abuse it. But the ocean always has to lie to you before she does it.

He looked again at her gentle rise and fall that showed the Minervas as regularly and attractively as though she were trying to sell them as a choice location.

"Want to get me a sandwich?" he asked Ara. "Corned beef and raw onion or ham and egg and raw onion. After you get breakfast, bring a four-man watch up here and check all the binoculars. I'm going outside before we go in to Antón."

"Yes, Tom."

I wonder what I would do without that Ara, Thomas Hudson thought. You had a wonderful sleep, he told himself, and you couldn't feel better. We've got orders and we are right on their tails and pushing them toward other people. You're following your orders and look what a beautiful morning you have to follow them in. But things look too damned good.

They moved down the channel keeping a good lookout, but there was nothing but the calm, early morning sea with its friendly undulations and the long green line of Romano inland with the many keys between.

"They won't sail very far in this," Henry said.

"They won't sail at all," Thomas Hudson said.

"Are we going in to Antón?"

"Sure. And work all of that out."

"I like Antón," Henry said. "There's a good place to lay to, if it's calm, so they won't eat us up."

"Inside they'd carry you away," Ara said.

A small seaplane showed ahead, flying low and coming

toward them. It was white and minute with the sun on it.

"Plane," Thomas Hudson said. "Pass the word to get the big flag out."

The plane came on until it buzzed them. Then it circled them twice and went off flying on down to the eastward.

"He wouldn't have it so good if he found one," Henry said. "They'd shoot him down."

"He could send the location and Cayo Francés would pick it up."

"Maybe," Ara said. The two other Basques said nothing. They stood back to back and searched their quadrants.

After a while the Basque they called George because his name was Eugènio and Peters could not always say Eugenio said, "Plane's coming back to the eastward between the outer keys and Romano."

"He's going home to breakfast," Ara said.

"He'll report us," Thomas Hudson said. "So in a month maybe everybody will know where we were at this time today."

"If he doesn't get the location mixed up on his chart," Ara said. "Paredón Grande, Tom. Bearing approximately twenty degrees off the port bow."

"You've got good eyes," Thomas Hudson said. "That's her, all right. I better take her in and find the channel in to Antón."

"Turn port ninety degrees and I think you'll have her."

"I'll hit the bank anyway and we can run along it until we find that damned canal."

They came in toward the line of green keys that showed like black hedges sticking up from the water and then acquired shape and greenness and finally sandy beaches. Thomas Hudson came in with reluctance from the open channel, the promising sea, and the beauty of the morning on deep water, to the business of searching the inner keys. But the plane working the coast in this direction, turning to run over it with the sun behind it, should mean no one had picked the boats up to the eastward. It could be only a routine patrol, too. But it was logical that it should mean the other. A routine patrol would have been out over the channel both ways.

He saw Antón, which was well wooded and a pleasant island, growing before him and he watched ahead for his marks while he worked in toward the bank. He must take the highest tree on the head of the island and fit it squarely into the little saddle on Romano. On that bearing, he could come in even if the sun were in his eyes and the water had the glare of a burning glass.

Today he did not need it. But he did it for practice and when he found his tree, thinking, I should have something more permanent for a bearing on a hurricane coast, he eased along the bank until he fitted the tree carefully into the slot of the saddle, then turned sharp in. He was in the canal between marly banks that were barely covered with water and he said to Ara, "Ask Antonio to put a feather out. We might pick up something to eat. This channel has a wonderful bar on the bottom."

Then he steered straight in on his bearing. He was tempted not to look at the banks but to push it straight through. But then he knew that was one of the things of too much pride Ara had spoken of and he piloted carefully on the starboard bank and made his turn to starboard when it came by the banks and not by the second bearing that he had. It was like running in the regular streets of a new subdivision and the tide was racing in. It came in brown at first, then pure and clean. Just before he came into the part that he thought of as the turning basin where he planned to anchor, he heard Willie shout, "Feesh! Feesh!!" Looking astern, he saw a tarpon shaking himself high in the sun. His mouth was open and he was huge and the sun shone on his silvered scales and on the long green whip of his dorsal fin. He shook himself desperately in the sun and came down in a splash of water.

"Sábalo," Antonio called up disgustedly.

"Worthless sábalo," the Basques said.

"Can I play him, Tom?" Henry asked. "I'd like to catch him even if he is no good to eat."

"Take him from Antonio if Willie hasn't got him. Tell Antonio to get the hell forward. I'm going to anchor."

The excitement and the leaping of the big tarpon continued astern, with no one paying attention to it except to grin, while they anchored.

"Do you want to put out another?" Thomas Hudson called forward. His mate shook his head. When they swung well to the anchor, his mate came up on the bridge.

"She'll hold in anything, Tom," he said. "Any kind of a squall. Anything. And it doesn't make any difference how she swings, we can't have any motion."

"What time will we get the squalls?"

"After two," his mate said, looking at the sky.

"Get the dinghy over," Thomas Hudson said. "And give me an extra can of gas with the outboard. We have to get the hell going."

"Who's going with you?"

"Just Ara and Willie and I. I want her to travel fast."

X

IN the dinghy the three of them had their raincoats wrapped around the *niños*. These were the Thompson submachine guns in their full-length sheep-wool cases. The cases were cut and sewn by Ara, who was not a tailor, and Thomas Hudson had impregnated the clipped wool on the inside with a protective oil which had a faintly carbolic smell. It was because the guns nestled in their sheep-lined cradles, and because the cradles swung when they were strapped open inside the branch of the flying bridge, that the Basques had nicknamed them "little children."

"Give us a bottle of water," Thomas Hudson said to his mate. When Antonio brought it, heavy and cold with the wide, screw-on top, he passed it to Willie, who stowed it forward. Ara loved to steer the outboard and he was in the stern. Thomas Hudson was in the center and Willie crouched in the bow.

Ara headed her straight in for the key and Thomas Hudson watched the clouds piling up over the land.

As they came into the shallow water, Thomas Hudson could see the grayish humps of conches bulging from the sand. Ara leaned forward to say, "Do you want to look at the beach, Tom?"

"Maybe we'd better before the rain."

Ara ran the dinghy ashore, tilting his motor up just at the last rush. The tide had undercut the sand to make a little channel at the point and he drove the boat in, slanting her up onto the sand.

"Home again," Willie said. "What's this bitch's name?"

"Antón."

"Not Antón Grande or Antón Chico or Antón El Cabrón?"

"Just Antón. You take it up to that point to the eastward and then keep going. We'll pick you up. I'll work along this beach fast and Ara will leave the dinghy down somewhere past the next point and work on ahead. I'll pick him up in the dinghy and we'll come back around for you."

Willie had his *niño* wrapped in his raincoat and put it on his shoulder.

"If I find any Krauts, can I kill them?"

"The Colonel said all but one," Thomas Hudson said. "Try to save a smart one."

"I'll give them all IQ tests before I open up."

"Give yourself one."

"Mine's goddam low or I wouldn't be here," Willie said, and he set out. He walked contemptuously and he watched the beach and the country ahead as carefully as a man could watch.

Thomas Hudson told Ara in Spanish what they were going to do and then shoved the dinghy off. He started down the beach with his *niño* under his arm and he felt the sand between his bare toes. Ahead, the dinghy was rounding the small point.

He was glad that he had come ashore and he walked as fast as he could go and still check the beach. It was a pleasant beach and he had no forebodings about it as he had had earlier in the day on the sea.

It was spooky this morning, he thought. Maybe it was just the calm. Ahead he could see the clouds still building up. But nothing had started to come out. There were no sand flies now in the hot sun and no mosquitoes and ahead of him he saw a tall white heron standing looking down in the shallow water with his head, neck, and beak poised. He had not flown when Ara passed with the dinghy.

We have to search it carefully even though I do not believe there is anything here, he thought. They are becalmed today so we lose nothing and it would be criminal to overrun them. Why don't I know more about them? he thought. It is my own fault. I should have gone in and looked at the hut they built and at the tracks. I questioned Willie and Ara and they are both truly good. But I should have gone in myself.

It is the repugnance that I feel toward meeting them, he thought. It is my duty and I want to get them and I will. But I have a sort of fellow death-house feeling about them. Do people who are in the death house hate each other? I don't believe they do unless they are insane.

Just then the heron rose and flew further up the beach. Braking widely with his great wings, and then taking a few awkward steps, he landed. I am sorry I disturbed him, Thomas Hudson thought.

He checked all of the beach above high tide. But there were no tracks except where one turtle had crawled twice. She had made a wide track to the sea and back and a wallowing depression where she had laid.

I haven't time to dig for the eggs, he thought. The clouds were beginning to darken and to move out.

If they had been on this side of the key they certainly would have dug for them. He looked ahead but he could not see the dinghy because there was another curving point.

He walked along just where the sand was firm from the

dampness of the high tide and he saw the hermit crabs carrying their shells and the ghost crabs that slipped across the stretch of sand and into the water. To his right, in the shallow channel, he saw the grayness that a school of mullet made and their shadow on the sand bottom as they moved. He saw the shadow of a very big barracuda that was stalking the mullet and then he saw the lines of the fish, long, pale, and gray, and seeming not to move. He walked steadily and soon he was past the fish and was coming up on the heron again.

I'll see if I can pass him without making him fly, he thought. But just when he was coming almost even with the heron, the school of mullet burst from the water jumping stiffly, big-eyed and blunt-headed, silvery in the sun but not beautiful. Thomas Hudson turned to watch them and to try to see the barracuda who was cutting into them. He could not see the predatory fish; only the wild leaping of the frightened mullet. Then he saw that the school was re-formed into a gray moving mass and when he turned his head the heron was gone. He saw him flying with his white wings over the green water and ahead was the yellow sand beach and the line of the trees along the point. The clouds were beginning to darken behind Romano and he walked faster to round the point and see where Ara had left the dinghy.

Walking faster gave him an erection and he thought there can't be any Krauts around. That wouldn't happen if there were any Krauts around. I don't know, he thought. It could happen if you were wrong enough and didn't know it.

At the end of the point there was a patch of bright white sand and he thought, I'd like to lie down here. This would be a good place. Then he saw the dinghy at the end of the long beach and he thought, the hell with it. I'll sleep tonight and I will love the air mattress or the deck. I might as well love the deck. We have been around together long enough to get married. There is probably a lot of talk about you and the flying bridge now, he thought. You ought to do right by her. And all you do is step on her and

stand on her. What sort of a way is that to act? And spill
cold tea on her, too. That's not nice. What are you saving
her for anyway? To die on her? She would certainly appreciate that. Walk on her, stand on her, and die on her.
Treat her really nice. One thing practical you can do now
is cut out this crap and get this beach checked and pick
up Ara.

He walked on down the beach and he tried not to think
at all but only to notice things. He knew his duty very well
and he had tried never to shirk it. But today he had come
ashore when someone else could have done it just as well,
but when he stayed aboard and they found nothing, he
felt guilty. He watched everything. But he could not keep
from thinking.

Maybe Willie's side is hotter, he thought. Maybe Ara
will have hit something. I know damn well this is where
I would come if I were they. It is the first good place. They
might have passed it and gone straight on. Or they might
have turned in between Paredón and Cruz. But I don't
believe they would because somebody would see them
from the light and they never could get in and through
there at night, guide or no guide. I think they will have
gone further down. Maybe we will find them down by
Coco. Maybe we'll find them right in behind here. There's
another key that we ought to work out. I must remember
that they are always working on the chart. That is, unless they picked up a fisherman here. I haven't seen any
smoke from anybody burning charcoal. Well, I am glad
we will get this key worked out before the rain. I love
doing it, he thought. I just don't like the end.

He shoved off the dinghy and stepped into her, washing
the sand off his feet as he got in. He stowed the *niño,* in its
rubber coat, where he could reach it and started the motor.
He had no love for the outboard as Ara had and he never
started it without remembering blowing out and sucking
out clogged fuel lines and remembering shorted plugs and
other delights of the small motor. But Ara never had igni-
tion trouble. When the motor misfunctioned, he regarded

it as a chess player might admire a brilliant move on the part of his opponent.

Thomas Hudson steered along the beach but Ara was far ahead and he could not see him. He must be halfway to Willie, he thought. But when he saw him he was nearly to the mangrove bay where the sand stopped and the mangroves grew heavy and green into the water, their roots showing like tangled brown sticks.

Then he noticed the mast sticking up out of the mangroves. It was all he could see. But he could see Ara was lying behind a small sand dune so that he could just see over the top.

He could feel his scalp prickle as it does when you meet a car coming fast, suddenly, on the wrong side of the road. But Ara heard the motor and turned his head, and waved him in. Thomas came in on a tangent behind Ara.

The Basque came aboard carrying his raincoated *niño*, barrel first, over the right shoulder of his old striped beach shirt. He looked pleased.

"Get as far out as the channel will let you," he said. "We'll find Willie."

"Is it one of the boats?"

"Sure," Ara said. "But I'm sure it's abandoned. It's going to rain, Tom."

"Did you see anything?"

"Nothing."

"Me either."

"It's a nice key. I found an old trail to water. But it wasn't used."

"There's water on Willie's side, too."

"There's Willie," Ara said. He was sitting on the sand. His legs were drawn up and his *niño* was in his lap. Thomas Hudson ran the dinghy in to him. Willie looked at them, his black hair down over his forehead and wet with sweat and his good eye blue and mean.

"Where you two fuck-offs been?" he asked.

"When were they here, Willie?"

"Yesterday by the turds," Willie said. "Or should I say their excrement?"

"How many?"

"Eight that could execremenate and three of these with the bubbleshits."

"What else?"

"They got a guide or a pilot or whatever his rating is."

The guide they had picked up was a fisherman who had a palm-thatched shelter and had been salting barracuda strips on a rack to sell them later to the Chinese who bought fish for the Chinese retail grocers who would sell the dried fish in their shops as codfish. The fisherman had salted and dried a good quantity of fish by the looks of the rack.

"Krauts eat 'em plenty codfish now on in," Willie said.

"What language is that?"

"My own," Willie said. "Everybody has a private language around here, like Basque or something. You got an objection if I speak mine?"

"Tell me the rest."

"Sleepum here one smoke," Willie said. "Eatum pig meat. All sameee from Massacre Key. Kraut master no gottum tin goods or save 'em."

"Cut out the shit and tell it straight."

"Ole Massa Hudson going to lose all afternoon anyway due huge rainfall accompanied squall winds all along same. Might as well listen alongside Willie all same famous scout of the Pampas. Willie tell his own way."

"Cut it out."

"Listen, Tom, who found Krauts twice?"

"What about the boat?"

"Boat all same finish. She alongside too many rotten planks. One drop out by stern."

"They hit something coming in with a bad light."

"I guess so. Well, I'll cut out the shit. They've gone on into the westward sun. Eight men and a guide. Maybe nine if the captain couldn't shit on account of his great responsibilities like our own leader himself has trouble sometimes and now it is starting to rain. The boat they left was stunk up and beshat with pigs and chickens and that comrade we buried. There's one other guy is wounded but it doesn't look bad from the dressing."

"Pussy?"

"Yeah. But clean pus. You want to see it all or you take my word for it?"

"I take your word on all of it but I want to see it."

He saw everything, the tracks, the fire, where they had slept and cooked, the dressing, the part of the brush they had used as a latrine, and the groove the turtle boat had made in the sand when they beached her. It was raining hard now and the first gusts of the squall were coming.

"Put on the coats and put the niños under them," Ara said. "I have to take them down again tonight anyway."

"I'll help you," Willie said. "We're breathing down their necks, Tom."

"There's an awful lot of country and they have someone with local knowledge now."

"You just keep thinking the way you are," Willie said. "What local knowledge has he got that we haven't got?"

"Certainly he'll have plenty."

"The hell with him. I'm going to wash on the stern with soap. Jesus, I want to feel that fresh water and that soap."

It was raining so hard now that it was hard to see the ship as they came around the point. The squall had moved out toward the ocean and it was so violent and the rain so heavy that trying to see the ship was like looking at an object from behind a falls. Her tanks will fill like nothing with this, Thomas Hudson thought. She'll probably be running off through the galley faucets and the head right now.

"How many days since it rained, Tom?" Willie asked.

"We'll have to check with the log. It's something over fifty."

"It's like the goddam monsoon breaking," Willie said. "Give me a gourd so I can bail."

"Keep the cover on your niño dry."

"Her butt is in my crotch and her nose is under the left shoulder of my coat," Willie said. "She never had it better in her life. Give me the gourd."

On the stern they were all bathing naked. They soaped themselves and stood on one foot and another, bending against the lashing of the rain as they soaped and then leaning back into it. They were really all brown but they looked white in this strange light. Thomas Hudson thought of the canvas of the bathers by Cézanne and then he thought he would like to have Eakins paint it. Then he thought that he should be painting it himself with the ship against the roaring white of the surf that came through the driving gray outside with the black of the new squall coming out and the sun breaking through momentarily to make the driving rain silver and to shine on the bathers in the stern.

He brought the dinghy up and Ara tossed a line and they were home.

XI

THAT night after the rain had stopped and he had checked all leaks from the long dry spell, and seen that pans were put under them, and the point of actual leakage, not the drip, was pencilled, the watches were set, the duties apportioned, and everything discussed and agreed on with his mate and Ara. Then when the supper was ended and the poker game underway, he went up on the flying bridge. He had a Flit gun with him and his air mattress and a light blanket.

He thought that he would lie down and think about nothing. Sometimes he could do this. Sometimes he could think about the stars without wondering about them and the ocean without problems and the sunrise without what it would bring.

He felt clean from his scalp to his feet from the soaping in the rain that had beaten down on the stern and he thought, I will just lie here and feel clean. He knew there was no use thinking of the girl who had been Tom's mother nor all the things they had done and the places they had been nor how they had broken up. There was no use thinking about Tom. He had stopped that as soon as he had heard.

There was no use thinking about the others. He had lost them, too, and there was no use thinking about them. He had traded in remorse for another horse that he was riding now. So lie here now and feel clean from the soap and the rain and do a good job at nonthinking. You learned to do it quite well for a while. Maybe you will go to sleep and have funny or good dreams. Just lie quiet and watch the night and don't think. Ara or Henry will wake you if Peters gets anything.

He was asleep in a little while. He was a boy again and riding up a steep canyon. The canyon opened out and there was a sandbar by the clear river that was so clear he could see the pebbles in the bed of the stream and then watch the cutthroat trout at the foot of the pool as they rose to flies that floated down the current. He was sitting on his horse and watching the trout rise when Ara woke him.

The message read CONTINUE SEARCH CAREFULLY WESTWARD with the code name at the end.

"Thanks," he said. "Let me have anything else."

"Of course. Go back to sleep, Tom."

"I was having a fine dream."

"Don't tell it to me," Ara said. "And maybe it will come true."

He went to sleep again and when he went to sleep he smiled because he thought that he was carrying out orders and continuing the search westward. I have her pretty far west, he thought. I don't think they meant this far west.

He slept and he dreamed that the cabin was burned and someone had killed his fawn that had grown into a young buck. Someone had killed his dog and he found him by a tree and he woke sweating.

I guess dreams aren't the solution, he said to himself. I might as well take it the same as always without any hope of anaesthetics. Go on and think it out.

All you have now is a basic problem and your intermediate problems. That is all you have so you better like it. You will never have good dreams any more so you might as well not sleep. Just rest and use your head until it won't work any more, and when you go to sleep, expect to have the horrors. The horrors were what you won in that big crap game that they run. You put it on the line and made your point and let it ride and finally you dragged down the gift of uneasy unpleasant sleep. You damned near dragged down not sleeping at all. But you traded that in for what you have so you might as well like it. You're sleepy now. So sleep and figure to wake up sweating. And what of it? Nothing at all of it. But do you remember when you used to sleep all night with the girl and always happy and never woke unless she woke you to make love? Remember that, Thomas Hudson, and see how much good it will do you.

I wonder how many dressings they have for that other wounded character? If they had time to get dressings they had time to get other stuff, too. What stuff? What do you think they have besides what you know they have? I don't think much. Maybe pistols and a few machine pistols. Maybe some demolition charges they could make something out of. I have to figure that they have the machine gun. But I don't think so. They wouldn't want to fight. They want to get the hell away and on a Spanish ship. If they had been in shape to fight they would have come back that night and taken Confites. Maybe no. Maybe something made them suspicious and they saw our drums on the beach and thought we might be basing there nights. They wouldn't know what we were. But they would see the drums and figure there was something around that burned plenty of gas. Then too they probably didn't want to fight with their wounded. But the boat with the wounded could have laid off at night while they came in and took the wireless station if they wanted to get off with that other sub. I wonder what happened with her. There's something very strange about that.

Think about something cheerful. Think about how you start with the sun at your back. And remember they have local knowledge now, along with all that salt fish, and you are going to have to use your head. He went to sleep and slept quite well until two hours before daylight when the sand flies awakened him. Thinking about the problems had made him feel better and he slept without dreaming.

XII

THEY left before the sun was up and Thomas Hudson steered down the channel that was like a canal with the gray banks showing on either side. By the time the sun was up he was out through the cut between the shoals and he steered due north to get into blue water and past the dangerous rocky heads of the outer reef. It was a little longer than running on the inside but it was much safer.

When the sun rose, there was no wind and not enough swell for the sea to break on any of the rocks. The day would be hot and muggy, he knew, and there would be squalls in the afternoon.

His mate came up and looked around. Then he looked carefully at the land and along it to where the high, ugly tower of the light showed.

"We could have run down easily on the inside."

"I know it," Thomas Hudson said. "But I thought this was better."

"Another day like yesterday. But hotter."

"They can't make much time."

"They can't make any time. They're becalmed somewhere. You're going to check with the light whether they went into the cut between Paredón and Coco, aren't you?"

"Sure."

"I'll go in. I know the keeper. You can lay just inside the little key at the tip. I won't be gone long," Antonio said.

"I don't even need to anchor."

"You've got plenty of strong-backed people to get anchors up."

"Send up Ara and Willie if they've eaten. Nothing should show here this close to the light and you can't see a damned thing looking into the sun. But send up George and Henry, too. We might as well do it right."

"Remember the rocks make right up to your blue water here, Tom."

"I remember and I can see them."

"Do you want your tea cold?"

"Please. And a sandwich. Send the men up first."

"They'll be right up. I'll send the tea up and have everything ready to go ashore."

"Be careful how you talk to them."

"That's why I am going in."

"Put out a couple of lines, too. It will look better coming in on the light."

"Yes," his mate said. "We might get something we could give them at the light."

The four came up and took their usual posts and Henry said, "Did you see anything, Tom?"

"One turtle with a sea gull flying around him. I thought he was going to perch on his back. But he didn't."

"*Mi capitán*," said George, who was a taller Basque than Ara and a good athlete and fine seaman, but not nearly as strong as Ara in many ways.

"*Mi señor obispo*," said Thomas Hudson.

"OK, Tom," George said. "If I see any really big submarines do you want me to tell you?"

"If you see one as big as you saw that one time keep it to yourself."

"I dream about her nights," George said.

"Don't talk about her," Willie said. "I just ate breakfast."

"When we closed I could feel my *cojones* going up like an elevator," Ara said. "How did you really feel, Tom?"

"Scared."

"I saw her come up," Ara said. "And the next thing I heard Henry say, 'She's an aircraft carrier, Tom.'"

"That's what she looked like," Henry said. "I can't help it. I'd say the same thing again."

"She spoiled my life," Willie said. "I've never been the same since. For a nickel I'd have never gone to sea again."

"Here," said Henry. "Take twenty cents and get off at Paredón Grande. Maybe they'll give you change."

"I don't want change. I'll take a transfer."

"Would you really?" Henry asked. There had been a certain amount of bad blood between them since the last two times they had been in Havana.

"Listen, expensive," Willie said. "We're not fighting submarines or you wouldn't have come up without sneaking a quick one. We're only chasing Krauts to kill them in a decked-over half-open boat. Even you ought to be able to do that."

"Take the twenty cents anyway," Henry said. "You'll need it some day."

"To stick up—"

"Cut it out the two of you. *Cut it out,*" Thomas Hudson said. He looked at both of them.

"I'm sorry, Tom," Henry said.

"I'm not sorry," Willie said. "But I apologize."

"Look, Tom," said Ara. "Almost abeam inshore."

"That's the rock that's just awash," Thomas Hudson said. "It shows further to the eastward on the chart."

"No. I mean further in about a half a mile."

"That's a man crawfishing or hauling fish traps."

"Do you think we ought to speak to him?"

"He's from the light and Antonio's going in to talk with them at the light."

"Feesh! Feesh!" his mate called and Henry asked, "May I take him, Tom?"

"Sure. Send Gil up."

Henry went down and in a little while the fish jumped and showed he was a barracuda. Then, a little later, he heard Antonio grunt as he hit him with the gaff and then he heard the thunking knocks of the club on its head. He waited for the splash of the fish being thrown back and looked at the wake to see his size. There was no splash and he remembered that barracuda were good to eat on this stretch of the coast and Antonio was saving him to take in to the light. Just then he heard the double shout of "Feesh!" and this time there was no jumping and the line was singing out. He turned out further into the blue water and slowed down both engines. Then as the line kept going out he threw out one motor and made a half-turn toward the fish.

"Wahoo," his mate called up. "Big one."

Henry brought the fish in and they looked down over the stern and saw him long and oddly pointed, his stripes showing clearly in the blueness of the deep water. When he was nearly within reach of the gaff he turned his head and made another fast deep run that took him out of sight in the clear water in less time than a man could snap his fingers.

"They always have that one run," Ara said. "It goes like a bullet."

Henry brought him in fast and they watched over the stern as he was gaffed and brought aboard rigid and trembling. His stripes showed a bright blue and his jaws, that could cut like razors, opened and closed with spasmodic uselessness. Antonio laid him in the stern and his tail beat against the deck.

"*¡Qué peto más hermoso!*" Ara said.

"He's a beautiful wahoo," Thomas Hudson agreed. "But we'll be out here all morning if this keeps up. Leave out the lines but take the leaders off," he said to his mate. He steered for just outside the light on its high point of rock and tried to make up the time they had lost and still act as though they were fishing. The friction of the lines in the water bent the rods.

Henry came up and said, "He was a beautiful fish, wasn't he? I'd love to have had him on light tackle. Don't they have an extraordinarily shaped head?"

"What will he weigh?" Willie asked.

"Antonio said he'd weigh about sixty, Willie. I was sorry I didn't have time to call you. He really should have been yours."

"That's all right," Willie said. "You caught him faster than I could and we have to get the hell along. I bet we could catch plenty good fish all along here."

"We'll come sometime after the war."

"I'll bet," said Willie. "After the war I'm going to be in

Hollywood and be a technical adviser on how to be a horse's ass at sea."

"You'll be good at it."

"I ought to be. I've been studying it now for over a year to train me for my career."

"What the hell have you got so much black ass about today, Willie?" Thomas Hudson asked.

"I don't know. I woke up with it."

"Well, go down to the galley and see if that bottle of tea is cold and bring it up. Antonio's butchering the fish. So make a sandwich will you, please?"

"Sure. What kind of sandwich?"

"Peanut butter and onion if there's plenty of onion."

"Peanut butter and onion it is, sir."

"And try to get rid of your black ass."

"Yes sir. Black ass gone, sir."

When he was gone Thomas Hudson said, "You take it easy with him, Henry. I need the son of a bitch and he's good at his stuff. He's just got black ass."

"I try to be good with him. But he's difficult."

"Well try a little harder. You were needling him about the twenty cents."

Thomas Hudson looked ahead at the smooth sea and the innocent-looking deadliness of the reef off his port bow. He loved to run just off a bad reef with the light behind him. It made up for the times when he had to steer into the sun and it made up for several other things.

"I'm sorry, Tom," Henry said. "I'll watch what I say and what I think."

Willie was back up with the empty rum bottle full of tea wrapped in a paper towel and with two rubber bands around it to keep the towel in place.

"She's cold, skipper," he said. "And I have insulated her."

He handed a sandwich, wrapped in a paper towel segment, to Thomas Hudson and said, "One of the highest points in the sandwich-maker's art. We call it the Mount Everest Special. For Commanders only."

In the calm, even on the bridge, Thomas Hudson smelled his breath.

"Don't you think it's a little early in the day, Willie?"

"No sir."

Thomas Hudson looked at him speculatively.

"What did you say, Willie?"

"No sir. Didn't you hear me, sir?"

"OK," Thomas Hudson said. "I heard you twice. You hear this once. Go below. Clean up the galley properly and then go up in the bow where I can see you and stand by to anchor."

"Yes sir," said Willie. "I don't feel well, sir."

"Fuck how you feel, you sea lawyer. If you don't feel well you are going to feel a damned sight worse."

"Yes sir," Willie said. "I don't feel well, sir. I should see the ship's surgeon."

"You'll find him in the bow. Knock on the door of the head and see if he's there as you go by."

"That's what I mean, sir."

"What do you mean?"

"Nothing, sir."

"He's skunk-drunk," Henry said.

"No, he's not," Thomas Hudson said. "He's drinking. But he's closer to crazy."

"He's been strange for quite a while," Ara said. "But he was always strange. None of us has ever suffered as he has. I have never even suffered at all."

"Tom's suffered," Henry said. "And he's drinking cold tea."

"Let's not talk morbid and let's not talk wet," Thomas Hudson said. "I never suffered and I like cold tea."

"You never did before."

"We learn something new all the time, Henry."

He was coming up well on the light and he saw the rock he should keep outside of now, and he thought this was a worthless conversation.

"Go up forward with him, Ara, and see how he's doing. Stick around with him. You get the lines in, Henry. George, get down and help Antonio with the dinghy. Go in with him if he wants you to."

When he was alone on the bridge he smelled the bird

guano from the rock and he rounded the point and anchored in two fathoms of water. The bottom was clean and there was a big tide running. He looked up at the white-painted house and the tall old-fashioned light and then past the high rock to the green mangrove keys and beyond them the low, rocky, barren tip of Cayo Romano. They had lived, off and on, for such a long time within sight of that long, strange, and pest-ridden key and knew a part of it so well and had come in on its landmarks so many times and under such good and bad circumstances that it always made him an emotion to sight it or to leave it out of sight. Now it was there at its barest and most barren, jutting out like a scrubby desert.

There were wild horses and wild cattle and wild hogs on that great key and he wondered how many people had held the illusion that they might colonize it. It had hills rich in grass with beautiful valleys and fine stands of timber and once there had been a settlement called Versailles where Frenchmen had made their attempt at living on Romano.

Now all the frame buildings were abandoned but the one big house and one time when Thomas Hudson had gone in there to fill water, the dogs from the shacks were huddled with the pigs that had burrowed in the mud and dogs and pigs both were gray from the solid blanket of mosquitoes that covered them. It was a wonderful key when the east wind blew day and night and you could walk two days with a gun and be in good country. It was country as unspoiled as when Columbus came to this coast. Then, when the wind dropped, the mosquitoes came in clouds from the marshes. To say they came in clouds, he thought, is not a metaphor. They truly came in clouds and they could bleed a man to death. The people we are searching for would not have stopped in Romano. Not with this calm. They must have gone further up the coast.

"Ara," he called.

"What is it, Tom?" Ara asked. He always swung up onto the bridge and landed as lightly as an acrobat but with the weight of steel.

"What's the score?"

"Willie's not himself, Tom. I took him out of the sun and I made him a drink and made him lie down. He's quiet now but he looks at things too fixedly."

"Maybe he had too much sun on his bad head."

"Maybe. Maybe it is something else."

"What else?"

"Gil and Peters are sleeping. Gil had the duty to keep Peters awake last night. Henry is sleeping and George went in with Antonio."

"They should be back soon."

"They will be."

"We must keep Willie out of the sun. I was stupid to send him forward. But I did it for discipline, without thinking."

"I am disassembling and cleaning the big ones and I checked all the fuses from the dampness and rain of last night on the other stuff. Last night after the poker game we disassembled and cleaned and oiled everything."

"Now, with the dampness, we have to make a daily check, whether anything is fired or not."

"I know," Ara said. "We ought to disembark Willie. But we can't do it here."

"Cayo Francés?"

"We could. But Havana would be better and have them ship him from there. He's going to talk, Tom."

Thomas Hudson thought of something and regretted it.

"We never should have taken him after he had a medical discharge and with the bad head," Ara said.

"I know. But we did. How many damn mistakes have we made?"

"Not too many," Ara said. "Now may I go down and finish the work?"

"Yes," Thomas Hudson said. "Thank you very much."

"*A sus órdenes,*" Ara said.

"I wish to hell they were better orders," Thomas Hudson said.

Antonio and George were coming out with the dinghy and Antonio came up on the bridge immediately and let George and Henry hoist the motor and the dinghy aboard.

"Well?" Thomas Hudson said.

"They must have gone by in the night on the last of the breeze," Antonio said. "They would have seen them at the light if they came into the cut. The old man who has the skiff and the fish traps hadn't seen any turtle boat. He talks about everything and he would have mentioned it, the lightkeeper said. Do you think we ought to go back and check with him?"

"No. I think they're down at Puerto Coco or else at Guillermo."

"That's about where they would have reached with what wind they had."

"You're sure they couldn't have gone through the cut at night?"

"Not with the best pilot that ever lived."

"Then we have to find them in the lee of Coco or down by Guillermo. Let's get the anchor up and go."

It was a very dirty coast and he kept outside of everything and ran the edge of the hundred-fathom curve. Inshore there was a low rocky coast and reefs and big patches of banks that came out dry with the low tide. There was a four-man watch and Gil was on Thomas Hudson's left. Thomas Hudson looked toward the shore and saw the beginning of the green of the mangroves and thought, what a hell of a place to be now in this calm. The clouds were piled high already and he thought the squalls would come out earlier. There are about three places past Puerto Coco that I must search, he thought. I had better hook her up a little more and get in there.

"Henry," he said. "Steer 285 will you? I want to go below and see Willie. Sing out if you sight anything. You don't need to watch inshore, Gil. Take the starboard watch forward. That's all too shallow inshore for them to be in there."

"I'd like to watch inshore," Gil said. "If you don't mind, Tom. There's that crazy channel that makes in almost against the beach and the guide could have taken them there and put them in the mangroves."

"Good," said Thomas Hudson. "I'll send up Antonio."

"I could see her mast in the mangroves with these big glasses."

"I doubt it like hell. But you might."

"Please, Tom. If you don't mind."

"I agreed already."

"I'm sorry, Tom. But I thought a guide might take her in there. We went in there once."

"And we had to come out the same way we went in."

"I know. But if the wind failed them and they had to hide in a hurry. We don't want to overrun them."

"Right. But we are a long way out for you to see a mast. Besides they would probably cut mangroves to hide the mast from the air."

"I know," Gil said with Spanish stubbornness. "But I have very good eyes and these are twelve-power glasses and it is calm so I see well and—"

"I said it was OK before."

"I know. But I had to explain."

"You've explained," Thomas Hudson said. "And if you find a mast you can stick it up my ass with peanuts on it."

Gil felt a little hurt at this but he thought it was funny, especially about the peanuts, and he searched the mangroves until the big glasses almost pulled the eyes out of his head.

Below, Thomas Hudson was talking with Willie and watching the sea and the land. It was always strange how much less you saw when you were down from the bridge, and, as long as things went well below, he felt a fool to be anywhere but at his post. He tried always to keep the necessary contact and avoid the idiocy of the uninspecting inspection. But he had delegated more and more authority to Antonio, who was a much better sailor than he was, and to Ara who was a much better man. They are both better men than I am, he thought, and yet I still should be in command, using their knowledge and talent and their characters.

"Willie," he said. "How are you really?"

"I'm sorry about acting like a fool. But I'm sort of bad, Tom."

"You know the rules about drinking," Thomas Hudson said. "There aren't any. I don't want to use chickenshit words like the honor system."

"I know," Willie said. "You know I'm not a rummy."

"We don't ship rummies."

"Except Peters."

"We didn't ship him. They gave him to us. He has his problems, too."

"Old Angus is his problem," Willie said. "And his goddam problems get to be our problems too damn fast."

"We'll skip him," Thomas Hudson said. "You have anything else eating you?"

"Just in general."

"How?"

"Well I'm half crazy and you're half crazy and then we've got this crew of half saints and desperate men."

"It isn't bad to be half saint and half desperate man."

"I know it. It's wonderful. But I was used to things being more regular."

"Willie, there's nothing eating you really. The sun bothers your head and I'm sure drinking isn't good for it."

"I'm sure, too," Willie said. "I'm not trying to be a fuck-up, Tom. But did you ever go really crazy?"

"No. I always missed it."

"It's a lot of bother," Willie said. "And however long it lasts, it lasts too long. But I'll stop drinking."

"No. Just drink easy like you always did."

"I was using the drinking to stave it off."

"We're always using drinking for something."

"Sure. But this wasn't any gag. Do you think I'd lie to you, Tom?"

"We all lie. But I don't think you'd lie on purpose."

"Go on up on your bridge," Willie said. "I see you watching the water all the time like it was some girl that was going to get away from you. I won't drink anything except sea water maybe and I'll help Ara break them to pieces and put them together again."

"Don't drink, Willie."

"If I said I won't, I won't."

"I know."

"Listen, Tom. Can I ask you something?"

"Anything."

"How bad is it with you?"

"I guess pretty bad."

"Can you sleep?"

"Not much."

"Last night?"

"Yes."

"That was from walking the beach," Willie said. "Go on up and forget about me. I'll be working with Ara at our trade."

XIII

THEY had searched the beach for tracks at Puerto Coco and they searched the mangroves beyond with the dinghy. There were some really good places for a turtle boat to hide. But they found nothing and the squalls came out earlier with heavy rain that made the sea look as though it were leaping into the air in white, spurting jets.

Thomas Hudson had walked the beach and gone back inland behind the lagoon. He had found the place where the flamingoes came at high tide and he had seen many wood ibis, the *cocos* that gave the key its name, and a pair of roseate spoon-bills working in the marl of the edge of the lagoon. They were beautiful with the sharp rose of their color against the gray marl and their delicate, quick, forward-running movements, and they had the dreadful, hunger-ridden impersonality of certain wading birds. He could not watch them long because he wanted to check in case the people they were looking for had left the boat in the mangroves and camped in the high ground to be clear of the mosquitoes.

He found nothing but the site of an old charcoal-burning and he came out onto the beach after the first squall hit and Ara had picked him up in the dinghy.

Ara loved running the outboard in the rain and a bad

squall and he had told Thomas Hudson none of the searchers had found anything. Everybody was on board but Willie who had taken the furthest stretch of beach beyond the mangroves.

"And you?" Ara asked.

"Me, nothing."

"This rain will cool off Willie. I'm going to get him when I put you on board. Where do you think they are, Tom?"

"At Guillermo. That's where I'd be."

"Me too. That's what Willie thinks, too."

"How was he?"

"He's trying hard, Tom. You know Willie."

"Yes," said Thomas Hudson. They came alongside and he climbed aboard.

Thomas Hudson watched Ara pivot the dinghy on her stern and go off into the white squall. Then he called down for a towel and dried himself off on the stern.

Henry said, "Don't you want a drink, Tom? You were really wet."

"I'd like one."

"Do you want straight rum?"

"That's nice," Thomas Hudson answered. He went below to get a sweatshirt and shorts and he saw that they were all cheerful.

"We all had a straight rum," Henry said and brought him a glass half-full. "I don't think that way if you dry off quickly anyone can catch cold. Do you?"

"Hi, Tom," said Peters. "Have you joined our little group of health drinkers?"

"When did you wake up?" Thomas Hudson asked him.

"When I heard a gurgling noise."

"I'll make a gurgling noise some night and see if that wakes you up."

"Don't worry, Tom. Willie does that for me every night."

Thomas Hudson decided not to drink the rum. Then, seeing them all having had a drink and being cheerful and happy on an uncheerful errand, he thought it would be pompous and priggish not to take it. He wanted it, too.

"Split this with me," he said to Peters. "You are the

only son of a bitch I ever knew that could sleep better with earphones on than without them."

"That split's nothing," Peters said, entrenching himself in the retreat from formal discipline. "That split doesn't give either of us anything."

"Get one of your own, then," Thomas Hudson said. "I like the goddam stuff as well as you do."

— The others were watching and Thomas Hudson could see Henry's jaw muscles twitching.

"Drink it up," Thomas Hudson said. "And run all your mysterious machines tonight as well as you can. For yourself and for the rest of us."

"For all of us," Peters said. "Who is the hardest-working man on this ship?"

"Ara," Thomas Hudson said and sipped the rum for the first time as he looked around. "And every fucking body else on board."

"Here's to you, Tom," Peters said.

"Here's to you," Thomas Hudson said and felt the words die cold and stale in his mouth. "To the earphone king," he said, in order to recover something he had lost. "To all gurgling noises," he added, being now a long way ahead as he should have been at the start.

"To my commander," Peters said, running his string out too far.

"Any way you want to take it," Thomas Hudson said. "There are no articles that cover that with us. But I'll settle for that. Say it again."

"To you, Tom."

"Thanks," Thomas Hudson said. "But I will be a sad son of a bitch before I drink to you until all your radios and you are functioning."

Peters looked at him and into his face there came the discipline and into his body, which was in bad shape, the carriage of a man who had served three hitches in something that he had believed in and left for something else, as Willie had, and he said, automatically and without reservations, "Yes sir."

"Drink to you," Thomas Hudson said. "And crank up all your fucking miracles."

"Yes, Tom," Peters said, without any cheating and without reservations.

Well, I guess that is enough of that, Thomas Hudson thought. I better leave it as it lays and go back to the stern and watch my other problem child come aboard. I can never feel about Peters the way the rest of them all feel. I hope I know as well as they do what his defects are. But he has something. He is like the false carried so far that it is made true. It is certain that he is not up to handling what we have. But maybe he is up to much better things.

Willie's the same, he thought. One is as bad one way as the other. They ought to be in now.

He saw the dinghy coming through the rain and the white drifted water that curled and blew under the lash of the wind. They were both thoroughly wet when they came aboard. They had not used their raincoats but had kept them wrapped around their *niños*.

"Hi, Tom," Willie said. "Nothing but a wet ass and a hungry gut."

"Take these children," Ara said and handed the wrapped submachine guns aboard.

"Nothing?"

"Nothing multiplied by ten," Willie said. He was standing on the stern dripping and Thomas Hudson called to Gil to bring two towels.

Ara pulled the dinghy in by her painter and climbed aboard.

"Nothing of nothing of nothing," he said. "Tom, do we get overtime for rain?"

"We ought to clean those weapons right away," Willie said.

"We'll get dry first," Ara said. "I'm wet enough. First I could never get wet and now I have gooseflesh even on my ass."

"Tom," Willie said. "You know those sons of bitches can sail in these squalls if they reef down and have the balls to."

"I thought of that too."

"I think they lay up in the daytime with the calm and then run with these afternoon squalls."

"Where do you put them?"

"I don't put them past Guillermo. But they could be."

"We'll start at daylight and catch them at Guillermo tomorrow."

"Maybe we'll find them and maybe they'll be gone."

"Sure."

"Why the hell haven't we got radar?"

"What good would it do us right now? What do you see in the screen, Willie?"

"I'll pipe the hell down," Willie said. "Excuse me, Tom. But chasing something with UHF that hasn't got a radio . . . ?"

"I know," said Thomas Hudson. "But do you want to chase any better than we've been chasing?"

"Yes. Is that OK?"

"OK."

"I want to catch the sons of bitches and kill every one of them."

"What good would that do?"

"You don't remember the massacre?"

"Don't give me any of that massacre shit, Willie. You've been around too long for that."

"OK. I just want to kill them. Is that all right?"

"It's better than the massacre thing. But I want prisoners from a U-boat operating in these waters who can talk."

"That last one you had didn't talk much."

"No. Neither would you if you were up the creek like he was."

"OK," Willie said. "Can I draw a slug of the legal?"

"Sure. Get on dry shorts and a shirt and don't make trouble."

"With nobody?"

"Grow up," Thomas Hudson said.

"Drop dead," Willie said and grinned.

"That's the way I like you," Thomas Hudson told him. "Keep it that way."

XIV

THAT night there was heavy lightning and thunder and it rained until about three o'clock in the morning. Peters could get nothing on the radio and they all slept hot and muggy until the sand flies came out after the rain stopped and wakened them, one after the other. Thomas Hudson pumped Flit down below and there was coughing and then less restless moving and slapping.

He waked Peters by Flitting him thoroughly and Peters shook his head with the earphones on and said softly, "I've been trying hard, Tom, all the time. But there's nothing."

Thomas Hudson looked at the glass with a torch and it was rising. That will give them a breeze, he thought. Well, they can't say they haven't had luck again. Now I must figure that.

He went back to the stern and sprayed all the Flit he could into the cabin without waking the people.

He sat in the stern and watched the night clear and flitted himself occasionally. They were short of repellent but had plenty of Flit. It burned where a man had been sweating but it was better than sand flies. Their effect differed from mosquitoes in that you could not hear them before they hit and there was an instant itching from the bite. The bites made a swelling about the size of a very small pea. In some places on the coast and on the keys, they were more virulent than in others. At least their bites seemed to be much more annoying. But, he thought, that could be the condition that our hides are in and how much they are burned and toughened. I do not know how the natives stand them. They have to be hardy people to live on this coast and in the Bahamas when the trades aren't blowing.

He sat in the stern watching and listening. There were

two planes, high in the sky, and he listened to the throbbing of the motors until they no longer could be heard.

Big bombers going to Camagüey on the way to Africa or going straight through to somewhere and nothing to do with us. Well, he thought, they are not bothered by sand flies. Neither am I. The hell with them. The hell with them and the hell I'm not. But I'd like to get some daylight and get out of here. We've checked all the way up to the end of the point, thanks to Willie, and I'll run the little channel right along the edge of the bank. There's only one bad place and with the morning light I can see it OK even in a calm. Then we'll be at Guillermo.

They were underway at daylight and Gil, who had the best eyes, was watching the green shore line with the twelve-power glasses. They were close enough to shore for him to see a cut mangrove branch. Thomas Hudson was steering. Henry was watching out to sea. Willie was backing up Gil.

"They're past this part, anyway," Willie said.

"But we have to check," Ara said. He was backing up Henry.

"Sure," Willie said. "I was just commenting."

"Where's that Dawn Patrol from that damned Molasses ship at Cayo Francés?"

"They don't patrol on Sundays, do they?" Willie asked. "This must be a Sunday."

"There's going to be a breeze," Ara said. "Look at the cirrus."

"I'm afraid of one thing," Thomas Hudson said. "That they've gone in through the pass at Guillermo."

"We'll have to see."

"Let's hook the hell up and get there," Willie said. "This is getting on my nerves."

"That's the impression I get sometimes," Henry said.

Willie looked at him and spat over the side. "Thank you, Henry," he said. "That's the impression I wish to give."

"Break it up," Thomas Hudson said. "See that big coral head to starboard that's just awash? That's what we have to not hit. On the inside, gentlemen, is Guillermo. See how green she is and full of promise?"

"One more goddam key," Willie said.

"Can you make out any smoke from charcoal burning?" Thomas Hudson asked.

Gil swept it very carefully and said, "No, Tom."

"The way it rained last night there wouldn't be any smoke," Willie said.

"You're wrong for once, boy," Thomas Hudson said.

"Maybe."

"No. It could rain like hell all night and not put one of those big burnings out. I've seen it rain three days and hardly bother one."

"You know more about them than me," Willie said. "OK, there could be smoke. I hope there is."

"That's a bad shoal," Henry said. "I don't believe they could run in those squalls along here."

In the morning light they could see four terns and two gulls working around the shoal. They had found something and were diving. The terns were crying and the gulls were screaming.

"What are they into, Tom?" Henry asked.

"I don't know. It looks like a school of bait fish that is too deep for them to work."

"Those poor bastard birds have to get up earlier in the morning than we do to make a living," Willie said. "People don't appreciate the work they put in."

"How are you going to run, Tom?" Ara asked.

"Just as close in to the bank as I can and right up to the head of the key."

"Are you going to check that half-moon key with the wreck?"

"I'll make a turn around it close in and everybody glass it. Then I'll anchor in the bight inside the tip of Guillermo."

"We'll anchor," Willie said.

"That's implied. Why do you get so ornery this early in the morning?"

"I'm not ornery. I'm just admiring the ocean and this beautiful coast Columbus first cast his eyes on. I'm lucky I didn't serve under that Columbus."

"I always thought you did," Thomas Hudson said.

"I read a book about him in the hospital at San Diego," Willie said. "I'm an authority on him and he had a worse fucked-up outfit than this one."

"This isn't a fucked-up outfit."

"No," said Willie. "Not yet."

"OK, Columbus boy. Do you see that wreck that bears about twenty degrees to starboard?"

"That's for your starboard watch to see," Willie said. "But I can see it OK with my one eye that works and there is a booby bird from the Bahamas perched on it. He's probably come to reinforce us."

"Good," said Thomas Hudson. "He's what we need."

"I probably could have been a great ornithologist," Willie said. "Grandma used to raise chickens."

"Tom," Ara said. "Do you think we can work a little closer in? The tide is high now."

"Sure," Thomas Hudson answered. "Ask Antonio to get up in the bow and let me know how much water I have."

"You've got plenty of water, Tom," Antonio called. Right in to shore. You know this channel."

"I know. I just wanted to be sure."

"Do you want me to take her?"

"Thanks," said Thomas Hudson. "I do not."

"Now we can see the high ground beautifully," Ara said. "You take all of her, Gil. I'll just back you up. Glass her really well."

"Who takes the first quarter of the sea?" Willie asked. "How come you switched on me, anyway?"

"When Tom asked you to look at the wreck. We switch automatically. When you went to starboard I went to port."

"That's too nautical for me," Willie said. "When you want to be nautical, be right or not at all. Why don't you say right or left the same as in steering?"

"It was you who said the starboard watch," Henry said.

"That's right. And from now on I'm going to say downstairs and upstairs and the front and the back of the boat."

"Willie, get over with Gil and Ara and glass the beach, will you please?" Thomas Hudson said. "The beach and carry it up to the first third of the key."

"Yes, Tom," Willie said.

It was easy to see if there was anyone living on Cayo Guillermo on this which was the windward side for nearly all of the year. But there was nothing showing as they moved close in along the coast. They came abeam of the point and Thomas Hudson said, "I'll circle the half-moon key as close as I can and you all glass it. If you notice anything we can stand by and put the dinghy in."

The breeze was starting to rise and the sea was beginning to move but it did not break yet on the shoals because of the high tide. Thomas Hudson looked ahead at the small rocky key. He knew there was a sunken wreck at the western end of it but it showed only as a red brown bulge with this high tide. There was a shallow bank and a sandy beach on the inside of this key but he would not see the beach until he had rounded the wreck.

"There's somebody living on the key," Ara said. "I see smoke."

"Right," said Willie. "It's on the leeward side and the wind is carrying it to the west."

"The smoke is about at the center of where the beach should be," Gil said.

"Can you see a mast?"

"No mast," Gil said.

"They could step the goddam mast daytimes," Willie said.

"Go to your stations," Thomas Hudson said. "Ara, you stay here with me. Willie, tell Peters to get hooked up to talk whether anybody can hear him or not."

"What do you think?" Ara asked when the others were gone.

"I think if I were fishing and drying fish that I would have come off here from Guillermo when the calms came and brought the mosquitoes."

"Me, too."

"They aren't burning any charcoal on this key and the smoke is small. So it must be a fresh fire."

"Unless it is the end of a bigger one."

"I thought of that."

"Then we'll see in five minutes."

They rounded the wreck, which had another booby bird sitting on it, and Thomas Hudson thought, our allies are checking in fast. Then they were coming up into the lee of the key and Thomas Hudson saw the sand beach, the green behind it, and a shack with smoke coming from it.

"Thank God," he said.

"Equally," Ara said. "I was afraid of the other thing, too."

There was no sign of any boats.

"We're really close to them, I think. Get in fast with Antonio and tell me what you find. I'll lay her in right along the bank. Tell them to stay at their stations and act natural."

The dinghy spun and moved in to the beach. Thomas Hudson watched Antonio and Ara walking toward the thatched shack. They were moving as fast as they could without running. They called to the shack and a woman came out. She was dark as a sea Indian and was barefooted and her long hair hung down almost to her waist. While she talked, another woman came out. She was dark, too, and long-haired and she carried a baby. As soon as she finished speaking, Ara and Antonio shook hands with the two women and came back to the dinghy. They shoved off and started the motor and came out.

Antonio and Ara came up onto the flying bridge while the dinghy was being hoisted aboard.

"There were two women," Antonio said. "The men are outside fishing. The woman with the baby saw a turtle boat go into the channel that goes inside. It went in when this breeze came up."

"That would be about an hour and a half ago," Thomas Hudson said. "With the tide falling now."

"Very strong," Antonio said. "It is dropping very fast, Tom."

"When she is down, there is not enough water to carry us through there."

"No."

"What do you think?"

"It's your ship."

Thomas Hudson swung the helm hard over and put in both motors up to twenty-seven hundred revolutions and headed for the point of the key.

"They may run aground themselves," he said. "The hell with it."

"We can anchor if it gets too bad," Antonio said. "It's a marl bottom if we run aground. Marl and mud."

"And rocky spots," Thomas Hudson said. "Get Gil up here for me to watch for the stakes. Ara, you and Willie check all the weapons. Stay up here, please, Antonio."

"The channel is a bastard," Antonio said. "But it is not impossible."

"She is impossible in low water. But maybe the other son of a bitch will ground, too, or maybe the wind will fail."

"The wind won't fail, Tom," Antonio said. "It's firm and solid now for the trade wind."

Thomas Hudson looked at the sky and saw the long white hackles of clouds of the east wind. Then he looked ahead at the point of the main key, at the spot of key and the flats that were beginning to show. There he knew his trouble would start. Then he looked at the mess of keys ahead that showed like green spots on the water.

"Can you pick up the stake yet, Gil?" he asked.

"No, Tom."

"It's probably only the branch of a tree or maybe a stick."

"I can't see anything yet."

"It ought to be dead ahead as we go."

"I see it, Tom. It's a tall stick. Dead ahead as we go."

"Thank you," Thomas Hudson said.

The flats on either side were white yellow in the sun and the tidal stream that came pouring out of the channel was the green water of the inner lagoon. It was not fouled nor cloudy from the marl of the banks because the wind had not had time to raise a sea that would disturb them. This made his piloting easier.

Then he saw how narrow the cut was beyond the stake end and he felt his scalp prickle.

"You can make it, Tom," Antonio said. "Hang close to the starboard bank. I'll see the cut when it opens up."

He hung close to the starboard bank and crawled along. Once he looked to the port bank and saw it was closer than the starboard and he inched over to the right.

"Is she throwing any mud?" he asked.

"Clouds."

They came to the wicked turn and it was not as bad as he thought it would be. The narrow part they had come through was worse. The wind had risen now and Thomas Hudson felt it blowing strongly on his bare shoulder as they ran broadside to it through this cut.

"The stake is dead ahead," Gil said. "It's only a branch of tree."

"I've got it."

"Hold her hard against the starboard bank, Tom," Antonio said. "We have this one beat."

Thomas Hudson hugged the starboard bank as though he were parking a car against a curb. It did not look like a curb, though, but like the indented muddy terrain of an old battlefield, when they fought with great concentrations of artillery, that had suddenly been revealed from the bottom of the ocean and spread out, like a relief map, on his right.

"How much mud are we throwing?"

"Plenty, Tom. We can anchor when we get through this cut. This side of Contrabando. Or in the lee of Contrabando," Antonio suggested.

Thomas Hudson turned his head and saw Cayo Contrabando looking small and green and cheerful and he said, "The hell with that. Sweep that key and the channel that shows for a turtle boat, please, Gil. I see the next two stakes."

This channel was easy. But ahead he could see the sandbar on the right that was beginning to uncover. The closer they came to Cayo Contrabando, the narrower the channel became.

"Hold her to port of that stake," Antonio said.

"That's what I'm doing."

They passed the stake which was only a dead branch. It was brown and blowing in the wind and Thomas Hudson thought that with this wind blowing up they would have much less than the Mean Low Water depths.

"How's our mud?" he asked Antonio.

"Plenty, Tom."

"Do you see anything, Gil?"

"Only the stakes."

The water was beginning to be milky now from the sea that had risen with the wind and it was impossible to see the bottom nor the banks except when the ship sucked them dry.

This is no good, Thomas Hudson thought. But it is no good for them either. And they have to tack in it. They must really be sailors. Now I have to decide whether they would take the old channel or the new one. That depends on their pilot. If he is young, he would probably take the new one. That is the one the hurricane blew out. If he is old, he will probably take the old channel from habit and because it is safer.

"Antonio," he said. "Do you want to take the old canal or the new one?"

"They're both bad. It doesn't make much difference."

"What would you do?"

"I'd anchor in the lee of Contrabando and wait for the tide."

"We won't get enough tide to make it in daylight."

"That's the problem. You only asked me what I would do."

"I'm going to try to run the son of a bitch."

"It's your ship, Tom. But if we don't catch them, somebody else will."

"But why isn't Cayo Francés flying patrols over all this all the time?"

"They made their patrol this morning. Didn't you see it?"

"No. And why didn't you tell me?"

"I thought you saw it. One of those baby seaplanes."

"Shit," Thomas Hudson said. "It must have been when I was in the head and the generator was running."

"Well, it doesn't make any difference now," Antonio said. "But, Tom, the next two stakes are out."

"Can you see the next two stakes, Gil?"

"I can't see any stakes."

"The hell with it," Thomas Hudson said. "All I have to do is hug that next chickenshit little key and keep off the sand-spit that runs north and south of it. Then we'll case that bigger key with the mangroves and then we'll try for the old or the new channel."

"The east wind is blowing all the water out."

"The hell with the east wind," Thomas Hudson said. As he said the words, they sounded like a basic and older blasphemy than any that could have to do with the Christian religion. He knew that he was speaking against one of the great friends of all people who go to sea. So since he had made the blasphemy he did not apologize. He repeated it.

"You don't mean that, Tom," Antonio said.

"I know it," Thomas Hudson said. Then he said to himself, making an act of contrition and remembering the verse unexactly, "Blow, blow, thou western wind. That the small rain down may rain. Christ, that my love were in my arms and I in my bed again." It's the same goddam wind only with the difference in latitude, he thought. They come from different continents. But they are both loyal and friendly and good. Then he repeated to himself again, Christ, that my love were in my arms and I in my bed again.

The water was so muddy now that there was nothing to steer by except the ranges and the suction the ship made of water from the banks. George was in the bow with the lead and Ara had a long pole. They measured their depths and called back to the bridge.

Thomas Hudson had the feeling that this had happened before in a bad dream. They had run many difficult channels. But this was another thing that had happened sometime in his life. Perhaps it had happened all his life. But now it was happening with such an intensification that

he felt both in command and at the same time the prisoner
of it.

"Can you make out anything, Gil?" he asked.

"Nothing."

"Do you want Willie up here?"

"No. I see whatever Willie would see."

"I think he ought to be up anyway."

"As you wish, Tom."

Ten minutes later they were aground.

XV

THEY were aground on a patch of mud and sandy bottom
that should have been marked with a stake, and the tide
was still falling. The wind was blowing hard and the water
was muddy. Ahead was a medium-sized green key that
looked set low in the water and there was a scattering of
very small keys to the left. To the left and the right there
were patches of bare bank that were beginning to show
as the water receded. Thomas Hudson watched flocks of
shore birds wheeling and settling on the banks to feed.

Antonio had the dinghy over and he and Ara ran out
a bow anchor and two light stern anchors.

"Do you think we need another bow anchor?" Thomas
Hudson asked Antonio.

"No, Tom. I don't think so."

"If the wind rises it can push us against the flood when
it comes."

"I don't think it will, Tom. But it could."

"Let's get a small one out to windward and shift the
big one further to leeward. Then we don't have anything
to worry about."

"All right," Antonio said. "I'd rather do that than run
aground again in a bad place."

"Yeah," Thomas Hudson said. "We went into all that
before."

"It's still the right thing to anchor."

"I know it. I just asked you to put out another small one and shift the big one."

"Yes, Tom," Antonio said.

"Ara likes to lift anchors."

"Nobody likes to lift anchors."

"Ara."

Antonio smiled and said, "Maybe. Anyway I agree with you."

"We always agree sooner or later."

"But we mustn't let it be when it is too late."

Thomas Hudson watched the maneuver and looked ahead at the green key that was showing dark now at the roots of the mangroves as the tide fell. They could be in the bight on the south side of that key, he thought. This wind is going to blow until two or three o'clock in the morning and they could try to break out and run either of the channels in daylight when the flood starts. Then they could run that big lake of a bay where there is nothing to worry about all night. They have lights and a good channel to get out with at the far end. It all depends on the wind.

Ever since they had grounded he had felt, in a way, reprieved. When they had grounded he had felt the heavy bump of the ship as though he were hit himself. He knew it was not rocky as she hit. He could feel that in his hands and through the soles of his feet. But the grounding had come to him as a personal wound. Then, later, had come the feeling of reprieve that a wound brings. He still had the feeling of the bad dream and that it all had happened before. But it had not happened in this way and now, grounded, he had the temporary reprieve. He knew that it was only a reprieve but he relaxed in it.

Ara came up on the bridge and said, "It's good holding-ground, Tom. We have them in there good with a trip line to the big one. When we raise the big one we can get out fast. We buoyed both the stern anchors with trip lines."

"I saw. Thank you."

"Don't feel bad, Tom. The sons of bitches may be just behind that other key."

"I don't feel bad. I just feel delayed."

"It's not like smashing up a car or losing a ship. We're just aground waiting for a tide."

"I know."

"Both wheels are sound. She's just in mud up to her ass."

"I know. I put her there."

"She'll come off as easy as she went in."

"Sure she will."

"Tom. Are you worried about anything?"

"What would I be worried about?"

"Nothing. I only worried if you were worried."

"The hell with worry," Thomas Hudson said. "You and Gil go down. See everybody eats well and is cheerful. Afterwards we'll go in and check that key. That's all there is to do."

"Willie and I can go now. We don't have to eat."

"No. I'm going in later with Willie and Peters."

"Not me?"

"No. Peters speaks German. Don't tell him he's going in. Just wake him up and see he drinks plenty of coffee."

"Why can't I go, too?"

"The dinghy is too damn small."

Gil left him the big glasses and went down with Ara. Thomas Hudson studied the key carefully with the big glasses and saw that the mangroves were too high for him to learn anything about what was inside. There were other trees mixed with the mangroves on the solid part of the key and they brought the height up even more so that he could not possibly see if there was any mast showing in the horseshoe-shaped shelter on the far side. The big glasses hurt his eyes and he put them in their case and hung the strap of the case on a hook and laid the glasses flat on the frag rack.

He was happy to be alone again on the flying bridge and he relaxed for the short time of his reprieve. He watched the shore birds working on the flats and he remembered what they had meant to him when he was a boy. He could not feel the same about them now and he had no wish to kill them ever. But he remembered the early days with his father in a blind on some sand-spit with tin decoys out and how they would come in as the tide lowered and bared the flats and how he would whistle the flock in as they were circling. It was a sad whistle and he made it now and turned one flock. But they veered off from the stranded ship and went far out to feed.

He swept the horizon with the big glasses once and there was no sign of any boat. Maybe they have made it out through the new channel and into the inside passage, he thought. It would be nice if someone else caught them. We can't catch them now without a fight. They will not surrender to a dinghy.

He had been thinking so long in their heads that he was tired of it. I am really tired finally, he thought. Well, I know what I have to do, so it is simple. Duty is a wonderful thing. I do not know what I would have done without duty since young Tom died. You could have painted, he told himself. Or you could have done something useful. Maybe, he thought. Duty is simpler.

This is useful, he thought. Do not think against it. It helps to get it over with. That's all we are working for. Christ knows what there is beyond that. We've chased these characters quite well and now take a ten-minute break and then proceed with your duty. The hell with quite well, he thought. We've chased them very well.

"Don't you want to eat, Tom?" Ara called up.

"I don't feel hungry, kid," Thomas Hudson said. "I'll take the bottle of cold tea that's on the ice."

Ara handed it up and Thomas Hudson took it and relaxed against the corner of the flying bridge. He drank from the bottle of cold tea and watched the biggest key that was ahead. The mangrove roots were showing plainly now and the key looked as though it were on stilts. Then he saw a flight of flamingoes coming from the left. They were flying low over the water, lovely to see in the sunlight. Their long necks were slanted down and their incongruous legs were straight out; immobile while their pink and black wings beat, carrying them toward the mud bank that was ahead and to the right. Thomas Hudson watched

them and marvelled at their downswept black and white
bills and the rose color they made in the sky, which made
their strange individual structures unimportant and still
each one was an excitement to him. Then as they came
up on the green key he saw them all swing sharply to the
right instead of crossing the key.

"Ara," he called down.

Ara came up and said, "Yes, Tom."

"Check out three *niños* with six clips apiece and put
them in the boat with a dozen frags and the middle size
aid kit. Send Willie up here, please."

The flamingoes had settled on the bank to the far right
and were feeding busily. Thomas Hudson was watching
them when Willie said, "Look at those goddam filla-
mingoes."

"They spooked flying over the key. I'm pretty sure
that boat or another boat is inside there. Do you want to
go in with me, Willie?"

"Of course."

"Did you finish chow?"

"The condemned man ate a hearty lunch."

"Help Ara, then."

"Is Ara going with us?"

"I'm taking Peters because he speaks German."

"Can't we take Ara instead? I don't want to be with
Peters in a fight."

"Peters may be able to talk us out of a fight. Listen,
Willie. I want prisoners and I don't want their pilot to get
killed."

"You're making a lot of conditions, Tom, with them
eight or nine maybe and we three. Who the hell knows
we know they have the pilot anyway?"

"We know."

"Let's not be so fucking noble."

"I asked you if you wanted to come."

"I'm coming," Willie said. "Only that Peters."

"Peters will fight. Send Antonio and Henry up, will
you, please."

"Do you think they are in there, Tom?" Antonio asked.

"I'm pretty sure."

"Can't I go with you, Tom?" Henry asked.

"No. She will only take three. If anything happens to us, try and nail her with the .50's if she tries to come out on the first of the tide. Afterwards you'll find her in the long bay. She'll be damaged. She probably won't even be able to make it out. Get a prisoner if you can and get into Cayo Francés and check in."

"Couldn't I go in instead of Peters?" Henry asked.

"No, Henry. I'm sorry. But he speaks German. You have a good crew," Thomas Hudson said to Antonio. "If everything goes well with us I'll leave Willie and Peters on board with whatever there is and bring a prisoner back in the dinghy."

"Our last prisoner didn't last very long."

"I'll try and bring a good, strong, healthy one. Go on down and see everything is secured. I want to watch the flamingoes for a little while."

He stood on the flying bridge and watched the flamingoes. It is not just their color, he thought. It's not just the black on that rose pink. It is their size and that they are ugly in detail and yet perversely beautiful. They must be a very old bird from the earliest times.

He did not watch them through the glasses because he did not want details now. He wanted the roseate mass on the gray brown flat. Two other flocks had come in now and the banks were colored in a way that he would not have dared to paint. Or I would have dared to paint and would have painted, he thought. It is nice to see flamingoes before you make this trip. I better not give them time to worry or to think too much.

He climbed down from the bridge and said, "Gil, get up there and keep your glasses on the key. Henry, if you hear a lot of noise and then the turtle boat should come out from behind the key, shoot her fucking bow off. Everybody get up and glass where the survivors are and you can hunt them tomorrow. Plug the dinghy where she is shot up and use her. The turtle boat has a skiff and you can plug her up and use her too if we don't damage her too badly."

Antonio said, "Do you have any other orders?"

"Just keep your bowels open and try to lead clean lives. We'll be back in a little while. Come on, you two gentlemen bastards. Let's go."

"Grandmother always claimed I wasn't a bastard," Peters said. "She said I was the nicest-looking, most legitimate little baby in the county."

"Mother claimed I wasn't a bastard, too," Willie said. "Where do you want us, Tom?"

"She trims best with you in the bow. But I'll take the bow if you like."

"Get in and steer her," Willie said. "You got a really good ship now."

"I got my finger on my number," Thomas Hudson said. "I'm working up. Come aboard, Mr. Peters."

"Happy to be on board, admiral," Peters said.

"Good hunting," Henry said.

"Drop dead," Willie called. The motor caught and they were off toward the silhouette of the key that was lower in the water now because of their lack of altitude.

"I'm going alongside and we'll board her without hailing."

The two men nodded, one amidships and one in the bow.

"Get your junk hung. I don't give a shit if it shows," Thomas Hudson said.

"I don't know where I'd hide it," Peters said. "I feel like one of grandma's mules now."

"Then be a mule. It's a fucking good animal."

"Tom, do I have to remember all that shit about the pilot?"

"Remember it but use your head."

"Well," said Peters. "We haven't any fucking troubles anymore."

"We better all pipe down," Thomas Hudson said. "We'll all three board at the same time and if they are below, you ask them in Kraut to come out with their hands up. We have to stop talking because they can hear voices a long way above the noise of an outboard."

"What do we do if they don't come out?"

"Willie throws in a grenade."

"What do we do if they're on deck?"

"Sweep the deck according to our sectors. Me the stern. Peters amidships. You the bow."

"Then do I throw in a grenade?"

"Sure. We ought to get woundeds that we can save. That's why I brought the kit."

"I thought that was for us."

"Us too. Now let's pipe down. Do you have it clear?"

"Clearer than shit," Willie said.

"Has there been an issue of asshole corks?" Peters asked.

"They dropped it from the plane this morning. Didn't you get yours?"

"No. But grandma always said I had the slowest digestion of any baby in the whole of the South. They got one of my diapers in the Smithsonian Institute of the Confederacy."

"Cut out the shit," Willie said, leaning back in order not to talk loudly. "Are we doing all this in daylight, Tom?"

"Now."

"I'll be a sad son of a bitch," said Willie. "I have fallen among thieves and bastards."

"Shut up, Willie, and let's see you fight."

Willie nodded his head and looked ahead with his good eye toward the green mangrove key which lay tiptoed on its brown red roots.

He only said one more thing before they rounded the point, "They've got good oysters on those roots."

Thomas Hudson nodded.

XVI

THEY saw the turtle boat when they rounded the point of the key and passed through the channel which separated

it from another small key. She was lying with her bow
close in to shore and there were vines hanging from her
mast and her deck was covered with new-cut mangrove
branches.

Willie leaned back and with his voice almost against
Peter's ear, said in a low voice, "Her skiff's missing. Pass
the word."

Peters leaned his blotched, freckled face back and
said, "Her skiff's missing, Tom. There must be some
ashore."

"We'll board her and sink her," Thomas Hudson said.
"Same plan. Pass the word."

Peters bent forward and spoke into Willie's ear and
Willie's head started to shake. Then he held up his hand
with the familiar zero. Zero as in asshole, Thomas Hudson
thought. They came up on her as fast as the little coffee
mill of an engine would take them and Thomas Hudson
put her smartly alongside without bumping. Willie lifted
the grapple over the gunwale of the turtle boat and pulled
it fast and the three of them were on the deck almost at
the same time. Underneath their feet there were mangrove
branches with their dead fresh smell and Thomas Hudson
saw the vine draped mast as though now it were a dream
again. He saw the hatch open and a forward hatch open
and covered with branches. There was no one on deck.

Thomas Hudson waved Willie forward past this hatch
and covered the other one with his submachine gun. He
checked that the safety lever was on full automatic. Under
his bare feet he could feel the hard roundness of the
branches, the slipperiness of the leaves, and the heat of the
wooden deck.

"Tell them to come out with their hands up," he said
quietly to Peters.

Peters spoke in rough, throaty German. Nobody answered and nothing happened.

Thomas Hudson thought, grandma's boy has a good delivery, and he said, "Tell them again we give them ten
seconds to come out. We will treat them as prisoners of
war. Then count ten."

Peters spoke so it sounded like the voice of all German

doom. His voice holds up magnificently, Thomas Hudson thought, and turned his head fast to see if the skiff were in sight. He could only see the brown roots and the green of the mangroves.

"Count ten and put one in," he said. "Watch that fucking forward hatch, Willie."

"It's got those fucking branches covering it."

"Push one in with your hands when Peters goes. Don't throw it."

Peters reached ten and standing there, tall, loose-jointed like a pitcher on the mound, holding his sub-machine gun under his left arm, he pulled the pin of the grenade with his teeth, held it spurting smoke a moment as though he were warming it, and tossed it with the underhand motion of a Carl Mays into the darkness of the hatch.

As Thomas Hudson watched him, he thought, he's a great actor and he doesn't think there is anything down there.

Thomas Hudson hit the deck, covering the mouth of the hatch with his Thompson. Peter's grenade exploded with a flashing crack and a roar and Thomas Hudson saw Willie opening the brush to drop a grenade in the forward hatch. Then to the right of the mast, where the vines hung, he saw the muzzle of a gun come up from between the branches on the same hatch where Willie was working. He fired at it but it fired five quick flashes, clattering like a child's rattle. Then Willie's grenade went with a big flash and Thomas Hudson looked and saw Willie, in the scuppers, pull the pin on another grenade to throw in. Peters was on his side with his head on the gunwale. Blood was running from his head into the scuppers.

Willie threw and the grenade had a different sound because it rolled further into the boat before it burst.

"Do you think there are any more of the cocksuckers?" Willie called.

"I'll put one more in from here," Thomas Hudson said. He ducked and ran to get out of any fire from the big hatch and pulled the pin on another grenade, gray, heavy, solid, and notched in the grip of his hand, and crossing

forward of the hatch he rolled it down into the stern. There
was the crack, boom, and smoke where pieces of the deck
came up.

Willie was looking at Peters and Tom came over and
looked at him too. He did not look very different than
usual.

"Well, we've lost our interpreter," Willie said. His
good eye was twitching but his voice was the same.

"She's settling fast," Thomas Hudson said.

"She was aground already. But she's going over on her
beam ends now."

"We've got a lot of uncompleted business, Willie."

"And we traded even. One for one. But we sunk the
damned boat."

"You better get the hell back to the ship and get back
here with Ara and Henry. Tell Antonio to bring her
abreast of the point as soon as he gets the tide."

"I have to check below first."

"I'll check."

"No," Willie said. "That's my trade."

"How do you feel, kid?"

"Fine. Only sorry to hear of the loss of Mr. Peters.
I'll get a rag or something to put over his face. We ought
to straighten him out with his head uphill now she's
careening like this."

"How is the Kraut in the bow?"

"He's a mess."

XVII

WILLIE was gone now to bring Ara and Henry. Thomas
Hudson lay behind the parapet the high gunwale of the
turtle boat made. His feet were against the hatch and he
was watching for the skiff. Peters lay feet downward on
the other side of the hatch and his face was covered by a

German navy fatigue shirt. I never realized he was so tall, Thomas Hudson thought.

He and Willie had both searched the turtle boat and it was a mess. There had only been one German on board. He was the one who had shot Peters and he had evidently taken him for the officer. There was one other Schmeisser machine pistol aboard and close to two thousand rounds of ammunition in a metal case which had been opened with pliers or a can opener. Presumably, the men who had gone ashore had been armed because there were no weapons on board. The skiff was at least a sixteen-foot, heavy turtler from the chocks and the marks that she had left on the deck. They still had a quantity of food. It was mostly dried fish and hard roasted pork. It was the wounded man who had been left on board who had shot Peters. He had a bad thigh wound that was nearly healed and another nearly healed wound in the fleshy part of his left shoulder. They had good charts of the coast and of the West Indies and there was one carton of Camels without stamps and marked Ships Supplies. They had no coffee, nor tea, nor any liquors of any sort.

The problem now was what they would do. Where were they? They must have seen or heard the small fight on the turtle boat and they might return to pick up their stores. They would have seen one man leave by himself in the dinghy with the outboard and from the shots and the explosion of the frags there could easily be three men dead or incapacitated aboard. They would come back for stores or anything else that might be hidden and then break for the mainland in the dark. They could shove the skiff off anything that she might ground on.

The skiff must be a sturdy craft. Thomas Hudson had no radio operator and it was therefore impossible to give a description of the skiff and nobody would be looking for her. Then, if they wanted to, and had the will to try it they could try to assault the ship at night. That seemed extremely unlikely.

Thomas Hudson thought it out as carefully as he could. Finally, he decided, I believe that they will go inside the mangroves and haul the skiff in and hide it. If we go in after them, they can ambush us easily. Then they will run for the open inside bay and push on and try and pass Cayo Francés at night. That is easy. They may pick up supplies, or raid for them, and they will keep on pushing to the westward and try to make one of the German outfits around Havana where they will hide them and pick them up. They can easily get a better boat.

They can jump one. Or steal one. I have to report at Cayo Francés and deliver Peters and get my orders. The trouble won't come until Havana. There's a lieutenant commanding at Cayo Francés and we won't have any trouble there and they can keep Peters.

I have enough ice to handle him to there and I gas there and get ice at Caibarién.

We are going to get these characters for better or for worse. But I am not going to put Willie and Ara and Henry into one of those burp-gun massacres in the mangroves for fuck-all nothing. There are eight of them, anyway, from the looks of everything on board. I had a chance to catch them today with their pants down and I blew it because they were too smart or too lucky and they are always efficient.

We've lost one man and he is our radio operator. But we have cut them down to a skiff now. If I see the skiff we will destroy it and blockade the island and hunt them down on it. But I'm not going to stick our necks into any of those eight against three traps. If it is my ass afterwards, it is my ass. It is going to be my ass, anyway. Now that I've lost Peters. If I lost any irregulars, nobody would give a damn. Except me and the ship.

I wish they would get back, he thought. I don't want those bastards coming out to see what gives aboard this vessel and have the battle of no-name key by myself. I wonder what they are doing in there, anyway? Maybe they went for oysters. Willie mentioned the oysters. Maybe they just didn't want to be on this turtle boat in daylight if a plane came over and spotted her. But they must know the hours those planes work on by now. Hell, I wish they would come out and get it over with. I've got good cover and they'd have to get in range before they try to come aboard. Why do you suppose that wounded man didn't open up on us when we came over the side? He must have heard the outboard. Maybe he was asleep. The outboard makes very little noise anyway.

There are too many whys in this business, he thought, and I am not at all sure I have it figured properly. Maybe I should not have jumped the boat. But I think I had to do that. We sunk the boat and lost Peters and killed one man. That is not very brilliant but it still adds up.

He heard the hum of the outboard and turned his head. He saw her coming around the point but he could only see one man in her. It was Ara in the stern. But he noticed she was loaded deep and he realized that Willie and Henry must be lying flat. Willie's really smart, he thought. Now the people on the key don't know but that there may be only one man in the dinghy and they will see it is a different man from the one that took her away. I don't know whether that is smart or not. But Willie must have figured it.

The dinghy came up in the lee of the turtle boat and Thomas Hudson saw Ara's great chest, his long arms, and his brown face that was serious now, and he could see the nervous twitching of his legs. Henry and Willie lay flat with their heads on their arms.

When the dinghy came into the lee of the turtle boat that was careened away from the key and Ara held the rail, Willie turned on his side and said, "Get aboard, Henry, and crawl up there with Tom. Ara will hand you your junk. You've got Peters' junk too."

Henry climbed cautiously up the steep deck on his belly. He took one look at Peters as he crawled by him.

"Hi, Tom," he said.

Thomas Hudson put his hand on Henry's arm and said softly, "Get up in the bow and keep absolutely flat. Don't let anything show over the gunwale."

"Yes, Tom," the big man said, and began inching down to crawl up to the bow. He had to crawl over Peters' legs and he picked up his submachine gun and clips and stuck the clips in his belt. He felt in Peters' pockets for frags and hung them on his belt. He patted Peters on the legs and holding the two submachine guns by the muzzles he crawled up to his post in the bow.

Thomas Hudson saw him look down into the blasted forward hatch as he crawled up the steep deck over the broken mangroves. His face gave no sign of what he saw there. When he was under the lee of the gunwale, he put the two submachine guns by his right hand and then tested the functioning of Peters' gun and put in a fresh clip. He laid the other clips along the gunwale and unhooked the grenades from his belt and laid them out within reach. When he saw him in position and looking out at the greenness of the key, Thomas Hudson turned his head and spoke to Willie who was lying in the bottom of the dinghy with his good and his bad eye shut against the sun. He was wearing a faded khaki shirt with sleeves and ragged shorts and he had a pair of sneakers on. Ara was sitting in the stern and Thomas Hudson noticed his thatch of black hair and the way his big hands gripped the gunwale. His legs were still jumping but Thomas Hudson had known for a long time how nervous he always was before action and how beautiful he was once things started.

"Willie," Thomas Hudson said. "You have anything figured?"

Willie opened his good eye and kept his bad eye closed against the sun.

"I ask permission to go in on the far side of the key and see what the hell gives. We can't let them get out of here."

"I'll go in with you."

"No, Tommy. I know this shit and it's my trade."

"I don't want you to go in alone."

"That's the only way on this. You trust me, Tommy. Ara will come back here and back up your play if I flush them. He can come in and pick me up on the beach if there isn't any trouble."

He had both eyes open and he was looking hard at Thomas Hudson the way a man looks who is trying to sell an appliance to someone who should really have it if they can afford it.

"I'd rather go in with you."

"Too fucking much noise, Tom. I tell you truly I know this shit good. I'm a fucking expert. You'll never find anybody like me."

"OK. Go in," Thomas Hudson said. "But bust up their skiff."

"What the hell you think I'm going to do? Go in there and jerk off?"

"If you're going in, you better get in."

"Tom. Now you've got two traps set. The ship and here. Ara makes you mobile. You have one expendable, medically discharged Marine to lose. What's holding you up?"

"You talking so much," Thomas Hudson said. "Get the hell in and shit bless you."

"Drop dead," Willie told him.

"You sound in good shape," Thomas Hudson said and explained rapidly in Spanish to Ara what they were going to do.

"Don't bother," Willie said. "I can talk to him lying down."

Ara said, "I'll be right back, Tom."

Thomas Hudson watched him yank the motor alive and watched the dinghy move out with Ara's broad back and black head in the stern and Willie lying in the bottom. He had turned around so that his head was close to Ara's feet and he could talk to him.

The good, brave, worthless son of a bitch, Thomas Hudson thought. Old Willie. He made up my mind for me when I was starting to put things off. I would rather have a good Marine, even a ruined Marine, than anything in the world when there are chips down. And we have chips down now. Good luck, Mr. Willie, he thought. And don't drop dead.

"How are you, Henry?" he asked softly.

"Fine, Tom. It was very gallant of Willie to go in, don't you think?"

"He never even heard of the word," Thomas Hudson said. "He just conceived it to be his duty."

"I'm sorry we haven't been friends."

"Everybody is friends when things are bad enough."

"I'm going to be friends from now on."

"We're all going to do a lot of things from now on," Thomas Hudson said. "I wish from now on would start."

XVIII

THEY were lying on the hot deck watching the line of the key. The sun was strong on their backs but the wind cooled them. Their backs were nearly as brown as the sea Indian women they had seen this morning on the outer key. That seemed as long ago as all his life, Thomas Hudson thought. That and the open sea and the long breaking reefs and the dark depthless tropic sea beyond were as far away as all of his life was now. We could have just gone up the open sea with this breeze and made Cayo Francés and Peters would have answered their blinker and we all would have had cold beer tonight. Don't think about it, boy, he thought. This is what you had to do.

"Henry," he said. "How are you doing?"

"Splendidly, Tom," Henry said very softly. "A frag couldn't blow up from getting too hot in the sun could it?"

"I've never seen it. But it can increase their potency."

"I hope Ara's got some water," Henry said.

"Don't you remember them putting it in?"

"No, Tom. I was looking after my own equipment and I didn't notice."

Then against the wind they heard the noise of the outboard on the dinghy. Thomas Hudson turned his head carefully and saw her round the point. The dinghy was riding high and Ara was in the stern. He could see the width of his shoulders and his black head at this distance. Thomas Hudson turned his head again to watch the key and he saw a night heron rise from the trees in the center and fly away. Then he saw two wood ibis rise and wheel and fly off with quick-flapping, then coasting, then quick-flapping wing beats downwind toward the little key.

Henry had watched them, too, and he said, "Willie must be getting pretty well in."

"Yes," Thomas Hudson said. "They came off the high ridge in the center of the key."

"Then nobody else was there."

"Not if it was Willie who scared them."

"That's about where Willie would be by now if he didn't have too bad going."

"Keep down low now when Ara comes."

Ara brought the dinghy along the careened lee of the turtle boat and put the grapnel aboard against the gunwale. He climbed carefully aboard with the ease of a bear. He had a water bottle and a bottle of tea in an old gin bottle each tied to a piece of heavy fishing line that suspended them over his neck. He crawled up to lie beside Thomas Hudson.

"What about some of the damn water?" Henry asked.

Ara laid his stuff down beside Thomas Hudson's, untied the water bottle from the fish line and crawled carefully along the slanted deck above the two hatches to where Henry was stationed.

"Drink it," he said. "Don't try to bathe with it."

He slapped Henry on the back and crawled back to lie beside Thomas Hudson.

"Tom," he said, speaking very low. "We saw nothing. I landed Willie on the far side almost directly opposite us and went out to the ship. There I went aboard on the lee side away from the key. I explained everything to Antonio and he understood well. Then I filled the outboard with gas and filled the reserve can and brought out the iced tea and the water."

"Good," said Thomas Hudson. He dropped down the

deck a little way and took a long pull at the bottle of iced tea.

"Thank you very much for the tea."

"It was Antonio thought of it. We forgot certain things in our hurry at the start."

"Move down toward the stern so you can cover it."

"Yes, Tom," Ara said.

They lay there in the sun and the wind and each one watched the key. Occasionally a bird, or a pair of birds would fly up, and they knew these birds had been frightened either by Willie or by the others.

"The birds must make Willie angry," Ara said. "He didn't think about that when he went in."

"He might just as well be sending up balloons," Thomas Hudson answered.

He was thinking and he turned to look over his shoulder.

He did not like any of it now. There were too many birds getting up from the key. And what reason now had they to believe that the others were in there now? Why would they have gone in there in the first place? Lying on the deck he had a hollow feeling in his chest that both he and Willie had been deceived. Maybe they haven't sucked us in. But it does not look good with so many birds getting up, he thought. Another pair of wood ibis rose not far from the shore and Thomas Hudson turned to Henry and said, "Get down in the forward hatch, Henry, please, and keep watch inland."

"It's awfully messy in there."

"I know."

"All right, Tom."

"Leave your frags and clips. Just take a frag in your pocket and the *niño*."

Henry eased himself down into the hatch and looked out toward the inside keys that masked the channel. His expression had not changed. But he was tight-lipped keeping it in order.

"I'm sorry about it, Henry," Thomas Hudson said to him. "It's just the way it has to be for a while."

"I don't mind it," Henry said. Then the studied severity of his face cracked and he smiled his wonderful good smile. "It's that it isn't exactly the way I would plan to spend a summer."

"Me either. But things don't look so open and shut right now."

A bittern came out from the mangroves and Thomas Hudson heard it squawk and watched its nervous swooping flight downwind. Then he settled down to trace Willie's progress along the mangroves by the rising and the flight of the birds. When the birds stopped rising he was sure he was headed back. Then after a time they were being put up again and he knew Willie was working out the windward curve of the key. After three-quarters of an hour he saw a great white heron rise in panic and start its slow heavy wing-beats to windward and he said to Ara, "He'll be out now. Better go down to the point and pick him up."

"I see him," Ara said in a moment. "He just waved. He's lying down just in from the beach."

"Go get him and bring him back lying down."

Ara slid back down to the dinghy with his weapon and with a couple of frags in his pockets. He got into the stern of the dinghy and cast her off.

"Toss me the tea bottle, will you, Tom?"

Ara caught it using both hands for surety instead of the one-hand catch he would usually have made. He enjoyed catching frags one-handed and the hardest way possible just as he enjoyed crimping detonator caps with his teeth. But this tea was for Willie and he appreciated what Willie had been through, even though there were no results and he placed the bottle carefully under the stern and hoped it was still cool.

"What do you think, Tom?" Henry asked.

"We're fucked. For the moment."

In a little while the dinghy was alongside and Willie was lying in the bottom with the bottle of tea in both hands. His hands and face were scratched and bloody, although he had washed them with sea water, and one

sleeve was torn off his shirt. His face was bulging with
mosquito bites and there were lumps from mosquito bites
wherever his flesh was bare.

"There's not a goddam thing, Tom," he said. "They
never were on that key. You and I weren't too damned
smart."

"No."

"What do you think?"

"They went inside after they grounded. Whether for
keeps or to make a recon of the channels I don't know."

"Do you think they saw us board?"

"They could have seen everything or nothing. They're
pretty low in the water to see."

"They ought to have heard it downwind."

"They should have."

"So now?"

"You get out to the ship and send Ara back for Henry
and me. They might still be back."

"What about Peters? We can take him."

"Take him now."

"Tommy, you're parapeted up on the wrong side,"
Willie said. "We've both been wrong and I'm not offering
any advice."

"I know it. I'm going down in the afterhatch as soon
as Ara loads Peters."

"He better load him by himself," Willie said. "They
could see silhouettes. But they couldn't make out an
object flat on the deck without glasses."

Thomas Hudson explained to Ara and Ara climbed up
and handled Peters quite easily and impersonally but he
knotted the cloth behind his head. He was neither tender
nor rough and all he said as he lifted him and slid him
head first into the dinghy was, "He is very rigid."

"That's why they call them stiffs," Willie said. "Didn't
you ever hear?"

"Yes," Ara said. "We call them *fiambres* which means
cold meats as in a restaurant when you can have fish or
cold meats. But I was thinking of Peters. He was always
so limber."

"I'll get him right back, Tom. Do you need anything?"

"Luck," Thomas Hudson said. "Thank you for the recon, Willie."

"Just the usual shit," Willie said.

"Have Gil put Merthiolate on the scratches."

"Fuck the scratches," Willie said. "I'm going to run as a jungle man."

Thomas Hudson and Henry were looking out from the two hatches toward the broken and indented line of keys that lay between them and the long bay that formed the inland channel. They spoke in a normal tone of voice since they knew the others could not be closer than those small green islands.

"You watch," Thomas Hudson said. "I'm going to throw that ammunition of theirs overboard and have another look around below."

Below he found several things he had not noticed before and he lifted the case of ammunition out onto the deck and pushed it over the side. I suppose I should have scattered all the cartons, he thought. But the hell with it. He brought up the Schmeisser pistol and found it was not functioning. He laid it down with his own stuff.

I'll let Ara break it down, he thought. At least we know why they did not take it with them. Do you suppose they left that wounded man behind just as a reception committee and pulled out? Or do you suppose they made him comfortable and went off for a recon? How much do you think they saw and how much do they know?

"Don't you think we might have kept that ammo for evidence?" Henry asked.

"We're way past the evidence stage now."

"But it's always good to have it. You know how stuffy they are and they'll probably just evaluate the whole thing as doubtful. Maybe ONI won't even give it a doubtful. Do you remember the last one, Tom?"

"Yes, I remember."

"She went all the way up the mouth of the Mississippi and she's still doubtful."

"That's correct."

"I think we might have kept the ammo."

"Henry," Thomas Hudson said. "Please take it easy.

The deads from the massacre are on the key. We have Schmeisser bullets from them and from the dead Kraut. We have another dead Kraut buried with the location in the log. We have this turtle boat sunk and a dead Kraut in her bows. We have two Schmeisser pistols. One is nonfunctioning and the other is smashed by the frag."

"A hurricane will come along and blow everything away and they will say the whole thing is doubtful."

"All right," said Thomas Hudson. "Let's concede the whole thing is doubtful. And Peters?"

"One of us probably shot him."

"Sure. We'll have to go through all that."

They heard the outboard and then saw Ara round the point. That dinghy rides as high in the bow as a canoe, Thomas Hudson thought.

"Get your junk together, Henry," he said. "We're going back to the ship."

"I'm glad to stay aboard this thing if you want me to."

"No. I want you on the ship."

After Ara came alongside Thomas Hudson changed his mind.

"Stay here, Henry, a little while and I'll send Ara for you. If they come out, get a frag into the skiff if they come alongside. Take this back hatch where you have lots of room. Use your head."

"Yes, Tom. Thank you for letting me stay."

"I'd stay and send you in. But I have to talk things over with Antonio."

"I understand. Shouldn't I fire on them when they are alongside before I throw the frag?"

"If you want. But keep your head down and then throw the frag in from the other hatch. And hold it all you can."

He was lying in the lee scuppers passing his things to Ara. Then he lowered himself over the side.

"Is there too much water for you down there?" he asked Henry.

"No, Tom. It's quite all right."

"Don't get claustrophobia and keep a good lookout.

If they come in, let them get right alongside before you make your play."

"Of course, Tom."

"Think of it as a duck blind."

"I don't have to, Tom."

Thomas Hudson was lying flat on the planking of the dinghy now.

"Ara will be back as soon as you ought to come in."

"Don't worry, Tom. I can stay here all night if you like but I'd like Ara to bring out something to eat and a little rum perhaps and some more water."

"He'll be back and pick you up and we'll have a little rum on board."

Ara pulled the cord on the motor and they headed for the ship. Thomas Hudson felt the frags along his legs and the weight of the *niño* across his chest. He put his arms around it and cuddled it and Ara laughed and leaned down and said, "This is a bad life for good children."

XIX

THEY were all on board the ship now and it was cool in late afternoon wind. The flamingoes were gone from the flat although it was still uncovered. The flat was gray in the afternoon light and there was a flock of willets working over it. Beyond was the shallow water, the channels that could not be seen for the mud, and in the background were the keys.

Thomas Hudson was standing now on the flying bridge, leaning against a corner of it, and Antonio was talking to him.

"We don't get a high tide until after eleven tonight," Antonio said. "This wind is emptying the water right out of the bay and the flats and I don't know what sort of depths we will have."

"Will it float her or will we have to kedge off?"

"It will float her. But we haven't any moon."

"That's right. That's why we have these big springs."

"She only made last night," Antonio said. "She's new. We didn't see her last night because of the squall."

"That's right."

"I sent George and Gil in to cut some brush to stake the channel so we can get out. We can always sound it with the dinghy and get stakes on the points."

"Look. What I'd like to do when she floats is get in to where I can bring the searchlight and the .50's to bear on the turtle boat and put somebody on board to blink to us if they come out in the skiff."

"That would be ideal, Tom. But you can't get in there in the dark. You could get in there with the searchlight and the dinghy sounding ahead of you and calling the soundings and staking. But nobody would come out then. They'd never come out."

"I guess so. I've been wrong twice today."

"You were wrong," Antonio said. "But it was just chances. Like drawing a card."

"What's important is that I was wrong. Now tell me what you think."

"I think that if they haven't gone and if we make no move to act as though we were not aground they will come out to board the ship tonight. We do not look like anything except a pleasure craft. I'm sure they were inside the keys when it happened. They will feel contempt for us and they will be sure we are weak because they have seen only one man all day in the dinghy if they have watched."

"We tried to play it that way."

"Then if they find how things are on the turtle boat what then?"

"Ask Willie to come up here," he said to Antonio.

Willie came up, still lumpy-looking from the mosquito bites. His scratches looked better, though, and he was wearing only a pair of khaki shorts.

"How are you, jungle man?"

"I'm fine, Tom. Ara put some chloroform on the bites and they've stopped itching. Those damn mosquitoes are about a quarter of an inch long and black as ink."

"We've got ourselves pretty well fucked-up, Willie."

"Hell. We've been fucked-up from the start."

"Peters?"

"We've got him sewed up in canvas and some ice on him. He won't bring anything in the market. But he'll hold a couple of days."

"Listen, Willie. I was telling Antonio what I'd like to do was get in to where the .50's and the searchlight would bear on that hulk. But he says we can't get in without spooking the whole ocean and that it's no good."

"Sure," Willie said. "He's right. That's three times you've been wrong today. I'm leading you by one less."

"Do you think they will come out and try and board the ship?"

"I doubt it like hell," Willie said.

"But they could."

"They aren't crazy. But they could be desperate enough to try it."

The two of them were sitting on the deck of the flying bridge leaning back against the stays and the canvas. Willie rubbed the part of his right shoulder that had begun to itch again on the canvas.

"They could come out," he said. "They did a crazy thing when they made that massacre."

"Not from their point of view then. You have to remember it was when they had just lost their ship and they were desperate."

"Well, they lost another ship today as well as a comrade. Maybe they were fond of the son of a bitch."

"Probably. Or they wouldn't have let him take up space."

"He was a pretty good guy," Willie said. "He took all that surrender talk and a grenade before he even made his play. He must have thought Peters was the captain because of his commanding manner and the way he spreched Kraut."

"I guess so."

"You know the frags went off below decks. They might never have heard them. How many rounds did you fire, Tom?"

"Not more than five."

"The character fired one burp."

"How loud did it all sound to you, Antonio?"

"It didn't sound loud," Antonio said. "We are down-wind and to the north of it with the key between. It didn't sound loud at all. But I could hear it clearly."

"They might never have heard it," Thomas Hudson said. "But they must have seen the dinghy running around and their ship careened. They're sure to think she's a trap. I don't think they will go near her."

"I think that's right," Willie agreed.

"But do you think they'll come out here?"

"You and God know just as much about that as I do. Aren't you the one who's always thinking in the Germans' minds?"

"Sure," Thomas Hudson said. "Sometimes I'm pretty good at it. But I'm not so hot today."

"You're thinking all right," Willie said. "You just ran into a bad streak."

"We could set a trap over there."

"You're just as trapped as you're trapping on her," Willie said.

"You go over and booby-trap her while it's still light."

"Now you're talking," Willie said. "That's the old Tom. I'll booby-trap both hatches and that dead Kraut and the lee rail. You're thinking your way out of it now."

"Use plenty of stuff. We've got lots of stuff."

"She'll be booby-trapped till Christ won't have her."

"They're coming in with the dinghy," Antonio said.

"I'll get Ara and the necessary and get over there," Willie said.

"Don't blow yourself up."

"Don't think too much," Willie said. "Get some rest, Tom. You're going to be up all night."

"So are you."

"The hell I am. When you want me they can wake me."

"I'll take the watch," Thomas Hudson said to Antonio. "When does our tide turn?"

"It's turned already but it is fighting with the current that the strong east wind blows out from the bay."

"Put Gil on the .50's and give George a break. Tell everybody to get a rest for the night."

"Why don't you take a drink, Tom?"

"I don't want one. What are you giving them to eat tonight?"

"A big piece of that wahoo boiled with Spanish sauce and black beans and rice. There aren't any more canned fruits."

"There were some on the list at Confites."

"Yes. But they were crossed off."

"Do you have any dried fruits?"

"Apricots."

"Soak some tonight and give them to them for breakfast."

"Henry won't eat them for breakfast."

"Well, give them to him the first meal he eats well. Have you plenty of soup?"

"Plenty."

"How is ice?"

"We have plenty for a week if we don't use too much on Peters. Why don't you bury him at sea, Tom?"

"Maybe I will," Thomas Hudson said. "He always said he'd like it."

"He said so many things."

"Yeah."

"Tom, why don't you take a drink?"

"All right," said Thomas Hudson. "Do you have any gin left?"

"Your bottle is in the locker."

"Do you have any water coconuts?"

"Yes."

"Make me a gin and coconut water with some lime in it. If we have limes."

"We have plenty of limes. Peters has some Scotch of his hidden if I can find it. Would you rather have that?"

"No. Find it and lock it up. We might need it."

"I'll make yours and hand it up."

"Thank you. Maybe we'll have good luck and they will come out tonight."

"I can't believe they will. I am of the school of Willie. But they might."

"We look awfully tempting. And they need some sort of craft."

"Yes, Tom. But they are not fools. You would not have been able to think in their heads if they were fools."

"OK. Get the drink." Thomas Hudson was glassing the keys with the big binoculars. "I'll try to think in their heads some more."

But he did not have any luck thinking in their heads. He was not thinking very well at all. He watched the dinghy, Ara in the stern and Willie out of sight, round the point of the key. He watched the flock of willet fly up finally and turn and head for one of the outer keys. Then he was alone and he sipped the drink that Antonio had made.

He thought how he had promised himself that he would not drink this trip, not even the cool one in the evening, so that he would not think of anything but work. He thought how he had planned to drive himself so he would sleep completely exhausted. But he made no excuses for this drink nor for the broken promise.

I drove myself, he thought. I did that all right. Now I might as well have this drink and think about something besides those other people. If they come out tonight we'll have everything set for them. If they do not come out, I will go in after them tomorrow morning on the high tide.

So he sipped the drink, which was cold and clean-tasting, and he watched the broken line of the keys straight ahead and to the westward. A drink always unlocked his memory that he kept locked so carefully now and the keys reminded him of the days when they used to troll for tarpon when young Tom was a small boy. Those were different keys and the channels were wider.

There were no flamingoes but the other birds had been

nearly all the same except for the flocks of big golden plover. He remembered the seasons when the plover were gray and the others when the black feathers had the golden tinge and he remembered young Tom's pride at the first one he had ever brought home when he had his first single barrel twenty-gauge. He remembered how Tom had stroked the plump white breast and touched the lovely black under-markings and how he had found the boy asleep that night in his bed with his arms around the bird. He had taken the bird away very softly hoping he would not wake the boy. The boy did not wake. His arms just closed up tightly and he rolled onto his back.

As he had taken the golden plover into the back room where the icebox was, he felt he had robbed the boy of it. But he had smoothed its plumage carefully and laid it on one of the grilled shelves of the icebox. The next day he had painted young Tom a picture of the golden plover and the boy had taken it with him when he went off to school that year. In the picture he had tried to get the fast, running quality of the bird and the background was a long beach with coconut palms.

Then he remembered one time when they were in a tourist camp. He had wakened early and Tom was still asleep. He lay on his back with his arms crossed and he looked like the sculpture of a young knight lying on his tomb. Thomas Hudson had sketched him that way using a tomb that he remembered from Salisbury Cathedral. He was going to paint a canvas of it later but he did not do it because he thought it could be bad luck. A lot of good that did, he thought.

He looked into the sun that was low now and he could see Tom high up in the sun in a Spitfire. The aircraft was very high and very tiny and it shone like a fragment of broken mirror. He liked it up there, he said to himself. And it was a good rule you made about not drinking.

But over half of the drink was still in the paper-wrapped glass and there was still ice in it.

Courtesy of Peters, he thought. Then he remembered when they lived on the island in the old days and how

Tom had read about the ice age at school and he was afraid it would come again.

"Papa," he had said. "That is my only worry."

"It can't hit here," Thomas Hudson had said.

"I know. But I can't stand to think what it will do to all those people in Minnesota and Wisconsin and Michigan. Even Illinois and Indiana."

"I don't think we really have to worry about it," Thomas Hudson had said. "It's a dreadfully slow process if it comes."

"I know," young Tom had said. "But that's the only thing I every really worry about. That and the extinction of the passenger pigeon."

That Tom, he thought, and put the drink into one of the empty frag holes and glassed the keys carefully. He saw nothing that might be a sailing skiff and he put the glasses down.

The best times they had, he thought, were on the island and out West. Except Europe, of course, and if I think about that I'll think about the girl and it will be worse. I wonder where she is now. Sleeping with some general, I suppose. Well, I hope she gets a good one.

She looked awfully well and very beautiful when I saw her in Havana. I could think about her all night. But I won't. It is indulgence enough to think about Tom. I wouldn't do that without the drink. I'm glad I took it, though. There is a time to break all your rules. Maybe not all. I will think about him for a while and then I will work out our small problem for tonight when Willie and Ara get back. They're a wonderful team. Willie learned that awful Spanish in the Philippines but they understand each other perfectly. Some of that is because Ara is a Basque and speaks bad Spanish, too. Christ, I'd hate to go aboard that hulk after Willie and Ara rig her.

Go ahead and drink the rest of your drink and think about something good. Tom's dead and it's all right to think about him. You'll never get over it. But you are solid on it now. Remember some good happy times. You had plenty.

What were the happiest times? he thought. They were

all happy, really, in the time of innocence and the lack of useless money and still being able to work and eat. A bicycle was more fun than a motorcar. You saw things better and it kept you in good shape and coming home after you had ridden in the Bois you could coast down the Champs Élysees well past the Rond-Point and when you looked back to see what was behind you there, with the traffic moving in two streams, there rose the high gray of the great arch against the dusk. The horse chestnuts would be in bloom now. The trees would be black in the dusk as he pedalled now toward the Place de la Concorde and the upstanding blooms would be white and waxen. He would get off the racing bicycle to push it along the gravel path and see the horse chestnut trees slowly, and feel them overhead as he pushed the bicycle and felt the gravel under the thin soles of his shoes. He had bought this pair of racing shoes second-hand from a waiter he knew at the Select who had been an Olympic champion and he had paid for them by painting a canvas of the proprietor the way the proprietor had wished to be painted.

"A little in the style of Manet, Monsieur Hudson. If you can do it."

It was not a Manet that Manet would have signed but it looked more like Manet than it did like Hudson and it looked exactly like the proprietor. Thomas Hudson got the money for the bicycle shoes from it and for a long time they could have drinks on the house as well. Finally one night when he offered to pay for a drink, the offer was accepted and Thomas Hudson knew that payment on the portrait had been finished.

There was a waiter at the Closerie des Lilas who liked them and always gave them double-sized drinks so that by adding water they needed only one for the evening. So they moved down there. They would put Tom to bed and sit there together in the evenings at the old café, completely happy to be with each other. Then they would take a walk through the dark streets of the Montagne Sainte-Geneviève where the old houses had not yet been torn

down and try to come home some different way each
night. They would go to bed and hear Tom breathing in
his cot and the purring of the big cat that slept with him.

Thomas Hudson remembered how people were hor-
rified that they let the cat sleep with the small boy and
that they left him alone when they went out. But Tom
always slept well and if he woke up, there was the cat,
who was his best friend. The cat would let no one near the
bed and he and Tom loved each other very much.

Now Tom was—the hell with that, he said to himself.
It is something that happens to everybody. I should know
about that by now. It is the only thing that is really final,
though.

How do you know that? he asked himself. Going away
can be final. Walking out the door can be final. Any
form of real betrayal can be final. Dishonesty can be final.
Selling out is final. But you are just talking now. Death
is what is really final. I wish Ara and Willie would get
back. They must be rigging that hulk up like a chamber
of horrors. I've never liked to kill, ever. But Willie loves
it. He is a strange boy and very good, too. He is just
never satisfied that a thing cannot be done better.

He saw the dinghy coming. Then he heard her purring
hum and then he watched her get clearer and bigger
and then she was alongside.

Willie came up. He looked worse than ever and his
bad eye was showing too much white. He drew himself up,
saluted smartly, and said, "Permission to speak to the
captain, sir?"

"Are you drunk?"

"No, Tommy. Enthusiastic."

"You've been drinking."

"Sure, Tom. We took a little rum with us for working
around that cadaver. And then when we got through
Ara urinated in the bottle and then booby-trapped the
bottle. It's double booby-trapped."

"Did you rig her good?"

"Tommy, a little tiny gnome no bigger than a man's
hand couldn't get on her without being blown clean back
to gnome land. A cockroach couldn't crawl on her. Ara

was afraid the flies on the cadaver would set her off. We trapped her beautifully and delicately."

"What's Ara doing?"

"He's disassembling and cleaning everything in a frenzy of enthusiasm."

"How much rum did you guys take?"

"Less than half a bottle. It was my idea. It wasn't Ara's."

"OK. Get the hell down with him and clean the weapons and check the .50's."

"You can't check them really without firing them."

"I know. But you check them completely without firing them. Throw away the ammo that's been in the breeches."

"That's smart."

"Tell Henry to come up here and bring me a small glass of this and tell him to bring a drink for himself. Antonio knows what this drink is."

"I'm glad you're drinking a little again, Tom."

"For Christ's sake, don't be glad or sad about whether I'm drinking or not drinking."

"OK, Tom. But I don't like to see you ride yourself like a horse riding on a horse's back. Why don't you be like a centaur?"

"Where did you learn about centaurs?"

"I read it in a book, Tommy. I'm educated. I'm educated far beyond my years."

"You're a good old son of a bitch," Thomas Hudson told him. "Now get the hell down and do what I told you."

"Yes sir. Tommy, when we finish this cruise will you let me buy one of the sea paintings out at the joint?"

"Don't shit me."

"I'm not doing that. Maybe the hell you don't understand all the time."

"That could be. Maybe all my life."

"Tommy, I kid a lot. But you chased pretty."

"We'll see tomorrow. Tell Henry to bring a drink up. But I don't want any."

"No, Tommy. All we have tonight is a simple fight and I don't think we'll have it."

"All right," said Thomas Hudson. "Send it up. And get down off this fucking bridge and get to work."

XX

HENRY passed the two drinks up and swung up himself after them. He stood beside Thomas Hudson and leaned forward to look at the shadow of the far keys. There was a thin moon in the first quarter of the sky to the westward.

"Here's to your good health, Tom," Henry said. "I didn't look at the moon over my left shoulder."

"She's not new. She was new last night."

"Of course. And we didn't see her for the squall."

"That's right. How's everything below?"

"Excellent, Tom. Everybody's working and cheerful."

"How are Willie and Ara?"

"They drank a little rum, Tom, and it made them very cheerful. But they're not drinking now."

"No. They wouldn't."

"I look forward to this very much," Henry said. "So does Willie."

"I don't. But it's what we are here to do. You see, we want prisoners, Henry."

"I know."

"Because they made that mistake on the massacre key they don't want to be taken prisoner."

"I think that's putting it mildly," Henry said. "Do you think they will try to jump us tonight?"

"No. But we have to be alerted in case they do."

"We will be. But what do you really think they are going to do, Tom?"

"I can't figure it, Henry. If they are really desperate they will try for the ship. If they have a radio operator left, he could fix our radio up and they could go across to Anguilas and just call a taxi and wait for it to take them home. They have every reason to try for the ship. Somebody could always have talked around Havana and they might know what we are."

"Who would talk?"

"Never speak ill of the deads," Thomas Hudson said. "But I'm afraid he might have when he was drinking."

"Willie is sure he did."

"Does he know anything?"

"No. He's just sure."

"It's a possibility. But they could also just try to make the mainland and make their way overland to Havana and get a Spanish ship out. Or an Argentine ship. But they don't want to be picked up on account of the massacre business. So I think they'll try something desperate."

"I hope so."

"If we can set it up," Thomas Hudson said.

But nothing happened all night long except the movement of the stars and the steady blowing of the east wind and the sucking of the currents past the ship. There was much phosphorescence in the water from the weed that the big tides and the sea made by the wind had torn up from the bottom, and it floated in and out and in again like cold strips and patches of white, unhealthy fire in the water.

The wind dropped a little before dawn and when it was light Thomas Hudson lay down and slept on the deck, lying on his belly with his face against a corner of the canvas. Antonio covered him and his weapon with a piece of canvas but Thomas Hudson was asleep and did not feel it.

Antonio took over the watch and when the tide was high so they swung free, he woke Thomas Hudson. They got the anchors in and started in with the dinghy going ahead and sounding and staking any dubious points. The water on this flood tide was clean and clear by now and the piloting was difficult but not as it had been the day before. They had staked a branch of a tree in the channel where they had grounded the day before and Thomas Hudson looked back and saw its green leaves moving in the current.

Thomas Hudson looked ahead and followed the dinghy closely as she worked out the channel. They passed a long green key that had looked like a small round key

when they had been head on to it. Then ahead in what
looked like an unbroken but indented line of mangrove
keys Gil, who had the glasses, said, "Stake, Tom. Dead
ahead of the dinghy against the mangroves."

"Check," Thomas Hudson said. "Is it the canal?"

"It looks to be but I can't see the opening."

"It is very narrow on the chart. We will just about
brush the mangroves on each side."

Then he remembered something. How could I be so
stupid? he thought. But we had better go on now,
anyway, and out through the channel. Then I can send them
back. He had forgotten to tell Wilie and Ara to detrap
the hulk of the turtle boat. That is a hell of a thing to leave
around if some poor fisherman comes onto it. Well, they
can go back and detrap it.

The dinghy was signalling him now to keep hard over
to the right of the three tiny spots of key and close against
the mangroves. Then, as if to make sure he understood,
they wheeled and came up. "The channel's right in along
the mangroves," Willie shouted. "Leave the stake on
your left. We're going ahead through. As long as you don't
hear from us keep on steaming. It's just a deep creek."

"We forgot to detrap that turtle boat."

"I know," Willie shouted. "We'll go back after."

Ara grinned and spun the dinghy around and they
went on ahead, Willie signalling that it was OK. They
turned left and right and went out of sight into the
green.

Thomas Hudson steered in their wake. There was
plenty of water although no such water showed on the
chart. This old channel must have been scoured out by a
hurricane, he thought. Many things have happened since
the U.S.S. *Nokomis* had boats sounding in here.

Then he saw there were no birds rising from the mangroves as the dinghy went into the narrow brush river
of the channel.

While he steered he spoke into the tubes to Henry in
the forward cockpit, "We may get jumped in this channel.
Have your .50's ready to fire from either bow and

abeam. Keep behind the shield and watch for the flashes and pour it onto them."

"Yes, Tom."

To Antonio he said, "We may get jumped here. Keep well down and if we are fired on, aim below the flashes and pour it on. Keep way down."

"Gil," he said. "Put your glasses away. Take two frags and straighten the pins and put them there in the rack by my right hand. Straighten two pins on those extinguishers and then put your glasses away. They'll probably hit us from both sides. That's how they ought to."

"Tell me when to throw, Tom."

"Throw when you see the flashes. But loft it plenty because it has to fall through brush."

There were no birds at all and since the tide was high he knew that the birds had to be in the mangroves. The ship was entering the narrow river now and Thomas Hudson, bareheaded and barefooted and only wearing a pair of khaki shorts, felt as naked as a man can feel.

"You lie down, Gil," he said. "I'll tell you when to get up and throw."

Gil lay on the floor with the two fire extinguishers that were loaded with dynamite and a booster charge and were fired by the detonating assembly of a regulation frag, with its charger hacksawed off at the juncture of the fuse and a dynamite cap fitted and crimped on.

Thomas Hudson looked at him once and saw how he was sweating. Then he looked at the mangroves on either side.

I could still try to back her out, he thought. But I don't believe I could, the way the tide is flowing.

He looked ahead at the green banks. The water was brown again now and the mangrove leaves were as shiny as though they were varnished. He looked to see where any had been cut or disturbed. But he saw nothing but the green leaves, the dark branches, and the roots that were exposed with the suction of the ship. There were a few crabs that showed when their holes under the mangrove roots were exposed.

They went on and the channel narrowed but he could

see it opening wider ahead. Maybe I just had the jitters, he thought. Then he saw a crab come sliding out fast from the high mangrove roots and plop into the water. He looked hard into the mangroves but he could see nothing beyond the trunks and branches. Another crab came out very fast and went into the water.

Just then they opened on him. He did not see the blinking flash and he was hit before he heard the stutter of the gun and Gil was on his feet beside him. Antonio was firing tracers where he had seen the gun flash.

"Where the tracers are going," Thomas Hudson said to Gil. Thomas Hudson felt as though someone had clubbed him three times with a baseball bat and his left leg was wet.

Gil lobbed the bomb with a high overhand motion and Thomas Hudson saw its long brass cylinder and conic nose shining in the sun. It was spinning, not going end over end.

"Down, Gil," he said and thought he ought to drop himself. Then he knew he shouldn't but should hold the ship as she was. The twin .50's had opened up and he could hear them pounding and he felt the jolt of them through his bare feet. Very noisy, he thought. That will keep the bastards down.

He saw the blinding burst of the bomb before the roar came and the smoke started to rise. He smelled the smoke and the smell of broken branches and burned green leaves.

"Get up, Gil, and throw two frags. One on each side of the smoke."

Gil did not lob the frags. He threw them like the long throw from third base to first and in the air they looked like gray iron artichokes with a thin trickle of smoke coming from them.

Before they burst cracking white in the mangroves Thomas Hudson said into the tube, "Shoot the shit out of it, Henry. They can't run in there."

The smoke from the frags smelled differently from the bomb and Thomas Hudson said to Gil, "Throw two more frags. One beyond the bomb and one in this side close."

He watched the frags go and then hit the deck. He did

not know whether he hit the deck or the deck hit him because the deck was very slippery from the blood that had been running down his leg and he fell hard. At the second burst he heard two fragments tear through the canvas. Others hit the hull.

"Help me up," he said to Gil. "You threw that last one close enough."

"Where are you hit, Tom?"

"A couple of places."

Ahead he saw Willie and Ara coming up the channel in the dinghy.

He spoke in the tube to Antonio and asked him to hand up a first aid kit to Gil.

Just then he saw Willie drop flat in the bow of the dinghy and start firing into the mangroves on the right. He could hear the dat-dat-dat of his Thompson gun. Then there was a longer burst. He put in both his motors and headed for them with all the speed the channel would allow. His idea of this speed was not completely accurate because he felt very sick. He felt sick into his bones and through his chest and his bowels and the ache went into his testicles. He did not feel weak yet but he could feel the first onslaught of weakness.

"Get your guns to bear on the right bank," he said to Henry. "Willie's found more of them."

"Yes, Tom. Are you all right?"

"I'm hit but I'm all right. What about you and George?"

"We're fine."

"Open up any time you see anything."

"Yes, Tom."

Thomas Hudson stopped his engines and commenced to go astern again slowly to hold the ship outside the angle where Willie was firing. Willie had a clip in now with tracers in it and he was trying to spot the target for the ship.

"You got it, Henry?" he asked through the tube.

"Yes, Tom."

"Work on it and around it with short bursts."

He heard the .50's start slamming and he waved Ara and Willie in. They came in as fast as the little motor would bring them. Willie was firing all the time until they were under the lee of the ship.

Willie jumped aboard and came up on the flying bridge while Ara made the dinghy fast.

He looked at Tom and at Gil who was putting a tourniquet on his left leg as close to the crotch as he could tighten it.

"Jesus Christ," he said. "What you got, Tommy?"

"I don't know," Thomas Hudson said. He did not know, either. He could not see any of the wounds. All he saw was the color of the blood and it was dark so he did not worry. But there was too much of it and he felt very sick.

"What's in there, Willie?"

"I don't know. There was a guy with a burp gun fired on us and I got him. Or I'm pretty sure I did."

"I didn't hear it with the noise you made."

"You guys sounded like an ammunition dump going up. Do you think there's anything still back there?"

"Still, maybe. We gave it the treatment."

"We'll have to work it out," Willie said.

"We can let these sons of bitches hang and rattle," Thomas Hudson said. "Or we can go in now and finish it."

"I'd rather take care of you."

Henry was probing with the .50's. He was as delicate as he was rough with a machine gun and with a pair of them all his qualities were doubled.

"Do you know where they are, Willie?"

"There's only one place they can be."

"Then let's go in blasting and blow the shit out of them."

"Spoken like an officer and a gentleman," Willie said. "We sunk their skiff."

"Oh. We didn't hear that either," Thomas Hudson said.

"It didn't make much noise," Willie said. "Ara chopped her open with a machete and cut the sail up. Christ couldn't repair her in a month the best day he was in that carpenter shop."

"You get up forward with Henry and George and have

Ara and Antonio on the starboard side and let's go in,"
Thomas Hudson said. He felt very sick and strange,
although there was no dizziness yet. The dressings Gil had
put on contained the bleeding too easily and he knew it
was internal. "Put lots of fire on and you signal me how
to go. How close are they?"

"Right up against the shore behind the little rise of
ground."

"Can Gil reach it all right with the big ones?"

"I'll shoot tracers to show him the target."

"They'll still be there?"

"They got no place to go. They saw us break up the
skiff. They're fighting Custer's Last Stand in the mangroves. Christ, I wish I had some Anheuser Busch."

"Ice cold in cans," Thomas Hudson said. "Let's get in."

"You're awfully white, Tommy," Willie said. "And
you've lost a lot of blood."

"Let's take her in fast then," Thomas Hudson said.
"I'm still all right."

They closed fast with Willie with his head up over
the starboard bow sometimes waving a correction.

Henry was traversing before and behind the rise that
showed by the higher trees and George was working on
what should be the lip of the rise.

"How is it, Willie?" Thomas Hudson said into the tube.

"You got enough hulls up here to start a brass foundry,"
Willie answered. "Lay her goddam bow up against the
bank and swing her broadside so Ara and Antonio can
bear."

Gil thought he saw something and fired. But it was the
low branch of a tree that Henry had cut loose.

Thomas Hudson watched the bank come closer and
closer until he could see individual leaves again. Then
he swung her broadside until he heard Antonio firing
and saw his tracers going in a little to the right of Willie's.
Ara was firing now, too. Then he came a little astern on
his motors and swung her close to the bank but not so
close that Gil could not throw.

"Throw an extinguisher," he said. "Where Willie's been
shooting."

Gil threw and again Thomas Hudson marvelled at the throw and at the shine of the brass cylinder whirling high through the air to drop almost exactly where it should. There was the flash and the roar and then the rising smoke and then Thomas Hudson saw a man walking toward them out of the smoke with his hands clasped over his head.

"Hold up the fire," he said as rapidly as he could into two tubes.

But Ara had already fired and he saw the man slump forward into the mangroves on his knees with his head forward.

He spoke again and said, "Resume fire." Then he said to Gil, very tiredly, "Put in another one about the same place if you can. Then put in a couple of frags."

He had had a prisoner. But he had lost him.

After a while he said, "Willie, you and Ara want to have a look?"

"Sure," Willie said. "But keep some fire on while we go in. I want to go in from the back."

"Tell Henry what you want. When do you want it off?"

"As soon as we clear the entrance."

"All right, jungle man," Thomas Hudson said and for the first time he had time to realize that he was probably going to die.

XXI

HE heard the noise of a grenade bursting behind the small ridge. Then there was no more noise and no firing. He leaned heavily on the wheel and he watched the smoke of the grenade thin out in the wind.

"I'm going to take her on through as soon as I see the dinghy," he said to Gil.

He felt Antonio's arm around him and heard him say, "You lie down, Tom. I'm taking her."

"All right," he said and he took a last look down the narrow, green-banked river. The water was brown but clear and the tide was flowing strong.

Gil and Antonio helped him to lie down on the planking of the bridge. Then Antonio took the wheel. He went astern a little more to hold her against the tide and Thomas Hudson could feel the sweet rhythm of the big motors.

"Loosen the tourniquet a little," he said to Gil.

"We'll get the air mattress," Gil said.

"I like it on the deck," Thomas Hudson said. "I think it is better if I don't move much."

"Get a cushion under his head," Antonio said. He was looking down the channel.

In a little while he said, "They're waving us in, Tom," and Thomas Hudson felt the motors go ahead and the ship slide forward.

"Anchor her as soon as we're out of the channel."

"Yes, Tom. Don't talk."

Henry came up and took the wheel and the controls when they anchored. Now that they were in the open again, Thomas Hudson felt her swing into the wind.

"There's lots of water in here, Tom," Henry said.

"I know. All the way to Caibarién and the two channels are clear and well marked."

"Please don't talk, Tom. Just lie quiet."

"Have Gil get a light blanket."

"I'll get it. I hope it doesn't hurt too much, Tommy."

"It hurts," Thomas Hudson said. "But not too bad. It doesn't hurt any worse than things hurt that you and I have shot together."

"Here's Willie," Henry said.

"You old son of a bitch," said Willie. "Don't talk. There were four in there with the guide. It was the main party. Then there was the one Ara got by mistake. He feels awful about it when you wanted a prisoner so much. He's crying and I told him to stay below. He just loosed off like anybody would."

"What did you throw the grenade at?"

"Just a place I didn't like the look of. Don't you talk, Tom."

"You have to go back and detrap that hulk."

"We're going right away and we'll check the other place. I wish the Christ we had a speed boat. Tommy, those goddam fire extinguishers are better than an .81mm mortar."

"Not the same range."

"What the hell we want with range? That Gil was throwing them into a bushel basket."

"Get going."

"How bad are you, Tommy?"

"Pretty bad."

"Think you can make it?"

"I'm going to try."

"Keep perfectly still. Don't move for anything."

They were not gone long but it seemed a long time to Thomas Hudson. He lay on his back in the shade of a canopy Antonio had rigged for him. Gil and George had unlaced the canvas from the windward side of the flying bridge and the wind came fresh and friendly. It was not as strong as it had been yesterday but it was steady from the east and the clouds were high and thin. The sky was the blue sky of the eastern part of the island where the trades blow strongest and Thomas Hudson lay and watched it and tried to hold his pain in control. He had refused the hypodermic of morphine that Henry had brought him because he thought he might still have to think. He knew he could always take it later on.

He lay there under the light blanket with the dressings on his three wounds. Gil had sifted them all full of sulfa when he dressed them and he could see sulfa spilled like sugar on the part of the deck where he had stood at the wheel while Gil had worked on him. When they had taken down the canvas, so he would have more air, he had noticed the three small holes where the bullets had come through and the others to the left and to the right. He had seen the gashes in the canvas from the grenade fragments.

As he lay there, Gil watched him and saw his salt-bleached head and his gray face above the light blanket. Gil was a simple boy. He was a great athlete and nearly as strong as Ara and if he could have hit a curve ball he would have been a very good ball player. He had a great throwing arm. Thomas Hudson looked at him and smiled, remembering the grenades. Then he smiled just to look at Gil and the long muscles of his arms.

"You should have been a pitcher," he said and his voice sounded strange to him.

"I never had control."

"You had it today."

"Maybe it wasn't really necessary before," Gil smiled. "You want some water on your mouth, Tommy. Just nod your head."

Thomas Hudson shook his head and looked out at the lake that was the inside passage. It showed white caps now. But they were the small waves of a good sailing breeze and beyond them he could see the blue hills of the Turiguaño.

That's what we'll do, he thought. We'll head for the Central or for the other place and they may have a doctor there. No, it's too late in the season. But they can fly a good surgeon in. They are all fine people in there. A bad surgeon is worse than none and I can lie quiet until he comes and they move me. I ought to take a lot of sulfa. But I shouldn't drink water. Don't worry about it, boy, he said to himself. All your life is just pointed toward it. But why couldn't Ara not have shot that son of a bitch so we would have something to show for it all so it would have done some good. I don't mean good. I mean so it would have been some use. Hell, if they had had the firepower we had. They must have pulled the other stakes on the channels to suck us into that one. But maybe if we had the prisoner he would be stupid and know nothing. He would have been useful to have had though. We are not being very useful now. Sure we are. We are detrapping that old turtle boat.

Think about after the war and when you will paint again. There are so many good ones to paint and if you paint as well as you really can and keep out of all other

things and do that, it is the true thing. You can paint the
sea better than anyone now if you will do it and not get
mixed up in other things. Hang on good now to how
you truly want to do it. You must hold hard to life to do
it. But life is a cheap thing beside a man's work. The
only thing is that you need it. Hold it tight. Now is the
true time you make your play. Make it now without hope
of anything. You always coagulated well and you can
make one more real play. We are not the lumpen-
proletariat. We are the best and we do it for free.

"Tom, do you want some water?" Gil asked again.

Thomas Hudson shook his head.

Three chickenshit bullets, he thought, to fuck good
painting and prove nothing. Why did the poor bastards
ever make that error on the massacre key? They could
have surrendered and been all right. I wonder who the
one was who came out to surrender when Ara shot. He
could have been like the boy they shot at massacre key.
Why do they have to be such damned fanatics? We chased
good and we will always fight. But I hope we are not
fanatics.

Then he heard the noise of the outboard coming. He
could not see it join them from where he lay and then
Ara and Willie came up. Ara was sweating and they both
were scratched by the brush.

"I am sorry, Tom," Ara said.

"Shit," said Thomas Hudson.

"Let's haul ass out of here," Willie said, "and I'll tell
you. Ara, get the hell down on the anchor and send
Antonio up here to take her."

"We're going in to the Central. It's faster."

"Smart," Willie said. "Now don't talk, Tom, and let
me tell you." He stopped and put his hand on Thomas
Hudson's forehead lightly and reached under the blanket
and felt the pulse accurately but very gently.

"Don't die, you bastard," he said. "Just hold it and
don't move."

"Roger," Thomas Hudson said.

"At the first fight there were three deads," Willie explained. He was to windward of Thomas Hudson sitting on

the deck and he smelled sour of sweat and his bad eye was swung wild again and all the plastic surgery on his face showed white. Thomas Hudson lay very quietly and listened to him.

"They had two burp guns only but they were set up good. Gil's first extinguisher got them and the .50's cut the shit out of them. Antonio hit them too. Henry can really shoot the .50's."

"He always could."

"I mean with the heat on. So we detrapped that joint and it is very high now. Ara and I cut all the wires but we left the stuff. She's OK and I'll pinpoint the location of these other Krauts on the chart."

The anchor was up and the motors were turning.

"We didn't do so good, did we?" Thomas Hudson said.

"They outsmarted us. But we had the firepower. They didn't do so good either. Don't say anything to Ara about the prisoner. He feels bad enough. He says he squeezed off before he thought."

The ship was heading toward the blue hills and gathering speed.

"Tommy," Willie said. "I love you, you son of a bitch, and don't die."

Thomas Hudson looked at him without moving his head.

"Try and understand if it isn't too hard."

Thomas Hudson looked at him. He felt far away now and there were no problems at all. He felt the ship gathering her speed and the lovely throb of her engines against his shoulder blades which rested hard against the boards. He looked up and there was the sky that he had always loved and he looked across the great lagoon that he was quite sure, now, he would never paint and he eased his position a little to lessen the pain. The engines were around three thousand now, he thought, and they came through the deck and into him.

"I think I understand, Willie," he said.

"Oh shit," Willie said. "You never understand anybody that loves you."

THE END

Bantam Book Catalog

Here's your up-to-the-minute listing of every book currently available from Bantam.

This easy-to-use catalog is divided into categories and contains over 1400 titles by your favorite authors.

So don't delay—take advantage of this special opportunity to increase your reading pleasure.

Just send us your name and address and 25¢ (to help defray postage and handling costs).